I Am a Damn Savage

What Have You Done
to My Country?

Indigenous Studies Series

The Indigenous Studies Series builds on the successes of the past and is inspired by recent critical conversations about Indigenous epistemological frameworks. Recognizing the need to encourage burgeoning scholarship, the series welcomes manuscripts drawing upon Indigenous intellectual traditions and philosophies, particularly in discussions situated within the Humanities.

Series Editor

Dr. Deanna Reder (Cree-Métis), Associate Professor of English and Chair of First Nations Studies and English, Simon Fraser University

Advisory Board

Dr. Jo-ann Archibald (Stó:lō), Professor Emeritus, Educational Studies, Faculty of Education, University of British Columbia

Dr. Kristina Bidwell (NunatuKavut), Professor of English, University of Saskatchewan

Dr. Daniel Heath Justice (Cherokee Nation), Professor of First Nations and Indigenous Studies/English and Canada Research Chair in Indigenous Literature and Expressive Culture, University of British Columbia

Dr. Eldon Yellowhorn (Piikani), Associate Professor, First Nations Studies, Simon Fraser University

For more information, please contact:

Dr. Deanna Reder
First Nations Studies and English
Simon Fraser University
Phone 778-782-8192
Fax 778-782-4989
Email dhr@sfu.ca

Eukuan nin matshi-manitu innushkueu

I Am a Damn Savage

Tanite nene etutamin nitassi?

What Have You Done to My Country?

An Antane Kapesh

Sarah Henzi, translation from French and afterword

WILFRID LAURIER UNIVERSITY PRESS

Inspiring Lives.

Wilfrid Laurier University Press acknowledges the support of the Canada Council for the Arts for our publishing program. We acknowledge the financial support of the Government of Canada. This work was supported by the Research Support Fund.

Library and Archives Canada Cataloguing in Publication

Title: Eukuan nin matshi-manitu innushkueu = I am a damn savage ; Tanite nene etutamin nitassi? = What have you done to my country? / An Antane Kapesh ; translation from French and afterword by Sarah Henzi.
Other titles: Works | I am a damn savage | Tanite nene etutamin nitassi? | What have you done to my country?
Names: Kapesh, An Antane, 1926–2004 author. | Henzi, Sarah, 1977– translator, writer of afterword. | container of (work): Kapesh, An Antane, 1926–2004 Eukuan nin matshi-manitu innushkueu. | container of (expression): Kapesh, An Antane, 1926–2004 Eukuan nin matshi-manitu innushkueu. English. | container of (work): Kapesh, An Antane, 1926–2004 Tante nana etutamin nitassi. | container of (expression): Kapesh, An Antane, 1926–2004 Tante nana etutamin nitassi? English.
Description: Eukuan nin matshimanitu innu-iskueu previously published in Innu with French translation: Montréal: Leméac, 1976. | Tanite nene etutamin nitassi? previously published under title: Tante nana etutamin nitassi? Montreal: Éditions Impossibles, 1979. | Includes bibliographical references. | Text in English with original Innu on facing page.
Identifiers: Canadiana (print) 2019023864X | Canadiana (ebook) 20190240539 | ISBN 9781771124089 (softcover) | ISBN 9781771124102 (PDF) | ISBN 9781771124096 (EPUB)
Subjects: LCSH: Kapesh, An Antane, 1926–2004 | LCSH: Montagnais Indians—Biography. | LCSH: Montagnais Indians—Québec (Province)—Social conditions. | LCSH: Montagnais Indians—Québec (Province)—Government relations. | LCGFT: Autobiographies. | LCGFT: Fiction.
Classification: LCC E99.M87 A58 2020 | DDC 971.4004/97.—dc23

Cover image: *11 Novembre* by Roger Kupaniesh Dominique. Used with kind permission from the Institut Tshakapesh. Cover design by Heng Wee Tan. Interior design by Daiva Villa, Chris Rowat Design.

© 2020 Wilfrid Laurier University Press
Waterloo, Ontario, Canada
www.wlupress.wlu.ca

This book is printed on FSC® certified paper. It contains recycled materials and other controlled sources, is processed chlorine free, and is manufactured using biogas energy.

Printed in Canada

Every reasonable effort has been made to acquire permission for copyright material used in this text, and to acknowledge all such indebtedness accurately. Any errors and omissions called to the publisher's attention will be corrected in future printings.

CONTENTS

An Antane Kapesh. © John André.

Eukuan nin matshi-manitu innushkueu

I Am a Damn Savage

Nitauassimat umenu nishuaush etashiht

*Ume mashinaikan ka tutaman ka itashiht ka uitshiht
tshetshi tutaman ninashkumauat kassinu. Kie nipa
minueniten tshetshi uapataman kutak innu tshetshi
mashinaitshet e innushtenit.*

for my eight children

*I thank all those who helped me with this book
that I made. And I would be happy to see other Innu
people writing, in the Innu language.*[1]

Tshitshipanu aimun

Ute nimashinaikanit apu takuannit kauapishit utaimun.
Ka ishi-mamitunenitaman tshetshi mashinaitsheian
tshetshi tshishpeuatitishuian kie tshetshi tshishpeuatamuk
nitauassimat utinniunuau, pitama niminu-mamituneniteti
uesh ma nitshisseniteti e mashinaitshenanut namaieu
nin nitinniun kie miam e papamipanian anite itetshe
mishta-utenat ne ut mashinaikan ka itenitaman tshetshi
tutaman, apu shuk{u} ut minuataman. Katshi minu-
mamitunenitaman kie tiapuetatishuian e innushkueuian
tshetshi mashinaitsheian, eukuan nitishi-nishtuteti :
kassinu auen ka itenitak tshekuannu tshetshi tutak tshika
takuannu tshetshi ut animiut muk{u} iapit apu nita tshika
ut ui patshitenimut. Uemut iapit nanitam peikutau tshika
ui ishi-mamitunenitam{u} kie apu tshika ut takuannit
tshekuannu tshetshi ui nanakanikut. Kie nete tshek
tshika peikussu, apu tshika ut taniti uitsheuakana. Iapit
namaienu nenu tshe ut patshitenimut. Uemut iapit anu
tshika ui tutam{u} nenu tshekuannu ka itenitak tshetshi tutak.

Kaiatushkanut, ushkau-pishim{u} 1975

Preface

In my book, there is no White voice. When I thought about writing to defend myself and to defend the culture of my children, I had to first think carefully because I knew that writing was not a part of my culture and I did not like the idea of having to leave for the big city because of this book I was thinking of doing. After carefully thinking about it and after having made, me, an Innu woman, the decision to write, this is what I came to understand: any person who wishes to accomplish something will encounter difficulties but nonetheless, she should never get discouraged.[2] She will nevertheless have to constantly follow her idea. Nothing will make her want to give up, until this person will find herself alone. She will no longer have any friends but that is not what should discourage her either. More than ever, she will have to accomplish the thing she had thought of doing.

Schefferville, September 1975

Eshi-takuak

Contents

I

Kauapishit ushkat ka takushinit nitassinat

Kauapishit ka ui apashtat kie ka ui pikunak nitassinannu, apu ut natuenitamuat auennua kie apu ut kukuetshimat innua miam tshetshi tapuetakukue. Kauapishit ka ui apashtat nitassinannu kie ka ui pikunak, apu ut minat innua mashinaikanuiannu tshetshi mashinatautishuniti tiapuetakut tshetshi apashtat kie tshetshi pikunak nutim eshpishanit nitassinannu, muk^u uin natshishk tshetshi pakassiuatshet. Kauapishit ka ui tutuat innua tshetshi ishinniuniti miam kauapishiniti, apu ut kukuetshimat innua kie apu ut minat innua mashinaikanuiannu tshetshi mashinatautishuniti tiapuetakut innua tshe ishpish inniuniti tshetshi nakataminiti utinniunnu.

Kauapishit ka itenitak tshetshi apashtat kie ka iteni-tak tshetshi pipikunak nutim eshpishanit nitassinannu, kuishk^u ninatuapamikutan. Katshi takushinit ute nitassi-nat ekue nutinikutan tshetshi tshishkutamuimit nenu uin utinniun kie ekue nimaminikutan kassinu tshekuannu nenu uin utinniun kie nenua utaitapashtauna kauapishit kassinu tshekuannu nutinamakutan : mitshuapa, katshish-kutamatsheutshuapinu kie miam natukunitshuapinu. Kauapishit ka ut tshishkutamuimit nenu utinniun kie ka ut maminimit kassinu tshekuannu, miam mate nenu shu-nianu aiapishish ka minimit peikuau peikupishimua kassinu innu papeik^u kautishkuemit kie nenua mitshuapa ka minimit kie nenu ka utinamuimit kassinu eishinakuannit

I

The White man's arrival in our territory

When the White man[3] wanted to exploit and destroy our territory, he did not ask anyone for permission, he did not ask the Innu if they agreed. When the White man wanted to exploit and destroy our territory, he did not give the Innu a document to sign saying they approved that he exploit and destroy all our territory so that only he might earn a living indefinitely. When the White man wanted for the Innu to live like the White men, he did not ask them for their opinion and he did not give them a document to sign saying they agreed to give up their culture for the rest of their days.

When the White man had the idea to exploit and destroy all of our territory, he simply came to see us. After he arrived, he took us so as to teach us his way of life, he gave us all the things of his culture and he provided us with all the White man's services: houses, school, health centre. If the White man taught us his culture and if he gave us all sorts of things – for instance the allowance he doled out once a month to each Innu family, the houses and different services he provided – it is because he wanted to make sure that we, the Innu, would remain in the same place so as not to disturb him while he exploited and destroyed our territory. By the same token, the

utaitapashtaun, kauapishit nui tutakutan e inniuiat
peikutau tshetshi apiat tshetshi eka mamashitshit nenu
nitassinannu tshe apashtat kie tshe pipikunak. Ek^u ninan
e inniuiat, kauapishit ashit nui tutakutan tshetshi nipatat
nitinnu-inniunnannu kie ashit nitinnu-aimunnannu.
Kauapishit katshi takushinit ute nitassinat, ka utinimit
tshetshi tshishkutamuimit nenu uin utinniun kie nenua
ashit nitauassiminana ekue utinepan tshetshi kakusseshiu-
tshishkutamuat muk^u tshiam tshetshi nanuiat mak muk^u
tshiam tshetshi tutuat tshetshi unitaniti utinniunnu e
inniuniti kie muk^u tshiam tshetshi tutuat tshetshi unitaniti
utinnu-aimunnu, miam ka tutuat mishueshkamit innua.

Kauapishit umenu ka ui ishi-utinimit, apu peikuau
ut tutak kautshimau-aiminanunit tshetshi minu-
nishtutamuniat innua tan ka ishi-mamitunenitak tshe
ishi-uieshimat innua. Kauapishit apu nita ut petutshit
tshetshi ishimit kie mashinaikanuian apu nita ut
utitaukuiat tshetshi mashinaimuimit tshetshi ishimit :

« *Nin kauapishit ek^u tshinuau innuat. Ne assi etaiek^u,
tapue tshinuau e inniuiek^u tshitassiuau, nitshisseniten
namaieu nin nitassi. Muk^u tshui uitamatinau tshekuan,
tshui kukuetshimitinau tshekuan kie tshui natuenitama-
tinau tshekuan.* »

Kauapishit apu nita ut ishimit :

« *Innitik^u ma tshitapuetenau tshetshi natuapamitikut
anite tshitassiuat ? Ma tshitapuetenau tshetshi apashtaian tshitassiuau ? Ma tshitapuetenau tshetshi pikunaman tshitassiuau ? Ma tshitapuetenau tshishipimuaua
tshetshi tshipaiman mak ashit tshetshi uinakamitaian
tshishipimuaua kie tshishakaikanimuaua ? Eshk^u
eka tapuetuiek^u ume eshi-natuenitamatikut, pitama*

White man wanted to kill our Innu culture at the same time as our Innu language. After he came to our territory, by taking us to teach us his way of life, the White man also took our children to give them a White education, solely to taint them and solely to make them lose their Innu culture and language, as he did with all the Indigenous Peoples of America.

When he wanted to seize us thus, the White man did not call even one assembly so as to make the Innu understand how he planned to dupe them. We never heard the White man tell us and we never received an official letter in which he said:

> "Me, I am White and you, you are Innu. The lands on which you are, it is true they belong to you, Innu; I know, they are not my lands. But I will tell you something, I will ask you something, I will make a request of you."

The White man never said to us:

> "You the Innu, do you agree that I join you in your territory? Do you agree that I exploit your territory? Do you agree that I destroy your territory? Do you agree that I build dams on your rivers and that I pollute your rivers and lakes? Before agreeing to what I am asking you, think hard and try to understand. You might come to regret in the future that

*minu-mamitunenitamuk[u] kie kutshipanitak[u] tshetshi
minu-nishtutamek[u]. Uesh ma nete aishkat tshipa tshi
ishinakuan tshetshi mitatamek[u] tapuetuiekui tshetshi
natuapamitikut nete tshitassiuat. Uesh tapuetamekui
tshetshi takushinian nete tshitassiuat, nika ituten tshetshi
unuitishinaman ashini. Ne ashini tshi unuitishinamani
nete tshitassiuat, nete aishkat uemut nutim eshpishat
tshitassiuau nika apashtan kie nutim eshpishat nika
pikunen. Kie nenua tshishipimuaua kassinu etatiki
nika katshipain kie kassinu tshishakaikanimuaua nika
uinakamitan. Tan ma tshinuau etenitamek[u] ? Tshika
minuatenau a tshetshi miniek[u] nipi e uinakamit ? »*

Kauapishit apu nita ut ishi-uauitamuat innua :

*« Kie ne tshitassiuau tshe apashtaian kie tshe pikunaman
kashikat, tshuapatenau, eshk[u] mishta-uashkamau kie
ne tshitinnu-aueshishimuau, tshitshissenimauau, kashikanit eshk[u] kassinu eishinakushit uashkamishiu. Eshk[u]
kassinu minushiu tshetshi muek[u]. Nete aishkat tshitaueshishimuau, innu-aueshish kassinu eishinakushit nika
nanuiau kie nika uinnakuiau tanite ume tshitassiuau nete
aishkat apu tshika ut ishpish uashkamat miam kashikat
kie ne tshitaueshishimuauat apu tshika ut ishpish uashka-
mishiht miam kashikanit. Tan ma tshinuau etenitamek[u] ?
Ne tshitaueshishimuau tshe nanuik kie tshe uinnakuik,
tshinuau e inniuiek[u] tshika minuatauau a tshetshi muek[u]
eka e uashkamishit ? Miam mate ne tshinameshimuau
kassinu eishinakushit nete aishkat ui nipaiekui tshetshi
muek[u], nete meiaput ekute tshe ut utinek[u]. »*

Kauapishit apu nita ut ishi-nishtutamuniat umenu innua.

*you have allowed me to join you, because if you
agree that I go into your territory, I will go so as
to open a mine. Once the mine is open, I will then
have to exploit and ruin your land, to its whole
extent. And I will dam all your rivers and dirty
all your lakes. What do you think? Will you like
drinking polluted water?"*

The White man never spoke of this to the Innu.

*"I will exploit your territory and I will destroy it.
Today, you see, it is still very clean and, you know
it, all of the kinds of animals that you have, the
Innu animals, are still clean. All are still good to
eat. Later, I will waste and dirty your animals, all
of the species of Innu animals. In the future, your
territory will not be as clean as it is now and your
animals will not be as clean as they are now. What
do you think? After I have wasted and dirtied your
animals, will you, the Innu, like to eat them even if
they are not clean? For instance, it is in the sewage
that you will catch all the fish that you have, if in
the future you want to kill them for your food."*

Never did the White man explain that in this way
to the Innu.

« *Kie ne kakusseshiu-atusseun tshe shenaman anite*
tshitassiuat, nin muk[u] e kakusseshiuian nika pakassiua-
tshen tshe ishpish inniuian tanite kakusseshiu-atusseun
ume nin e kakusseshiuian eukuan nin nitinniun.
Minu-mamitunenitamuk[u] ne kakusseshiu-atusseun
tshe shenaman anite tshitassiuat. Tshinuau e inniuiek[u],
akua uin uieshimitikuti kie akua uin uieshimitishuiekui.
Uesh ne kakusseshiu-atusseun tshe takuak nete tshi-
tassiuat, namaieu tshinuau e inniuiek[u] tshetshi minue-
nitamikuiek[u] uesh ma namaieu tshinuau e inniuiek[u]
ka ishi-pakassiuiek[u]. Kie tshipa tshi put ishinakuannu
kauapishit tshetshi eka ui apatshiat innua anite
kakusseshiu-atusseunit miam ne innu eka kanuenitak
netess.[1] Ek[u] tshinuau e inniuiek[u], tan ma eshi-mamitune-
nitamek[u] tshetshi ishi-pakassiuiek[u] nete aishkat ?

« *Uesh ma, mate ne tshitassiuau tapuetuiekui tshetshi*
apashtaian, tshinuau e inniuiek[u] apu tshika ut tapuetatikut
tshetshi mamashiek[u] tshi miniekui tshetshi apashtaian.
Kie ne tshitinnu-aueshishimuau, tshitshissenimitinau kie
tshinuau e innuiek[u] tshitshissenitenau, ne innu-aueshish
kassinu eishinakushit kashikanit eshk[u] tshinuau tshitipe-
nimauau. Ek[u] miam tapuetamekui tshitassiuau tshetshi
apashtaian, kakusseshiu-atusseun tutakaniti anite tshi-
tassiuat, ne tshitaueshishimuau tshika tshitaimatinau
tshetshi nipaiek[u]. Apu tshika ut tapuetatikut tshetshi ne
ut inniuiek[u] innu-aueshish. Kie ne kakusseshiu-atusseun
tshe tutakanit anite tshitassiuat, eukuan tshe itapash-
tat kauapishit nenu atusseunnu : muk[u] tatupipuna
tshika natshi-atusseu anite tshitassiuat, tshishi-mautati
shunianu, kau tshe tshiuet anite utassit. Eukuan muk[u]
tshe itapashtaiat ne kakusseshiu-atusseun, tapuetamekui
tshetshi pipikunakanit tshitassiuau. Kie ume ninan e
kakusseshiuiat nika mitshetinan tshe ut uenutishiat anite
tshitassiuat ek[u] tshinuau e inniuiek[u] nanitam tshika

"As for the construction site that I will open on
your land, there will be only me, who is White,
who will earn a living as long as I live because paid
work is part of my culture, the White man. Think
hard about the paid work that I will bring to your
territory. You the Innu, beware that I deceive you
and beware that you deceive yourselves. The paid
work that will be in your territory, it will not be to
make you happy, you the Innu: it is not your way
of earning your living. It might come to be that on
the site the White man will not need the Innu, the
one who does not have his competency certificate
for instance. And you, the Innu, how will you earn
your living in the future, do you think?

"If you give me permission to exploit your territory, I will not accept that you disturb me after
you have given me your lands for my use. Your
Innu animals – I know it and you the Innu, you
know it too – all the kinds of animals still belong
to you today. But if you accept that I exploit your
territory, if we establish paid work on your lands,
I will forbid you from killing your animals. I will
not allow you to live on Innu animals. Once paid
work is established in your territory, this is how it
will serve the White man: he will go work there for
a few years only and once he has accumulated his
money, he will return to his country. It is in this
way only that we will use paid work if you agree
that your territory be destroyed. We, the White
men, will be many to get rich by means of your territory and you, Innu, will always be poor. Perhaps
you will even come to see how all of this will bring
upon you more misery than today, while you are

tshitimaunau. Kie put tshipa tshi ishinakushinau tshetshi
mishkamek^u anu tshetshi animiuiek^u mak kashikat, eshk^u
tshinuau tshitinniunuau eshinniuiek^u kie eshk^u tshinuau
eshi-pakassiuiek^u tshitishi-pakassitishunau. »

Kauapishit apu nita ut ishi-uauitamuat umenu innua.

« Ne tshe tutaman kakusseshiu-atusseun anite
tshitassiuat, apu tshika ut tapuetatikut tshetshi
mamashiek^u kie ne tshitaueshishimuau tshe
tshitaimatikut. Tshinuau e inniuiek^u, eukuan muk^u
tshetshi tutatikut : kassinu innu papeik^u kautishkuemit
peikuau peikupishimua tshika minitinau aiapishish
shuniau mak mitshuapa tshika minitinau mak nitinniun
tshe tshishkutamatikut. Eukuan ne tshe tutatikut e
inniuiek^u nanitam peikutau tshetshi apiek^u. Tan ma
tshinuau etenitamek^u ? Tshika minuatenau a tshe
ishpish inniuiek^u nanitam peikutau tshetshi apiek^u kie
tshititenitenau a tshetshi eka nita mueshtatapiek^u ?
« Ne shuniau kie nenua mitshuapa tshe minitikut
kie kassinu kutak tshekuan tshe ishi-maminitikut e
kakusseshiuian nitaitapashtauna kie tshe tshishkuta-
matikut nitinniun, minu-mamitunenitamuk^u. Akua
uieshimitikuti kie tshinuau e inniuiek^u akua uieshimi-
tishuiekui. Uesh ne shuniau kie nenua mitshuapa tshe
minitikut kie kassinu kutak tshekuan tshe ishi-minitikut,
eukuan e atauatsheiek^u tshitassiuau kie ashit tshitinniu-
nuau. Eshk^u kashikat tshiminitinau kassinu tshekuan
eshi-natuenitamuiek^u muk^u nete aishkat, miam tshishi-
atauatsheiekui tshitinniunuau kie tshitassiuau, eka uin
itenitamuk^u tshetshi ishi-maminitikut tshekuan miam
kashikat eshi-maminitikut tshekuan. Kie tshinuau e
inniuiek^u tshika ishi-pimipannau miam kauapishit
eshi-pimipanit, pikutaiekui kie eka pikutaiekui, uemut

still living according to your own culture and that
you have your own way to provide for yourselves."

The White man never spoke of this to the Innu
in these terms.

"After I have established paid work on your land,
you will not disturb me and I will forbid you your
animals. This is all that I will do for you, the Innu:
to each family, once a month, I will give a little
money, I will give you houses and I will teach you
my culture. This is what I will do so that you,
Innu, become sedentary. What do you think?
Will you like living forever in the same place for
your whole lives, do you think you will not know
boredom?

"The money and houses that I will give you, as
with all the other things I will hand out to you
under the form of my White man's services, my
culture that I will teach you, think about it care-
fully. Beware that I deceive you and beware that
you deceive yourselves. It is through the money
and houses that I will give you and all of the other
things I will hand out to you that you will sell your
territory and your culture. Today still, I give you
all that you ask for but later, once you have sold
your culture and your territory, do not think that
I will give you things the way I do now. And you,
Innu, you will function as the White man func-
tions; whether you are capable or not, you too, this
is how you will have to function. Even if you are

kie tshinuau e inniuiek[u] *eukuan tshe ui ishi-pimipa-
niek*[u]. *Kie tshinuau, at e inniuiek*[u], *kassinu tshekuan
tshika tshishikashunau miam kauapishit. Kie ne tshitinnu-aueshishimuau, itenitamekui tshetshi ut pakassiti-
shuiek*[u], *kie tshinuau e inniuiek*[u] *tshika tshishikashunau
miam peikuan kauapishit.* »

Kauapishit umenu apu nita ut ishi-uauitamuimit kie
apu tshekuannu anite ut nishtutamunimit. Kauapishit
katshi takushinit ute nitassinat ekue nutinikutan tshetshi
tshishkutamuimit nenu uin utinniun kie nenua nitauassiminana ekue utinepan tshetshi kakusseshiu-tshishkutamuat eka tshekuannu anite e uauitamuimit kie eka
tshekuannu anite e nishtutamunimit. Kauapishit, nenua
nitauassiminana ka utinat tshetshi kakusseshiu-tshishkutamuat, apu umenu ut ishimit :

« *Tshinuau innitik*[u], *anitshenat tshitauassimuauat ma
tshitapuetenau tshetshi kakusseshiu-tshishkutamukau
muk*[u] *tshetshi nipatauk utinniunuau mak utaimunuau ?
Ume anutshish tshe ishi-uauitamatikut, minu-mamitunenitamuk*[u]. *Akua uieshimitikuti kie tshinuau akua
uieshimitishuiekui uesh ma tshipa tshi put ishinakuan
nete aishkat tshetshi mitatamek*[u] *anitshenat ut tshitauassimuauat. Anitshenat tshitauassimuauat tapuetamekui tshetshi kakusseshiu-tshishkutamukau, eukuan
ushkat tshekuan uet tshitshipanit tshetshi ut unitaiek*[u]
*tshitinnu-inniunuau. Kie eukuan metikat tshe ut naka-
tamek*[u] *tshitinniunuau. Mate ne tshinuau e inniuiek*[u],
*anite tshitishinikashunuat mishta-uipat apu tshika ut
tshissenitakushiek*[u] *e inniuiek*[u], *tshika peikutanan tshi-
tishinikashunnua kauapishit mak e inniuiek*[u]. *Tshinuau
e inniuiek*[u], *kassinu anite mashinaikanit nianatuapa-
tamekui tshitinnu-ishinikashunuaua, apu nita tshika ut*

Innu, you too will have to spend money for eve-
rything, just like the White men. And if you think
you will live off your Innu animals, you too will
have to pay, just like the White men."

The White man never spoke to us of this in this
way and did not explain anything to us. After his
arrival here, in our territory, he took us so as to
teach us his own way of life and he took our children to give them a White man's education without
telling us anything, and without explaining anything. When the White man took our children to
educate them in his way, he did not tell us this:

"You, the Innu, do you agree that I give your child-
ren a White man's education for the sole purpose of
destroying their culture and their language? Think
carefully about what I am going to tell you. Beware
that I deceive you and beware that you deceive
yourselves because you might come to have regrets
in the future because of your children. If you agree
that I give them a White man's education, it will
be the beginning of the end of your Innu culture.
This is what will make you gradually give up your
culture. For instance, soon it will not be possible
to tell from your family names that you are Innu.
Whites and Innu, we will have the same names.
When you will look for your Innu names in books,
you will never find yourselves there. There will
come a time when you will not recognize yourselves
among each other. Maybe later, your children,

mishkatishuiek[u]. Kie e inniuiek[u] nete aishkat tshek apu tshika ut nishtuapamituiek[u] e inniuiek[u]. Ek[u] anitshenat tshitauassimuauat tshe tutukau tshetshi unitaht utinnu-inniunuau, put nete aishkat kau tshika nanatuapatamuat nenu muk[u] apu nita tshika ut kau mishkahk. Kie nenu utinnu-aimunuau tshe unitaht, apu nita kau tshika ut katshitinahk. »

Kauapishit apu umenu ut ishi-uauitamuat innua. Kauapishit eukuannu eka ut ishi-uauitamuat innua : tshimut ui nipatapan nitinniunnannu kie tshimut ui nipatapan nitaimunnannu kie nitassinannu nitshimutamakutan.

Kauapishit kashikanit uin nenu unanua[2] eukuannu e tutak ute nitassinat kie nenua unekakanima[3] nitutamakunan kie ninan e inniutshit tshetshi nashamat miam peikuan kauapishit. Kauapishit kashikanit nenu unanua ka tutak kie nenua unekakanima ka tutak, ninan e inniuiat ninashkumanan, apu apashtautshit uesh ma ninan e inniuiat, ne kakusseshiu-nanua peikuan apu tshekuan anite nishtutamat. Kauapishit unanua kie nenua unekakanima tshika kanuenitam[u] kie tshika apashtau muk[u] uin e kakusseshiut uesh ma uin nenu utinniun. Nin eukuan etenitaman. Kauapishit kashikanit tutamakuti innua unanuaminu tshetshi tshishkutamatishuatshet, ushtuin atut tshekuannu anite tshipa nishtutam[u] kie ushtuin atut tshekuannu anite tshipa pikutau. Kie ashit ute innu utassit, muk[u] uin innu ishinakuannipan tshetshi tutak nanua kie tshetshi minat kauapishiniti tshetshi tshishkutamatishuatsheniti, miam mate kauapishit ka takushinit ute innua utassinit, tshetshi tshissenitak kassinu tshekuannu kie tshetshi tshiaminniut, uin katshi natuapamat innua utassinit, kie tshetshi nakatuenitak tshetshi eka ushikuiat innua kie tshetshi minu-nishtuapatak passikannu kie

*whom I will make lose their Innu culture, they
will look for it but they will never be able to find
it again. They will never find that Innu language
that they will have lost."*

The White man did not say this to the Innu.
What he did not say was that he wanted to kill our
culture without our knowledge, that he wanted to
kill our language without our knowledge, and he
was stealing our territory from us.

Nowadays, he is the one who makes the laws in
our territory and upon us Innu, he makes us follow his rules, like White men. We thank the White
man for his laws and rules but they are of no use to
us because we, who are Innu, we do not understand
anything of the White man's law anyway. May the
White man keep for himself his laws and rules and
may he use them for himself because it is of his
culture. This is what I think. If nowadays the Innu
were to make the laws that the White man had to
follow, maybe he would not understand them and
would not be able to abide by them. Also, in Innu
territory, only the Innu had the right to make the
laws and to make the White men respect them so
that newcomers would know all things; that they
behave after coming to find the Innu in their territory; that they be careful not to cause harm to the
Innu; that they know how to handle firearms well
so as not to shoot recklessly; that they not play with
the Innu animals so as not to waste the Innu's food
that comes from Innu animals. This is the law that

tshetshi eka natamikᵘ papassitshet kie ashit tshetshi eka
metuatshet innu-aueshisha tshetshi eka nanutauat innua
umitshiminu nenua ut innu-aueshisha. Kauapishit eukuannu
umenu nanua tshipa minikupan innua tshetshi tshishkutamatishuatshet katshi takushinit ute innua utassinit.

Kauapishit umenu innu-nanua kie umenua innu-
nekakanima eka tshekuannu anite nishtutakakue kie eka
pikutatakue tshetshi tutak, tshipa tshiuepan tanite nete ka
ututet, anite e takuanniti uin e kakusseshiut unanua kie
unekakanima. Ekᵘ ne kauapishit eka nishtutakakue kie
eka pikutatakue tshetshi tutak innu-nanua, uemut kie uin
tshipa uakaikupan innua. Miam mate ninan e inniuiat
shash tshitshue nuakaikunan kauapishit usham anumat
anu uin ui mishta-tipenitamᵘ ute nitassinat. Nitishpannan
ka tatupipuna tipenimimit kie nitishpannan ka tatupipuna matshi-tutuimit kie nitishpannan ka tatupipuna
manenimimit kauapishit.

Kauapishit ka ut takushinit ute nitassinat, eukuannu
mukᵘ tshetshi nanatuapatak pakassiunnu. Kauapishit
katshi mishkak tshetshi ut pakassiut ute innua utassinit, eka pissenimatakue innua tshetshi ui tipenimat kie
tshetshi ui tshishkutamuat kassinu tshekuannu. Kauapishit ishi-mamitunenitakakue : « Ka takushinian ute
innu utassit, ne innu shash uin uetshit aitutatishuipan kie
shash kassinu tshekuannu uin uetshit utinamatishuipan. »
Kauapishit ushkat ka uapamat innua, eukuannu umenu
tshipa tshi ishi-mashinataimupan. Kauapishit tipan
kanuenitakakue utinniun, kie ninan e inniuiat tipan nipa
kanuenitetan nitinniunnan e inniuiat. Kashikat atut ut
ishpish matshipanu kauapishit mak innu.

Kauapishit eukuannu nanitam ka itenitak : « Mukᵘ nin
nitinnishin. » Kauapishit nitshissenimanan uin ituteu anite

the Innu would have asked the White man to follow after his arrival in Innu territory.

If the White man had not understood these Innu laws and rules, and if he had not been able to abide by them, he would have returned to where he came from, where there are White man's laws and rules. If the White man had not understood the Innu law and if he was unable to abide by it, he would not have been able, either, to escape being harassed by the Innu. We, for instance, are truly harassed by the White men because they want by all means to be master in our own territory. But we are tired of being, for a number of years now, regulated by the White men. We are tired of being, for a number of years now, mistreated by them, and we are tired of seeing them, for a number of years now, disrespect us.

If the White man came to us, it is solely to earn a livelihood. After finding it in Innu territory, the White man should have left them in peace, he should not have tried to govern them or tried to teach them everything. He should have said to himself: "When I arrived in Innu territory, the Innu were self-governed and self-sustainable." This is what the White man should have noticed when he saw them for the first time. If the White man had kept his culture to himself, we too would have kept ours and today there would not be as many conflicts as there are between the Whites and the Innu.

The White man has always thought: "There is only me who is intelligent." We are well aware that

ninipassite[4] kie kanuenitam^u netshipenum[5] ka ishinikatet. Ek^u innu ka uauiepit anite kakusseshiu-katshishkuta-matunit, kanuenitam^u kie uin netshipenum muk^u innu uin apu nita ut uapatiniuet e kanuenitak kie apu nita ut apashtat nenu unetshipenum. Innu eshk^u utinniun ka ishinniut anite nutshimit, uapatinitishuipan e kanuenitak netshipenum kie apashtapan. Innu katshi natuapamikut kauapishiniti ute utassit ekue tshishkashtapan nenu unetshipenum usham, innu ushkat ka uapamat kauapi-shiniti, itenimepan : « Ushtuin anu uin innishitshe mak nin. » Innu eukuannu ka ut tshishkashtat nenu unetshipe-num. Katshi natuapamikut kauapishiniti ute utassit, innu pitama tshimut tshitapamepan tan tshe itutakut, miam tshetshi matshi-tutakut kie miam tshetshi manenimikut ute utassit. Tatupipuna tshimut katshi nakatuapamat kauapishiniti, kashikanit innu shash tshissenitam^u eteni-mikut kauapishiniti : innu apu innishit.

Kauapishit ushtuin apu nita ut tshissenimat innua e kanuenitaminiti netshipenum tanite kauapishit ka natuapamat innua utassinit, katuakupan e kanuenita-miniti netshipenum. Kashikanit innu apu shakuenimut tshetshi uapatiniat kauapishiniti kie uin e inniut katshi kanuenitak netshipenum kie apu shakuenimut uin unetshipenum tshetshi apashtat. Innu apu taniti uka-numa e kanuenitak netshipenum tshetshi akuashkuauat anite ashtamitat tanite uin innu e kanuenitak netshipe-num, anite ushtikuanit kanuenitam^u.

the White man goes to university and has a diploma. The Innu, whom the White man's school system puts in the zeroth class, also has a diploma but he, he never showed that he had one and it has never been of any use to him. When he still lived his own life on the land, he would show to himself that he had a diploma and proved its value. When the White man met him in his territory, the Innu put his diploma away because, seeing the White man for the first time, he thought: "He is probably more intelligent than me." This is why he put his diploma away. After the arrival of the White man, he started to observe him discreetly to see how he would act towards him. He wanted to see if the White man would harm him and if he would be disrespectful towards him on his own territory. After observing him for a few years, the Innu knows, today, that the White man thinks he is unintelligent.

The White man probably never knew that the Innu had a diploma: when he sought him out in his territory, the Innu hid it from him. But today, he is not embarrassed to show the White man that he too, in his capacity as Innu, has a diploma and he is not ashamed to assert its value. The Innu, he does not have a certificate to hang on the wall confirming he has graduated: it is in his mind that his diploma can be found.

2

Ashini ka mishkakanit ute Tshiuetinit

Ume tipatshimun eukuannu umenu Tshishennish-Pien utipatshimun mak kauapikuesht Kakushkuenitak mak kauapikuesht Kauashkamuesht. Ume tipatshimun apu uiesh tshika ut mishkamekᵘ anite mashinaikanit uesh ma e inniuiat, kauapishit eshkᵘ eka ka tshishkutamuimit utinniun, apu nita ut ishinniuiat tshetshi mashinai-tsheiat tshetshi uauitamat kassinu tshekuan nete utat ka pet aishpanit. Anutshish kashikanit kauapishit katshi tshishkutamuimit utinniun kie katshi pikunak nitin-niunnannu, kashikat e mitatamat nitinniunnan, eukuan ka ut itenitamat kie ninan e inniuiat tshetshi mashinai-tsheiat miam peikuan kauapishit. Nititeniten, e inniuiat tshetshipaniat tshetshi mashinaitsheiat, anu ninan nikanuenitenan tipatshimuna uesh ma ninan kashikat nishuait eshinniunanut nuapatenan. Kauapishit tapueu nenu essishuet : « Innu apu takuannit umashinaikan. » Innu tapue apu takuannit umashinaikan mukᵘ nin eukuan etenitaman : kassinu innu papeikᵘ kanuenitamᵘ tipatshimunnu anite ushtikuanit, kassinu papeikᵘ innu tshipa tshi tipatshimu anite utat eshkᵘ nitinniunnan ka ishinniuiat mak ume kashikat eshinniuiat kauapishit utinniun tshetshi uauitamat kauapishit ka ishpish uin aiatinimit tan ka ishi-uieshimimit. Nin nititenitamun, kashikat anu ninan ishinakuan tshetshi aimiat kassinu anite tipatshimu-mashinaikanit kie anite katshitapatakanit

2

The discovery of ore in the North

This is the story of Tshishennish-Pien and Fathers Babel and Arnaud. You will not find this story anywhere in a book because before the White man taught us his culture, we, the Innu, never lived in such a way as to have to write to relate things from the past. Now that the White man has taught us his way of life and destroyed ours, we miss our culture. It is for this reason that we have been thinking, we too, the Innu, to write like the White man does. And I think, now that we are starting to write, we are the ones who have the most to tell because we, we are today the witnesses of the two cultures. The White man speaks the truth when he says: "The Innu does not have any books." It is true, the Innu do not have any books but this is what I think: each Innu has stories in his or her mind, each Innu could tell of the life we used to live in the past and of the life of the White men that we live today, each Innu could say to what extent the White man deceived us since he started administering us. In my opinion, today it is rather up to us to speak up in the newspapers and on television because here, in our territory, there is no White man who knows better than the Innu how things were before the arrival of the first White man in the North.

uesh ma ute nitassinat apu tat kauapishit anu uin tshetshi
minu-tshissenitak mak innua tan ka ishpannit ute nitassinat eshkᵘ eka peikᵘ kauapishit ka takushinit ute Tshiuetinit.

Tshipetenau anutshish kashikanit kauapishit
essishuet : « Kauapikuesht Kakushkuenitak eukuan uin
ushkat ka mishkak ashininu. » Kauapishit nenu essishuet nin eukuan etenitaman : kauapikuesht Kakushkuenitak ka itenitak tshetshi takushinit ute nitassinat,
tshekuennua eukuannu eshinniuniti peshukupan ute
Tshiuetinit ? Eukuannua innua mautania⁶ peshukupan.
Kie peikuan kauapikuesht Kauashkamuesht ka itenitak
tshetshi takushinit ute nutshimit, iapit eukuannua innua
peshukupan kie eukuannua innua atusseshtakupan
tshetshi ut inniut anite innu-mitshuapit kie eukuannua
innua ashamikupan ishpish peikupipuna nenu ut e natauniti kassinu eishinakushiniti innu-aueshisha. Ne Kakushkuenitak kie ne Kauashkamuesht ka takushiniht ute
Tshiuetinit, pikutatakuenit e papeikussiht tshetshi ituteht,
ushtuin atut ut apatshiepanat innua, kuishkᵘ tshipa
takushinipanat e papeikussiht ute Tshiuetinit.

Nishuasht-tatunnu ka itashtet, metuenanuipan ute
Kaiatushkanut. Ne mietuenanut eukuan ushkat nipetetan ume tipatshimun, kauapikuesht Kakushkuenitak uin
katshi mishkak ashininu ute. Ume tipatshimun apu nita
ut petuk nutaui tshetshi tipatshimut kie peikuan kutakat innuat kie tshishennuat apu nita ut petukau tshetshi
tipatshimuht. Ka metuenanut ute Kaiatushkanut, ushtuin
takupan innu eka uet minu-tshissenitak tshekuan ne tshe
ut metuenanut.

Uiauitakanit tshe metuenanut nete utenat, kie ninan
e inniuiat ekue uishamikauiat tshetshi uitshiaushiat
tshe uaueshtakanit nete utenat, innuat tshetshi tutahk
innu-mitshuapinu kie innushkueuat tshetshi piminueht
miam tshetshi tshissuaht shaieua mak ashit tshetshi

Nowadays, you will hear the White man say:
"It is Father Babel who discovered iron ore." This
is what I think. When Father Babel thought about
coming to our territory, who brought him to the
North? It is the Montagnais Innu[4] who brought him
there. It is the same thing with Father Arnaud, when
he thought to go inland, it is also the Innu who
brought him there and it is the Innu who worked so
that he would survive in a tent, it is the Innu who
fed him during a whole year, by hunting all kinds
of Innu animals. If Father Arnaud and Father Babel
could have fended for themselves on their own
when they came to the North, they probably would
not have brought any Innu with them; they would
have come straight to the North, by their own
means.

In 1970, we celebrated a centennial here in
Schefferville. It is during that celebration that we
heard for the first time the story that it was Father
Babel who discovered iron ore here. I had never
heard that story from my father, or from any other
Innu, or from other Elders. During the centennial,
there were probably some Innu who did not really
know the reason for the festivities.

When it was announced that there would be a
celebration over there, in town, we were invited as
well, to help with the preparations. It was asked
of the Innu men to put up a tent and of the Innu
women to cook, to prepare baked beans and to bake

tutuaht kaianauakuakanniti. Uesh kashikat eshinniuiat
kauapishit utinniun, mietueiati e inniuiat, eukuanat
muk^u shaieuat nanitam emuakaniht anite mietuenanuti.
Ueshkat nitinnu-inniunnan ka ishinniuiat, e makusheiati,
eukuan atiku-pimi nimitshitan. Kie ne atiku-pimi apu
takuak kutak tshekuan anu tshetshi uikak mak atiku-
pimi namaieu miam shaieuat. Eshk^u eka tshitshipannanut
e metuenanut, e inniuiat ekue uishamikauiat tshetshi
tshishuashpishuiat e inniuiat ka ishi-tshishuashpishuiat,
innushkueuat kie napeuat kie innu-auassat. Mak peik^u
napeu tshishuashpitakanu miam peikuan shashish kauapikueshiht ka itashpishuht, Kautshipaiatikumiht ka ishini-
katakaniht. Ne innu-mitshuap ka tutakanit, shaputuan
ishinakutakanipan muk^u atiku-pimi apu takuak anite
pitukamit. Kie ne shaputuan ka tutakanit, tauat anite
innuat pitukamit. Eukuanat uinuau tshe ashuapamaht
nenua innua nish^u kautishkuemiht tshika takushinuat
anite shaputuanit. Anitshenat innuat nish^u kautishkuemiht
tshika pimishkauat, innu-uta tshika apashtauat. Ek^u ne
innu ka tshishuashpitakanit miam kauapikuesht kie uin
ekute tshe peshuakanit, innu-utit tshika pushiakanu.

Uiapamakanih innuat nish^u kautishkuemiht pieshtash-
tamishkaht, anitshenat innuat pessish etaht anite shaputuanit, nuapamanan kauapikuesht kie uin takushinu mak
innua peshuku, anite innu-utit pushiakanu. Anitshenat
innuat nish^u kautishkuemiht ka takushiniht ekue kapaht
anite ututuat, kassinu innua anite shaputuanit ka taniti ekue
pushukataht. Kie ne innu ka tshishuashpitakanit miam
shashish kauapikuesht ekue kapat anite ut innu-utit kie uin
ekue pushukatat kassinu innua. Ne innu ka tshishuashpitakanit miam kauapikuesht, eukuan ne tshissinuatshitakan
kauapikuesht Kakushkuenitak ek^u nenua innua ka pushikut
anite innu-utit, eukuan ne tshissinuatshitakan ne Kakushkuenitak innua katshi peshukut ute Tshiuetinit.

bannock[5] in the sand. Today, now that we are living
the White man's life, whenever there is a celebration, all we ever eat is beans. When in the past we
lived our life as Innu, if we had a *makushan*,[6] it was
caribou fat that we ate. There is nothing better than
caribou fat and baked beans cannot compare to
caribou fat. Before starting the celebration, we were
asked, men, women, and children, to dress up in
our traditional Innu clothes. An Innu was made
to dress up like one of those Oblate Fathers from
the past. The tent that had been put up was a
shaputuan but inside, the caribou fat was missing.
Inside the *shaputuan*[7] were Innu: they were the ones
who would wait for the two Innu families to arrive
at the *shaputuan*. They would arrive by water, in a
canoe. And it is also there, by canoe, that the man
dressed up as a missionary would be brought.

Upon the arrival of the two Innu families close
to where the *shaputuan* stands, we saw the priest
arriving as well, brought in a canoe by an Innu.
Upon their arrival, the two families got out of their
canoes and shook hands with everyone of the
shaputuan. As for the Innu disguised as a priest, he
too got out of the canoe and he too shook hands
with all the Innu. The man dressed up as a priest
was the replica of Father Babel, and the man who
brought him in the canoe was the replica of the
Innu who had brought Father Babel to the North.

Ne kametuenanut ute Kaiatushkanut ne ut ashini
uiesh nishtutshishikua ishpish metuenanuipan. Ushkat
tshishik[u] ka metuenanut, Tukuitu[7] takushinipan tshetshi
shatshuapatak nenu mietuenanunit tanite eukuan tshe
unuipanit ussi-tipatshimun, ne kauapikuesht Kakushkuenitak uin katshi mishkak ashininu ute Tshiuetinit. Katshi
apita-tshishikat eshk[u] eka tshiuenanut ekue petamat eimi-
nanut anite ut katshikauemakak, innu-aiminanu ashit
mishtikushiu-aiminanu : « Kauapikuesht Kakushkuenitak kashikanit eukuannu peikumitashumitannuepipuna
eshpish tshi mishkak ashininu ute Tshiuetinit. Kashikat
eukuan uet metuenanut », issishuenanu.

Ne tipatshimun katshi petaman, nimashkateniten
tanite apu nita ut petuk nutaui tshetshi tipatshimut
kie kutakat innuat kie tshishennuat apu nita ut petukau tshetshi tipatshimuht. Nutaui mishta-tshishenniu,
peikushteu-tatunnu ashu peik[u] tatupipuneshu. Mitshetuau nipetuati tepatshimut nete utat aianishkat kassinu
tshekuannu ka uapatak kie tan ka ishi-petak anite utat
aianishkat tipatshimunnu. Kie nutaui kashikanit nenu
eshpitishit, niminueniteti tshetshi natutuk tepatshimuti
miam tshekuan nete utat ka pet aishpanit. Uesh ma nutaui
namaienu muk[u] uin ka kanuenitak tipatshimunnu, utauia
mak umushuma, utanishkutapana. Eukuannu ka ut
kanuenitak tipatshimunnu tan ka ishpanit eshk[u] eka peik[u]
kauapishit ka takushinit ute Tshiuetinit.

Katshi punnanut ekue tshiuenanut. Tekushiniat anite
nitshinat ninapem shash ekue tshitshipaniat tshetshi
uauitamat ne ka ishi-petamat tipatshimun. Mekuat e
uauitamat ne ka ishi-petamat tipatshimun ekue pitutshet nutaui. Tekushinit anite nitshinat, shash ekue
tipatshimushtuk tan ka ishi-petaman tipatshimun. Nutaui
eshk[u] apu tshishtauk nenu ka ui tipatshimushtuk, shash
ekue papit ekue ishit : « Eka ma natuta ne katshinaun,

The iron ore celebrations in Schefferville went on for three days. On the first day, Trudeau[8] came to see the festivities because it was at that moment that the untold story of who discovered iron ore, that is, Father Babel, here in the North, would be revealed. In the afternoon, before people went home, we heard someone speaking into the microphone, in French and in Innu: "We are celebrating today the centennial of the discovery of iron ore in the North by Father Babel," they said.

After hearing that, I was surprised: I had never heard my father, or the other Innu or the Elders, tell that story. My father is very old, he is ninety-one years old. I had often heard him tell of all that he had seen and of the stories he had heard about the past generations. Given his age today, I was happy to listen to my father tell of things of the past. It is not only my father who keeps these stories, there was also his father, his grandfather, and his great-grandfather. This is how he knows the stories that tell of how things were done in the North before the first White man arrived.

At the end, everyone went home. Upon arriving home, my husband and I, we started to talk about the news we had heard. While we were talking, my father came in. Upon his arrival, I immediately told him what I had heard. I had not finished telling him what I wanted to before my father started laughing and told me: "Come on, do not listen to that lie. The story that you heard today, the White man just

nitik[u]. Ne tipatshimun ka petamin kashikat, kauapishit nenu anutshish tutam[u] tipatshimunnu », nitik[u]. Minuat ekue ishit nutaui : « Ume nin tshe tipatshimushtatan, shuka minu-natutui », nitik[u] :

> « *Nananat Kauashkamuesht mak Kakushkuenitak, nitishipetetan e inniuiat, muk[u] aiamieunnu eukuannu ka ut takushiniht ute Tshiuetinit tshetshi uapamaht innua ute Tshiuetinit ka taniti tshetshi tshishkutamuaht aiamieunnu kie tshetshi shukaituaht innua ute nutshimit. Nananat kauapikueshiht e nishiht ka takushiniht ute Tshiuetinit, e inniuiat apu nita ut petamat tshetshi nanatuapatahk ashininu kie apu nita ut petamat tipatshimun Kakushkuenitak tshetshi mishkak ashininu ute Tshiuetinit », issishueu nutaui.*

Nutaui minuat ekue issishuet :

> « *At tapuenanutakue Kakushkuenitak uin katshi mishkak ashininu ute Tshiuetinit, nititeniten nin, issishueu nutaui, namaienu uin utishinikashun tshipa takuannipan umenu ashininu, tshekunnu eukuan ka peshuat ute Tshiuetinit Kakushkuenitaminiti, eukuan uin tshipa takuannipan utishinikashun umenu ashininu ka mishkakannit ute Tshiuetinit, issishueu nutaui. Uesh ma ne uin kauapikuesht Kakushkuenitak ka itenitak tshetshi takushinit ute Tshiuetinit, atut nita ut tshi peshutishuipan e peikussit ute nutshimit kie atut nita ut tshi kanuenimitishuipan e peikussit anite innu-mitshuapit ishpish peikupipuna, issishueu nutaui. Ne akunikan kashikanit uiapamekui ekuashkuauakanit anite Shepaniekanautshuapit[8], Kakushkuenitak mak peik[u] innukautishkuemit. Ek[u] ne innu eukuan uin Atshapi Antane eshinikatakanit », issishueu nutaui.*

invented it." My father also told me: "Now, me, I will tell you something, listen carefully:

"We the Innu, we heard that Fathers Babel and Arnaud only came to the North for a religious purpose: they came to see the Innu that lived here to teach them religion and to baptize them, here, inland. We never heard anyone say that the two priests who came here were looking for ore and we never heard the story according to which Father Babel would have found ore in the North."

My father further said:

"And even if it were true that Father Babel had found ore here, I myself think that it is not his name but that of the Innu who brought him to the North that should be associated with the ore that was found. When Father Babel thought to come here, he never could have reached the inland by his own means and he never would have been able to take care of himself on his own, in a tent, for a whole year. The portrait that you see today hanging in the hall of the Knights of Columbus is that of Father Babel and an Innu family. The man's name is Atshapi Antane."

Kashikat uiapamaki akunikan anite uiesh kie tshesse-
nimak ne innu eshinikatakanit ka peshuat Kakushkuenitaminiti ute Tshiuetinit, nimishta-ashinen tanite ne innu
Atshapi Antane eshinikatakanit, eukuan uin ninapem
utanishkutapana, ninapem utauia umushuminua. Kie
kashikat tekuak atusseu-utenau ute ninataun-assinat kie
kakusseshiu-atusseun tekuak ute nutshimit, ninishtuten
eukuan innu ka ut tshi takuak. Kie nipa mishta-ashinen
tshetshi uapataman e inniuian meshkanaua tshetshi
ishi-uitshishutakaniti e innu-aiminanut miam ume
INNU ATSHAPI ANTANE mak ashit INNU TSHISHEN-
NISH-PIEN. Uesh ma ne innu Atshapi Antane eukuan
uin ka peshuat kauapikueshiniti Kakushkuenitaminiti ute
nutshimit ek^u ne innu Tshishennish-Pien eukuan uin ushkat ka mishkak ashininu ute Tshiuetinit.

Kashikanit uiapamaki ne akunikan, nitapueten eukuan
Kakushkuenitak kie eukuan Atshapi Antane, ninapem
utanishkutapana. Muk^u peik^u tshekuan apu tapuetaman ne
ut akunikan : ne innu-kautishkuemit ishi-tshishuashpishu
miam peikuan anite kamatau-pikutakannit e nukushit
innu. Uesh ma ume eshinniuiat mautania nasht namaieu
ninan nititashpishutan. Nutaui minuat ekue tshitshipanit
tshetshi tipatshimut ekue issishuet :

*« Tshishennish-Pien eshk^u eka ka mishkak ashininu ute
Tshiuetinit, nete utat apu nita ut petamat kutak eshinniut tshetshi aimuatak ashininu », issishueu nutaui.*

Nutaui kashikanit nenu eshpitishit, nete e auassiut
uapameu nanani Tshishennish-Piena :

*« Nin eshk^u nitauassiuti ek^u ne innu Tshishennish-Pien
shash mishta-tshishenniuipan », issishueu nutaui.*

Today, when I see that painting, since I know the
name of the Innu who brought Father Babel to the
North, I am full of pride because the man whose
name is Atshapi Antane is the great-grandfather of
my husband, the grandfather of his father. If today
there is a mining town in our hunting territories
and paid work has been established inland, I understand that it is thanks to that Innu. And so I would
be very proud, as an Innu woman, to see streets
with Innu names like INNU ATSHAPI ANTANE
and INNU TSHISHENNISH-PIEN. Because the
Innu Atshapi Antane is the one who brought Father
Babel inland and the Innu Tshishennish-Pien is the
first to have found iron ore here in the North.

Today, when I see that portrait, I admit that it
is indeed Father Babel and Atshapi Antane, the
great-grandfather of my husband. But there is one
thing that I do not agree with: the Innu family in
the painting is dressed as are the Indians[9] we see
in films. That is absolutely not the way we used to
dress, we the Montagnais Innu.[10] My father went on
with his story. He said:

> *"Before Tshishennish-Pien discovered ore in the
> North, we had never heard of another people who
> spoke of ore."*

Given his great age, my father had seen, in his
youth, Tshishennish-Pien:

> *"Me I was still young whereas the Innu Tshishen-
> nish-Pien was already very old," my father said.*

Kashikanit eukuannu uet issishuet :

« *Shash tshekat nishumitashumitannuepipunitshe ka*
ishpish petamat e inniuiat tipatshimun Tshishennish-
Pien ka mishkak ashininu, issishueu nutaui. Ne innu
Tshishennish-Pien katshi mishkak ashininu, eshk[u] anite
mitshetupipuna apu nita ut petamat e inniuiat kutak
eshinniut tshetshi takushinit ute tshetshi nanatuapatak
kie tshetshi mishkak ashininu, issishueu nutaui. Ek[u]
ne innu Tshishennish-Pien katshi mishkak ashininu,
anitshenat kauapikueshiht e nishiht eukuanat uinuau
tshitaimuepanat Tshishennish-Piena akua tshetshi uaui-
taminiti tanite itetshe ka mishkaminiti nenu ashininu kie
akua tshetshi uapatinianiti kutaka auennua eshinniuniti
nenu ashininu, issishueu nutaui. Kauashkamuesht mak
Kakushkuenitak eukuannu umenu uinuau utaimunuau
ka minaht Tshishennish-Piena, issishueu nutaui : "Ne
ashini ka mishkamin nete tshitassiuat, uauitamini kie
uapatiniti kutak auen eshinniut, tshika uitamatin tshe
tutashk : tshin muk[u] e peikussin tshipa tshi minu-tutak[u],
nuash peik[u] napekuian e shakassinet tshipa tshi ishpish
minik[u] tshekuannu. Muk[u] nete tshitassiuat aishkat
aianishkat tshika tshitimauat tshitshinnuat uesh ma nete
tshitassiuat tshika mishkutishkakuau kutak eshinniut.
Tshitassiuau nutim eshpishat tshika apashtakanu kie
nutim eshpishat tshika pikunakanu. Tshitaueshishimuau
innu-aueshish nete aishkat kassinu tshika nanushu.
Kie nete aishkat innu-aueshish nete tshitassiuat
tshek apu tshika ut tat. Kie nete tshitassiuat aishkat
eshakumitshishikua tshika petenau e matuetik kie
kassinu kutak tshekuan e tatueuetakanit. Kie tshe ishpish
mitshetinanut nete tshitassiuat etussenanut, e inniuiek[u]
tshika katshitinenau kassinu eishinakuak akushun. Kie
nete tshitassiuat aianishkat takuaki kassinu tshekuan

And for this reason, he said:

"*It must be for about two hundred years now
that we, the Innu, have been hearing the story
of Tshishennish-Pien who discovered the mine.
After Tshishennish-Pien had discovered the ore,
many years went by without us hearing of foreign
people who had come here to look for ore, had
found it, said my father. After the discovery of ore
by Tshishennish-Pien, it was the two priests who
warned him not to disclose the place where he
had discovered it or to show it to strangers. This,
said my father, is what Father Arnaud and Father
Babel's speech to Tshishennish-Pien was: 'If you
speak of the ore that you found on your land and
if you show it to the Foreigner, I will tell you what
will happen: you will be the only one that he can
favour, he might go so far as to give you a full
schooner of goods. But in your territory, in future
generations, your people will be destitute because
another race will replace them there. Your territory, in its entirety, will be exploited and destroyed.
Later on, all your animals, the Innu animals, will
be wasted. And the day will come when, in your
territory, there will no longer be any Innu animals.
Later on, you will hear every day explosions and
all sorts of other noises. There will be so many
workers that you, the Innu, will contract all kinds
of diseases. And when there will be all sorts of
machines, you too will have accidents because of
them and you will even come to die. And later on,
from your territory, all kinds of evil animals will
emerge. In future generations, the day will come
that you, the Innu, will be wretches.*'"

*pemipanit, kie tshinuau eukuan tshe ut ushikuiek*u *kie
nuash eukuan tshe ishi-nipiek*u*. Kie nete tshitassiuat
aishkat tshika nitautshu kassinu eishinakushit manitush.
Kie tshek nete aishkat aianishkat e inniuiek*u *tshika
matshinnutishunau."»*

*Kauashkamuesht mak Kakushkuenitak eukuannu
umenu ishi-uauitamuepanat Tshishennish-Piena,
itatshimuipanat innuat kie tshishennuat kie nukum kie
peikuan nikaui kie nutaui, issishueu nutaui. Nananat
kauapikueshiht e nishiht namaienua muk*u *Tshishennish-
Piena e peikussiniti katshi ishi-uauitamuaht umenu,
issishueu nutaui. Kauashkamuesht mak Kakushkuenitak
anite Pessamit ekute takuannipan utaiamieutshuapuau.
Ek*u *menashtakanniti enameshikananuniti ketshe-
ssimataui innua, ashit eukuannu umenu nanitam
ishi-uauitamuepanat innua, itatshimuipanat innuat kie
tshishennuat, issishueu nutaui, miam mautania-innu
ka utshipanit ute nutshimit, tshetshi eka nita utinak
ashininu ute nutshimit tshetshi petat anite uinipekut kie
tshetshi eka nita uapatiniat ashininu auennua kutaka
eshinniuniti anite uinipekut ka taniti, itatshimuipanat
innuat kie tshishennuat, issishueu nutaui.*

*Tshishennish-Pien eukuan uin atusseshtuepan
kauapikueshiniti e nishiniti anite uitshinit kie eukuan
nikamuipan enameshikananuniti anite aiamieutshuapit,
itatshimuipan nukum kie kutakat innuat. Nukum mak
nimushum eshpitishiht eukuanat uiesh tatapishkut ish-
pitishipanat miam Tshishennish-Pien, issishueu nutaui.
Ek*u *anite Pessamit takuanipan pineshaush piapanit
mani. Ne pineshaush piapaniti anite Pessamit, apu ut
natakamipanit uesh ma pakupeutshikan eshk*u *apu ut
takuak anite. Ek*u *e inniuiat metapeiati anite Pessamit,
nutinnu-mitshuapitan. Ek*u *ne pineshaush piapaniti,
ekutiki anite taukam, tapanat innuat eshitshimeht anite*

This is what Father Arnaud and Father Babel said to Tshishennish-Pien. This is what the Innu and Elders have told, my grandmother and also my mother and my father, said my father. The two priests did not only tell this to Tshishennish-Pien. The church to which belonged Fathers Arnaud and Babel was in Bersimis.[11] According to the Innu and the Elders, during their Sunday sermons, they were constantly warning the Innu[12] – the Montagnais Innu that were coming from the bush – to never take ore from the inland to bring it to the coast and show it to the Foreigner who lives along the coastline.

Tshishennish-Pien worked at the presbytery for the two priests and was a cantor in the church, so said my grandmother and other Innu. My grandmother and my grandfather were about the same age as Tshishennish-Pien, said my father. There was a schooner that came regularly to Bersimis.[13] When it arrived, it did not come up close as there was not a quay there yet. When we came out of the woods at Bersimis, we would stay in our tents. Upon its arrival, the schooner would anchor off the coast and the Innu would go to the boat in their canoes, so said my grandmother. It is there, on

*pineshautit, innu-uta apashtakanipani, itatshimuipan
nukum, issishueu nutaui. Kie ne Tshishennish-Pien ekute
anite pineshautit uiapatiniat kutaka auennua eshinniuniti nenu ashininu ka mishkak nete nutshimit.*

*Tshishennish-Pien uetutet anite pineshautit ekue
pimutet pessish nitshinat, nitshitapamikunan kie ninan
nitshitapamanan muk^u apu auat natshikapaut kie apu
aimimit, muk^u tshiam ninamishkuenishtakunan. Ninan
apu tshi aimitshit. Tshishennish-Pien nenu pemutet anite
tshipishkuat nitshinat, itashpishuipan miam peikuan
mishta-utshimau. Nenua umatshunishima kakash-
teuanit ishinakuannipani, akup ka pushkukutet anite
utat uassekutenu mak utakunishkueun kashteuanu,
miam kaiakuaiat muk^u etatu ishpananu, mak ushash-
kauteunu mak tushkapatshikannu tshikamutau anite
uiat, itatshimuipan nukum, issishueu nutaui. Tshishennish-Pien nenu uiapamitshit menuashpishut uetutet
anite pineshautit, e inniuiat nititenimatan eukuannu
nenu uiapatiniat kutaka eshinniuniti anite pineshautit
nenu ashininu ka mishkak ute Tshiuetinit. Tshishennish-
Pien nenu katshi uapatiniat kutaka eshinniuniti nenu
ashininu ka mishkak ute Tshiuetinit ek^u nenu ka uapamitshit menuashpishut peikuau etashpishut, e inniuiat
eukuannu muk^u nitshissenimatan tshekuannu ka minakanit, itatshimuipan nukum, issishueu nutaui.*

*Tshishennish-Pien tshessenimikut Kauashkamueshi-
niti kie Kakushkuenitaminiti katshi uapatiniat kutaka
eshinniuniti nenu ashininu, minuat ekue aimikupan
kauapikueshiniti e nishiniti : « Ne ashini ka mishkamin anite tshitassiuat katshi uapatinit kutak eshinniut,
kukuetshimikauini tanite ka mishkamin ne ashini, eka
uin nita uitamu kie kukuetshimishki kutak eshinniut
tshetshi itutait tanite ka mishkamin ashini, eka uin nita
itutai », itikupan Tshishennish-Pien Kauashkamueshiniti*

the schooner, that Tshishennish-Pien showed the Foreigner the ore that he had found inland.

Returning from the boat, he walked by close to our tent, he looked at us, we looked at him, but he did not even stop and he did not speak to us, he just nodded at us. We were not able to speak to him. When Tshishennish-Pien walked by the entrance of our tent, he was dressed like a gentleman. He was wearing a black-tailed suit and a top hat, he had a cane and a telescope was dangling alongside his body, so said my grandmother. Seeing Tshishennish-Pien all dressed up coming back from the schooner, we thought he had shown the Foreigner, on the boat, the ore that he had found in the North. After Tshishennish-Pien had shown him the ore, all that he received from him, from what we knew, was to have been dressed up from head to toe, just as we had seen, said my grandmother.

When Father Babel and Father Arnaud found out that Tshishennish-Pien had shown the ore to the Foreigner, they both spoke to him again: "Now that you have shown him the ore, if he asks you where you found it, never tell him and if he asks you to bring him to where you found it, never bring him," said Fathers Babel and Arnaud to Tshishennish-Pien, as told by my grandmother.

mak Kakushkuenitaminiti, itatshimuipan nukum, issi-
shueu nutaui.

   Tshishennish-Pien katshi uapatiniat kutaka eshin-
niuniti nenu ashininu ka mishkak ute Tshiuetinit, eshk^u
anite mitshetupipuna apu nita ut petamat e inniuiat
kutak eshinniut tshetshi aimuatak ashininu kie tshetshi
mishkak ashininu ute kie kakusseshiu-katipaitshesht eshk^u
apu nita ut uapamitshit ute nutshimit. Tshishennish-Pien
katshi tshissenimikut innua nenu ka tutak, apu ut minue-
nitamat tanite nanitam nikushtatan kutak eshinniut
tshetshi takushinit ute nutshimit, itatshimuipan nukum,
issishueu nutaui. Kie ushkat ka uapamitshit kutak
eshinniut ka kutshipanitat tshetshi itutet nete nutshimit,
eukuan Tshishennish-Pien uishamikupan kie tapuetue-
pan. Muk^u apu ut itutaiat katak^u nutshimit kie apu ut
uitamuat tanite anite ka mishkak ashininu. Eukuannu
umenu Tshishennish-Pien utipatshimun ka ishi-ti-
patshimut nukum kie kutakat innuat, issishueu nutaui.

   Ek^u ne kakusseshiu-katipaitshesht apu tshi uauina-
kanit tan ka tatupipunnit ka takushinit ute Tshiuetinit
usham mitshetipanat innuat ka uapamaht ushkat ka
takushinniti kakusseshiu-katipaitsheshiniti ute, issishueu
nutaui. Kakusseshiu-katipaitshesht ka takushinit ute,
innu shash mishta-shashish tshishi-tipaimupan nutim
eshpishanit utassi, ushkata e apashtat, kie shash nete
mishta-shashish uinishtam innu uauitamupan tshe
ishinikatenit nutim eshpishanit utassi : shipua, sha-
kaikana, utshua kie shipissa. Uesh innu ueshkat apu
ut takuannit unataun-assi, kassinu innu mishue nete
aitutepan nutim eshpishanit innu utassi tshetshi nana-
tuapatak tshetshi ut inniut, issishueu nutaui.

   Kie innu shashish apu ut minuatak tshetshi uauapa-
tiniat kutaka eshinniuniti ute katak^u nutshimit, issi-
shueu nutaui. Mate kakusseshiu-katipaitshesht ushkat

Afterwards, many years went by without us hearing the Foreigner speak about the ore to say he had found it here and without us seeing any White surveyors on the land. After the Innu found out what Tshishennish-Pien had done we were not happy, we were always afraid the Foreigner would come into our territories, so said my grandmother, said my father. In the beginning, when we saw the Foreigner trying to make his way inland, it was Tshishennish-Pien who was asked to bring him there. He accepted but he did not bring him far inland and he did not tell him where he had found the ore. This is the story of Tshishennish-Pien as told by my grandmother and the other Innu, said my father.

As for the White surveyors, it is not worth recalling how many years it has been since their arrival in the North, many Innu saw them upon their arrival, said my father. When they arrived here, the Innu had long finished surveying all of his territory on his own two legs and had long since, he the first, said how, throughout his territory, the rivers, lakes, mountains, and streams would be named. That is because in the past, the Innu did not have hunting grounds so to speak, each individual would hunt throughout Innu territory in search of what he needed to live, said my father.

In the past, the Innu did not like to show the Foreigner the territory inland, said my father. For instance, when the White surveyors tried at first

*ka kutshipanitat tshetshi natshi-tipaik Tshiuetinnu, apu
ut mishkuat peik^u innua tshetshi uitsheukut muk^u iapit
kutshipanitapan tshetshi kushpit eka peik^u innua e uitsheukut. Ne kakusseshiu-katipaitshesht ka kutshipanitat
tshetshi natshi-tipaitshet ute katak^u nutshimit, uiesh
muk^u nishunnuemin ishpish tshi itutetshe anite minashkuat, ekute uet tshiuekue, apu tshi itutet eka mishkuat
peik^u innua tshetshi uitsheukut. Ne kakusseshiu-katipaitshesht ka ui natshi-tipaik nitassinannu, tapanat innuat
eka uet tapuetahk tshetshi uapatiniaht utassiuau ute
nutshimit kau iapit tshek tapan innu, katshi uieshimikut
kutaka auennua eshinniuniti, tiapuetuat tshetshi
uauapatiniat assinu ute katak^u nutshimit.*

*Kashikat eukuan tshinanu uiapatamak^u ka issishueht
Kauashkamuesht kie Kakushkuenitak : ute tshitassinat
tshinanu e inniuiak^u tshitanimiunan. Ute tshitassinat
kauapishit ka natuapamitak^u, nin eukuan eshi-nishtutaman, maniteu ka tshitimut, tshinatuapamikutan tshetshi
ut inniut ute tshitassinat, issishueu nutaui.*

Eukuannu umenu nutaui utipatshimun ka petuat
uikanisha tepatshimuniti, ukauia kie ukuma kie kutaka
tshishennua. Ne Tshishennish-Pien ukussa ka uitshima-
niti innushkueua, ekute ute nipipan ne ishkueu Kaiatushkanunit kie shash mishta-tshishenniuipan ka nipit.
Ne innushkueu kie nin mitshetuau nipetuati tepatshimut
nenu tipatshimunnu utshishennima – Tshishennish-
Piena – katshi mishkaminiti ashininu ute.

Nutaui ka ishpish petuk tepatshimut kie kutakat
innuat, peikushu tshekuan niminueniteti kie nimish-
ta-ashineti : ka itashit eishinniut ka itenitak tshetshi
takushinit ute nitassinat, tapue eukuannua innua nanitam
kanuenimikupan ute nutshimit. Kie ka itashit eishinniut
innua ka kanuenimikut e peikussit ute nutshimit, apu

to come survey the North, they did not find a single
Innu who would accompany them but nonetheless,
they tried to go into the territory. When they wanted
to survey the far-away territories inland, they at best
made it about twenty miles into the woods. From
there, they apparently turned back, they were unable
to reach their destination because not a single Innu
would accompany them. When the surveyors wanted
to survey our land, there were Innu who did not want
to show them the territory, here, inland, but one day
there were some who, after they had been duped by
the Foreigner, agreed to show him the territory, the far
interior.

  Today, we are witnesses to what Father Arnaud
and Father Babel had said: our own way of life, Innu,
is difficult in our territory. This is how I understand
these things, when the Foreigner came to us, it is him
who was poor, he came to us to earn a living in our
territory, said my father.

This is the story my father heard told by his parents, by his mother, by his grandmother and by many
other Elders. The Innu woman who married the son of
Tshishennish-Pien died here in Schefferville, she died
very old. Me too I have often heard that woman tell the
story of her father-in-law Tshishennish-Pien who had
discovered ore here.

Since I heard my father and the other Innu tell this
story, there is one thing that made me feel happy and
very proud: it has always been the Innu who took care,
on the land, of all the foreigners who had the idea to
come into our territory. And we never heard that any
one of those foreigners, who had been taken care of by

nita ut petamat tshetshi matshi-tutakut innua kie tshetshi
manenimikut miam uin kauapishit kashikanit etutuimit e
inniutshit.

Kashikat eukuan uet issishueian : kauapishit eshk^u eka
peik^u ka takushinit ute nitassinat, shash nete nikanuenitetan innishun. Kauapishit ka ishpish uitshimakanitu-
tutshit, tshekat eshakumitshishikua nipetenan essishuet :
« Innuat apu innishiht. » Kauapishit eshpish uitshimaka-
nitututshit ute nitassinat, e inniuiat mitshetuau nimishke-
nan kauapishit anu uin eka innishit mak ninan.

the Innu in the woods, and who though was alone,
had been mistreated or offended by them the way the
White man, him, treats us, the Innu.

It is for this reason that I say today: before any
White man came here to our territory, we were already
civilized. Since the White man has been our neighbour, almost every day we hear him say: "The Indians
are not civilized."[14] Since he has been our neighbour
on our land, we, the Innu, we often see that the White
man is less civilized than us.

3

Kakusseshiu-tshishkutamatun

Ume ninan eshinniuiat mautania, anite minashkuat ka ut
inniuiat, tutakanipan nikatshishkutamatsheutshuapinan,
patetat-tatunnu ashu nisht^u ka itashtet mishta-atshitashun.
Ne katshishkutamatsheutshuap ka uapatamat ka
tutakanit, apu nita ut ishi-mamitunenitamat tshetshi ne
ut unitaiat nitinniunnan kie apu nita ut ishi-mamitunenitamat tshetshi ne ut animiuiat nete aishkat. Nikatshishkutamatsheutshuapinan ka ui tutakanit, kassinu tshekuan
e minuat nitaitikautan kie kassinu tshekuan e minuat
nitaishi-uapatinikautan. Ishi-tshitshipannanuipan muk^u
tshetshi minuenitamat. Kauapishit ka ishi-mamitunenitak
tshetshi kakusseshiu-tshishkutamuat nitauassiminana,
nititenimau nin, uin shash minu-tshissenitamukupan
anite nikan tshe ishi-matshipanimit e inniutshit. Ek^u
uin tapue ninan e inniuiat ueshkat ka ishi-uauitamuimit
kauapishit tshetshi ishinniuiat miam kauapishit, apu
tshekuan anite ut nishtutamat kie apu tshekuan anite ut
mamitunenitamat tan tshe ishpaniat nete nikan, tatupipuna tshi ishinniuiati kauapishit utinniun.
    Anitshenat katshishe-utshimau-atusseht eukuannu
ushkat tshitshue nuapamatanat kie eukuannu tshitshue
ushkat nipetuatanat eimiaht innua. Kie e inniuiat anitshenat katshishe-utshimau-atusseht ushkat ka uapamitshit,
nitishi-utinatanat eukuanat uinuau tepenimimit. Kassinu
eissishueht uemut ishinakuan tshetshi tapuetutshih, nitishi-

3

White education

At the time when we were living in the woods, we the Montagnais Innu,[15] a school was built for us. That was in 1953. When we saw it being built, we never thought that school would make us lose our culture and we never imagined that it would be a source of misery for us later on. When they were thinking of building us a school, we were told all sorts of good things and we were shown all kinds of nice things. This was done in the beginning, but only so as not to displease us. So when the White man thus thought to give our children a White education, I myself think he knew exactly that in the future, he would cause us problems. As for us, Innu, when he spoke to us in the past about living like him, we did not understand it at all and we did not think about what would happen to us in the future, once we had lived the White man's life for a certain number of years.

It is then that we saw for the first time real officials from the Department of Indian Affairs and it was the first time that we heard them speak to the Innu. That time, we thought of them as those who governed us. We understood that we had to agree with everything they would say and that is

nishtutetan. Eukuan ka ut ishpish mishta-uieshimikauiat anite pet utat e inniuiat. Uesh ma anitshenat katshishe-utshimau-atusseht nenu ka ishi-utinitshit uinuau tipenitamuat, eukuannu minuenitamukupanat tshetshi katshinassimimiht. Mate katshishkutamatsheutshuap ka ui tutakanit ut ninan e inniuiat, anitshenat katshishe-utshimau-atusseht eukuan issishuepanat :

« Ne tshikatshishkutamatsheutshuapuau tshe tutaka-nit anumat tshika minuashu anite pitukamit, kassinu tshekuan tshika takuan kie anitshenat tshitauassimuauat nenu anutshish tshe tshishkutamuakaniht. Ne tshe tutaka-nit tshikatshishkutamatsheutshuapuau tshika ishinakuta-kanu tshetshi kanuenimakaniht tshitauassimuauat anite katshishkutamatsheutshuapit, tshetshi eka mamashitakut tshinuau ui tutamekui iapit ka tutamek^u, ui kushpiekui anite nutshimit, issishuepanat. Kie anitshenat tshitauassi-muauat tshe kanuenimakaniht anite katshishkutama-tsheutshuapit, anumat tshika minu-tutuakanuat, kassinu tshekuannu tshika minakanuat, tshika minu-ashamaka-nuat tshetshi ut minuinniuht, unushushkun-piminu tshika miniakanuat tshetshi shutshishiht. Anitshenat tshitauassi-muauat nenu uet ui kakusseshiu-tshishkutamuakaniht, ui minu-tshishkutamuakanuat kie tshika minuenite-nau uapamekuti tshishi-tshishkutamuakanitaui. Mate tshe uapamek^u innu-auass e kauapikueshiut kie tshe uapamek^u innu-auass e natukunishiut kie tshe uapamek^u innushkuess e kakashteukupeshkueut kie tshe uapamek^u innu-auass e takuaikanut kie tshe uapamek^u innu-auass kaimisht e ishi-atusset », nitaitikutanat anitshenat katshishe-utshimau-atusseht.

Nitauassiminanat ka utinakaniht tshetshi kanue-nimakaniht anite innu-katshishkutamatsheutshuapit,

why we have been deceived so often in the past, we the Innu. Since we considered the officials from the Department of Indian Affairs to be those who governed us, they most certainly had a good laugh lying to us. For instance, when they wanted to build us a school, they said:

"We will build you a school, it will be beautiful inside, it will have everything you need. From now on, your children will go to that school. We will build it so as to keep your children so that you will not be prevented from doing what you want, if you want to go out onto the land, they said. Your children will be kept in the boarding school. They will be very well taken care of, everything will be given to them. They will be well fed so as to stay healthy and we will give them cod liver oil so that they become strong. The reason why we want to send your children to the White man's school is because we want them to have a good education and you will be happy to see them when they will be done with their studies. You will see, for instance, the young Indian boy become a priest and a doctor, you will see the young Indian girl become a nun, you will see the young Indian boy become a superintendent and a lawyer," said the officials from the Department of Indian Affairs.

When they took our children away to put them in the Indian residential school, it is true that they

tapue apu tshekuannu nanatuenitamuakaniht tshetshi
tshishikashuht, tshishuashpitakanipanat shetshen,
kassinu tshekuannu shetshen aitutakupanat innu-
tshishe-utshimaua. Kie tapue ne nikatshishkutamatsheutshuapinan katshi tshishtakanit, anite pitukamit
miam peikuan atauitshuap ishinakuanipan, nenu
nitauassiminanat kassinu tshekuannu tshe aitapash-
taht : umitshimuau, umatshunishimuaua kie kassinu
eishinakuak ka tipashkunakanit patshuian ashit tshetshi
tutakanniti umatshunishimuaua. Kie tapue muk^u
uinuau e innu-auassiuht tshishkutamuakanipanat anite
innu-katshishkutamatsheutshuapit.

   Ne katshishkutamatsheutshuap ka tutakanit ut ninan,
nitishi-katshinassimikutan tshetshi kanuenimakaniht
nitauassiminanat anite katshishkutamatsheutshuapit,
ne innu nanitam ka kushpit anite nutshimit tshetshi eka
mamashikut nenu utauassima, iapit tshetshi kushpit.
Muk^u innu nenua utauassima ka utinakanniti tshetshi
tshishkutamuakanniti, uipat nenu shash ekue tshisseni-
tamupan kassinu tshekuannu tshe eka miminupannit uin
innu utaitun kassinu ka ishinniut tanite ne katshishkutamatsheutshuap katshi tshishtakanit, kauapikueshiht mak
ushteshimauat mak kakashteukupeshkueuat eukuanat
kanuenimepanat innu-auassa. Ek^u ne innu nanitam ute
nutshimit ka pet kanuenimat utauassima, mamituneni-
tamupan nenu uesh ma innu uin utinniun ka ishinniut,
apu nenu ut ishinakuannit utinniun tshetshi tatipan taniti
nutim utauassima, innu-auass patush napauti nakatepan
utauia kie ukauia. Innu-auass ka utinakanit tshetshi tshishkutamuakanit kie nenu tshe kanuenimakanit anite katshishkutamatsheutshuapit, innu apu shuk^u ut minuenitak
uiapamat utauassima aitshinnua tshetshi kanuenimikuniti.

   Ne ka ishi-uauitamakauiat tshetshi ishinniuiat
miam ueshkat, tshetshi iapit kushpiat anite nutshimit,

were not asked for money, they were clothed for
free, the federal government provided for everything. And it is true that once our school had been
built, the inside looked like a store, there was everything that our children would need: food, personal
effects of all sorts, and all kinds of cloth by the yard
to make them clothes. And it is true that the boarding school was reserved for the Innu children.

We were made to believe that the school was
built to keep our children so that the Innu who
was used to going out into the bush could do so
without being prevented by his children, so that he
could still go out onto the land. But the Innu whose
children were taken away and put in school knew
early on that nothing would work again in his way
of life because, once the construction of the school
was over, it was the priests, the brothers and the
nuns who would have the duty to care for the Innu
children. This preoccupied the Innu, he who was
used to always taking care of his children himself
in the bush. When the Innu lived his own life, his
culture did not allow him to be separated from each
of his children. The youth left his father and mother
later, when he got married. When the Innu child
was taken to be educated and kept as a boarder, the
Innu was not happy to see his child under the care
of strangers.

We tried to live like before, to go out onto the
land anyway, as we were told. But that did not suit

nikutshipanitatan. Muk^u apu ut mitshetupipuna minupa-
nikauiat tanite e inniuiat apu ut ishi-nakanauiat tatipan
tshetshi taiat kassinu papeik^u kautishkuemit utauassima.
Shash apu tshi kushpit innu ishpish kutunnuepishimua
tanite nenua utauassima kanuenimakanniti anite katshishkutamatsheutshuapit, uemut ui uapameu, uemut ui
tshissenimeu tan tshe aitutuakanniti tshetshi minu-tutuakannikueni kie ma tshetshi eka minu-tutuakannikueni.
Nititeniten nin eukuannu nenu ka ut itenitak kie uin innu
tshetshi kakusseshiu-atusset.

Ne uin ishkuteutapan shash pimipanipan eshpanit ute
nutshimit kie ne kauapishit shash tshitshipanipan tshetshi
itutet anite itetshe nutshimit ninan e inniuiat nanitam ka
ut pet inniuiat. Ek^u ne kauapishit mishkut nui tutakutan
anite itetshe uin utassit uinipekut peikutau tshetshi apiat.
Kauapishit eukuannu muk^u ka ut tutak nikatshishkuta-
matsheutshuapinannu anite itetshe uinipekut Uashat.
Kauapishit nui mishkutunamakutan nitassinannu,
mishkut nenu uin utassi nui minikutan eka tshekuannu
anite ut e tshissenitamunimit. Kauapishit ka ui itutet
nutshimit nitassinat, kassinu nitaishi-maminuashiku-
tan anite itetshe uin utitaunit uinipekut; e inniuiat nete
itetshe uinipekut tutamupan nitshinana kie nikatshish-
kutamatsheutshuapinannu nete itetshe uinipekut tutamupan. Ek^u uin kauapishit niatshi-manukatishut ute itetshe
nutshimit, ninan e inniuiat nanitam ka ut inniuiat.

Ne katshishkutamatsheutshuap ka tutakanit ut ninan,
kashikat eukuan eshi-mamitunenitaman : ushtuin atut ut
minuau ut ninan e inniuiat kie ushtuin atut ut tshekuan
ishpitenitakuan ut ninan e inniuiat. Kashikat e mami-
tunenitakanit, peik^u e nishiki anite ishinakuanikupan
katshishkutamatsheutshuap ka ut tutakanit ut ninan e
inniuiat : put e ui minu-tutakauiat kie ma put muk^u e
ui matshi-tutakauiat. Muk^u nin anu nui ishi-nishtuten

us for long because we are not used to, we Innu,
each family living apart from their children. The
Innu could therefore no longer go out onto the land
ten months at a time because his children were
being kept as boarders. Of course he wanted to see
them and to check how they were being taken care
of, if they were being treated well or not. And it is
for this reason, I believe, that the Innu then thought
about getting him too a job.

The train that went up all the way into the territory was working by then and the White man
had already begun to go there where we had always
lived. In exchange, he wanted to make sure we
would settle next to his own territory, by the coast.
This is the only reason why it was in Sept-Îles, by
the coast, that he built our school. He wanted, without letting us know, to move us from our territory
and in return he gave us his. When he wanted to go
out onto our lands, inland, the White man made
our eyes shimmer with all the goods of his own
settlement on the coast; it is along the coastline
that he built our houses, that is where he built our
school. And he went to live inland, there where we
had always lived, we the Innu.

This is what I think now of that school they built
us: probably it was not good for us and probably it
had no value for us, the Innu. When we think today
about the reasons why the school was built for us,
there are two possibilities: either it was built for our
good or it was built to harm us. As for me, I tend
to think that it was solely to harm us, to make us
disappear, to have us settle, we the Innu, so that we

muk^u tshiam nui matshi-tutakautan, muk^u nui tutakautan
tshetshi eka tshissenitakushiat e inniuiat mak muk^u nui
tutakautan e inniuiat peikutau tshetshi apiat tshetshi eka
katshepishkutshit kauapishit nenu nitassinannu muk^u
uin ka ui pakassiuatshet. E inniuiat eukuan muk^u ka ut
tutakanit nikatshishkutamatsheutshuapinan. Kauapishit
ka ui natuapamimit tshetshi natshi-pakassiuatshet nitassinannu, ishkuteutapan-meshkanau ka ui itamutakanit ute
nitassinat, nitishi-uauinikutan kie nitishi-pamipanikutan
miam ume ninan e inniuiat eka ut minuat nitinnniunnan
ka ishinniuiat mak atut nut innishinan. Kauapishit, nititenimau nin, eukuannu umenu ka ishi-mamitunenitak
ka tutak innu-katshishkutamatsheutshuapinu tshetshi
tshishkutamuat innu-auassa, muk^u tshetshi pipikunamuat
utinnniunnu.

Anitshenat nitauassiminanat nishtam ka utinakaniht tshetshi kakusseshiu-tshishkutamuakaniht, tapue
pissik^u innu-tshishe-utshimaua aitutakupanat. Katshi
tatupipuna, apu auat ut matenitamat nitauassiminanat e
ashu-patshitinakanikuenit anite kakusseshiu-katshishkutamatsheutshuapit. Kauapishit nenu ka itenitak tshetshi
ishi-tutak, apu ut kukuetshimimit e inniutshit. Kie
anitshenat nitauassiminanat katshi ashu-patshitinakanih
anite kakusseshiu-katshishkutamatsheutshuapit,
kauapishit ekue pikuaimupan nenu ueshkat ka tutak
nitinnu-katshishkutamatsheutshuapinannu anite Uashat.

Kashikanit nitauassiminanat etuteht anite
kakusseshiu-katshishkutamatsheutshuapit, nitshissenitenan muk^u kamashikatunanut eukuan tekuak
innu-auassat mamu kakusseshiu-auassat. Nitauassiminanat nitshissenimananat mishta-ait eishi-utinakanih
anite kakusseshiu-katshishkutamatsheutshuapit. Itashuat
innu-auassat essishueht : « E innu-auassiuiat nimatshi-tu-
takaunan, nimanenimikaunan kie nuaushinakaunan,

would not disturb the White man while he earned
his livelihood in our own territory. These are the
only reasons why they built us a school. When the
White man thought to seek us out so as to exploit
our territory, when he thought to build the railway
there, he started speaking about us and insinuated
that the culture that we had was not good and that
we were not civilized. In my opinion, the only thing
the White man was thinking about when he built a
residential school to educate the Innu children was
to destroy their culture.

When, in the beginning, they took our children
to give them a White man's education, it is true that
they answered solely to the federal government.
A few years later, we did not even realize that they
were being transferred to the school board. When
the White man thought of this transfer, he did not
consult with us, we the Innu. Once our children
transferred to the provincial school, the White man
demolished the residential school he had built for us
in Sept-Îles.

Now that our children are in a school run by
the school board, we know that there is constant
fighting between the White children and the Innu
children. We know that our children are treated
in a rather peculiar way there. A certain number
of them say: "We the Innu children, we are bul-
lied, we are insulted, and we are made fun of. For
instance, the White children and even the teachers

issishueuat. Mate e innu-auassiuiat nitishinikatikunanat
« pikauish » kakusseshiu-auassat kie peikuan katshishkutamatsheshiht », issishueuat. Ne aimun PIKAUISH
namaieu ninan nitaimunnan, namaieu mautania-innu-
aimun. Ne aimun PIKAUISH nashpit apu tshissenitamat
tanite uetshipanit kie apu nishtutamat tan essishuemakak.
Innu-auassat uinuau eukuan eshi-nishtutahk : « Nitinnu-aimunnan nitishi-manenimikaunan ». Eukuannu
uet eka minuenitahk pietuataui auennua essishueniti
« pikauish » kie ma « matshi-manitu-pikauish » anite
kakusseshiu-katshishkutamatsheutshuapit.

Kie anitshenat nitauassiminanat etuteht anite
kakusseshiu-katshishkutamatsheutshuapit, mitshetuau
nipetenan essishuet kauapishit : « Innu-auassat utikumuat. » Mate ne kapakashimunanut nete utenat ueshkat
mamu apashtapanat kakusseshiu-auassat mak innu-
auassat. Tshek innu-auassat ekue nakauakanniht tshetshi
ituteht anite kapakashimunanunit : « Usham utikumuat
innu-auassat », issishuepanat kauapishiht. Kie anitshenat
nitauassiminanat tekushinitaui nitshinat, mitshetuau issishueuat : « Nishikauikautan shikauniss ekue uitamakauiat
tat^u e mishkuakaniht nitikuminanat », issishueuat. Ek^u
anitshenat katshishkutamatsheshiht katshi uauapatamua-
taui innu-auassa upishkueunnua ekue tutahk mitshet
mashinaikanuiana ekue minaht nenu innu-auassa papeik^u
mashinaikanuiannu tshetshi tshiuetataniti uitshuanit,
kassinu ukaumau innushkueu tshetshi tshitapatak nenu
mashinaikanuiannu. Mate nika tipatshimun. Peikuau
nitauassim ekue petat nenu mashinaikanuiannu nitshinat.
Ne mashinaikanuian ekue tshitapataman, eukuan etashtet : « Ue tshitauassim nuauapatamuatan upishkueuna
kie nishikauiatan shikaunissinu kie nimishkamuatan
utikuma. Ue tshitauassim uinakuannua upishkueuna
kie tshika shikauiau shikaunissinu kie tshinuau anite

call us Pikauish." The word PIKAUISH is not one
of our words, it does not belong to the Montagnais
Innu language.[16] We have no idea where this expression comes from and we do not understand what
it means. But this is how the Innu children, they
understand it: "They are making fun in this way of
our Innu language." This is the reason why they are
not happy when they hear someone say, at school,
"Pikauish" or "Damn Pikauish."

Also, now that our children go to a school run
by the school board, we often hear the White man
say: "The Indian children have lice." In the past, for
instance, Innu children and White children would
go to the municipal pool, then one day, the pool was
forbidden to Innu children: "They have lice," said
the White men. And when our children come home
from school, they often say: "They fine-combed
our hair and then they told us how many lice they
found." After examining the Innu children's hair,
the teachers would prepare a pile of notes and hand
one out to each child so that they would take it
home to their Innu mothers to read. I will tell you.
Once, one of my children brought home one of
these notes. I read it. On it, there was written: "We
examined your child's hair, we fine-combed it and
we found lice. Your child's hair is dirty. You will
fine-comb him, along with every other member of
your family, once a week," said the White man from
the White school, over there. After I read the note, I
tore it up and threw it in the garbage.

tshitshiuat kassinu etashiekᵘ tshe shikauiekᵘ shikauniss
peikuau peikuminashtakana », nitikᵘ kauapishit nete ut
kakusseshiu-katshishkutamatsheutshuapit. Ne mashinaikanuian katshi tshitapataman ekue pikuetshipitaman
ekue uepimitaman anite kauepinashunanut.

Anitshenat uin ikuat nanitam pietamani uiauinakanitaui anite kakusseshiu-katshishkutamatsheutshuapit, apu
tshekuan ishi-mamitunenitaman uesh ma nin nitishi-
utinen ikᵘ apu tshekuan ishpitenitakushit. Kauapishit katshi
nanuiat nitauassima e innu-auassiuniti, kashikat eukuan
tekuak tshekuan tshetshi ut mishta-mamitunenitaman
tshe ishpish inniuian. Kassinu eitashtet mashinaikanuian ka utshipanit anite kakusseshiu-katshishkutamatsheutshuapit, apu minuat ui uapataman tanite nitauassim
etutet anite kakusseshiu-katshishkutamatsheutshuapit,
namaienu ninishtam nititenitamun, uin kauapishit ush-
kuishtuepan nitauassima e innu-auassiuniti mukᵘ tshetshi
nanuiat mak mukᵘ tshetshi shuniauatshet. Uesh ma e
inniuiat niminu-tshissenitenan innu-tshishe-utshimau
mishta-ashtau shunianu anite kakusseshiu-katshishkutamatsheutshuapit nenua ut nitauassiminana. Peikushu
tshekuan nin meshkatenitaman : kauapishit apu nita uaka-
tamuat kie apu nita manenitamuat innua ushuniaminu.

Kauapishit kashikanit mitshetuau issishueu :
« Innu-auassat nitaniminikunanat, apu ui ituteht anite
katshishkutamatsheutshuapit. » Kauapishit tapueu nenu
essishuet mukᵘ apu mashkatenitakuak. Innu-auass
tan tshipa ishi-minuatamᵘ nenu ? Mukᵘ issishuetau e
inniuiat kauapishit uishamitshiti tshetshi uitsheuimit
anite nitinnu-inniunnat minashkuat ; ne kauapishit eka
minuataki tshetshi uitsheuimit, e inniuiat atut nita nipa
utinenan mishtikᵘ tshetshi ut ututamautshit tshetshi
ushkuishtutshit tshetshi uitsheuimit. Ekᵘ uin kauapishit ka uishamat nitauassima e innu-auassiuniti tshetshi

The fact that there is constant talk of lice in
the school run by the school board, I do not care:
I myself think that lice are a detail. What worries
me greatly now, and I will always worry about it for
the rest of my life, is that the White man sullied my
children. I never want to see one of those notes that
comes from a White school again. If my children go
to a school run by the school board, it was certainly
not me who had the idea, it is the White man who
compelled them, if only to ruin them and to make
money off of them. Because we, the Innu, know
very well that the federal government pays a lot
of money to those school boards for our children.
There is one thing that surprises me: the White
man never hates or insults the Innu's money...

Nowadays, the White man often says: "The
Indian children cause us problems, they do not
want to go to school." The White man is telling the
truth. But that is not surprising, how could the Innu
child like that? Nonetheless, let us speculate that we
Innu invited the White man to accompany us in our
culture, in the bush; if the White man did not want
to come with us, we never would have hit him, us,
with a stick to force him to accompany us. When the
White man, he, incited my children to get a White
man's education, he forced them terribly, he went so

kakusseshiu-tshishkutamuat, mishta-ushkuishtuepan
nuash mishtikunu apashtapan. Kauapishit tatupipuna ka
ushkuishtuat nitauassiminana e innu-auassiuniti tshetshi
kakusseshiu-tshishkutamuat, nitapuetuau tapue animi-
nikutshe. Muk^u nititenimau nin kauapishit uin kashikanit
shash apu mishta-mamitunenitak kie shash apu aieshkushit
nenua ut nitauassiminana uesh ma kauapishit kashikanit
shash tshissenitam^u tshe ishpish inniunnanunit uin tshe
uitsheukut nenua nitauassiminana e innu-auassiuniti.
Nititenimau nin kauapishit kashikanit uin apu tshekuannu
mitatak nenua ut nitauassiminana. Kashikat ninan e
inniuiat kuessipan tekuak tshetshi ut mishta-mamituneni-
tamat kie tshetshi ut mishta-animiuiat kie tshetshi ut mish-
ta-mitatamat anitshenat ut nitauassiminanat.

   Tanite anitshenat nitauassimat nenu ut katshi
kakusseshiu-tshishkutamuakaniht, kashikanit utinnu-inniunuau apu tshekuannu anite nishtuapatahk,
utinnu-aimunuau unitauat, utinnu-mitshimuau shash
minaush mitshuat, ka itashpishuht e innu-auassiuht
unitauat. Kashikanit nitauassiminanat nenu ut katshi
kakusseshiu-tshishkutamuakaniht, miam tetaut tauat :
apu pikutaht tshetshi ishi-pakassiuht utinnu-inniunuau
kie apu nakanauiht tshetshi kakusseshiu-pakassiuht.
Kashikanit nitauassimat nuapamauat, eukuannu muk^u e
takuannit tshekuannu tshetshi tutahk, natamik^u meshkanat tshetshi papamuteht. Uesh ma nitauassimat e
innu-auassiuht kie uinau takuannipan utinniunuau
kie anu minuanipan. Uesh ma kassinu innu utauassima
utinniun ka ishi-tshishkutamuat, uemut mishta-kutshipanitapan tshetshi minu-tshishkutamuat utinniun tshetshi
uapamat utauassima tshetshi minu-pakassitishuniti nenu
ut e natauniti kassinu eishinakushiniti innu-aueshisha.

   Nitauassiminanat ka utinakaniht tshetshi kakusseshiu-
tshishkutamuakaniht, eukuan ka ishi-mamitunenitaman :

far as to use a stick. Over the many years that the White man has forced our children to get a White man's education, I believe it, it is true that they must cause him problems. But I think that today, he no longer really worries about nor makes an effort with our children: he is already certain that it is he that our children will follow forever. I myself believe that the White man has no regrets today about our children. It is now our turn, we the Innu, to have reasons to worry greatly and to have, because of them, serious problems and deep regrets.

Because of the White man's education that they received, today my children know nothing of their Innu culture, they are losing their Innu language, they barely eat their Innu food, they have forgotten their customary clothing. Because they went to the White man's school, our children now find themselves in an in-between: they are not able to provide for themselves through their Innu culture and they are not used to earning a livelihood the White man's way either. Today, I see my people, all they have left to do, is to loaf around. Yet my Innu children did have a culture and it was that one that was the better one: each Innu who taught his own culture to his children went to great lengths to teach them carefully in the hopes that he would see them provide well for themselves, by hunting all the kinds of Innu animals.

When they took our children away to give them a White man's education, this is what I thought:

« Tapue anu uin tshika innishu mak nin. Nitauassim
nenu tshe kakusseshiu-tshishkutamuakanit, nete aishkat
nika uapamau anu uin tshika minupu mak nin tanite
ne nitauassim nete aishkat nanitam tshika mishkam[u] e
minuanit kakusseshiu-atusseunnu kie eukuan uin tshe
tshishpeuashit. Uesh ma nin tshe ishpish inniuian apu
nita tshika ut pikutaian tshetshi tshishpeuatitishuian
anite itetshe kauapishit utinniunit », nititeniteti. Uesh ma
nitauassimat e innu-auassiuht ka utinakaniht tshetshi
kakusseshiu-tshishkutamuakaniht, nin nitshisseniteti
tshe eka nita tshishkutamakauian. Kashikat uiapatamani
kakusseshiu-tshishkutamatun, apu tshekuan anite
mitataman uesh ma niminu-nishtuten, apu tshekuan
ishpitenitakuak ut ninan e inniuiat.

Anutshish innu-tshishkutamuakanuat nitauassiminanat. Tshishe-utshimau kashikanit kutshipanitakashu
kau tshetshi innu-tshishkutamuat innu-auassa muk[u]
tshetshi minuenitamat e inniuiat. Eukuannu nanitam ka
ishi-tutuimit e inniutshit tshishe-utshimau. Nititeniten
nin, innu-auass katshi unitat utinnu-aimun, anumat
tshika animannu kau tshetshi katshitinak. Uesh ma
kashikat eshinniuiat kauapishit utinniun, nititeniten nin
namaieu tshitshue innu-aimun eshi-aimiat. Uesh ma
kashikat e inniuiat kakusseshiu-mitshuapit nitapinan
kie kassinu eishinakuak kauapishiu-apashtaun eukuan
e apashtaiat; eukuan ka ut tshishipanit tshetshi unitaiat
nitinnu-aimunnan uesh ma e inniuiat nitinniunnan ka
ishinniuiat anite nutshimit, aitanipan ka ishi-aimiat.
Nana nitinnu-aimunnan anite nutshimit ka apashtaiat, eukuan nana tshitshue nitinnu-aimunnan. Ek[u]
nin nititenitamun, nana tshitshue nitinnu-aimunnan
ka unitaiat, namaieute anite kakusseshiu-katshishkutamatsheutshuapit tshe ut unuimakak kie namaieute
kakusseshiu-ninipassite.

"My child will be smarter than me. He will get an education, I will see him later on in a better situation than my own because in the future he will always find a good job and he will be able to help me. Me, I will never be able to manage on my own in the White man's culture," I thought. Indeed, when they took my children to give them an education, I knew that I would never go to school. Nowadays, when I see that White man's education, I have no regrets because I understand all too well that the White man's education is not worth anything to us, Innu.

Now our children are getting courses in Innu. The government today pretends to provide again Innu children with an Innu education, only to please us. It is always in this way that the government has behaved towards us, the Innu. Me, I think that once an Innu child has lost his Innu language, it will be very hard for him to regain it. Now that we live the White man's life, in my opinion it is not the real Innu language that we speak. We now live in the White man's houses and we use all of the things of the White man's culture; it is for this reason that we are rapidly losing our Innu language. When we lived our real Innu lives in the bush, the language that we spoke was different. Our real Innu language is the one that we used in the bush. In my opinion, the real Innu language that we have lost will not come out of a provincial school or a White man's university.

Nititeniten nin, tshishe-utshimau ishpitenitakakue nitinnu-aimunnannu miam nenu umishtikushiu-aimun eshpish mishta-ishpitenitak, ka tshitshipanit innu-auassa tshetshi kakusseshiu-tshishkutamuat, ushtuin tshipa mishta-kutshipanitapan tshetshi eka nipatauat utinnu-aimunnu. Kauapishit kashikanit mitshetuau nipetuanan essishuet : « Innu ishinakuannu kie uin tshetshi ishpitenitakannit utinnu-inniun. » Kauapishit nenu essishuet, nin apu tapuetuk tanite eukuan uin ka nikuashkatak nitinnu-inniunnannu kie nitinnu-aimun-nannu. Kashikanit kauapishit kutshipanitau innu-auassa tshetshi innu-tshishkutamuat mamash muk^u tshetshi minuenitamat e inniuiat. Kauapishit nenu innu-auassa ua innu-tshishkutamuat, ekute anite iapit etishauat anite kakusseshiu-katshishkutamatsheutshuapit kie ashit mishtikushiu-tshishkutamueu. Kie ne kauapishit nenua innu-auassa ua innu-tshishkutamuat, ishpish peikumi-nashtakana apu auat peikutipaikana patshitinak tshetshi innu-tshishkutamuakanniti. Mak innu-auass nenu ua innu-tshishkutamuakanit, ute ninan Kaiatushkanut, ut tshitshipaniakanu neu ka itapit. Ne innu-auass neu ka itapit anite kakusseshiu-tshishkutamatunit, shash unitau utinnu-aimun. Nititeniten nin, tapueti kauapishit nenu ua innu-tshishkutamuat innu-auassa, namaienu uin tshetshi tshissenitak tan tshe ishi-tutuakaniht nitauassiminanat nenu ua innu-tshishkutamuakaniht, ninan e inniuiat ishinakuannu kauapishit tshetshi kukuetshimimit tan eishi-mamitunenitamat tshe ishi-tshishkutamuakaniht nitauassiminanat.

Kauapishit tapueti innu-auassa tshetshi innu-tshish-kutamuat, ne auass ushkat etutet anite katshishkutama-tsheutshuapit, nishtam tshipa tshishkutamuakanu pissik^u utaimun tshetshi minu-tshissenitak eshk^u eka nishtuapa-tak kutaka eshinniuniti utaimunnu. Kie tshipa tau innu

I believe that if the government had as much
respect for our Innu language as it does for its
own French language, once they started giving a
White man's education to our Innu children, they
would have made some serious efforts so as not to
kill their Innu language. Today we often hear the
White man say: "The Indian too must be proud of
his Indian culture." I do not believe the White man
when he says that because he is the one who buried
our Innu culture and language. Now he tries to give
a rudimentary education in Innu to our children,
only to appease us. When the White man wants
to give an Innu education to our children, he still
sends them to the school run by the school board
and in parallel, gives them an education in French.
And he does not even give them an hour a week of
Innu courses. Moreover, here in Schefferville, Innu
courses start in the fourth grade. The child who is
in fourth grade in the White man's education system has already lost his Innu language. If the White
man is telling the truth when he says he wants to
teach Innu to Innu children, I think that it is not up
to him to know how that education is to be given to
our children, he must ask us, Innu, how we foresee
such an education for our children.

If the White man truly wants to give an Innu
education to the Innu child, when the child first
arrives at school, he should first receive an education entirely in his language so that he knows it
properly before learning the language of another

tshetshi tshishkutamuat auassa anite minashkuat tshetshi
nishtuapatak innu-auass. Uesh ma e inniuiat nitissishue-
nan innu-auass tshipa apatannu tshetshi nishtuapatak
anite minashkuat uesh ma tau innu-auass menuatak
tshetshi itutet anite minashkuat. Ek^u e inniuiat nitissi-
shuenan innu-auass eituteti anite minashkuat, kushpine-
nitakushu tshetshi ushikut, miam mate anite nipit, kie ma
tshetshi unishinit anite minashkuat kie ma e pipunniti
tshetshi shikatshit. Nititeniten nin, napess kie peikuan
ishkuess mishta-apatannu tshetshi nishtuapatak anite
minashkuat kie tshetshi tshissenitak tan tshe ishi-
tshishuashpishut pepunniti ua ituteti anite minashkuat.
Nititeniten nin mishta-apatan tshetshi minu-tshishku-
tamuakanit innu-auass, napess kie peikuan ishkuess, kassinu eishinakuak nitinnu-inniunnan uesh ma innu-auass
eka nashpit nishtuapatak utinniun, tshipa tshi tau tshetshi
mitatak nete aishkat. Uesh ma mate anite aitassit ka itashit
innu ka unitat utinnu-inniun kie utinnu-aimun, kashikat
mitshetuau nipetenan e mitatak nenu.

Miam mate ninan e inniuiat takuanipani nitinnu-
ishinikashunnana ek^u anite eshukaitashuiat ekute uet
utshipanit tshetshi ut unitaiat. At ma eshukaitashuiati,
uemut kie ninan ishinakuanipan tshe ishpish inniunanut
tshetshi kanuenitamat nitinnu-ishinikashunnana.

Mate nin kashikat nitishinikashun Matam^9 Antane.
Ek^u nitinnu-ishinikashun, ninapem utishinikashu-
nuau aianishkat KAPESH. Ek^u ne Kapesh tshimisha-
kanu ne ishinikashun, ninapem umushum tshitshue
utinnu-ishinikashunnu, eukuan SHUKAPESH. Ek^u ne
Shukapesh, eukuan issishuemakak : napeu e shukate-
nitakushit. Eukuannu ka ut ishinikatakanniti ninapem
umushuma Shukapesh. Ume ishinikashun Shukapesh
apu nita petaman kauapishit tshetshi ishinikatakanit
ek^u ne ishinikashun Antane mitshetuau nipeten

ethnic group. And there could be Innu who teach
him out on the land so that he learns about the
bush. We, the Innu, think it is important that the
Innu child knows the bush, there are children who
like going out into the bush. When the child goes
out into the bush, we tell ourselves, it is dangerous,
he might have an accident, in the water for instance,
or he might get lost in the forest or he could freeze
in the winter. I myself think that it is very important that both boys and girls know the bush, that
they know how to dress in the wintertime if they
want to go there. I believe that it is very important
to teach the Innu children – boys and girls – properly all of the aspects of our Innu culture because
if they do not know their culture at all, some may
come to regret it later on. Nowadays, we often hear
that all the other Indigenous Peoples elsewhere
who have lost their culture and their language, they
regret it.

For instance, we used to have Innu names and
it is because we were baptized that we lost them.
Despite the fact that we were baptized, we should
have been able to keep our Innu names until the
end of time.

Me for instance, today I am called Madam
André. My Innu name, that of my husband's ances-
tors, is KAPESH. Kapesh is an abbreviation, the real
Innu name of my husband's grandfather was SHU-
KAPESH, which means "man with great abilities."
That is why they called my husband's grandfather
Shukapesh. I have never heard of a White man being
called Shukapesh but I have often heard them being
called André. Today I would be a lot prouder to
be called AN KAPESH because that is my Innu

kauapishit eshinikatakanit. Kashikat anu nipa mishta-
ashinen AN KAPESH tshetshi ishinikatikauian uesh
ma eukuan nitinnu-ishinikashun. Nititeniten nin
tshipa mishta-apatan tshetshi nanatuapatamat nitinnu-ishinikashunnana, kie ninan e inniuiat tshe ishpish
inniunanut tshetshi kanuenitamat. Uesh ma anite aishkat
tshipa tshi put tau innu-auass tshetshi mitatak, nasht
nipimakakaui nitinnu-ishinikashunnana kie ma kashikanit shash put tatshe innu-auass eka minuatak nenu
umishtikushiu-ishinikashun.

   Nititeniten nin, innu-auass nishtam e tshitshipania-
kanit utinnu-aimun tshetshi tshishkutamuakanit, mauat
muk^u peikupipuna kie mauat muk^u nishupipuna ishpish
tshetshi innu-tshishkutamuakanit. Ne innu-auass tshipa
minuanu uiesh patetat-tatupipuna tshetshi ishpish tshishkutamuakanit pissik^u utinnu-aimun mak tshetshi eka
nashpit petuat kakusseshiu-katshishkutamatsheshiniti
ashit tshetshi mishtikushiu-aimikut nuash tshe ishpish
minu-nishtuapatak nenu uin utaimun. Uesh ma anitshenat kakusseshiu-katshishkutamatsheshiht apu ishinakuannit anu uinuau mak nin tshetshi nishtutakut nitauassima
kie apu ishinakuannit anu uinuau mak nin tshetshi
nishtutuaht nitauassima. Kashikat nin nitanimiun anitshenat ut nitauassimat e tshishkutamuakaniht : kashikat
e innushkueuian nitauassimat ennu-aimikaui apu nish-
tutuht kie uinuau eimitaui apu minu-nishtutukau tanite
kashikanit shash minaush pikutauat tshetshi innu-aimiht.

   Tshishe-utshimau ka tshitshipanit innu-auassa tshetshi
mishtikushiu-tshishkutamuat, mishta-ashtapan shunianu,
apu ut mamanashat. Kashikanit netueitamakuti innua
tshetshi innu-tshishkutamuakanit innu-auass, eukuannu
tshitshue eshinakuannit tshetshi ashat kie tshetshi eka
mamanashat shunianu. Kie tshipa ishinakuan tshetshi
mitshetiht innuat tshetshi tshishikuakaniht tshetshi

name. I think it would be very important for us
to look for our own names and to keep them until
death. Later on, there may be some youth who will
regret that our Innu names have been completely
erased and maybe already today there are young
Innu who do not like their French names.

In my opinion, if we start by teaching the Innu
language to the children first, we should not do it
for only one or two years: it would be good that
for at least five years the child receives an education entirely in his language and during that time,
he does not hear a White teacher speak to him in
French until he understands his own language
properly. It does not make sense that my children
understand their White teachers better than me and
it does not make sense that the White professors
understand my children better than me. Today I
have trouble with my children who go to school: me,
who am an Innu woman, when I speak Innu to my
children, they do not understand me, and when they
speak to me, I do not understand them well because
already, my children can barely speak Innu today.

When the government started to teach French
to the Innu children, they invested a lot of money,
without sparing it. Now that the Innu ask of the
government that they teach Innu to the Innu
children then they really should invest their money
and should not spare it either. There should be
several Innu who are paid to contribute to the

uauitshiaht innu-auassa tshetshi innu-tshishkutamuakanniti, miam ka ishpish mitshetiht kauapishiht ka tshishikuakaniht tshetshi mishtikushiu-tshishkutamuaht
innu-auassa. Mate mashinaikana e innushteti tshipa ishinakuan tshetshi mitsheki tshetshi tshitapatahk auassat.
Kie nenua mashinaikana e innushteti namaieute muk^u
peik^u innu-assit tshetshi tutakaniti, tshipa ishinakuan
kassinu papeik^u innu-assit tshetshi tutakaniti mashinaikana e innushteti.

Nititeniten nin mishta-apatan tshetshi mishta-kutshi-
panitaiat tshetshi nanatuapatamat kie tshetshi kanuenitamat nitinnu-inniunnan kie nitinnu-aimunnan. Nin
nititenitamun, etashit auen eishinniut ushtuin atut tau
peik^u eshinniut tshetshi ashineuatshet kutaka eshinniuniti utinniunnu kie utaimunnu. E inniuiat takuanipan nitinnu-inniunnan kie nitinnu-aimunnan tshetshi
ashineuatsheiat.

Innu education of the children, as many as there were White men who were paid to teach them French. There should be many books written in Innu so that the children can read them. And there should not only be books in Innu on one reserve, there should be such books in all Indigenous communities.

Me, I feel it is very important to make big efforts to search for our Innu culture and our language and to preserve them. In my opinion, of all the peoples that exist on earth, there is likely not one that is proud to live according to their neighbours' culture and language. We, Innu, had an Innu culture and an Innu language of which we can be proud.

4.

Katshitamishkuet

Nutaui ueshkat kueshpiti anite unataun-assit, tanipani
atikua kie nanitam nipaiepan atikua. Kashikanit nutaui
etuteti anite nakana ka nataut, apu taniti atikua tanite
ne nutaui anite unataun-assit mitakue uashka takuan-
nua kusseutshuapa. Namaieu muk[u] nutaui tekuanniti
kusseutshuapa anite unataun-assit, tauat kutakat innuat
tekuanniti kusseutshuapa anite unataun-assiuat. Mate
nutaui e peikussit unataun-assit, uiesh tshekat kutunnue-
makannitsheni kusseutshuapa.

Kauapishit kashikanit mitshetuau nenu issishueu :
« Innu apu itenitak tshetshi tutak miam ueshkat ka kushpit anite nutshimit. » Kashikat mitshetuau nipetenan essishuet kauapishit. Innu kashikanit tau eshi-mushtuenitak
tshetshi kushpit anite nutshimit. Innu apu ut uepinak
unataun-assi kie apu ut uepinak utinniun. Nititeniten
nin, innu nanitam mushtuenitam[u] tshetshi kushpit anite
nutshimit muk[u] kashikat mitshetuait anite tshekuan
shash apu minupanit.

Miam mate kauapishit kashikanit ishi-natau kie uin
miam peikuan innu. Miam mate ninan ute etaiat Kaiatushkanut, tapue nataun-assit nititanan muk[u] kashikat
shash anu mitshetu kauapishit mak innua. Innu kashikanit etuteti anite minashkuat tshetshi natshi-nataut,
nanitam mamashiku kauapishiniti. Kauapishit eukuan
uin ka mamashiat innua netauniti. Mak innu kashikanit

4

The game warden

In the past, when my father used to go to his hunting grounds, there was caribou and he always killed some. Nowadays, when he goes to where he used to hunt, there are no caribou because on his hunting grounds, he is surrounded with hunting and fishing clubs. It is not only on my father's territory that there are clubs, they are on the territories of other Innu. Just on my father's territory, there are about ten.

Today the White man often says: "The Indian no longer thinks to go out on the land the way he used to." We often hear the White man say this. There are Innu who still want to go out on the land. The Innu did not give up his hunting territory and he did not renounce his culture. I myself think that the Innu constantly wants to go out on the land but things are no longer as easy.

It must be said that nowadays the White man also goes hunting. Where we are, in Schefferville, it is true that we are on a hunting territory but already there are more White men than there are Innu. Nowadays when the Innu goes hunting in the woods, he is constantly bothered by the White man. It is the White man who disturbs the Innu while

etuteti anite minashkuat, mishue uapatam^u mitshuapa
ketshemateniti mak innu kashikanit kassinu anite eituteti, muk^u kakusseshiu-meshkanaua eukuannua uiapatak, utapan-meshkanaua mak neshkitu-meshkanaua.
Mak mishue anite eituteti minashkuat, natshishkueu
kauapishiniti.

Kauapishit kassinu anite eituteti minashkuat, mitshetuau mamashieu innua kie matshi-tutueu innua. Innu
mitshetuau unitau nenu unataun-apashtaun…Miam
mate utanipia unieu katshi tshikamuiati anite shakaikanit. Kie nanikutini utanipia katshi tshikamuiati anite
shakaikanit, pikuauakannua nenua ut ishkuteu-utissa
kashikat kassinu anite pepamipanniti shakaikanit. Kie
innu ekutati ukushkan mishkumit, kauapishit uia-
patamuati innu ukushkannu anite shakaikanit ekue
utinamuat ukushkannu ashit unameshiminua nutim
ekue tshimutamuat. Kassinu innu anite unataun-assit
mamashiku kauapishiniti kie tau innu shash nianutakan-
nit unataun-assi.

Mate ninapem ka shitshimikut kauapishiniti tshetshi
kakusseshiu-atusset kie ka tapuetuat, metenitak utassi
anite ka nataut, shash atamipekut takuannu mak
nutim utinnu-aueshishima atamipekut tanua. Eukuan
Tshishe-shatshiu-shipu ka tshipaikanit, ekute tekuak
ninataun-assinan. Mishta-minuashipan ninataun-
assinan, kassinu etatiki shakaikana nekaunipan, mishta-
minuashipan nekau. Ne ninataun-assinan ninapem
nanitam nipa itenitetan tshetshi apashtaiat usham
kashikat shash papanu tshetshi mueshtatapiat peikutau
epiat. Ninapem kashikanit shash tshekat nishunnuepipuna eshpish kakusseshiu-atusset. Nin eukuan etenitaman : apu tshekuan ishpitenitakuak nin e inniuian
kakusseshiu-atusseun.

he is hunting. When the Innu goes into the woods, he sees houses everywhere and everywhere he goes today, all he sees is evidence of the White man, roads and snowmobile trails. Wherever he goes, in the woods, he finds White men.

Not only is the White man everywhere in the woods but more often than not he bothers the Innu and harms him. Often the Innu lose their hunting equipment... For instance, they lose their fishing nets once they have set them in the lake. Sometimes the motorboats that coast along on the lake tear the nets that are set. If the Innu set night lines through the ice, the White men who find them take them and steal all the fish. All the Innu are bothered by the White man on their hunting territory. Some have even had their entire hunting territory destroyed.

My husband, for instance, was urged by the White man to take a White man's job and he accepted it. One day he realized that the territory where he used to hunt was under water, as were all his Innu animals. I am speaking of the Hamilton River,[17] where a dam was built, that is where our hunting territory is. It was a very beautiful hunting territory, all the lakes were sandy, the sand was beautiful. My husband and I were always thinking about using our hunting territory because nowadays, we are bored of always living in the same place. It has been almost twenty years now that my husband has been a wage earner. I myself think that a salaried job has no value to me as an Innu woman.

Kauapishit uin ka takushinit ute nitassinat, namaienu
tshetshi natshi-nataut ut takushinipan, kakusseshiu-
atusseun ka shenakanit ute nitassinat, kauapishit uin
eukuannu muk^u ut takushinipan. Kauapishit katshi
takushinit ute Tshiuetinit nataun-assit, uin ishinakuannipan tshetshi kukuetshimat innua peik^u innu-aueshisha ua nipaiat. Kie kauapishit ishinakuannipan tshetshi
kukuetshimat innua etenitak tshetshi tutak kusseutshuapa
anite innua unataun-assinit tshetshi eka mamashiat innua
anite unataun-assinit. Kie ishinakuannipan tshetshi
kukuetshimat innua nenu shipinu etenitak tshetshi
tshipaik. Mate nishipiminan Tshishe-shatshiu-shipu ka
tshipaikanit, innuat unataun-assiuau nutim atamipekut
takuannu kie innu-aueshish kassinu nanushu.

Mate kauapishit nenua shipua tshepaiki nenu ut
nanimissiu-ishkutenu, e inniuian apu tshi uapataman
tan tshe itapashtaian ne nanimissiu-ishkuteu. Uesh
ma nanimissiu-ishkuteu namaieu nitinniun, kauapishit nenu utinniun. Kashikat e inniuian, anu nimitaten
ninataun-assinan uesh ma eukuan nin e inniuian nitinniun. Kie namaieute mishta-utenat etaian, Tshiuetinit nataun-assit nititan. Nanimissiu-ishkuteu eukuan
muk^u uin kauapishit tshe apashtat eiapit kie eiapit kie
eukuan muk^u uin tshe shuniatsheuatshet tshe ishpish
inniunanunit.

Kauapishit katshi takushinit ute Tshiuetinit, innu
eukuan ishinakuannipan uenashk tshetshi ishi-tshitshipanit tshetshi ishi-atusset miam katshitamishkuet nenua
ut kauapishiniti ka takushinniti ute nataun-assit. Uesh
ma innu ute utassit uin natuapamikupan kauapishiniti
kie eukuan uin ishinakuannipan tshetshi ishi-atusset
miam katshitamishkuet. Uesh ma innu eukuan nishtam
ka tat ute Tshiuetinit nataun-assit kie eukuannu
utinniun e nataunanunit. Ne uin kakusseshiu-katshi-

When the White man came here, he did not come to hunt but to open a construction site in our territory. That is the only reason he came. After he arrived in the North, on the hunting grounds, he is the one who should have asked the Innu for permission to kill any one of the Innu animals. And he should have asked the Innu for permission before establishing the hunting and fishing clubs on the Innu's hunting territory so as not to bother the Innu on his own land. The White man should have also asked the Innu for permission when he thought about building dams on the rivers. For instance, on our river, the Hamilton River, which he dammed, the Innu hunting grounds are all under water and all the Innu animals are lost.

When the White man dams the rivers for electricity, I cannot see how that electricity will serve me, an Innu woman. Electricity is not a part of my culture, it is a part of the White man's. As an Innu woman, I worry a lot more about our hunting territory because that is my life as an Innu woman. Moreover, I do not live in a big city, I live in the North, on a hunting territory. That electricity will only benefit the White man for centuries and it is for him only that it will generate profits until the end of time.

After the White man came to the North, the Innu should have immediately started to watch over how the White man hunted in his hunting territories. It is the White man who sought out the Innu here in his territory, it is thus the Innu who had the right to act as the game warden. He was the first who was here in the North on his hunting territory and hunting was his life. It has only been about fifteen years that the White game wardens

tamishkuet muk^u kutunnuepipunnitshe ashu patetat
eshpish tshi takushinit ute nutshimit. Nete utat apu
nita ut uapamitshit katshitamishkuet tshetshi tshishkutamuat innua tshe ishi-natauniti kie tshe ishi-
passitsheniti. Kakusseshiu-katshitamishkuet anu uin
pikutatakue e nataunanunit, nipa minuenitetan etatu
uipat tshetshi katshitinitshit ute nataun-assit tshetshi
tshishkutamuat innua e nataunanunit kie tshetshi tshishkutamuat innua passikannu e nataunanunit. Uesh
ma uin innu apu tshissenitakannit pipunnu tan ka
ishpish tshitshipanit e natauti kie apu tshissenitakannit atshitashunnu tan ka ishpish tshitshipanit tshetshi
ishi-pakassiut pissik^u innu-aueshisha. Nititeniten nin,
innu tatutshishemitashumitannuepipuna anite utat ka
tshitshipanit e tshishkutamatishut e nataunanunit, ne
kakusseshiu-katshitamishkuet eukuannu tshipa tshitshipanipan tshetshi tshishkutamuat innua e nataunanunit.

Ne katshitamishkuet ka takushinit ute nutshimit,
kassinu innu mishta-shashish nishtuapatamupan passikannu kie minu-tshissenitamupan tshe ishi-nataut,
namaienua katshitamishkueniti tshishkutamakupan.
Kauapishit eshk^u eka ka takushinit ute nitassinat, katshitamishkuet apu nita ut uapamitshit ute nutshimit tshetshi
mamashiat innua netauniti kie tshetshi tipaimuat innua
utinnu-aueshishiminua. Ne katshitamishkuet tan eshpite-
nitakushit ut ninan e inniuiat ?

Katshitamishkuet eshk^u eka ka takushinit ute
nutshimit, innu apu nita ut nanuiat kie apu nita ut
metuatshet utaueshishima. Apu nita ut nipaiat shetshen
muk^u e minuashikut tshetshi ut nipaiat kie apu nita ut
uapamat innu atikua shetshen tshetshi nipiniti anite
minashkuat. Kakusseshiu-katshitamishkuet patush katshi
takushinit ute nutshimit, eukuannu tshitshipanipan kassinu eishinakushit innu-aueshish e metuatshenanut kie e

arrived on the land. Before that, we had never seen
a game warden teach an Innu how to hunt and how
to shoot a firearm. If the White game warden had
been better at hunting than the Innu, we would
have been happy to welcome him earlier on the territory so that he might teach the Innu how to hunt
and how to hunt with a gun. We do not know when
the Innu, he, started to hunt and we do not know
when he started to live solely on Innu animals. I
myself think it is during that time, thousands of
years ago, when the Innu started to learn how to
hunt that the game warden should have started to
teach him how to hunt.

When the game warden came inland, it had been
a very long time that the Innu had firearms and
knew how to hunt perfectly well: it is not the game
warden who taught them how. Before the White
man came to us, we had never seen, on the land, a
game warden bother the Innu while he was hunting
and ration his Innu animals. That game warden,
what does he bring to us, the Innu?

Before the game warden came, the Innu never
wasted his animals and would never play with them.
He did not kill them for no reason, out of pleasure to
kill only, and thus he never saw, in the woods, caribou who were dead for no apparent reason. When,
later, the White game wardens came, they started to
play around with all the Innu animals and to waste
them. The game wardens cannot do anything, they

nanuiakanit. Katshitamishkuet apu tshekuannu anite tshi
tutak, apu tshi tutak utatusseun nenua ut kauapishiniti.
Mate ne atik[u], eukuan peik[u] innu-aueshish kashikanit
anumat nianuiakanit kie mietuatshenanut. Innu uin
apu nita ut nipaiat atikua muk[u] uteshkannua tshetshi ut
nipaiat kie nenu uiashinu tshetshi uepinak. Mitshetuat
innuat ka uapatahk ume eshinakuak.

   Utat nishtupipuna tapan katshitamishkuet mak ashit
innu-kamakunuesht. E nishiht katshitamishkueuipanat
kie tapue tutamupanat utatusseunuau muk[u] nenua ut
innua. Ne katshitamishkuet mak innu-kamakunuesht
nanitam papamipaitupanat anite minashkuat, neshkitua[10]
apatshiepanat tshetshi nanatu-nakanaht innua niatshi-
natauniti. Ne katshitamishkuet mak innu-kamakunuesht
uiapamataui innua anite minashkuat peik[u] pineua nepaia-
niti ekue utinimaht, ashit upassikannu ekue utinamuaht.
Katshitamishkuet mak innu-kamakunuesht mishta-
uitsheuakanitutatuipanat tshetshi matshi-tutuaht innua.

   Mate nika tipatshimun peik[u] tshekuan ne ut katshitamishkuet mak innu-kamakunuesht. Nutaui mishta-
tshishenniu. Kushpipan, nishuasht-tatunnu ashu nish[u] ka
itashtet mishta-atshitashun. Nishtesha uitsheuku mak
kutaka peik[u] innua. Nutaui nenu tshe kushpit, uemut
upashtamakana utineu nenu ut utshishenniu-shuniam.
Ne nutaui nenu uet kushpit, innu-mitshiminu tshetshi
mitshit mak ashit e minuatak anite nutshimit. Nutaui etuteti anite utassit, apu tshekuannu anite takuannit, atikua
apu taniti. Ueshkat tanipani atikua eshk[u] eka ka tutakanniti kusseutshuapa anite utassit. Nutaui ueshkat nanitam
nipaiepan atikua tshetshi muat. Kashikanit miam anite
utassit mishta-mitshennua kusseutshuapa. Eukuannu muk[u]
etaniti namesha, kakua, uapusha mak pineua. Nutaui
katshi kushpit anite nutshimit, uemut
eukuannu muk[u] namesha – kukamessa – miaunat

cannot do their job when it comes to White men. The caribou, for instance, is one of the Innu animals that today is wasted and who is played with terribly. The Innu, he, has never killed a caribou just for his antlers and then thrown away the meat. Many Innu have seen how this happens.

Three years ago, there was a game warden and there was also an officer of the Royal Canadian Mounted Police. They both acted as game wardens and they only worked at the expense of the Innu. The game warden and the officer of the RCMP would constantly go around on their snowmobiles in the woods looking for Innu that were hunting. When they saw one who had just killed a partridge, they would seize the partridge and the firearm. The game warden and the royal police got along very well when it came to harming the Innu.

I will tell a story about the game warden and the RCMP officer. My father is very old. In 1972, he went into the bush with my elder brother and another Innu. He had chartered a plane with money from his old age pension. When he goes into the bush, it is to feed himself with Innu food and also because he likes being in the bush. When my father goes to his territory, there is nothing there, there are no caribou. In the past, before there were hunting and fishing clubs, there were caribou. In the past, my father would always eat caribou that he killed. Nowadays, there are many hunting and fishing clubs on his land. That is why there is only fish, porcupine, rabbit, and partridge. Once there, he was forced to only catch fish – lake trout – which he would bring back home with him. If he

tshetshi nashipetaiat nashipeti, miam ua mitshiti innu-
mitshiminu, tshetshi muat nenua unameshima.

Nutaui nishupishimua anite tau nutshimit. Uetitshi-
panniti tshetshi nashipet, uemut upashtamakana ekue
natauakanit nenu ut utshishenniu-shuniam. Ne upashtamakan tshe pet takushinit anite tueunanit, shash anite
tanishapani katshitamishkueniti mak innu-kamakunueshiniti. Nutaui nenua namesha ka nashipetaiat,
nutim ekue makunakanniti. Ne katshitamishkuet kie ne
innu-kamakunuesht katshi nishtupishimua ek^u manaka-
nit nutaui nenu unameshima. Anitshénat nameshat shash
apu ut minushiht tshetshi muakaniht, passe nutim piku-
panuat. Kie apu ut nutim minakanit kie apu tshekuannu
ut uitamuakanit nanana ut unameshima.

Ne katshitamishkuet mak innu-kamakunuesht
mishta-uitsheuakanitutatuipanat e nishiht tshetshi
matshi-tutuaht muk^u innua. Kie e nishiht apu ut tshi
minu-tshissenimitshit tanen eukuan tshitshue katshitamishkuet kie tanen eukuan tshitshue innu-kamakunuesht
tanite tatapishkut ishinakuannipan utatusseunauau :
katshitamishkuet ka ishinikatitshit, uapamakanipan e
makunat innua e minukashuniti ek^u innu-kamakunuesht
ka ishinikatitshit, kie uin katshitamishkueuipan nenua
ut innua. Mate nutaui unameshima ka makunakanniti,
eukuan uin innu-kamakunuesht uetinat nenua namesha,
issishuepan nishtesh.

Katshitamishkuet apu shakuenimut tshetshi tshishkutamuat innua tshe ishi-natauniti kie tshe ishi-nipaianiti
utaueshishiminua. Kassinu eishinakushit aueshish ute
nutshimit ka tat, innu nenua utaueshishima kie kassinu
eishinakushit namesh anite nutshimiu-shakaikanit ka tat,
innu nenua unameshima. Innu-aueshish kassinu eishinakushit anite nutshimit ka tat, apu tshekuannu anite
nishtuapatak kakusseshiu-katshitamishkuet. Mate nutaui

had wanted to eat Innu food, he would have had to eat that fish.

My father spent two months on the land and when the time came to return home, the plane he had chartered with money from his old age pension had to go pick him up. The plane had not yet arrived at the airport, but the game warden and the RCMP officer were already there, apparently. They seized all of the fish that my father had brought back. They gave it back to him three months later. Not only were the fish no longer good to eat, but some were decomposing. In addition, some were missing and he was not given an explanation.

The game warden and the RCMP officer got along very well when it came to causing trouble for the Innu. And we could not really tell which one was a real game warden and which one was a real police officer because they did the same job: the one whom we called the game warden, we saw him arrest an Innu who was drunk, and the one whom we called the mounted police would also act as a game warden at the expense of the Innu. For instance, when my father's fish was seized, according to my elder brother, it is the RCMP officer who seized it.

The game warden is not ashamed to teach the Innu how to hunt and how to kill his own animals. All of the kinds of animals that are here in the woods are the Innu's animals and all of the kinds of fish that are in the lakes in the interior are the Innu's fish. The White game warden does not know about the differences between the many kinds of Innu animals that are found inland. For instance,

unameshima ka makunakanniti, ne katshitamishkuet kie
ne innu-kamakunuesht e nishiht apu ut nishtuapamaht
tsheku-namesha nenua miakunaht. « Matamekuat nititenimatanat », issishueuat itakanuat. Kukamessa nenua
makunepanat.

Katshitamishkuet kie innu-kamakunuesht eka ka
nishtuapamaht tanenua eukuannua innu-aueshisha ua
makunaht, shetshen katshitamishkueuipanat ut innua.
Anu nutaui ishinakuannipan tshetshi katshitamishkueut
nenua ut uin utaueshishima, anu uin nishtuapameu kassinu eishinakushiniti innu-aueshisha. Nutaui katshitamishkueutakue nenua ut utaueshishima, atut ut pataimupan,
tshipa minu-nishtuapamepan tanenua eukuannua aueshisha tshe makunat.

Nutaui shash peikushteu-tatunnuepipuneshu ashu
peik^u, uemut shash nishuaush-tatunnuepipuna ashu nisht^u
eshpish nataut. Nutaui uemut anu uin ishinakuannit
tshetshi katshitamishkueut ute nutshimit : uin umenu
utassi, kie uin nenua utaueshishima kashikanit mietuatshenanuniti kie nianuiakanniti kie uinishtam ka tat ute
nutshimit. Katshitamishkuet eshk^u eka ka takushinit ute
nutshimit, kassinu papeik^u innu uin uetshit ishi-atusseshtatishuipan miam katshitamishkuet.

Kakusseshiu-katshitamishkuet eka tshekuannu e
nishtuapatak ute nutshimit kie eka e nishtuapamat
innu-aueshisha, shetshen tshipa takushinu ute nutshimit
tshetshi ishi-atusset miam katshitamishkuet ut innua kie
ut innu-aueshisha. Katshitamishkuet eka tshekuannu e
nishtuapatak ute nutshimit kie eka e nishtuapamat kassinu eishinakushiniti innu-aueshisha, e inniuiat apu ui
uapamitshit kie apu ui apatshitshit.

when my father's fish was seized, neither the game warden nor the RCMP officer knew what kind it was. "We thought it was speckled trout," they said, and they had seized lake trout.

If the game warden and the mounted police do not know how to identify the Innu animal that they want to seize, how can they control the Innu's hunting? It would have been better if my father had been the game warden for his own animals, he knew a lot better about the different wild species. If my father had controlled the hunting of his own animals, he would not have made a mistake. Upon seizure, he would have known exactly what kind of species it was.

My father is ninety-one years old and he has been hunting for eighty-three years. In all evidence, it would have been better if he had been the game warden, here in the interior: it is his own territory and it is with his animals that others are playing and are wasting and it was him who was here first. Before the game warden made his way inland, each Innu was his own game warden.

If the White game warden does not know anything about the forest here and if he does not know the wild animals, there is no point for him to come inland to control the Innu's hunting and to keep watch over their animals. If the game warden does not know anything about the interior and if he does not know anything about Innu animals, we, the Innu, have no use for him and we do not want to see him.

5

Ka atauatshet ishkutuapunu

Ne ka atauatshet ishkutuapunu ueshkat takushinipan ute nutshimit tshetshi nanatuapatak tshetshi ut pakassitishut. Ekue tutamupan kaminnanunit muk^u tshetshi tshitshipanit. Ne kaminnanut ushkat e tshimatakanit apu ut mishat kie apu ut takuak anite tshetshi mishta-minuashit, nutim eshpishat tapishkut ishinakuanipan. Kaminnanut ushkat katshi tshishtakanit kie innu ueshkat ka minakanit tshetshi minit ishkutuapunu, anite kaminnanut mamu minnanuipan kauapishiht mak innuat. Muk^u anitshenat innuat ueshkat ka ituteht anite kaminnanunit issishuepanat : « E inniuiat nenua kamikuakamiunakana ait ishinakuana iapashtatinikauiat. » Kie tapanat essishueht : « Innuat katshi pitutshetaui anite kaminnanunit ekue shekutakanniti pashpapuakana », issishuepanat innuat.

Innu ueshkat ka pitukaiakanit kaminnanunit, ne ka tipenitak kaminnanunit ushtuin atut ut minuateu innua, inishat pitukaiekupan innua. Muk^u ne ka atauatshet ishkutuapunu tatupipuna katshi pitutsheniti innua anite kaminnanunit, shash tshissenitamukupan tshe ut uenutishit nenua ut innua. Uesh ma kassinu auen tshekuannu tshetshipaniti tshetshi tutak, uipat tshissenitam^u utatusseun tshe minupannit kie tshe eka minupannit. Mate ne ka atauatshet ishkutuapunu ueshkat ka tshitshipanit tshetshi atauatshet ishkutuapunu ute nutshimit

5

The alcohol merchant

In the past, the alcohol merchant came into the territories to find a way to earn a living. And so, he started by building a bar.[18] The first bar was not very big and there was no lounge bar. When the bar was finished and the Innu were allowed to drink alcohol,[19] Whites and Innu would drink together at the bar. But the Innu who would go to the bar said: "The glasses they serve us in, us the Innu, are different." And others would say: "They open the windows when the Innu arrive at the bar."

In the past, when the Innu were allowed in the bar, the owner already did not really like them: it is rather willy-nilly that he let them come in. But it had only been a few years that they were coming to the bar when already, the alcohol merchant must have known he would make money off of them. All those who start something know early on if their business will succeed or not. For instance, when the alcohol merchant started to sell alcohol in our territory, here in the interior, he did not show the Innu

nitassinat, apu ut tutuat innua tshetshi unuishpimitat
anite ut kaminnanunit kie apu ut tutuat innua katshi
tshishi-apatshiati tshetshi uishamat kamakunueshiniti, ne
uin kamakunuesht kuessipan tshetshi shuniatsheuatshet
nenua innua.

Ne ka atauatshet ishkutuapunu tatupipuna katshi
natuapamikut innua, eukuannu meshitat nenu ukamin-
nanunim kie eukuannu etutak anite e minuashinit muk^u
kauapishiniti tshetshi pitukaiat. Kie nenua innua ekue
tutamuat anite itetshe tshe pitukaiat tshetshi eka pitutsheniti anite itetshe e minuashinit. Kie ne ka atauatshet
ishkutuapunu eukuannu tshetshipanit ua matshi-tutuat
kie ua manenimat innua. Ne ka atauatshet ishkutuapunu
anite nakapit e uinakuannit ekute muk^u patukaiat innua.
Ne kaminnanut anite nakapit mishta-uinakuan ashit
mishta-kashti-tipishkau. Anitshenat innuat tshitaimuaka-
nuat tshetshi ituteht anite e minuashinit ek^u ne kaminnanut, innuat nenu ushuniamuau.

Muk^u nin natshi-miniani anite kaminnanut, atut
nita nipa pitutshen anite nakapit e uinakuak. Uemut
anite itetshe e minuashit nipa natshi-min uesh ma nipa
mishta-ashinen uiapataman nishuniaminan e inniuiat
ne kaminnanut katshi tutamat tshetshi mishitaiat kie
tshetshi takuak anite e minuashit. Uesh ma kie nin
takuan anite nishuniam, miam ninapem ushuniam mak
anitshenat nitauassimat ushuniamuau. Kie anitshenat
nitauassimat etutetaui anite kaminnanunit passe eshk^u
apu tatupipuneshiht kie apu nita ut nakanakaniht patu-
tshetaui anite kaminnanunit. Peikuan kie nin pitutsheiani
anite kaminnanut, ituteiani anite e minuashit, nin nititeniten nashpit apu ishinakuak tshetshi nakanikauian uesh
ma nitauassimat apu nakanakaniht at eka etatupipu-
neshiht. Pitukaiakanuat anite kaminnanunit muk^u anite
itetshe e uinakuannit tanite ne ka atauatshet ishkutuapunu

the door and he did not, after he had exploited him, call the police so that the police might make money off of him as well.

The Innu had been going there for only a few years when the alcohol merchant decided to make his bar bigger and he put in a lounge bar that was for Whites only. And he made the Innu use the side door so that they would not go into the lounge bar. It is then that the alcohol merchant started to want to mistreat and insult the Innu. The alcohol merchant would only allow the Innu into a dirty basement. The cellar of the bar was very dirty and very dark. It was forbidden for the Innu to go into the lounge bar and yet this bar it is the Innu's money.

Me, if I were to go have a drink at the bar, I would never go into that dirty basement. I would most certainly go drink in the lounge bar because I would be proud to see how thanks to our money, we the Innu, we contributed to making the bar bigger and to having a lounge bar established. Me too I had money invested in there, as was my husband's money and my children's. Among my children who go to the bar, some of them are not legally old enough but no one has ever stopped them from entering. Me, if I were to go to that bar and if I were to go to the lounge bar, I think that nobody has the right to prevent me from doing so: they do not forbid entry to my children who are not even old enough. They are allowed in the bar but only in a filthy place. The alcohol merchant knows very well

kashikanit uapatam[u] shash nishtuau anu mishanu
mak ushkat ka tshimitat. Ne kaminnanut kashikat
uiapatamekui nishtuau anite anu meshat kie menuashit,
eukuan ninan e inniuiat nishuniaminan.

Ne ka tipenitak kaminnanunit, innua apishish
uekaikuti ekue utinat ekue unuishpimitat, muk[u] eshi-
nakushiniti napeua kie peikuan ishkueua kie muk[u] tatutipaikana, ua unuishpimitati unuishpimiteu, tshashikaniti
kie tepishkaniti unuishpimiteu kie muk[u] eshinakuannit
tshishikunu, ua unuishpimitati napinniti kie pepunniti,
peikuan unuishpimiteu. Kie ne ka atauatshet ishkutuapunu nenua innua uenuishpimitati, apu tshissenimat
tshetshi ishpish innishiniti tshetshi tshiuetaitishuniti
kie apu tshissenimat tshetshi kanuenitaminiti shunianu
tshetshi ut tshiuetaitishuniti, unuishpimiteu iapit tanite
shash ishpanu shunianu nenua ut innua. Ne ka atauatshet ishkutuapunu nenua innua katshi nutim utinamuati
ushuniaminu, eukuannu tshe ui unuishpimitat muk[u]
eshk[u] eka uenuishpimitati, pitama uishameu kamakunueshiniti tshetshi minat nenua innua tshe unuishpimitat.
Ne uin kamakunuesht ekue utinat nenua innua manaka-
nit kuessipan tshetshi shuniatsheuatshet...

Peikuau innu tipatshimuipan. Ne innu uapameshapan
nish[u] innu e makunakanniti anite unuitimit kaminnanunit anite pessish tshishtukanit. Ne innu uiapamat
nenua innua miakunakanniti, « pitama ekue tshitapama-
kau tshe aitutuakanikuenit nititenimauat », iteu ne innu.
Ne kamakunuesht uiapamak uetamauat nenua peik[u] anite
utashtamikunit, iteu, anitshenat kamakunueshiht ekue
natuapamakau anite utapanuat, iteu, ekue itakau : « Anitshenat innuat mamushatshinekut miam innua », nitauat
iteu. Anitshenat nish[u] innuat miakunakaniht unuishpimi-
takanuat anite ut kaminnanunit, issishueu ne innu. Anitshenat kamakunueshiht nenua nish[u] innua miakunaht,

that his bar today is three times bigger than it was when he built it. If you saw that bar today, which is three times bigger and nicer, it is thanks to our money, us the Innu.

If the Innu bothers the owner of the bar ever so slightly, he grabs him and throws him out, whether it is a man or a woman and no matter what time it is; if he wants to throw him out, he throws him out, whether it is during the day or at night, he throws him out and no matter the weather; if he wants to throw him out, whether it is summer or winter, he throws him out. When the alcohol merchant throws an Innu out, he does not know if his mind is clear enough to find his way home and he does not know if he has enough money to make it home: he throws him out anyway because he has already made his money off of him. It is only after he has taken the Innu for all his money that the alcohol merchant wants to throw him out, but before he does this, he calls the police first so as to hand the Innu over to them. Then the police officers seize the man that was given to them and in turn make money off of him...

Once, an Innu told a story about seeing two Innu being arrested outside the bar, near the door. When he saw the Innu being arrested, "first I thought to watch what they would do to them," said the Innu. When I saw one of the police officers hit one of them in the face, I went over to the police officers who were in their car and I told them: "Those Innu, pick them up like human beings." The two Innu who were being arrested had just been thrown out the door of the bar, he said. Before the police officers could leave in their car with the two who had just been arrested, two other Innu were thrown out

eshk^u eka tshi pushiaht anite utapanuat, minuat kutakat
nish^u innuat uet unuishpimitakaniht anite ut kaminnanunit, issishueu ne innu. Ne ka tipenitak kaminnanunit
ekue tepuatat nenua kamakunueshiniti, iteu : "Utshenat
kutakat matshi-manitu-innuat mamushatshinekut"
ishi-tepuateu nenua kamakunueshiniti », issishueu ne
innu ka tipatshimut.

Ne ka atauatshet ishkutuapunu kashikanit anumat
minuenitam^u tshetshi matshi-tutuat innua kie minue-
nitam^u tshetshi manenimat innua kie apu shakuenimut nenu tshetshi tutak. Muk^u kutunnuepipuna ashu
patetat nete utat apu nita ut uapatamat kaminnanut ute
nutshimit mitshetuait tshetshi ut aishi-matshi-tutakuiat
kie nitauassiminanat tshetshi nenu ut matshi-tutakuht.
Ne ka atauatshet ishkutuapunu katshi takushinit ute
nutshimit, e inniuiat kashikat eukuan anu tshekuan ka
ut mishat tshetshi ut ushtuenitamat. Miam mate anitshenat nin nitauassimat uemut ekute uetshipannit anite
tshekuannu tshetshi ut eka minuinniuht. Anitshenat
nitauassimat eshk^u euassiuht nanitam shetshishitaui nenu
ut ishkutuapunu kie eka nita minukuamutaui nenu ut
ishkutuapunu kie miam nutepanitaui mitshiminu nenu
ut ishkutuapunu, tanite tshe ut tshi minuenniuht ? Tanite
tshe ut tshi minu-nitautshiht ?

Ninan nitinniunnan ka ishinniuiat, apu nita ut uapatamat miam kashikat kassinu eishi-uapatamat nitanimiun-
nan. Kauapishit katshi utinak nitinniunnannu, eukuannu
muk^u niminikutan e matshikaunit inniunnu.

of the bar. The owner then yelled to the police officers: "Take these ones as well, these damn savages."
This is what the Innu said.

Nowadays, that alcohol merchant looks forward
to brutalizing and insulting the Innu and he has
no shame in doing so. Before fifteen years ago, we
had never seen a bar in the interior that caused us
so much harm in so many ways, to us and to our
children. The fact that the alcohol merchant came
to our territory is the primary source of our worries today. For instance, in all evidence, that is why
my children are not healthy. If, at their young age,
they are always afraid because of alcohol and if they
never sleep well because of alcohol and if they lack
food because of alcohol, how can those children be
healthy? How can they grow up normally?

When we lived according to our own ways, we
never saw all the miseries that we do today. After
he took our lives, all the White man gave us was a
bad life.

6

Kamakunueshiht mak kauaueshtakanit

Kamakunueshiht kie kauaueshtakanit namaieu ninan nitinniunnan, kauapishit nenu utinniun. Kauapishit katshi takushinit ute nitassinat Tshiuetinit, kassinu tshekuannu nitaitutakutan kie ninan e inniuiat tshetshi nashamat nenu utinniun, e matshi-tutuimit mak e tutak shunianu ut ninan. Kauapishit apu shakuenimut tshetshi matshi-tutuimit muk[u] ninan e inniuiat. Apu shakuenimut muk[u] ninan e inniuiat nanitam kamakunueshiutshuapit tshetshi pitutsheiat kie apu shakuenimut eshakumitshi-shikua anite kauaueshtakannit tshetshi pimipanimit.
E inniuiat nitinniunnan ka ishinniuiat, apu nita ut uapa-mitshit kamakunuesht, kamakunueshiutshuap apu nita ut uapatamat, kauaueshtakanit apu nita ut uapatamat.

Kamakunueshiht eshk[u] eka ka takushiniht ute nitassi-nat, kie ninan shash nikanuenitetan innishun. Namaieu kamakunuesht nitinnishiuikutan kie namaieu kamaku-nueshiutshuap nitinnishiuikutan kie namaieu kauauesh-takanit nitinnishiuikutan. Kashikat apu shakuenimuiat tshetshi issishueiat kauapishit katshi takushinit ute nita-ssinat, eukuan uin ka mamashitat nitinnu-innishunnannu uesh ma kauapishit eukuan uin ka tshishkutamuimit utinniun. Eukuan tshekuan apu nishtutamat e inniuiat kie ma put uin kauapishit atut nishtutatishu nenu e tutak : kauapishit katshi tshishkutamuimit kassinu eishinakuan-nit utinniun, kashikanit tshekuannu uet ishi-utinimit

6

The police and the courts

The police and the courts, that is not our culture, it is that of the White man. After his arrival here in our territory, in the North, the White man did everything so that we too, the Innu, would follow his way of life; he mistreated us and made money off of us. The White man feels no shame in only mistreating us, the Innu. He has no shame that we are the only ones to constantly go to prison and he has no shame in taking us to court every day. When we lived our Innu way of life, we never saw police officers, we never saw prisons, and we never saw courts.

Before the police officers arrived here in our territory, we already had a civilization as well. It is not the police that civilized us and it is not the prisons or the courts either. Today, we have no shame in saying that it is the White man who, after his arrival here, disturbed our Innu civilization: he is the one who taught us his culture. Here is one thing that we, Innu, do not understand or perhaps it is the White man who does not understand what he is doing either: after teaching us all of his culture, why does the White man now consider us as if we were not human? Why does he think of us as uncivilized beings? After teaching us his way of life, why does

miam eka innu ? Tshekuannu uet ishi-utinimit innu
apu innishit ? Kauapishit katshi tshishkutamuimit utinniun, kashikanit tshekuannu uet nanatuapatak nanitam
tshetshi anuenimimit ? Kauapishit uin eukuan ka pikunak
nitinnishunnannu.

Nin eukuan tshekuan meshkatenitaman. Kauapishit
katshi tshishkutamuimit kassinu eishinakuannit utinniun, kashikat mitshetuau nuapatenan e uauinikauiat
anite kakusseshiu-tipatshimu-mashinaikanit. Eukuan
eishi-uauinikauiat : « Innuat nanitam minukashuat »,
« Innuat nanitam matshi-tutamuat », « Innuat pipikuaimuat uitshuaua », « Innuat pikuaimuat kamaku-
nueshiu-utapana », « Innuat nimatshi-tutakunanat ».
Muk^u kauapishit apu nita ut tutak mashinaikannu
tshetshi tipatshimut tan ka ishi-matshi-tutuat innua, mate
anitshenat kamakunueshiht ka tatupipuna matshi-tutuaht
innua, kie ka tatupipuna shuniatsheuatsheht innua.

Anitshenat kamakunueshiht ka takushiniht ute,
nitishi-utinikutanat e inniuiat miam eka innishiat. Anitshenat kamakunueshiht nenu ka ishi-utinimit miam
eka innishiat, nin nititenimauat ushtuin uinuau nutepa-
nikupanat innishunnu. Miam mate anitshenat kamakunueshiht innua miakunataui, mitshetuau ushikuieuat
innua kie mitshetuau pitukaieuat anite akushiutshuapit.
Innua miakunataui kassinu aitutueuat : ututamaueuat
kie tatatshishkueuat kie nanatshipiteuat muk^u anite eshinakuannit. Anitshenat kamakunueshiht innua miakunataui, papamitatshimeuat anite ashinishkat kie anite kunit.
Nenua innua katshi pitukaiataui kamakunueshiutshuapit,
eshk^u anite minuat nenekatshieuat. Kamakunueshiht
peik^u innua miakunataui, uinuau nanitam nanishuat kie
nanikutini nishtuat ek^u ne innu peikussu miakunakaniti.
Muk^u innu pikutau tshetshi tipatshimushtuat mitshet

he now seek to constantly punish us? He is the one who killed our civilization.

Here is something that surprises me. After the White man taught us all of his own culture, we often see him today talk about us in the newspapers. In such terms: "The Indians are always drunk," "The Indians are always causing trouble," "The Indians are damaging their houses," "The Indians are damaging the police cars," "The Indians are causing us harm." But the White man never writes articles about how he has caused trouble for the Innu, how, for instance, the police officers have brutalized the Innu for a number of years and how, for a number of years now, they have exploited them.

Upon their arrival here, the police officers saw us as uncivilized beings. I myself think it is those who considered us as non-civilized who lacked civilization. While arresting the Innu, for instance, often the police officers hurt them and often they end up in the hospital. When they arrest the Innu, they do all sorts of things to them: they hit them, they kick them, and they shove them. When the police arrest an Innu, they drag him over rocks or through the snow. After they have put him in prison, they continue to torment him. When they arrest an Innu, there are always two, sometimes three police officers, but the Innu, he, is on his own. But that Innu is able, after he is released from prison, to tell a number of people how the police mistreated him.

innua, katshi unuit anite ut kamakunueshiutshuapit, tan
ka ishi-matshi-tutakut kamakunueshiniti.

Innu nanikutini tshitimatshenitakushu etatshimuti
eitutuakanit miakunakaniti. Innu peikuau tipatshimuipan. Ne innu katshi pitukaiakanit anite tshe tshipauakanit natshe ekue itat kamakunueshiniti : « Pet ashami,
uiash e minuat nui mitshin », iteu. Ne uin kamakunuesht ekue itat nenua innua : « Eka pitama ashuapata,
anutshish tshika minitin uiash e minuat. » Ne kamakunuesht ekue natuapamat anite ka tshipauat nenua innua
ekue mishta-utamauat anite utunnit. Ne innu katshi
utamaukut kamakunueshiniti iapit ekue tshitshipanit
tshetshi aimit anite ut ka tshipauakanit. Kamakunuesht uin minuat ekue natuapamat nenua innua anite
ka tshipauat ekue itat : « Tshui a minu-tshissenimau
nepinaiu[11] ? » iteu. Ekue utinat ekue ututamashkutauat
ushtikuannu anite nepinaiut. « Tshek ekue eka
tshissian », itatshimu ne innu.

Peikuau etuteian kamakunueshiutshuapit, nikuss
anite tapan. Ne nikuss nishtutshishikua katshi ishpish
tat anite kamakunueshiutshuapit niatshi-uapamak.
Nenu miakunakanit utamaukushapan kamakunueshiniti anite ussishikuapikanit, tshimaukushapan.
Nenu miakunakanit, anite Uashat natuenitamushapan
tshetshi natshi-uaueshiakanit nete etaniti tshitshue kai-
mishiniti. Nenu kashikanit tshe nashipetaiakanit, enut
nenu niatshi-uapamak. Umatshunishima nititutatauan
mak mitshiminu ekue itutatauk tanite nitshissenimau
eshpish mishta-shiuenit, nishtutshishikua shash eshpish
tat kamakunueshiutshuapit.

Patutsheian anite kamakunueshiutshuapit, eshapan
miam etat kamakunuesht ka utamauat nikussa. Nikuss
ekue itak : « Aua ne kamakunuesht ka utamaushk ne
ka-atusseua ? », nitau. Ekue ishit : « Eukuan nutamaukuti

Sometimes it is pitiful when the Innu speak of how they were treated when they were arrested. One of them told his story. Shortly after he had been locked up, he told the police officer: "Give me something to eat, I want to eat good meat." The police officer replied: "Hold on a little, I will give you some now." Then the police officer went into his cell and punched him in the mouth. After he had been hit by the police officer, the Innu still spoke up, from his cell. The officer went to see him again and said: "Do you want to know once and for all what plywood is?" He then grabbed the Innu and slammed his head several times against the plywood. "I suddenly fainted," the Innu said.

One day I went down to the police station. My son was in prison. He had been there for three days. At the time of his arrest, he had been, apparently, beaten up by the police, he had a cut on his eyebrow. When he was arrested, he had asked to be judged at the court in Sept-Îles, where there are real lawyers. The day he was supposed to be brought to Sept-Îles, I went to see him for the first time. I brought him clothes and food because I knew how hungry he must have been, after being in prison for three days.

When I arrived at the police station, the officer on duty was apparently the one who had hit my son. I asked my son: "The officer on duty, is he the one who hit you?" – "Yes, he is the one who hit me,

muk^u nashpit eka uin aimi, nenu nimashinaikanuiani-
minu tshika tutuau anu tshetshi matshitat », nitik^u. Ekue
itak : « Apu tshekuannu tshika ut itak », nitau. Ne nikuss
katshi tshipauakanit, kamakunuesht ekue natuapamak
anite umashinaikanitshuapit ekue itak : « Tshishpeu tapue
tshia innu-auass kashikanit eshpish nitau-matshi-tutak,
nitau. Innu-auass kashikanit nenu eshpish nitau-matshi-
tutak, kauapishit anite utshipanu tshia ? nitau. Utat
neunnuepipuna apu nita ut uapamitshit ute nutshimit
kauapishit kie innu-auass apu ut matshi-tutak », nitau.
Ekue ishit : « Ne tshikuss nenu uet makunakanit, anite
kaminnanunit matshi-tutamushapan », nitik^u. Minuat
ekue itak : « Peikuan nenua kaminnanuti utat neunnuepipuna apu nita ut uapatamat ute miam innu nenu kaminnanunit tshetshi ut matshi-tutakut kie uin innu tshetshi
matshi-tutuat nenua ka atauatsheniti ishkutuapunu »,
nitau. Ekue ishit : « Eukuan miam Utshimashkueu, niminueniten katshi uitamin etenitamin », nitik^u.

Anitshenat kamakunueshiht nasht kukuetu aishi-
nenekatshieuat innua. Mate ne nikuss nenu shiatshuapamak
anite kamakunueshiutshuapit, unipeunit – papatshitakut
nepinaiut – apu. Ekue itak : « Aua anite tshinipati ? »
nitau. Ekue ishit : « Ekute ute ninipati », nitik^u. « Uin put
muk^u tutuakanitshe », nititenimau. Ueshkat nuapateti
nenua nipeuna ashpishimununipani. Ne kutak innu ka
tipatshimut nenu ushtikuan uetutamashkutakannit, ekute
anite unipeunit nenu nepinaiut uetutamashkutakannit
ushtikuan.

Kutak innu tipatshimu miakunakanit. Katshi pitukaiakanit kamakunueshiutshuapit ek^u innu ka-ui-aimua iti-
tshe katshi tshipauakanit. Eukuan essishuet : « Uetinaka-
nit nipi shishtaitshipanu, anite ninipeunit ekue shishtau-
kauian, ninipeun tshek nasht pushapaueu, issishueu, kie
anite nimatshunishimit nutim nititapauen kie nashpit apu

he told me, but do not speak to him, you will only make my case worse." – "I will not say anything," I told him. After they locked him back up in his cell, I went to see the officer at his desk and told him: "It is really a shame that nowadays the young Innu are so good at causing trouble, isn't it? But that comes from the White man, doesn't it? Forty years ago, we never saw White men here in the interior and the young Innu never caused trouble," I told him. "The reason why your son was arrested, he said to me, is because apparently he was causing trouble at the bar." I further told him this: "Bars, either, forty years ago, we had never seen any here; the bar did not cause trouble for the Innu and the Innu did not cause trouble for the alcohol merchant." And then he said to me: "Very well, madam, I am glad that you gave me your opinion."

The police officers do not know what to think of next to hurt the Innu. For instance, when I went to see my son in prison, he was sitting on a bed made of plywood. And I asked him: "Is that where you slept?" He answered: "Yes this is where I slept." And then I thought: "He must be the only one that they treat like this." Before, I had seen that those beds had mattresses. But the Innu who had told how his head had been hit, it was against his plywood bed that it had been slammed.

Another Innu spoke of how he was arrested. After they put him in jail, he must have wanted to speak up, once he was in his cell. This is what he said: "They took a garden hose and they sprayed me while I was on my bed. My bed was quickly drenched and my clothes were soaked. I could not

mishkaman anite nipa akaushimun », issishueu ne innu.
Sheshtauakaniti ne innu nenu nipinu anumat, anumat
tshitimatshenitakuan.

Kamakunueshiht nanikutini mashkatenitakuan muk^u
nenu uiapamakanitaui eitutuaht innua. Nanikutini
muk^u natshishkuataui meshkanat innua ekue utinakue-
nit ekue uaueshiaht ekue ishi-pimipaniaht miam katshi
matshi-tutak ne innu. Peikuau innu tipatshimu netshish-
kuat innu-kamakunueshiniti ekue aimikut. Tshissenimeu ua tutakut, ui tutaku tshetshi mashikuat nenua
kamakunueshiniti. Ekue utamikueukut, apu matshishtuat. « Mishta-mitshetuau nutamikueuk^u tshek ekue ishit,
iteu nenua kamakunueshiniti : "Eku ek^u tshishpeuatiti-
shu", nitik^u », iteu. Ne innu iapit ekue eka matshishtuat
kie anumat mishta-shetshishitshe nenu etutakut
kamakunueshiniti eka auennua uiapamikut.

Peikuau nish^u kakusseshiu-kamakunueshiht ushikuie-
panat nikussa, peikuminashtakana pitukaiepanat
akushiutshuapit. Tatatshishkueshapanat kie ututa-
maueshapanat utashtamikunit ekue tshimauakuenit anite
ushkatikunit, uiesh nishumitshitin ishpish. Anite kamin-
nananunit unuitimit ekute miashikuakuenit ekue itutaiakue-
nit akushiutshuapit. Anitshenat nish^u kamakunueshiht
nenu etutaiaht akushiutshuapit, eshk^u eka pitukaiaht
akushiutshuapit, anite unuitimit ekute minuat pitama
tiatatshishkuaht. Anitshenat innuat ka pitukaiakaniht
akushiutshuapit, eukuanat uiapamaht nenua kamakunueshiniti kie eukuanat pietuaht auennua tieputepueniti
anite unuitimit. Uapameuat nish^u kamakunueshiniti
anite unuitimit akushiutshuapit tiatatshishkuaniti
innua. Anitshenat nish^u kamakunueshiht katshi ishpa-
niht e tatatshishkuaht nenua nitauassima, itakanuat, ek^u
patush uenikapauiaht, aitu ushpitunnit ut utineuat ekue
pitukaiaht akushiutshuapit. Nitauassim ka tshimaukut

find a place to hide," he said. A man who gets hosed down like that, that is terribly pitiful.

It is sometimes astonishing to see how the police officers treat the Innu. Sometimes, they just meet one along the way, they grab him, bring him to court, and make him believe that he did something reprehensible. Once, an Innu spoke about how he had met an officer of the RCMP who had spoken to him. The Innu knew what the officer wanted to do, he wanted him to fight with him. The officer slapped him but he did not respond. "The police officer slapped me several times and then suddenly he told me, 'Come on, defend yourself!'" The Innu still did not respond, and he must have been very scared, there were no witnesses.

Once, two municipal police officers injured my son, he was in the hospital for a week. It appeared they had kicked him and hit him in the face: he had a cut that was almost two inches long on his forehead. They had beaten him just outside of the bar and then brought him to the hospital. On the way to the hospital, before getting him there, the police officers kicked him again. Innu who were hospitalized then saw the officers and heard someone screaming outside. They saw two police officers outside the hospital kicking an Innu. When the two officers had had enough, so it is told, they stood him up, took him each by an arm, and walked him into the hospital. When my child had his forehead slit open by the officers, they had to give him stitches. Once his wound was stitched up, the two officers brought him back to the prison and locked him up again.

kamakunueshiniti ekue tshipukuatakanikue anite ush-
katikut. Katshi tshipukuatakanniti, anitshenat nish^u
kakusseshiu-kamakunueshiht kau ekue tshiuetaiakuenit
anite kamakunueshiutshuapit tshetshi tshipauaht.

Tshietshishepaushit uiesh nishuaush-tatutipaikana,
innushkueu nitaimik^u anite ut akushiutshuapit ekue ishit :
« Tshikuss tau a anite tshitshuat ? Tepishkanit peshua-
kanipan ute akushiutshuapit, nish^u kamakunueshiniti
peshukupan. Apu tat ute akushiutshuapit », nitik^u. Ne
ishkueu ekue itak : « Apu ut takushinit tepishkanit, put
kamakunueshiutshuapit tatshe », nitau. Uiesh peikushteu-tatutipaikana, ninapem ekue aimit anite kamakunueshiutshuapit ekue itat nenua kamakunueshiniti : « Tau
a anite nikuss ? », iteu. Ekue itikut kamakunueshiniti :
« Tshikuss tau ute. Ne tshikuss eka tshiaminniuti,
shash tshekat nika nakuatanan. » Ninapem ekue itat :
« Unuitishinek^u ne nikuss, iakushikue tshe itutaiek^u
akushiutshuapit », iteu. Anitshenat kamakunueshiht
nenua nikussa uenashk ekue unuitishinaht muk^u apu itu-
taiaht akushiutshuapit kie apu tshiuetaiaht. Ne nitauassim
katshi unuitishinakanit anite kamakunueshiutshuapit
ekue pet tshitutet e pimutet ishpish nishtuemin. Shash
tutamushapan katshishishunanunit. Nikuss tekushinit
nitshinat, nutim umatshunishimit shukushiu, utash-
tamik^u pikupannu, anite ushkatit nutim uaututshishiu
e tatatshishkakut kamakunueshiniti, ushtikuan nutim
eshpishanit mishta-patshipannu. Nikuss katshi pitutshet
nitshinat, uenashk ekue pimishinit nipeunit ekue ishit :
« Utina katshishishunanut, nimishta-akushin », nitik^u.
Peikumitashumitunnu ashu nish^u tutam^u katshishishunanunit ekue pitukaiakanit akushiutshuapit ishpish
peikuminashtakana.

Nikuss katshi pitukaiakanit akushiutshuapit ekue
itenitaman tshetshi shatshuapamak utshimau-

The next morning at about eight, an Innu woman phoned me from the hospital and said: "Is your son at home? Last night he was brought to the hospital by two police officers. He is not here," she told me. I said to the woman: "He did not come home last night, he must be in prison." At about nine o'clock, my husband phoned the police station and asked the police officer: "Is my son there?" The police officer replied: "Your son is here. If he does not stay quiet, we will hang him soon." My husband told him: "Let him out of there and if he is ill, take him to the hospital." The police officers immediately released my son but they did not take him to the hospital and they did not bring him home. After he was released from prison, my child left on foot for a three-mile walk. Evidently, he already had a fever. When he arrived home, his clothes were covered in blood, his face was swollen, his legs were bruised from having being kicked so much by the officers, and his head was covered in swollen cuts. After he arrived home, my son went to lie down on a bed and said: "Take my temperature, I am very ill." His temperature was a hundred and two. He was hospitalized for a week.

After he was admitted to hospital, I thought to go see the chief of police to tell him that two of the

kamakunuesht tshetshi uitamuk nikuss ka ushikuikut
nish[u] kakusseshiu-kamakunueshiniti. Nititenimati
ne utshimau-kamakunuesht anu uin innishitshe mak
ukupaniema. Ekue shatshuapamak mak peik[u] innu nuitsheuau. Ne utshimau-kamakunuesht shiatshuapamak,
nishatshuapamau tshiam kie nitaimiau tshiam, tanite
eshk[u] apu nita ut nishtuapamak... Ekue itak : « Tshipe-
teti a tepishkat ka ishpanit, nitau, nish[u] kamakunueshiht
ushikuieshapanat nikussa ? » Ne utshimau-kamakunuesht
ekue ishit : « Nipeteti », nitik[u]. Ekue ishit : « Tshikuss
nenu ueshikuikut kamakunueshiniti, namaietshenat nin
ninapemat ueshikuiaht, innu-kamakunuesht ushikuie-
tshe », nitik[u]. Ne utshimau-kamakunuesht minuat ekue
ishit : « Ne tshikuss nenu ueshikuikut kamakunueshiniti
mishku nin eka ka taian, tshikuss tshipa nipipan, » nitik[u].
Ne utshimau-kamakunuesht ekue uapatinit passikannu
ekue ishit : « Tshikuss eukuannu umenu passikannu nipa
passuati, anite ushtikuanit ekute nipa passuati. » Nenu
eshit ekue itak : « Ne nitauassim passuti, tshika mitshetu
kutak auen tshe passut », nitau.

Ume tipatshimun nikuss ka ushikuikut kamakunueshiniti ekue nipitukatati kauaueshtakanit. Kashikat
eshk[u] apu nita uapataman tshetshi pimipanitakanit,
kashikat uiesh kutuasht etatupipuk. Kie niminu-tshisse-
niten tshekuan ka ut eka pimipanitakanit anite kauaueshtakanit, usham kauapishiht nitapatshiatanat tshetshi
netemuanuht[12]. Nitshissenimikautanakupan uemut tshe
kanieuiat. Ne nikuss ka ushikuikut nish[u] kakusseshiu-
kamakunueshiniti, nimashkatenitetan. Tshekuan ka
ut mashkatenitamat, kamakunuesht nishtam ka uapamitshit, nitishi-utinatan namaieu natamik[u] napeu tanite
nitishi-petetan kassinu napeu ka ishi-atusset miam
kamakunuesht katapuenanunit tutuakanu kuishk[u] tshetshi
atusset. Eukuan uet mashkatenitamat kamakunueshiht

city's officers had injured my son. I thought that the
chief would be more intelligent than his men. So
I went to see him accompanied by another Innu. I
went to see him politely and I spoke to him politely,
I did not know him yet...I told him: "Did you hear
about what happened last night? Apparently two
officers injured my son." The chief of police told
me: "I heard about it." Then he added: "If your son
was injured by police officers, it cannot have been
by my men, it must have been by RCMP officers."
The chief of police then told me: "When the officers
injured your boy, you are lucky I was not there, he
would be dead!" Then he showed me a gun and
said: "It is with this gun that I would have shot your
boy and I would have shot him in the head." To this
I responded: "If you shoot my child, there will be
many others you will have to shoot."

This story about my son who was injured by
the police officers, I took it to court. Today, almost
six years later, the case has still not been heard
and I know exactly why: we had White people as
witnesses. They must have known that we would
certainly win the case. We were surprised that my
son was injured by two municipal police officers.
The reason for our surprise was, when we first saw
the police officer, we did not think of him as just
anyone. We had heard that all men who worked
as police officers had to take an oath so that they
would to their job with righteousness. This is why
we were surprised by the fact that it was always only
the Innu that the police officers mistreated and sent

muk^u innua miakunaht nanitam e matshi-tutuaht kie
muk^u innu patukaiaht akushiutshuapit. Ka tatupipuna
matshi-tutuimiht kamakunueshiht, apu nita ut petamat
peik^u kauapishiniti tshetshi ushikuiaht kie tshetshi
pitukaiaht akushiutshuapit.

Ninan e inniuiat apu tshi issishueiat anitshenat
kamakunueshiht nitishi-utinikutanat miam peikuan
atim^u tanite nitinniunnan ka ishinniuiat anite nutshimit,
ne atim^u nanitam niminu-kanuenimatan. Innu atimua
kenuenimati apu nita ut nanatu-matshi-tutuat, apu nita
ut utamauat shetshen kie apu nita ut tatatshishkuat. Kie
nenua atimua kenuenimati apu nita ut papamitapet anite
kunit kie anite ashinishkat. Kie ne innu nenua atimua
kenuenimati, kenuenitaki mitshiminu tshetshi ashamat,
ashamepan.

Anitshenat kamakunueshiht peik^u innua miakunataui
shetshen, mamitunenitamuat tan tshe tutuaht nenua
innua tshetshi ut shuniatsheuatsheht. Nenua innua ekue
tutamuaht umashinaikanuianiminu. Uinuau tshisse-
nitamuat tshe itashtauaht innua umashinaikanuianiminu muk^u tshetshi minupannit tshetshi ut pimipaniaht
kauaueshtakannit. Mitshetipan innu ka tipatshimut katshi
pimipaniakanit kauaueshtakannit, mishta-katshinau e
itashtakanikue nenu umashinaikanuianimuau. Peik^u
innu tipatshimu : « Miakunikauian, uiauitamakauian
ka ishi-matshi-tutaman, nimashinaikanuianim eukuan
etashtet, issishueu : "E minukashuin tshitishkuem
tshimashikatunauashapan, tshushikuitunauashapan
tshitishkuem, nitikaun. Mate ne tshissishik^u eshinakuak,
eukuannu tshitishkuem ka utamaushk," nitikaun.
Eukuan etashtet nimashinaikanuianim, » issishueu ne
innu. Ekue issishuet : « Pemipanikauian kauaueshtakanit, ne kamakunuesht ka utamaut anite nissishikut ekute
napaut anite upime. Shetshen ma uin at ui aimiani, atut

to hospital when they arrested them. After all this
time that police officers have been mistreating us,
we have never heard of but one White man who was
injured and sent to the hospital by them.

We the Innu, we cannot say that the police treat
us like dogs because when we lived our lives in
the woods, we would always take care of the dogs.
When the Innu kept a dog, he never sought to
mistreat him, he would never hit him unnecessarily and he would never kick him. When the Innu
had a dog, he would never drag him over rocks or
through the snow. If he had food to give to him, he
fed him.

When the police arrest an Innu for no reason,
they think about what they will do to make money
off of him. So they write up the file of this Innu.
They know what to write in his file so that it goes
to court. Many Innu have said, after they went
to court, that what was written in their file was
completely false. One of them said: "When I was
arrested, I was told what I had done wrong. This is
what my file showed: 'When you were drunk, you
apparently fought with your wife and you injured
each other. If your eye looks the way it does, it is
because your wife hit you.' This is what my indictment said." Then he said: "When I went to court,
the police officer who had hit me in the eye was
there, standing right next to us. It would not have
helped had I said anything, I would not have been
listened to and I never would have won." Remem-
bering how he was judged, this Innu did not know
what to think. When he spoke about it, he was

nita nut natutakaun kie atut nita nut kanieun », issishueu
ne innu. Ne innu nenu tepatshimut nenu eshi-uaueshia-
kanit, apu tshissenitak tshipa itenitam^u. Tepatshimut,
mishta-tshishuapu kie ashit apu tshi tutak tshetshi eka
papit. Tan ma ne uin kamakunuesht itikupan tshetshi
papit kie uin katshi tshishi-uaueshtakannit...

Innu kie innu-auass miakunakanitaui metshi-tutaku-
taui kamakunueshiniti, muk^u aiat shetshishu tshetshi
aimit, kushtam^u minuat makunakaniti anu tshetshi nene-
katshikut kamakunueshiniti. Innu mitshetuau tshisse-
nitam^u shetshen e makunakanit, iapit apu nita aimit,
kushtam^u minuat makunakaniti anu tshetshi matshashta-
niti kamakunueshiniti nenu umashinaikanuianim. Uesh
kamakunueshihit innua miakunataui, uinuau tshisseni-
tamuat tshe itashtauaht umashinaikanuianiminu.

Eishi-matshi-tutuimiht kamakunueshihit, apu taniti
auennua tshetshi kushtaht tanite tapue apu tat kauapishit
ka atusseshtuimit tshetshi nakatuapamimit kie tshetshi
tshishpeuashimit e inniuiat. Anitshenat uin katshishe-
utshimau-atusseht ka atusseshtuimit muk^u nenu uka-
nieunuau mak tshimut e atusseshtuaht kauapishiniti,
eukuannu muk^u miamitunenitahk. E inniuiat animan
tshetshi tshissenitamat, kie put nuash tshe nipiat apu
nita tshika ut tshissenitamat, ka itashiht kauapishiht ka
takushiniht tshetshi natshi-atusseshtuimit, miam Uepishtikueiat uetuteht kie peikuan Utauat uetuteht. Anitshenat
kauapishiht apu tshissenimitshiht tan ka ishi-katshe-
ssimakaniht nete uetuteht tshetshi ishi-atusseshtuaht
innua. Mak eukuan nimashkatenitenan, ka tatupipuna
matshi-tutuimiti kamakunueshiniti, apu nita ut mish-
kutshit peik^u kauapishit ka atusseshtuimit tshetshi tshishpeuashimit. Nin eukuan etenitaman : kassinu kauapishit
ka atusseshtuimit e inniuiat ishi-minushipan muk^u
tshimut tshetshi nanatshinimit e inniuiat inishat tshetshi

furious and at the same time, he could not help but
laugh. It is worth wondering whether the police
officer did not laugh as well after that hearing...

When an Innu, young or adult, is brutalized by the
police at the time of his arrest, he is more and more
afraid to speak, he is afraid he will be tormented even
more by the police officers during another arrest.
Often the Innu knows that he is arrested for no reason
but despite that he does not say anything, he is afraid
that during a possible arrest, the police officers will
only make his file look worse. When the police arrest
an Innu, they know how to write up his file.

When the police mistreat us like this, they have
no one to fear: among all the White people who
are at our service there really is no one to protect
us and defend us, we the Innu. The civil servants
who work for us only think about their salary and
about working secretly for the White man. It is
difficult for us to know – and perhaps we will not
know before we die – how many White people from
Québec and Ottawa came to work for us. And we do
not know what speech they are given when they are
hired, over there at Indian Services. What surprises
us is that, during all these years when the police
were mistreating us, we could never find but one to
defend us, among the White men who were at our
service. I think that all those White men who are at
our service, us the Innu, were only good at shoving
us along, without our knowledge, so that like it or
not, we would submit entirely to the White man's
regime. Today, all those White men who worked for

nashamat kassinu eishinakuak kakusseshiu-nanua. Kashikanit kassinu kauapishiht ka atusseshtuaht innua kassinu
tshishtauat utatusseunuau. Kashikat e inniuiat nipapan-
nan anite kassinu eishinakuak kakusseshiu-nanua.

Innu-auass kashikanit apishish metshi-tutaki, kauapishit shash ekue unuipanitat tipatshimu-mashinaikannu tshetshi matshi-uauinat innua kie innu-auassa.
Kakusseshiu-kamakunueshiht ueshikuiataui innua kie
innu-auassa nenu ut matshi-manitu-ishkutuapunu,
uinuau eshinniuht katshi petaht ute nitassinat, apu nita
mashinaitsheht anite tipatshimu-mashinaikanit.
Kie kakusseshiu-kamakunueshiht patukaiataui
innua anite akushiutshuapit, iapit apu nita unuipani-
taht tipatshimu-mashinaikannu uesh ma anitshenat
kakusseshiu-kamakunueshiht mishta-katauat nenu
etutahk. Katshi ushikuiataui innua kie katshi patukaiataui anite akushiutshuapit, apu tshi pimipaniaht anite
kakusseshiu-kauaueshtakannit.

Mate nika tipatshimun peik[u] tshekuan. Kutuasht-
tatunnu ashu peikushteu, nish[u] kakusseshiu-kamakunueshiht miam nuapamatiat patukaiaht nikussa anite
kamakunueshiutshuapit kie shash nipeteti kamakunueshiht miashikuaht innua kie innu-auassa miakunataui,
kakusseshiu-kamakunueshiht kie peikuan innu-kamaku-
nueshiht. Anitshenat nish[u] kakusseshiu-kamakunueshiht
katshi pitukaiaht nikussa anite kamakunueshiutshuapit
ekue pitutsheian anite mak peik[u] nitanish nuitsheuau.
Patutsheiat, tapue nuapamananat nish[u] kakusseshiu-
kamakunueshiht miam mashikueuat nikussa eshk[u] eka
pitukaiaht anite tshe tshipauaht. E nishiht ututamaueuat
anite ushkatanit kie kassinu anite uianit. Nitanish mak nin
ekue mishta-teputepueiat; pietuimiht tieputepueiat kie
uiapamimiht ekue puniaht nikussa e mashikuaht. Tshiam
ekue natshi-pitukaiaht nete tshe tshipauaht.

Indian Services have accomplished their work: we are moving towards a White man's regime.

When the young Innu does some harm, the White man immediately publishes an article that denigrates the Innu, youth and adults. But each time the municipal police officers injure the Innu, youth and adults, because of that damn alcohol that their own kind brought to our territory, they do not write about that in the newspapers. And each time the municipal police officers send an Innu to the hospital, they do not publish an article about that either because they carefully cover up their actions. After they have injured an Innu and sent him to hospital, they cannot risk taking him to the White man's court.

I will say something. In 1969, I saw two municipal police officers bring my son to the police station. I had already heard that the police – both the municipal police and the RCMP – would beat the Innu, youth and adults, when they arrested them. After the two municipal police officers brought my son to the police station, I went in with one of my daughters. Upon entering, we saw the two police officers beating my son before putting him in a cell. They were both hitting him in the stomach and everywhere else on his body. My daughter and I we then started to scream. Hearing us scream and seeing us, they stopped beating him and calmly locked him up in a cell.

Nitanish mak nin katshi unuiat anite ut kamakunueshiutshuapit ekue tepuashit peik[u] kamakunuesht,
eukuan ne peik[u] ka ishi-metuet miam peikuan kautamai-
tshenanut : « Matam Antane, ashtam ute », nitik[u]. Ekue
natuapamak ekue ishit : « Ashtam uitsheui, nika unui-
tishinau tshikuss, tshe tshiuetaiak[u] tshitshuat », nitik[u].
Ekue itak : « Eka pissenim, pitama tshika nipau uenapissish tshetshi ashteieshkushit », nitau. Ne kamakunuesht
minuat ekue ishit : « Matshi natshi-ataue anite atauitshuapit, tshishi-ataueini tshika tshiuetaitinan tshitshuat ashit
tshitatauan, » nitik[u]. Anitshenat nish[u] kakusseshiu-
kamakunueshihit nenu tshauetaimiht nitshinat ekue ishiht :
« Tshikuss uniti, nika tshiuetaianan tshitshuat kie apu
tshika ut pimipanit anite kauaueshtakannit », nitikuat.
Kie tapue nikuss apu ut pimipaniakanit anite kauaueshtakannit. Ume tipatshimun ka uapataman nikuss ka
mashikakut nish[u] kakusseshiu-kamakunueshiniti, tapue
nikushkupaniti kie minekash apu ut tshi uni-tshissian.
    Anitshenat kamakunueshiht tutamuat katshi
mashikuataui kie katshi ushikuiataui innua ekue akushi-
kashuht tshetshi nenu ishi-katshinaht miam uinuau
ueshikuikutau innua. Mate nikuss ka ushikuikut nish[u]
kakusseshiu-kamakunueshiniti, tshietshishepaushit
nipetenan tipatshimun anite ut akushiutshuapit, ne peik[u]
kamakunuesht ka ushikuiat nikussa tushkapamakanu,
itakanu, anite akushiutshuapit. E inniuiat takuanipan
tshekuan meshkatenitamat uiauitamati. Anitshenat
kamakunueshiht ueshukuiataui innua miakunataui
nenu ut ishkutuapunu, nanikutini uinuau uetshit itutaie-
panat akushiutshuapit. Kamakunueshiht patukaiataui
nenua innua ka ushikuiaht anite akushiutshuapit, tan ka
ishi-katshinaht...? Eukuan kutak tshekuan apu nita ut
tshissenitamat kie e inniuiat mitshetuau nuauitetan.

After we left the police station, one of the officers shouted at me – he was one of the beaters – "Madam André, come here!" he said. I went up to him and he said: "Come with me, I will release your son; we will bring him together to your home." Then I told him: "Leave him alone, he will first sleep and rest a bit." Then the police officer said to me: "Go do your shopping at the store. When you are done, we will bring you home with your parcels." While bringing me home, the two police officers told me: "When your son wakes up, we will bring him home and he will not go to court." And it is true, he did not go to court. I was truly astounded by that story of my son whom I had seen get beaten by two municipal police officers; for a long time I could not forget it.

After they have beaten and injured an Innu, the police pretend they are ill so that people think it was them who were hurt by the Innu. For instance, when my son was injured by two municipal police officers, we heard in the morning from people at the hospital that one of the police officers who had hurt him was getting an X-ray. One thing surprised us, us the Innu, when we talked together about it. When the police officers injured an Innu after they had arrested him for being drunk, sometimes it was the officers themselves who would bring him to the hospital. When the police officers brought an Innu whom they had hurt themselves to the hospital, what lies did they tell…? That is another thing that we never knew and that we often spoke about.

E inniuiat ka tatupipuna atusseshtuimit kamakunuesht, namaieu essishueian « Kamakunuesht apu ut kuishk^u atusseshtuimit » kie apu issishueian « Kamakunuesht kuishk^u nitatusseshtakutan » uesh ma e inniuian apu tshekuan anite nishtutaman kie apu tshekuan anite nish-tuapataman kamakunuesht utatusseun. Muk^u tatupipuna ka atusseshtuimit kakusseshiu-kamakunuesht kie peikuan innu-kamakunuesht, takuanipan tshekuan meshinatai-man : tshekuanitshe muk^u e inniuiat uet nanitam sha-kassinaimit kauapishit anite kamakunueshiutshuapit ? Kashikat e inniuiat pemipanikauiati anite kauaueshtaka-nit mamu kauapishit, nanitam anu innuat mitshetipanat pemipaniakaniht anite kakusseshiu-kauaueshtakannit mak at kauapishiniti.

E inniuiat nitshissenitenan mishta-ait eishi-pamipa-nikauiat kauaueshtakanit pemipanikauiati. Kauapishit uin apu uapamitshit eshakumiminashtakana tshetshi pimipaniakanit kauaueshtakannit ek^u innu tapue eshaku-miminashtakana pimipaniakanu kauaueshtakannit. Kie muk^u e inniuiat nitutakaunan tatuau pemipanikauiat tshetshi tshishikashuiat ne ut kauaueshtakanit. Auen tshetshi ishpish uenutishit eshakumiminashtakana tshetshi tshishikashut nenu ut kauaueshtakannit ? Ume eshinakuak kauaueshtakanit ut tshitshishipanipan innu ka minakanit tshetshi minit. Eukuannu ka ut tshitshipan-nit muk^u innu eshakumiminashtakana tshetshi tshishi-kashut nenu ut kauaueshtakannit. Nimashkatenitenan tanite ne uetshipanit muk^u uin innu eshakumitshishikua tshetshi matshi-tutak. Uesh ninan nitinniunnan ka ishinniuiat nutshimit, apu nita ut pitutsheiat kamaku-nueshiutshuap, kauaueshtakanit apu nita ut pimipaniat kie apu nita ut apashtaiat shuniau ut kauaueshtakanit. Kamakunueshiutshuap eshk^u eka nita ka pitutsheiat kie ne kauaueshtakanit eshk^u eka nita ka pimipanikauiat,

Now that it has been some years that the police officers have been at our service, Innu, I do not say "The police did not work for us righteously" and I do not say "The police worked for us righteously": I who am an Innu woman, I do not understand and I cannot conceive of a police officer's work. But of all the years that the municipal police and the RCMP worked for us, there is one thing that I noticed: for what reason are only the Innu injured by the police when they are arrested? For what reason is it only with us that the White man fills his prisons? Each time we were brought to court at the same time as White men, there were always more Innu than White men there.

We, the Innu, know that in court, we are treated in a very particular way. We do not see the White man in court each week but the Innu, he is brought to court truly every week. And only we are made to pay the fine each time. Who is rich enough to pay the fine each week? This weekly hearing only started when the Innu were given the right to drink alcohol. It is only then that only the Innu were made to pay the fine, each week. We wonder greatly how it has come to be that only the Innu do harm on a daily basis. When we lived our own lives, in the bush, we never went to prison, we were never brought to court, and we never spent money on the courts. In the past when we had never gone to prison and when we had never been brought to court, we were more civilized and our lives were more decent. It is neither the prisons nor the courts that civilized us. The fact that the police wanted to consider the Innu as non-civilized beings explains how they could do whatever they

anu nitinnishitan kie anu nitshiaminniutan. Namaieu
kamakunueshiutshuap nitinnishiuikutan kie namaieu
kauaueshtakanit nitinnishiuikutan. Kamakunueshiht
usham ui ishi-utinepanat « Innu apu innishit » eukuannu
ka ut aitutuaht innua muk^u ua aitutuaht kie eukuannu ka
ut mishta-shuniatsheuatsheht innua.

Anitshenat uin kakusseshiu-kamakunueshiht, innuat
nenua tshishikueuat, kassinu innu tshissenitam^u nenu.
Ne innu nenu eshakumiminashtakana pemipaniaka-
nit kauaueshtakanit apu nenu nita ut tepi-tshishikashut
umashinaikana. Ne innu nanitam nikan ashtenua
umashinaikana nenu ut kauaueshtakannit. Tanite eshakumiminashtakana e uaueshiakaniht muk^u innuat, tapan
innu nishuekannua umashinaikanuianima tshe tshishikashut muk^u peikuau e uaueshtakanit. Ne innu tshek
eshpish mishta-mashinaitshet nenu ut kauaueshtakannit,
anitshenat kamakunueshiht minuat ekue tshissenitahk
tshe tutahk tshetshi ut tshishipanniti e tshishikakutau
innua. Ne innu eka etusset eshakumipishimua minakanu
mitshim-shunianu tshetshi ut inniut. Ek^u ne tshishik^u
uetitshipanit tshetshi minakaniht innuat umitshim-
shuniamuau, kamakunueshiht eukuannu nenu minuat
tshe ui mamishkamaht innua.

Ne tshishe-utshimau-mashinaikanitshuap anite tshe
minakaniht innuat umitshim-shuniamuau, tshietshi-
shepaushiti uiesh peikushteu-tatutipaikana shenakanu.
Eshk^u eka shenakaniti, anitshenat kamakunueshiht
shash uinishtamuau papamipaituat utapanuat, nani-
shupuat, pitutsheuat mitshuapa nenua ut innua ka
mashinaitsheniti nenu ut kauaueshtakannit. Eukuannu
nenu miamushatshinaht eshk^u eka natuapataminiti
umitshim-shuniaminu ekue natshi-tshipauaht kamakunueshiutshuapit. Ne innu ka tshipauakanit kamaku-

wanted to them and it explains how they made so
much money off of them.

It is the Innu who maintain the municipal police
officers, every Innu knows it. The Innu who goes to
court each week will never be done paying his fines,
he constantly accumulates debt with the courts.
Because of the weekly hearings for the Innu, some
have been given two fines during the same hearing. But the Innu has never become discouraged,
he has always paid off his debt little by little. When
came the day that he owed the court a lot of money,
the police knew what to do in order to get paid
quickly. The Innu who does not have a job receives a
monthly food allowance. When the day comes that
rations are to be handed out, the police officers will
want to get him in their clutches again.

The office of the Department of Indian Affairs,
where the money for rations is handed out, opens
at about nine in the morning. Before it opens, the
police officers are the first to be seen driving by, two
by two. They go into the homes of the Innu who
owe the court money. That is where they pick them
up, before they leave to get their food allowance
money, and they lock them up in prison. The Innu
who is imprisoned in this way has to pay his fine to
be released. It has become habitual for the police to

nueshiutshuapit nenu ut umitshim-shuniam uemut
tshika ui tshishikashu umashinaikana nenu ut kauaueshtakannit, patush tshe unuitishinakanit anite kamakunueshiutshuapit. Anitshenat kamakunueshiht tshek
nakanauipanat nenu etutuaht innua. Ishi-utinepanat
innua miam eka innu.

Kauapishit katshi natuapamimit ute nitassinat,
katshi tshishkutamuimit utinniun kie katshi petat
ishkutuapunu ute nitassinat, kashikanit tshekuannitshe uet mishta-teputepuashimit pemipanimiti anite
kauaueshtakannit ? Kashikat e inniuiat patutsheiati
kamakunueshiutshuapit, eukuan uin kauapishit utinniun
uetshipanit uet pitutsheiat. E inniuiat kashikat eukuan
uin kauapishit utinniun uetshipanit uet pimipanikauiat
anite kauaueshtakanit. E inniuiat pemipanikauiati anite
kauaueshtakanit, kauapishit tshekuannu nenu nanitam
uet ishi-kukuetshimimit : « Tan tatuau minin peikupishimua ? », « Tan tatuputai kie tan tat^u nekaniss tshiminiti ? », « Tan eshinakuak ishkutuapui tshiminiti ? »,
« Tshekuan tshituteti uet eka nipain tepishkat ? », « Tan
tatutipaikana takuanipan patutshein kaminnanut ? »,
« Tan tatutipaikana takuanipan anite uet unuin kaminnanut ? », « Tshekuan uet eka atussein ? », nitaitikaunan
muk^u ninan e inniuiat anite kauaueshtakanit. Kauapishit
kashikanit tshekuannitshe uet kassinu aishi-kukuetshimi-
mit e inniutshit nenu ut utinniun ?

E inniuiat auen eukuan ka mishkutunak nitinniunnannu kie auen eukuan ka tshishkutamuimit utinniun
eka nita matshi-tutakakue muk^u nanitam minu-
tutakakue, nin eukuan etenitaman, ushtuin kie ninan
e inniuiat atut nita nipa matshi-tutetan uemut muk^u
nanitam nipa minu-tutetan. Tshekuannu ma kauapishit kashikanit nanitam uet nanatuapatak muk^u ninan e
inniuiat tshetshi anuenimimit ? Nititeniten nin, kashikat

act in this way towards the Innu. They did not consider them human beings.

After coming to find us in our homeland, after teaching us his culture, after bringing alcohol to our territory, why, when he brings us to court, does the White man now tell us off? If today we go to prison, it comes from the White man's culture. If we are brought to court, it comes from their culture. When we are brought before the judge, why does the White man ask us, tirelessly: "How many times a month do you drink?" "How many bottles and how many cans did you drink?" "What kind of alcohol did you drink?" "What were you doing that you were not sleeping last night?" "What time was it when you entered the bar?" "Why do you not work?" It is only to us, the Innu, that he says such things in court. Why now does he ask us all these questions about his own culture?

If the one who changed our culture and taught us his own had not acted badly but had always been irreproachable, I think neither would we have acted badly, we would have been required to always be perfect. Why does the White man constantly seek to punish only us, Innu? I believe it is the White man who is responsible for all of our bad actions today and for all of those of our children: he is the

e inniuiat kassinu eishi-matshi-tutamat kie nitauassiminanat kassinu eishi-matshi-tutahk, eukuan uin kauapishit
nanitam nianikanutet uesh ma kauapishit eukuan uin
ka mishkutunak nitinniunnannu. Kashikat eshinniuiat
kauapishit utinniun, kassinu innu kassinu anite kamakunueshiutshuapit e takuanniti umashinaikanuianima,
nititeniten nin namaienua nenua innu umashinaikanuianima, auen eukuan ka mishkutunak nitinnu-inniunnannu kie auen eukuan ka tshishkutamuimit utinniun,
eukuan uin kauapishit nutim umashinaikanuianima. Kie
kashikanit innu-auass miakunakaniti e matshi-tutaki
nenu ut ishkutuapunu, namaieu innu-auass metshitat nitishinikashunnannu e inniutshit, nititeniten nin
eukuan uin kauapishit metshitat nitishinikashunnannu.

Nutaui shash peikushteu-tatunnuepipuneshu ashu
peik[u]. Nutaui anite nutshimit ninitautshinikutan kie
anite nutshimit kassinu tshekuannu nitshishkuta-
makutan. Nutaui kie nikaui anite innu-mitshuapit ka
nitautshiniht kie anite nutshimit kassinu tshekuannu
ka tshishkutamuht, apu nita ut uapamakau tshetshi
pimipaniakaniht kauaueshtakannit kie apu nita ut
uapamakau katapuenanunit tshetshi tutahk. Nutaui uin
utinniun ka ishi-tshishkutamuimit, apu nita ut uapamak
kamakunueshiniti tshetshi aiatinikut miam tshetshi
makupitikut assikumaniapinu utitshit kie apu nita ut
uapamak kamakunueshiniti tshetshi ututamaukut kie
tshetshi tatatshishkakut nete mashten tshetshi pitukaikut
kukush-kamakunueshiutshuapit. Ninan nitinniunnan
ka ishinniuiat anite nutshimit innu-mitshuapit, nutaui
apu nita ut petuk tshetshi issishuet : « Ka makunikauian,
eukuan nitaitutakutiat kamakunueshiht », « Ka makunikauian, pissik[u] panune[13] eukuan eshamikuian », « Apu
ashamikauian », « Nipi apu minikauian », « Kamakunuesht apu tapuetut mishiutshuapit tshetshi ituteian ». Ne

one who changed our culture. And now that we are living the White man's life, according to me, it is not to the Innu that all the criminal records of the Innu belong, they belong to the one who changed our Innu lives and who taught us his own. These files all relate back to the White man. And now, when a young Innu is arrested for misbehaving while he is drunk, it is not he who tarnishes our name, the Innu, according to me, it is the White man.

My father is ninety-one years old, he raised us in the bush and it is in the bush that he taught us everything. My father and my mother who raised me in a tent and who taught me everything in the bush, I never saw them go to court and I never saw them be sworn in. When my father taught us his culture, I never saw him touched by police officers trying to put handcuffs on him. I never saw him get beaten by the police, kicked by them, and end up being thrown into that pigsty of a prison. When we, the Innu, lived our lives in the bush, in our tents, I never heard my father say: "When I was arrested this is what the police did," "When I was arrested all they fed me was baloney," "I was not given anything to eat," "I was not given water to drink," "The police officer would not let me go to the bathroom." When he lived his own life, I never heard my father say such things because before the White man's city existed in the interior, never, we the Innu, had we seen prisons or courts.

nutaui uin uetshit utinniun ka ishinniut, apu umenu nita
ut petuk tshetshi ishi-tipatshimut uesh ma ute nutshimit
eshk[u] eka takuak kakusseshiu-utenau, e inniuiat apu nita
ut uapatamat kamakunueshiutshuap kie kauaueshtakanit.

Kie ne katapuenanut apu nita ut uapatamat. Katapuenanut e inniuiat nitishi-nishtutenan namaieu natamik[u]
tshekuan. Ueshkat kamakunuesht apu nita ut uapamitshit
tshetshi nanatshinimit ne katapuenanut tshetshi katshi-
nau-tutamat. Kashikat eshinniuiat kauapishit utinniun,
kassinu tshekuan eishi-natshinikauiat tshetshi tutamat, kassinu nitutetan muk[u] e kushtatshikauiat at eka
menu-nishtutamati kie at eka menu-nishtutamunikauiati.
Peikuau nuishamikauti anite kauaueshtakanit miam nete-
mua tshetshi itapatshikauian. Kapishitshitak e inanunit
ekue ninatuenitamakuti tshetshi tutaman katapuenanut.
Apu ut tapuetaman e inniuian katapuenanut tshetshi
tutaman anite kauaueshtakanit uesh ma kauaueshtakanit kie peikuan katapuenanut e tutakanit, kauapishit
nenu utinniun. Katapuenanut etutakaniti, nin e inniuian
eukuan nitishi-peteti essishuenanut : namaieu natamik[u]
tshekuan kie namaieu e apishashit tshekuan etutakanit.
Eukuan ka ut eka tapuetaman e inniuian tshetshi tutaman
katapuenanut. Kie mitshetuau nitshitaimuatiat nitauassimat tshetshi tutahk nenu kakusseshiu-katapuenanunit
anite kauaueshtakannit.

Nitinniun ka ishinniuian anite nutshimit innu-
mitshuapit, eshk[u] eka peik[u] ka takushinit kakusseshiu-
kamakunuesht ute Tshiuetinit, kassinu innu-
auass apu nita ut ishi-mamitunenitak muk[u] tshetshi
nanatu-matshi-tutak tanite kassinu innu-auass apu
tshekuannu ut takuannit tshetshi minukashishkakut
tshetshi ut matshi-tutak. Uesh ne ishkutuapui namaieute
ute minashkuat uetshipanit kie namaieute shipit kie
namaieute shakaikanit uetshipanit. Kassinu innu-auass

Neither had we ever seen a swearing in. The way we understand things, for us the Innu, an oath is not something to be taken lightly. In the past, we had never seen police officers forcing us to take an oath in order to lie. Since we have been living the White man's life, we have done, out of fear, everything that we were made to do, without understanding them well and without things being explained to us. Once I was called to appear as a witness. The judge asked me to take an oath. I did not accept to take an oath because the court and the act of swearing in are part of the White man's culture. This is what I, an Innu woman, heard: to take an oath, it is not nothing, it is not a trifle. That is why I did not want to, as an Innu woman, be sworn in. And I often forbade my children from taking the White man's oath in court.

When I used to live my life in a tent, in the bush, before the first police officer came here to the North, the young Innu did not think about causing mischief. They did not have anything to get drunk with and then do bad things: alcohol does not come from the bush, it does not come from the rivers or the lakes. The only things that children aged from six to eight would find outside to play with were an axe and a toboggan. When

kutuasht etatupipuneshit nuash nishuaush etatupipuneshit, eukuannu muk^u tshekuannu mishkamupan
tshetshi metuatshet anite unuitimit : ushtashkunu mak
utapanashkua. Kassinu innu-auass uetakussiniti epuniti
e metuet unuitimit, uemut eukuannu muk^u takuannipan
tshetshi tutak, tshetshi nipat uipat. Kakusseshiu-kamakunuesht apu nita ut pitutshet innu-mitshuapit tshetshi
nanatu-mamushatshinat kie tshetshi tatatshishkuat
innu-auassa. Innu-auass ka kutunnuepipuneshit ashu
nish^u, shash tshitshipanipan e nataut. Innu-auass shash ka
tshitshipanit e nataut, uetakussiniti minekash eka patutshet uitshuat anite innu-mitshuapit, namaieute kaminnanunit apipan kie namaieute kamakunueshiutshuapit
apipan. Eukuannu ka tutak nenu peikutshishikua – e
nataut – kie takuannipan enutepanit tshishikunu, apu
ut ishpishit e nataut. Eukuannu muk^u tshekuannu ka
mamashikut ka ut ueshamapit tshetshi uipat pitutshet
uetakussiniti kie ka ut eka uipat nipat tepishkaniti.
Kassinu innu kie kassinu innu-auass mishta-
minuatamupan e nataut tanite nakanauipan nenu ka ishi-
pakassiut e nataut. Miam peikuan kauapishit nakanauiu
tshetshi kakusseshiu-atusset tanite kassinu eishinakuak
kakusseshiu-atusseun, kauapishit nenu utinniun. Anite
nutshimit innu-mitshuapit ka ishinniuiat, kassinu papeik^u
kautishkuemit uetakussiniti eshk^u eka nipananuti, aia-
miananuipan mamu utauassima kie kassinu papeik^u
kautishkuemit minukuamuipan tepishkaniti mamu
utauassima. Anite nutshimit innu-mitshuapit ka ishinniuiat, tapue iapit takuanipan tshishik^u eka uet takuak
tshe mitshiat innu-mitshim muk^u namaieu ishkutuapui
nitutakutan. Kie ne nitshinan innu-mitshuap apu nita
ut pipikuaimat tanite nitshissenitetan innu-mitshuap
eukuan ninan e inniuiat nitshinan. Kie ne nitshinan innu-
mitshuap apu ut tshikamut anite pashpapuakan tshetshi

they were done playing outside in the evening,
all that was left to do was to go to bed early. The
municipal police never went then into the tents
of the Innu to round up the children and kick
them. When they were twelve years old, the Innu
children started to hunt. If the child who had
begun hunting was late coming home in the evening, he would not be found either at a bar or in
a prison. Hunting was all that he had to do and
sometimes there would not be enough time to
hunt. That was the only thing that would make
him late, that prevented him from coming home
early in the evening and going to bed early. Every
adult and every youth liked to hunt enormously
because everyone was used to providing for himself by hunting. Just like the White man, he is
used to having a paid job because all the different kinds of paid work are a part of his culture.
When we lived in tents, in the bush, each family including the children would say the rosary
before going to sleep and they would sleep well
at night. When we lived in tents, in the bush,
it is true that there were days when we did not
have enough Innu food but it was not because of
alcohol. And we did not damage our houses, the
tents, because we knew that the tent is our home,
to us the Innu. And in our houses, the tents,
there were no windows to break with which to
hurt ourselves, us and our children. And old
battered cars, there never were any lying around
next to our tents and we were never injured by
cars and we did not die because of them. When
we lived in our tents, in the bush, you never
heard of our behaviour in the newspapers or on

pipikuaimat tshetshi ut ushikuitishuiat kie nitauassiminanat tshetshi ut ushikuitishuht. Kie ne matshutapan eshkua-apatak apu nita ut ashtet anite upime
innu-mitshuapit kie e inniuiat apu nita ut ishi-ushikuiat
utapan kie apu nita ut ishi-nipiat utapan. Kie tapue e
inniuiat anite nutshimit innu-mitshuapit ka ishinniuiat,
anite tipatshimu-mashinaikanit kie anite katshitapatakanit apu nita ut petamek^u tshetshi uauitakanit nitaiteni-
takushunnan. Innu kie innu-auass apu nita ut takuanniti
umashinaikanuianima metshi-tutaki kassinu anite
kamakunueshiutshuapit. Nutshimit innu-mitshuapit ka
ishinniuiat, apu ut takuak kamakunueshiutshuap kie ne
kauaueshtakanit apu ut takuak.

Kauapishit nenu utinniun ka ut ui tshishkutamuimit,
kashikat ninishtunenan kie nuapatenan muk^u tshiam nui
matshi-tutakutan mak muk^u tshiam nui uaushinaku-
tan mak muk^u tshiam nui manenimikutan. Uesh ma ne
kauapishit nimanenimikunan nenu etutuimit eshakumiminashtakana tshetshi tshishikashuiat kauaueshtakanit,
nuaushinakunan nenu etutuimit tshetshi natshikapaui-
mit anite kauaueshtakannit tshessenimimit e inniuiat
kauaueshtakanit eka tshekuan anite neshtutamat kie eka
nita ut uapatamat kauaueshtakanit kie eka neshtutamat
kakusseshiu-katapuenanut etutakanit. Kauapishit katshi
tshishkutamuimit utinniun mishkut nitinniunnannu
katshi pikunak, kashikanit tapue uin muk^u minuenita-
mitishu ek^u umenu ninan e inniuiat shash mishta-atamit
nitanikunan uesh ma apu tshi aishi-utinimit miam uin
eishi-utinitishut kie apu tshi aishi-pimipanimit miam uin
eishi-pimipanitishut.

Kashikat e inniuiat katshi tutakauiat peikutau tshetshi
apiat mamu kauapishit, kashikat ute Kaiatushkanut
pietakuaki metshi-tutakaniti, anitshenat kakusseshiu-
kamakunueshiht innua mak innu-auassa nishtam

the television. The Innu adult and youth did not have criminal records in every police station. When we lived in our tents, in the bush, there was no prison and there were no courthouses.

Nowadays, we see and understand the reasons why the White man wanted to teach us his culture: all he wanted was to harm us, all he wanted was to mock us, and all he wanted was to insult us. The White man insults us by making us pay a fine each week, he laughs at us when he puts us in front of the courts knowing perfectly well that we do not understand the courts – we who had never seen such things before – and that we do not understand the White man's oath. After teaching us his culture and in return destroying ours, the White man today is only truly satisfied with himself and we, the Innu, he relegates to the bottom: he is incapable of thinking of us the way he thinks of himself and he is incapable of giving us the same rights that he gives himself.

Now that we have been settled near the White men, if one hears of someone causing mischief, here in Schefferville, it is the Innu, young or adult, that the municipal police officers will pick

mamushatshineuat. Ninan e inniuiat kashikat eshinniuiat, anitshenat kamakunueshiht nitshissenimikunanat
anite itetshe kauapishit utinniunit etaiat, namaieu ninan
nitinniunnan. Kashikat apu tshekuan anite nishtuapata-
mat kie apu tshekuan anite nishtutamat e inniuiat. Apu
pikutaiat tshetshi tshishpeuatitishuiat e inniuiat anite itetshe kauapishit utinniunit. Kashikat eshpish ishinniuian
kauapishit utinniun, nin nimishken muk^u katshinaun
mak uieshitshemun. Eukuana muk^u anite tekuaki.

Eukuan eshpish mishta-mashkuat kashikat eishin-
niuiat katshi pikunakanit nitinnu-inniunnan. Ueshkat
kamakunuesht apu nita ut uapamitshit tshetshi nene-
katshimit kie tshetshi manenimimit. Kamakunuesht ka
tatupipuna ui innishiuimit, nasht ishinakuannipan uin
tshetshi innishiuitishut uesh ma anu uin apu innishit.
Mitshetuau umenu pet issishuepanat innuat.

E inniuiat nikan minuapan nitinniunnan. Kashikat
katshi tapuetamat ka pet aishi-uieshimikauiat, katshi
tutakauiat tshetshi nakatamat nitinnu-inniunnan kie
katshi patshitinitishuiat tshetshi tatakushkashimit kauapishit, kashikat nishuait eishinniunanut apu tshekuan
ishpitenitakushiat e inniuiat. Nin nititenitamun, anu
ma tshipa minuapan nitinniunnan kanuenitamatakue
ka ishi-minimit Tshishe-manitu tshetshi ishinniuiat e
inniuiat kie nitinnu-aimunnan kanuenitamatakue ka
ishi-minimit Tshishe-manitu tshetshi ishi-aimiat. Kauapishit ka takushinit ute nitassinat, tipan kanuenitakakue
utinniun kie nenu umishtikushiu-aimun kie ma kauapishit katshi takushinit ute nitassinat nenu nitassinannu
tshetshi uenutishiuatshet, eka matshi-tutuatakue innua
kie eka tutakakue innua nanitam tshetshi ui shuniatsheuatshet, kashikat ushtuin atut takuan kamashikatunanut e inniuiat mamu kauapishit.

up first. The police know very well that our way of living now is that of the White man, it is not our way. Today, we who are Innu, do not know it and we do not understand it. We cannot find a way out, as Innu, of the White man's culture. Since I have been living the White man's life, all that I find in it, personally, are lies and injustice. That is all there is.

It is to this extent that the lives we live today are difficult since our Innu culture has been destroyed. We had never before seen police officers hurt us or offend us. For years when the police officer wanted to "civilize" us, it would have been a lot better had he tried to civilize himself because he is the one who is less civilized. This is what the Innu have often said.

Our way of life, Innu, was better. But after agreeing to being duped, after we were made to abandon our Innu culture and after being trampled by the White man, we are not worth anything in either one culture or the other. In my opinion, it would have been better to keep the life that God[20] gave us to live as Innu and to keep the Innu language that God gave us to speak. If the White man, when he arrived in our territory, had kept his own culture and his own French language or even if, when he came here to make money with our land, he had not brutalized the Innu and had not always wanted to exploit them, today there probably would not be any conflict between him and us.

7

Katipatshimu-mashinaikani-tsheshiht mak kaiakunitsheshiht

Katipatshimu-mashinaikanitsheshiht kie kaiakunitsheshiht, kashikat eshinniuiat kauapishit utinniun,
mitshetuau ninatshishkuananat. Muk^u ninan nitinnu-
inniunnan ka ishinniuiat anite nutshimit, apu nita ut
uapamitshiht. Kashikat uiapatamekui uiauinikauiat e
inniuiat anite tipatshimu-mashinaikanit, nin nitishi-
utinen apu tshekuan anite tapuemakak kie uiapatamekui
nukuikauiat anite kamatau-pikutakanit kie anite
katshitapatakanit, apu tshekuan anite tapuemakak.

Uesh ma kashikat namaieu ninan nitinniunnan
eshinniuiat. Kashikat eshinniuiat kauapishit utinniun,
nin e inniuian nimishken e mashkuat inniun mak e
matshikaut inniun. Nimishken mishta-ait ishinakuan
kashikat nitinniun eshpish ishinniuian kauapishit utinniun. Kashikat eukuan muk^u uet minuenitaman tshetshi
natshishkukau katipatshimu-mashinaikanitsheshiht kie
kaiakunitsheshiht, muk^u tshetshi uapatinik kauapishit
katshi tutuimit tshetshi matshinakuimit. Nin e inniuian
eukuan muk^u uet tapuetaman tshetshi nanukushian anite
katshitapatakanit kie anite kamatau-pikutakanit, muk^u
apu tshekuan anite tapuemakak. Kie apu shakuenimuian
nukushiani anite kamatau-pikutakanit tanite nitshisseniten ishinniuianakue miam ueshkat innu, kashikat eshk^u
atut nita nut nanukushiti anite kamatau-pikutakanit kie

7

The journalists and the filmmakers

Now that we live the White man's life, we often meet journalists and filmmakers. When we lived our Innu life inland, we never saw them. I consider that today, when we are talked about in the newspapers, there is nothing true there, and when you see us in films or on television, there is nothing true there.

Because nowadays, it is not our own life that we are living. Me, an Innu woman, I find this life that we live now, which is the White man's, tiresome and harmful; I find my life is very different since I have been living according to White culture. The only reason why I am happy to meet journalists and filmmakers today is to show the White man that he did not bring us up well. As an Innu woman, this is the only reason that I agree to be seen on television and in films but there is nothing real in that. And I am not uncomfortable to appear in films because I know that had I lived the way the Innu used to in the past, today I would never have been seen in films or on television and no one would have talked about me in the newspapers.

anite katshitapatakanit kie anite tipatshimu-mashinaikanit atut nita nipa uauinikauti e inniuian.

Peikuau nuapateti tipatshimu-mashinaikan. Innuat
uiauinakanitaui, nin eukuan eshi-utinaman : muk[u] peik[u]
innu peikushu nutim innu. Ne tipatshimu-mashinaikan
eukuan itashtepan : « Innuat katshi manukuakaniht,
muk[u] tshiam minukashuat ek[u] nenua uitshuaua apu
itenitahk tshetshi akua tutahk kie anitshenat innushkueuat nenua uitshuaua apu itenitahk tshetshi naikahk,
anite ashtamitat mishta-uinakuannua kie innuat katshi
manukuakaniht nenua utshishtukanuaua apu tshissenitahk tshetshi tshipaihk, ueuepashtannua utshishtukanuaua tshek ekue manashtanniti natamik[u] ekue
papiushteniti. Innuat upashpapuakanuaua pipikuaimuat.
Mak innuat eiataui utapannu, pakupanniti, apu auat itenitahk tshetshi uaueshtaht, anite upime uitshuat ekute
eshtenit », itashtepan ne tipatshimu-mashinaikan ka
uapataman.

Kauapishit katshi tshishkutamuimit utinniun kie
katshi tshimutamuimit nitinniunnannu, kashikanit shetshen nenu tshipa ut aieshkushiuinitishu kassinu tshekuan
etutamat anite ut kauapishit utinniunit. Kauapishit
shetshen nenu tshipa ut tutam[u] tipatshimu-mashinai-
kana nenu ut ishkutuapunu katshi minimit tshetshi
miniat. Uesh ma ne eukuan uin ka ishi-tshishkutamuimit muk[u] nanitam tshetshi minukashuiat. Ek[u] nenua
uin nitshinana katshi manukakauiat, tshekuan uet eka
mamitunenitamat ? Ne mishtikushitshuap – kakusseshiu-
mitshuap – namaieu ninan e inniuiat nitshinan kie ne
mishtiku-tshishtukan namaienu nenu innu utshishtukan.
Ek[u] ne utapan kashikat uiapatamek[u] eshtet anite upime
nitshinat, eukuan kauapishit nenu umatshi-tutamun.
Kauapishit utapan eshkua-apashtati, eukuannua innua
nianatu-uieshimat nenu umatshutapan. Ne kauapishit

One day I read a newspaper. When they talk about the Innu, I myself see it as if they were talking about all Indigenous peoples, that all Indigenous peoples are one and the same. This is what was written in that newspaper: "Since we built them houses, all the Indians do is get drunk, they do not think about taking care of their houses and the Indian women do not think about cleaning them, the walls are very dirty; since we built them houses, the Indians do not know how to close their doors, they bang in the wind and they eventually fall off and lay around; the Indians break their windows; when the Indians buy a car, if it breaks down, they do not think about having it repaired and it just stays next to their house." That is what was written in the newspaper that I read.

After he taught us his culture and stole ours, the White man should not be tormented by every one of our actions that comes from White culture! He should not write newspaper articles about alcohol when he is the one who gave it to us! He is the one who taught us how to be constantly drunk. And why could we not care less about the houses that he built us? The White man's houses, houses made of wood, that is not our kind of house, the Innu, and wooden doors, that is not our kind of door. As for the cars you see lying around today next to our houses, that is the White man's misdoing. When the White man is done using his car, it is the Innu that he tricks with his old car. After he has found some- one to pass it on to, the White man, he buys himself a new car. Those are the old cars you see next to our

katshi mishkuat innua tshetshi uieshimat nenu umatshutapan, uin ekue ussi-utapanit. Eukuan ne matshutapan
kashikat uiapatamek[u] eshtet anite upime nitshinat.
Ninan uetshit nitshinan innu-mitshuap apu nita ut ashtet
matshutapan anite upime innu-mitshuapit.

Kauapishit kashikanit metshi-uauinimiti anite
tipatshimu-mashinaikanit, nin nitishi-nishtuten uin
nenu matshi-uauinitishu uesh ma eukuan uin ka
tshishkutamuimit utinniun kie eukuan uin ka tutuimit tshetshi uauinikauiat e inniuiat kashikat anite
tipatshimu-mashinaikanit kie eukuan uin ka tutuimit e
inniuiat kashikat tshetshi nukushiat anite kamatau-
pikutakanit kie anite katshitapatakanit.

Kaiakunitsheshiht kie anitshenat katipatshimu-
mashinaikanitsheshiht tshekuannitshe eka ut
takushiniht eshk[u] eka ka takuannit kakusseshiu-
atusseun-utenanu ? Etatu uipat itenitakakuenit tshetshi
shatshuapamimit ute Tshiuetinit, kie uinuau innua
apatshiatakuenit tshetshi itutaikutau ute nutshimit miam
ka tutak kutak kauapishit. Kassinu kauapishiht ka
itenitahk tshetshi shatshuapamimiht, eukuannua innua
utinepanat tshetshi itutaikutau ute nutshimit. Anitshenat
kaiakunitsheshiht kie anitshenat katipatshimu-
mashinaikanitsheshiht tshekuannu uet eka ut ishi-
mamitunenitahk tshetshi tutahk kie uinau ? Kie ninan
e inniuiat nipa mishta-ashinetan tshetshi uapatamat
tshitshue nitinniunnan anite kamatau-pikutakanit kie
anite katshitapatakanit.

Innu kashikanit enukuiakaniti anite katshitapatakannit namaienu nenu tshitshue innu utinniun, patush
umenu katshi utitikut kauapishiniti kie katshi mish-
kutunakannit innu utinniun. Kie innu-auass eshpish
kakusseshiu-tshishkutamuakanit, eukuannu nenu
patush katshi nukuiakanit anite katshitapatakannit.

houses today. Next to our houses, the tents, there were never any car carcasses lying around.

When the White man denigrates us in the newspapers, I myself consider that he is denigrating himself because he is the one who taught us this culture, he is responsible for the fact that today we are talked about in the newspapers, he is the reason why today we are seen in films and on television.

Why didn't the journalists and filmmakers come before there was a mining town in our territory? They should have thought earlier to come to us in the North and they should have, they too, asked the Innu to accompany them onto the land, as did the other White men. Any White man who thought to come meet us would bring Innu along to guide him into the interior. How come the journalists and filmmakers did not think of that? We would have been very proud too, the Innu, to see our true culture in films and on television.

Today when the Innu is shown on television, it is not his real way of life that is portrayed, it is the one that he has since the White man found him and changed his culture. And only the young people of today are shown, since they have been going to the White man's school. The Innu never sees himself

Innu apu nita uapamitishut anite kamatau-pikutakannit kie anite katshitapatakannit eshk^u eka ka apashtat
peik^u kakusseshiu-tshekuannu kie muk^u pissik^u innu-
mitshiminu ka ishinniut. Innu apu nita uapamitishut
ushkuai-utinu ka apashtat uin uetshit etutak kie ush-
kuanu kie ma atikuiana ka utapakuat kie ka mushe-kutuet
anite utinnu-mitshuapit. Innu apu nita uapamitishut
peik^u mishtikua ka apatshiat tshetshi tutak shimakannu
tshetshi ut nipaiat atikua kie apu nita uapamitishut,
atikua e minushiniti katshi nipaiat, tan ka ishi-aitutuat.
Ne innushkueu ekue tutamupan tamatshipeshikannu
kie eukuan nikan minuashipan innu-mitshim. Ne
tamatshipeshikan nin apu nita uapataman anite kamatau-pikutakanit. Innu apu nita uapamitishut miekuapi-
punniti mitshetuau ka papakuneuat mishkumia, nisht^u
ukutashkueua ishpish e tshishpatshishiniti mishkumia,
tshetshi tshikamuiat utanipia. Kie apu nita uapamitishut
miekuapipuki ka mishta-tshishik, ka ui apashtat tshi-
shikunnu etatu tshetshi eka ishpish mishta-tshishinnit.
Innu-napeu kie innushkueu kie innu-auass ka inniut
shetan-pishimua eukuan apatshiakanipan tshetshi tutak
etatu tshetshi minu-tshishikanit. Tapue mashkatenitakua-
nipan nenu ka tutak innu.

    Innu apu nita uapamitishut muk^u atikuiana ka tshi-
shuashpishuatshet. Kie uin innu-auass apu nita uapamitishut uin uetshit e innu-auassiut ka itashpishut anite
umatshunishimit. Mate nin kashikat nipa mishta-ashinen
uapamitishuiani ka itashpishuian e auassiuian atikuianiss
e minaushit ka tutak nikaui nipipunakupinu. Innu-auass
apu nita uapamitishut tan ka ishi-mitshishut kassinu
eishinakushiniti innu-aueshisha katshi nipaiakanniti
tanite anite anu ka ut minuatat tshetshi muat kie apu nita
uapamitishut tan ka ishi-metuet anite unuitimit kie anite
pitukamit innu-mitshuapit. Innushkuess apu nita

in a film or on television while using something other than from the White man's culture or when he only lived off Innu food. The Innu never sees himself using a bark canoe that he made, covering his dwelling with bark or caribou hide, and making a fire directly on the ground of his dwelling. The Innu never sees himself use a young tree to make a caribou spear and he never sees, after he has killed a nice caribou, the Innu woman preparing a *tama-tshipeshikan*.[21] That was the best kind of Innu food. I never see *tamatshipeshikan* in films. The Innu never sees himself, in the midst of winter, piercing several holes in ice as thick as three lengths of stove-pipe sheet, to set his nets and he never sees himself, in the midst of a very cold winter, trying to affect the weather so that it might ease up. Back then, the man, woman, or child born in July was asked to call upon better weather. That was a surprising thing that the Innu did.

The Innu never sees himself dressed only in caribou hide. The young Innu does not see himself either dressed in his children's clothes. Me, for instance, I would be very proud today to see myself, as a child, wearing the winter coat my mother made for me out of the hide of a young caribou of which she did not remove the fur. The Innu child never sees himself, after any one of the Innu animals has been killed, eating his favourite piece and he never sees himself playing outside or inside the tent. The little Innu girl never sees herself during a time when

uapamitishut eshk[u] eka nita ka tshimishakanniti
upishkueuna muk[u] ka apikatakanniti upishkueuna kie
ma ushetshipatuana ka tutakanniti. Ek[u] ne uin napess
apu nita uapamitishut tan ka ishi-tshitshipanit e nataut.
Nititenimau nin, kashikanit innu-auass uapamitishuti
umenu, tshipa mishta-ashineu.

Anitshenat kaiakunitsheshiht kie anitshenat katipatshimu-mashinaikanitsheshiht etatu uipat takushini-
takuenit ute Tshiuetinit tshetshi shatshuapamimit, muk[u]
innua eukuannua tshipa uapamepanat ute nutshimit mak
muk[u] innu-mitshuapa eukuannua tshipa uapatamupanat
mak muk[u] innua umeshkananua mak innu-aueshisha
umeshkananua eukuannua muk[u] tshipa uapatamupanat.
Kie atut tshekuannu ut petamupanat tshetshi tatueuetakannit ute nitassinat miam kashikat ute Tshiuetinit
eshakumitshishikua nipetenan e matuetet miam ne ut
kakusseshiu-atusseun e tatuetakanit ute nitassinat.

Nitshisseniten uin kashikat anumat animan tshetshi
uapatinikauian nitinniun e innuian tanite nin nitinniun kashikat apu takuak. Muk[u] miamitunenitamani,
anite nishtikuanit eukuan muk[u] kenuenitaman nin ka
ishinniuian.

her hair was never cut but when it was braided or
rolled up over her ears[22] and the little Innu boy,
he never sees himself going hunting on his own.
I myself think that if the Innu child saw all this
today, he would be filled with pride.

If the journalists and filmmakers had come to
meet us in the North earlier, they would have only
seen Innu in the hinterland, they would have only
seen tents, they would have only seen the paths of
the Innu and the tracks of the animals; they would
not have heard noises in our territory, like the
explosions that we hear now every day because of
the work the White man is doing on our land.

I know that it is very difficult today to show me
my real culture as an Innu woman because my life
of before no longer exists today. When I think about
it, it is only in my mind that I have kept my former
life.

8

Kakusseshiu-mitshuapa

Patetat-tatunnu ashu kutuasht itashtepan mishta-atshita-shun ka nakatamat nitshinana anite Uashat uinipekut ka tutakaniti, ka tshiueiat ute nitassinat. Tekushiniat ute ekue nuitshitan anite pessish utenat, nutinnu-mitshuapitan, tanite nititenitetan tshetshi minu-uitsheuimit Nakanau kie nititenitetan tshetshi tshitimatshenimimit, nenu tshe pikunak kie tshe shuniatsheuatshet ninataun-assinannu. Eukuan ka ut manukashuiat kie ninan e inniuiat anite pessish utenat.

Katshi manukashuiat innu-mitshuap, uemut ekue nanatu-atusset ninapem nishtam anite Nakanau. Apu mishku-atusset anite Nakanau. Minuat ekue natu-atusset anite kaiakuanashunit, ekute meshku-atusset. Kie uemut innu itenitamupan tshetshi mishkak atusseunnu uesh ma anitshenat nitauassiminanat, ka mamushatshinakanih tshetshi ituteht katshishkutamatsheutshuapit kakusseshit, eukuannu ushkat tshekuannu ka tshitshipanit tshetshi animishiuiat innu-auassa : anitshenat nitauassiminanat ka kanuenimakanih anite katshishkutamatsheutshua-pit eukuannu ut tshitshipannipan kie uinuau shunianu tshetshi ui apashtaht; nanitam nanatuenitamupanat shunianu kie anitshenat nitauassiminanat apu ut tapue-tuimiht minekash tshetshi kushpiat anite nutshimit miam ueshkat ka tutamat. Uesh anitshenat nitauassiminanat eshk[u] eka ka utinakaniht tshetshi tshishkutamuakaniht,

8

The White man's houses

In 1956, we left the houses that had been built for us in Sept-Îles, on the coast, and we went back to our territories. When we arrived here, we set up near the town, in tents. We thought that Iron Ore would be friendly towards us and take pity on us, given that they were going to destroy our hunting territories and make a big profit from them. That is the reason why we set up our camp there, us too the Innu, near the town.

After setting up our tent, my husband had to look for work, first at Iron Ore. He did not find any. Then he went to look in transport, and there he found work. The Innu had to think about finding paid work. When the White man had rounded up our children to send them to school, this is the first thing that made them become difficult children: since they were boarders, they started to need money too, they would ask constantly. And they did not want us to go out onto the land the way we used to. Before they took our children to send them to school, we were out on the land throughout the year and we would live in a tent throughout the year. We never stayed in the same place, we were constantly on the move. As for money, we never thought about it because it was not from paid work that we made a living.

ishkanipipuna nutshimit nititatan kie ishkanipipuna
innu-mitshuapit nitapitan. Kie apu nita ut minekash
peikutau apiat, nanitam nipapamipanitan. Ne uin
shuniau apu nita ut mamitunenitamat tanite namaieu
kakusseshiu-atusseun nitishinniutan.

Uiesh nishupishimua katshi apiat anite pessish utenat
e utinnu-mitshuapiat, nitishi-animiutan tshishtapakunat
shash katak[u] ninatuapamananat kie shash uiesh kutunnu
kautishkuemiht nititashitan epiat anite pessish utenat. Ek[u]
ume atusseun ka tshitshipannanut takuanipani mitshuapissa, miam anitshenat kamanutsheshiht umitshuapi-
ssimuaua kie nenua mitshuapissa shash takuanipani eka
iapashtakaniti. Eukuannua nenua eiaht innuat, miam
anitshenat innuat etatu uipat ka tshitshipaniht e atusseht
anite kaiakuanashunit kie kutakat tapanat etusseht anite
kaukutashkuetsheniti. Anitshenat innuat eiaht nenua
mitshuapissa tauat peikumitashumitunnu tshashikashuht
miam nenua mitshuapissa etatu minuati mak uiesh
kutunnueshit ishpish kashkatshakupani.

Kie ninan ninapem ekue uauitamat tshetshi nanatuapatamat matshi-mitshuapiss tshetshi aiaiat. Ninapem
pitshenik tshitshipanipan e atusset anite kaiakuanashunit.
Kie uin ekue nanatuapatak uitsh. Tekushinit ekue ishit :
« Shash nutim meshtinakanua mitshuapissa, nitik[u],
eukuan muk[u] eshkunakanit mishiutshuap kie peikuan
etutakanit peikumitashumitunnu. Nishuaush-tatushit
ishpish kashkatshau, nitik[u]. Ne mishiutshuap ishi-natue-
nitakanu peikuau tshetshi ashtaiak[u] peikumitashimi-
tunnu », nitik[u]. Ne mishiutshuap tshe ui aiaiat uemut
pitama nika aimuatenan tanite shuniau apu ishpaniat kie
uemut eukuan tshe ui aiaiat uesh ma eukuan mashten
tekuak mitshuap e atauatshenanut. Eukuan eshpish nutepaniat eshk[u] shuniau : patetat-tatunnu nikanuenitenan
ekue uauitamat tshetshi auiashuiat shuniau patetat-

We started to have difficulties barely two months after we had settled near the town, in the tents, because we had to travel far to collect fir branches.[23] We were already about ten families that had settled near the town. At the entrance of the site, there were little cabins, the carpenters'[24] little shacks. There were some of those little shacks that the carpenters no longer used. These, the Innu would buy them, those who had started to work first in transport or the others who worked in plumbing. Among the Innu who bought these shacks, some paid a hundred dollars for the best ones that were about ten feet long.

My husband and I talked about the possibility of looking as well for an old shack and buying it. My husband had only started to work in transport. He too started to look for a house. Upon his return, he said: "There are no more little shacks left, all that is left is a small outhouse but it is the same price: a hundred dollars. It is eight feet long. For that outhouse, they ask that we pay a hundred dollars in one instalment." We had to first talk about the purchase of this outhouse. We did not have enough money, but we were forced to buy it because it was the last house available. We did not have enough money, we had fifty dollars. We talked about borrowing fifty so as to give the required one hundred dollars in one instalment. We were able to borrow

tatunnu tshetshi peikuau patshitinamat ka natuenitama-
kauiat peikumitashumitunnu. Miam anitshenat innuat
uinuau etatu uipat ka tshitshipaniht e atusseht, ne patetat-
tatunnu ekue mishkamat tshetshi auiashuiat ekue
natshi-tshishikashut ninapem nenu umishiutshuapim.
Nin nimishta-minueniten tanite nitshisseniten shash
ninan nimishiutshuapiminan.

   Ne nimishiutshuapissiminan katshi tshishikashuiat
kie katshi petakanit, minuat peikuau ekue aimuatamat
ninapem tanite nashpit apu ishpishat tshetshi uitshitamat.
Ninapem ekue issishuet : « Nika maunauat matshi-papatshi-
takuat, tshe mishaiman minuat nishuaush-tatushit », nitik[u]
ek[u] apu nita ut uapamak tshetshi tutak mishtikushitshua-
pinu. Ekue tshitshipanit tshetshi mamushatshinat
matshi-papatshitakua e uepinakanniti ekue tshitshipanit
tshetshi mishaik nenu umishiutshuapissim.

   Kakusseshiu-atusseun ka tshitshipanit ute nitassinat, e inniuiat nimishta-tshitimatshenitakushitan. Ka
tshitshipanit Nakanau tshetshi manutshet, e inniuiat
eukuan nitshitshipanitan nanitam e manukashuiat, eshk[u]
kashikat apu nita puniat e manukashuiat. Nin eukuan uet
issishueian ume kakusseshiu-atusseun ka shenakanit ute
nitassinat, e inniuiat eukuan ut tshitshipanipan kassinu
tshetshi aishi-animiuiat.

   Uiesh katshi neupishimua apiat anite pessish utenat,
nipetenan katshishe-utshimau-atusset mishakau issishuenanu. Eukuannu tshe itshetishauimit Nakanau.
Ne katshishe-utshimau-atusset meshakat Uashat ututeu nenua Nakanaua mamu tshetshi uauitahk tan
tshe aitutakauiat, ne tshe itshetishaukauiat. Ne katshishe-utshimau-atusset ka mishakat nenua ut Nakanaua
eukuan uin uatamuat innua tan ka ishi-uaueshimit
Nakanau. Eukuan eshimit :

from other Innu who had started working earlier and my husband went to pay for his outhouse. Me, I was very happy because I knew that that outhouse belonged to us.

After we paid for our little outhouse and took delivery of it, my husband and I discussed once more: it was not at all big enough for us to settle into. My husband then said: "I will pick up old wood planks and extend it another eight feet." I had never seen my husband make a house out of wood. He started picking up leftover planks and started to make his little outhouse bigger.

When the site opened here, in our territory, we, the Innu, were pitiful to see. When Iron Ore started to build its houses, we too, the Innu, we started to build ourselves up. Still today, we are constantly building our houses. This is why I say: when the White man's work began on our land, our miseries, for us the Innu, also began.

After we had been settled for about four months near the town, we heard that an official from the Department of Indian Affairs had arrived. That is when we heard that Iron Ore was going to evict us. The official came from Sept-Îles to discuss with Iron Ore what would happen to us: we were being thrown out. It is this official from the federal government, who came on account of Iron Ore, who announced to the Innu how Iron Ore was going to seal our fates. This is what he told us:

« Nakanau eukuan essishuet, nitikunan : Nakanau
tshika minikuau assinu anite upime nishtuemin ishpish
tshetshi apiek[u]. Tapuetamekui tshetshi atapiek[u], mishkut
eukuan tshe minitikut atusseun tshitikuau Nakanau,
nitikunan. Usham ute e apiek[u] pessish utenat tshuina-
kamitanau nipi, tshitikuau Nakanau », *nitikunan ne*
katshishe-utshimau-atusset.

Nakanau ka takushinit ute nitassinat apu ut takuak
shakaikan e uinakamit, kashikanit eukuan uin
kauapishit uanakamitat shakaikana. Ne uin katshishe-utshimau-atusset ka mishakat nenu ut ka ui itshetishauimit Nakanau, anu tshipa minuanipan tshetshi
issishuet :

« Nakanau nenu essishuet ua itshetishautak[u], tan ma
tshinuau etenitamek[u] ? Uesh ma tshinuau ute tshitassiuat
tshititanau kie apu ma ut uishamek[u] Nakanau ute
tshitassiuat. Kie nenua shakaikana ka takuaki ute
tshitassiuat, tshinuau nenua tshishakaikanimuaua;
uinakamitaiekui, kuishk[u] e issishuenanut, tshinuau
tshitatusseunuau. Nakanau kie nin apu takuak ninan
nitatusseunnan. Ute tshitassiuat, Nakanau ishpish eka
takuannit tshetshi ueuetashumitak[u] minuat anu nin
apu takuak tshetshi ueuetashumitikut uesh ma nin
tshitatusseshtatinau. »

Uetitshipanit tshetshi atapinanut, eukuannu tekushinit
kashutshishit ne ka-tshinuashkushua. Nenua nitshinana
tshe tshitutatakaniti nitshissenitenan tshe pikupitaka-
niti, nitshissenitenan minuat peikuau tshe atushkatamat
nenua nitshinana. Tapue tshe tshitshitapaniti nitshinana etshetishauimit Nakanau muk[u] pashtapekatakanu
assikumaniapi. Uepinakaniti nitshinana uemut tshetshi

*"This is what Iron Ore has said: it will give you
some land over there, nearby, about three miles
from here where you can settle. If you agree to
move, Iron Ore said that in return they will give
you work. If you stay here near the town, Iron Ore
said you will pollute the water,"* this is what the
official said.

When Iron Ore arrived, there were no polluted
lakes in our territory. Nowadays, it is the White
man who pollutes the lakes. As for that official from
Indian Affairs who came because Iron Ore wanted
to evict us, it would have been better had he said:

*"You, what do you think about the fact that Iron
Ore wants to evict you? You are here in your territory and you did not invite Iron Ore to your territory. The lakes here are your lakes. If you pollute
them, to speak frankly, that is your problem, it
is not the problem of Iron Ore and it is not mine
either. Here, on your land, Iron Ore has no right
to give you orders and me, I have even less right
because I am at your service."*

When the time came to move, the crane arrived.
We knew that when our houses would be transported, they would break. We knew that once again
we would have to work on our houses. When they
transported them, when Iron Ore evicted us, all
they did was wrap a steel cable around them: when
they lifted them, of course they broke because not

pikupaniti uesh ma apu ut takuak mitshuap tshetshi nuti-
mat : kassinu innuat uitshuau mishaikannipan. Katshi
petakaniti nitshinana ute Tshuan-shakaikanit, nuapatenan nitshinana nutim pipikupanua, tapue nipatshite-
nimunan. Kie Nakanau katshi ueuepimetak nitshinana
nete nishtuemin ishpish, apu ishimit : « Nika peshuauat
papatshitakuat tshetshi uaueshtaiek^u tshitshuaua katshi
pikunaman. » Ume tipatshimun etshetishaukauiat patetat-tatunnu ashu kutuasht, uapikun-pishim^u, mekuat
mishta-mitshetipanat shatshimeuat. Uemut minuat ekue
tshitshipaniat tshetshi uaueshtaiat nitshinana tanite shash
papannipan kauapishit utipenitamun.

Ninishtutenan eukuan uet ishpish animiuiat katshi
atapiat Tshuan-shakaikanit. Kauapishit ekue tshitshipanipan tshetshi atamimit nipinu. Kauapishit ka takushinit
ute nitassinat, nititenimau ushtuin atut ut petau nipinu
tshetshi atauatshet. Nenu uin ishkutuapunu nipetetan
tshe petat tshetshi atauatshet. Ek^u nenu nipinu ka atamimit, ute nishakaikaniminat ut kuapaimupan nenu nipinu
ka atamimit.

Nakanau katshi itshetishauimit kie ka issishuet mishkut tshetshi minat innua atusseunnu, katshi atapiat
Nakanau peikuan apu ut tshinipit tshetshi minat innua
atusseunnu. Tiekunu nipetetan essishuet Nakanau :
« Anitshenat innuat eka etenitakushiht tshetshi atusseht
anu tshipa minuanu tshetshi nashipeht nete Uashat. »
Ute etaiat, nutshimit nititanan. Ne innu eka itenitakushit
tshetshi atusset anite Nakanau eshk^u takuanipan tshetshi
ishi-pakassiut e nataunanunit.

Nakanau ka tshitshipanit atusseunnu ute nitassinat,
uin utshimauipan, namaieu innu utshimauipan. Mate
nenu etshetishauimit Nakanau, uin uauapatamupan
assinu anite tshe minimit kie apu ut uauapatak anite e
minuanit tshetshi minimit, anite e papanatapishkanit

one house was made up of a single part, all the
houses of the Innu were made up of extensions.
Once our houses had been transported to Lake
John, we saw indeed that they had all been damaged. We were very discouraged. After they tossed
our houses over there, three miles away, Iron Ore
did not say to us: "I will bring you planks so that
you can repair your houses that I damaged." These
events took place in 1956, in June, when there are a
lot of mosquitoes. We had to start all over repairing
our houses. The White man's reign was in place.

We understand the reasons why we had so many
pitfalls after we were moved to Lake John: that is
when the White man started to sell us water. When
the White man came to our territory, I do not think
that he brought water to sell. Alcohol, of course, we
had heard he brought that to sell. But the water that
he sold to us, he was taking it from our own lakes.

Iron Ore evicted us and said that in exchange it
would give work to the Innu. After the move, they
were by no means in any hurry to do so. Worse, we
heard the company say: "It would be better if the
Indians who are not interested in working[25] go back
down to Sept-Îles." Here where we are, we are in the
middle of the woods. The Innu who was not interested in working for Iron Ore could still provide for
himself by hunting.

When Iron Ore opened a site in our territory, it
was queen, it was not the Innu who were king. For
instance, when they evicted us, they chose which
land they would give to us and they did not choose
the best: they gave us a rocky parcel of land, a plot

mak anite e matshiteueiapishkanit ekute niminikutan.
Nakanau nititshetishaukutan kie eukuan uin nitipai-
makutan nitassinannu. Nakanau ka takushinit ute, apu
ut tipaimatishut nitassinannu, uenashk nutim eshpishanit
ekue utinamatishuipan.

Uiesh kutunnuepipuna katshi atapiat ute Tshuan-shakaikanit, eshk^u nashpit apu tshekuan tshitshipanit tshetshi
tutakanit. Shash tshitshipannanu tshetshi uauitamakauiat
kau tshetshi atapiat nete ka ut itshetishaukauiat. Kie ne
assi uiauitamakauiat tshe minikauiat nete utenat anu
anite uet uinakuak mak muk^u anite e matshiteuiashit mak
anite anu mishta-apishish niminikaunan. Kauapishit ka
takushinit ute nitassinat, apu muk^u e matshiteuiashinit ut
utinamatishut nitassinannu, nutim eshpishanit Tshiuetinnu utinamatishuipan. Kauapishit anite katshi uinaku-
tat, ekute anite nianatuapatak tshetshi manukuat innua.

Kauapishit kashikanit muk^u e nanatu-kushtatshiat
innua mak e katshinassimat, eukuannu uet nanitam
kanieut muk^u uin etenitak tshetshi tutuat. Mate kau ka
uishamikauiat nete utenat tshetshi atapiat, muk^u katshinaun eukuan takuanipan. Anitshenat uin katshishe-
utshimau-atusseht ka pet atusseshtuaht innua nashpit apu
ut ishinakuannit tshetshi natutakutau innua. Katshishe-
utshimau-atusseht eimiataui innua netutakutaui, minuat
anu ekue nanatuapatahk tan tshe ishi-katshinassimaht
innua kie tan tshe ishi-kushtatshiaht innua tshetshi ut
kanieuht uinuau utitenitamunuau.

Mate anitshenat katshishe-utshimau-atusseht nenu ka
tshitshipaniht tshetshi aimuatahk tshetshi manukakauiat,
muk^u e katshinassimaht innua mak e kushtatshiaht innua,
eukuannu ka ut kanieuht tshetshi tutakanniti mitshuapa
nete utenat. Katshishe-utshimau-atusseht nin eukuan ete-
nimakau : muk^u nanatuapatamuat innua etusseshtuataui

situated on the edge of a rocky tip. Iron Ore sent us away and they measured for us our parcel of land. When the company came here, it did not do any calculations, it just quickly seized all of our land in all its extent.

About ten years after we were moved to Lake John, no construction had yet started. Then there was talk to move us back to where we had been evicted from. The parcel of land that they thought to give us in town was the dirtiest part and was very small, which would have meant even less space than before. When the White man came, he did not just take a little piece of our land, he took over the North in its entirety. After he has dirtied a place, it is in that place that the White man always tries to build houses for the Innu.

Nowadays, it is only by intimidating and by lying to the Innu that the White man manages to act towards them according to his own plans. For instance, when we were invited to come back to the town, there were only lies in that. No way should the Innu ever have listened to the civil servants who worked for Indian services. When they speak to them and when the Innu listen to them, they find even more ways to lie to them and to scare them so that it is their point of view that wins.

For instance, when the officials from the Department of Indian Affairs started to tell us about building us houses, it is only by lying to the Innu and by intimidating them that they were able to have them built in town. I think that when they work for the Innu, the civil servants only want to sow dissension

tshetshi matshipanituniti. Katshi tutuaht innua tshetshi
matshipanituniti, tapue ekue tshi tutahk uinuau utitenitamunuau tshetshi minu-pimipannit.

Mate ka ui atapinanut kau nete pessish utenat, nin
eukuan etenitaman : namaienu nenu nekaussei utitenitamun kie namaienu innuat utitenitamunuau, katshishe-
utshimau-atusseht eukuanat uinuau utitenitamunuau.
Nitshisseniten uet issishueian tanite neupipuna nititati
anite nekausseit, nishupipuna anite ushkat nekaus-
sseie nititati mak nishupipuna anite innu-utshimaunit.
Kie miam etaian anite innu-utshimaunit, katshishe-
utshimau-atusseht eukuannu tshitshue mishta-atush-
katamupanat tshetshi atapinanunit kau nete utenat. Nin
nimishta-atushkateti tshetshi eka atapinanut nete utenat.
Anitshenat katshishe-utshimau-atusseht mak nin mishta-
mishapan nitatusseunnan tanite nishuait nitishi-atussetan :
nin ute Tshuan-shakaikanit nitatushkaten tshetshi
manukuakaniht innuat ek^u uinuau nete utenat atushka-
tamuat tshetshi manikuakanniti innua.

Ne ut ka ui atapinanut kamashinatautishunanut apashtakanipan. Ushkat e mashinatautishunanut, anu mitshetipanat innuat eka ua atapiht nete utenat. Muk^u iapit apu
ut tshi tshitshipanit tshetshi manukuakaniht innuat ute
Tshuan-shakaikanit tanite ushkat ka mashinatautishunanut anu metshetiht innuat eka ua atapiht nete utenat,
anitshenat katshishe-utshimau-atusseht eshk^u namaienu
nenu uinuau utitenitamunuau. Eukuan ka ut eka tshitshipanit tshetshi manukuakaniht innuat ute Tshuan-shakaikanit. Katshishe-utshimau-atusseht eka kianieuht nenu
kamashinatautishunanunit, pitama minuat tatupipuna
ekue aimiepanat innua nianatu-kushtatshimaht kie nianatu-
katshinassimaht. Minuat mani ekue papanit tshetshi
mashinatautishunanut ne ut kaiatapinanut. Mitshetuau
katshi mashinatautishunanut, uemut anu tshetshi mitshetiht

among them. Once it has taken, they manage to make their idea seem the best.

For instance, the idea of a new move next to the town, in my opinion, that was not the idea of the Band Council nor that of the Innu population, it was that of the civil servants from the Department of Indian Affairs. I know what I am saying: I was part of the Band Council for four years. I was first councilperson during two years and during another two years, I was Band Chief. During my term as chief, the civil servants worked hard so that people would move back into the town. On my side, I worked hard so that they would not move back. The civil servants and I had an enormous task since we were working against each other: me it was so that they would build houses for the Innu here, in Lake John, and them, so that they would be built in town.

There was a referendum about the move. The first time there was a vote, the Innu who did not want to move to town were larger in number than the others. Despite that first vote, they did not start to build houses here: the fact that the major part of the Innu population refused to move into town did not line up with the plans of the civil servants. That is why they did not start to build houses here in Lake John. Since the civil servants lost the vote, they continued to lie and to intimidate the Innu, for a few more years. Then, from time to time, there came the moment to vote again about the move. After several referendums, obviously, the Innu who were in favour of the move came to be more numerous thanks to all the lies that the civil servants had told them.

innuat ua atapiht nete utenat tanite anitshenat katshishe-utshimau-atusseht nenu ut e katshinassimaht innua.

Nin eukuan etenitaman : kamashinatautishunanut kassinu eishinakuak namaieu ninan e inniuiat nitinniunnan. Kamashinatautishunanut nin eukuan etenitaman, eukuan kakusseshiu-nanua, kauapishit nenu utinniun. Muku ne kakusseshiu-nanua kassinu eishinakuak nimishta-katua-kautan : ne kakusseshiu-nanua apu takuak mashinaikan tshetshi tshitapatamat e innushtet tshetshi tshishkuta-matishuatsheiat. Kauapishit tapueu nenu essishuet uin tekuannit umashinaikan muku apu tutak mashinaikannu e innushtenit tshetshi uauitak kassinu eishinakuannit kakusseshiu-nanuanu. Uesh ma ne mashinaikan eka ka tutak e innushtenit tshetshi tshishkutamatishuatsheiat, eukuannu ka ut mishta-uieshimimit kauapishit.

Anitshenat katshishe-utshimau-atusseht, eukuannu aitepanat innua : « Ute etaieku Tshuan-shakaikanit eka uin nita itenitamuku tshetshi manukakauieku usham apu minuat, ashiniun ume assi kie usham mishta-shuniau tshipa apashtakanu ui manukakauiekui ute. » Anitshenat katshishe-utshimau-atusseht eshkuapekannit tutamupa-nat, kie nin apu nita ut patshitenimuian eshku etaian anite innu-utshimaunit. Peikuau etutakanit kautshimau-aiminanut, mishakauat katshishe-utshimau-atusseht. Eukuannu iapit uiauitahk tshetshi atapinanut nete utenat kie nin iapit ka ishi-uauitaman ute Tshuan-shakaikanit tshetshi manukakauiat. Ne peiku katshishe-utshimau-atusset Uepishtikueiat ututeu, eukuan uin tepenitak kama-nutshenanunit. Ekue issishuet : « Ishinakuanniti tshetshi manukuakaniht innuat ute Kaiatushkanut, nishtam nete utenat tshika tutakanua mitshuapa », issishueu. Ne katshi-she-utshimau-atusset nenu essishuet kueshte ekue aimik ekue itak : « Tshika tuten mitshuapa nishtam nete utenat muku nishuait tshika tuten mitshuapa miam peikuan

This is what I myself think: no kind of voting is part of our culture, the Innu. In my opinion, voting is a part of the White man's law, the White man's culture. But all the White man's laws were carefully hidden from us: there is no book of law written in the Innu language that we can read in order to find out about them. The White man is telling the truth when he says he has written texts but he does not write books in Innu to explain his different laws. It is because he did not write any books in Innu that would have helped us that the White man fooled us so.

This is what the civil servants said to the Innu: "Do not think that you will get houses built here where you are, in Lake John. This land is not good, it is rocky and it would cost far too much if we wanted to build for you here." The civil servants went as far as they could but I never got discouraged either, as long as I was in politics. One day when we were holding an assembly, the officials from the Department arrived. They spoke again of the move to town and I spoke again of building in Lake John. One of them came from Québec City, he was in charge of construction. He said: "If we ever build houses for the Indians of Schefferville, it will be in town that we first do so." To which I responded: "First, you will build houses in town, but you will build them in two places, like you did in Sept-Îles. First you built in Maliaténam and then you built in Sept-Îles." The official replied: "That could happen."

Uashat ka tutamin. Mani-utenam nishtam tshituteti
mitshuapa kie anite Uashat ekue tshituteti mitshuap »,
nitau. Ne katshishe-utshimau-atusset nenu etak ekue ishit :
« Tshipa tshi ishpanu. »

Ek^u minuat peikuau meshakat katshishe-utshimau-
atusset, Uepishtikueiat ututeu. Ne katshishe-utshimau-
atusset meshakat ekue uishamit anite tshishe-utshimau-
mashinaikanitshuapit ekue itenitaman ushtuin eukuannu
tshe uitamut tshetshi manukakauiat Tshuan-shakaikanit.
Ekue shatshuapamak ekue ishit : « Anitshenat innuat
eshpish nanitam minukashuht, ma tshipa tshi
kutshipanitan tshetshi tutamin kautshimau-aiminanut ?
Mitshetuau tshipa tuten kautshimau-aiminanut tshetshi
ashtanite itenitakushiht nenu e minukashuht, nitik^u. Tshi
tutamini ashtanite tshetshi itenitakushiht e minukashiht
ek^u patush tshe manukuakaniht nete utenat. » Ne katshishe-
utshimau-atusset nenu eshit nimishta-tshishimik^u ekue
itak : « Anitshenat innuat nenu nanitam menukashuht,
apu takuak anite nin nitatusseun, namaieu nin ka
minakau ishkutuapunu tshetshi miniht. Tshinuau
tutamuk^u kautshimau-aiminanut uesh ma anitshenat
innuat nenu nanitam menukashukuenit, tshinuau ka
minekut ishkutuapui, tshinuau tutamuk^u kautshimau-
aiminanut ! » nitau. Ne katshishe-utshimau-atusset
nenu etak nashpit apu aimit. Minuat kutak ekue mishakat katshishe-utshimau-atusset, eukuan kuekuetshimit
tshetshi tutaman kautshimau-aiminanut mamu napin[14].
Ne katshishe-utshimau-atusset nenu ka ui ishi-uieshimit
apu tapuetuk tanite anite pet utat apu nita ut petaman
anite innu-assit tshetshi tutakanit kautshimau-aiminanut
mamu kauapishit.

Nin kutuasht-tatunnu ashu nishuasht shash
nitshisseniteti tshe eka tat auen tshetshi itshetishaut ute
Tshuan-shakaikanit kie tshuapatenan kashikat nititan ute

Another time, a civil servant from Québec City came and asked that I meet him at the office of Indian Affairs. I thought he was going to tell me they would start building us houses in Lake John. I went to see him and he said: "Those Indians are so drunk, could you not try to arrange a meeting? You should have several meetings. If you can find a way for them to be less inclined to get drunk,"[26] he told me, "then we will build houses for them in town." As he was saying this, that civil servant made me furious. I replied: "If the Innu are always drunk, it is not my fault. I am not the one who gave them alcohol. You are the ones who should organize the meetings. If the Innu are always drunk as you say, you who gave them alcohol, you do the meetings!" I told him. He did not add anything else. Another civil servant came to me once and asked me to organize a meeting that municipal representatives would attend. That civil servant tried to fool me and I refused because in the past we had never heard of having meetings on the reserve with White men.

Me, already in 1967, I knew that no one would make me leave Lake John. Today, you and I both see it, I am in Lake John but I must admit that it never

Tshuan-shakaikanit muk^u tapue apu ut minupanit nishtam
tshetshi tutakaniti mitshuapa ute Tshuan-shakaikanit
tanite ka mashinatautishunanut, kakusseshiu-nanua
eukuan nanitam apashtakanipan. Uemut anite itetshe anu
metshetiht innuat ekute nishtam tutakanipani mitshuapa.
Eukuan « namashukite[15] » essishuenanut kakusseshiu-
nanua. Katshishe-utshimau-atusseht eukuannu tshitshue
ashineikupanat kie eukuannu minutamupanat nenu
aimunnu tanite eukuannu ka minuenitamikuht nenu
aimunnu « namashukite ». Ne aimun nin apu ut kush-
tatshikuian tanite nitishi-nishtuten e inniuian muk^u e
peikussian peikumitashumitunnu mak peikumitashumitunnu nitishpish kanueniten namashukite. Katshishe-
utshimau-atusseht eukuannu ka ut eka nita kushtatshiht
muk^u tapue uinuau kanieuipanat nishtam tshetshi tutahk
mitshuapa nete utenat. Ek^u nin ekue nitshitshipaniti
tshetshi atushkatishuian anite itetshe Kamamuituna-
nut innuat Uepishtikueiat tanite ninishtuteti anitshenat
katshishe-utshimau-atusseht namaienu tshe uitshiht
nenu ut eka ua atapian nete utenat. Anitshenat katshishe-
utshimau-atusseht eukuanat uinuau ka mishta-atush-
kashimiht ka itashiat ute Tshuan-shakaikanit tshetshi
atapiat nete utenat.

Katshishe-utshimau-atusseht ka tatupipuna atush-
kashimiht tshetshi atapiat nete utenat, nanikutini takuannipan tshetshi shetshishiaht innua. Muk^u miam auen e
shutshiteiet kie miam auen e nishtuapamat nenua katshi-
she-utshimau-atusseniti anu minupannipan tshetshi
papit mak tshetshi kushtatshikut. Mate nin eukuan
nititenimatiat ka ushkuishtuimiht tshetshi atapiat nete
utenat : nimishkamuatiat anu e uitenimakau mak tshetshi
kushtatshimiht. Mate nenua mitshuapa tshetshipannanuti
nete utenat, tshekat eshakumitshishikua papamuteuat,
pipitutsheuat mitshuapa nianatu-kushtatshimaht innua.

worked to get houses built for us here first because they constantly used the voting system as it exists in the White man's law. Of course, it was in the place that was most favoured by the Innu that the houses were built first. That is what is called "a majority" according to the White man's law. That word, "majority," made the officials from Indian Affairs very proud, they liked to hear it because it suited their designs. Me, that word did not scare me. The way I understand things, on my own, as an Innu woman, I have the majority one hundred percent. That is why I was never afraid of the civil servants. But it is true that they were able to first build the houses in town. I myself began to take care of my own business with help from the Indians of Quebec Association.[27] I knew that it would not be the civil servants who would support my opposition to the move: they were the ones who worked so hard to get the whole group to move from Lake John to town.

Over the years that they tried to make us move to town, it happened on occasion that the officials from the Department managed to scare the Innu. A person who was courageous and knew about the civil servants was better off laughing than being afraid. Me, for instance, this is what I thought of them when they were trying to force us to move: I found them more funny than menacing. When they first started building the houses in town, almost every day, they would walk around and go from door to door trying to intimidate the Innu. When

Katshishe-utshimau-atusseht eimiataui innua nanitam
kueshkaputshinamupanat utaimunuau, eukuannu ka ut
uitenitakushiht kie eukuannu ka ut uieshimaht innua.
Muk[u] anitshenat katshishe-utshimau-atusseht tanipani
innua neshtuapamaht, takuannipan mitshuapinu eka ka
tshi pitutsheht muk[u] iapit apu nita ut patshitenimuht. Nanitam mishkamupanat tshe tutahk tshetshi ut aimiaht innua.

   Mate nin apu nita ut tshi shatshuapamiht nitshit tshek
ekue niminikutiat atusseunnu kie nitatusseshtuatiat.
Eukuan ne atusseun ninan e innushkueuiat nitshishkuta-
makaunan tshe ishi-naikamat nitshinana nete utenat tshi
atapinanuti. Ek[u] miam uetshimau-aimiati ne ut nitatusseunnan, katshishe-utshimau-atusseht ashit nenu
mitshuapinu ekue nuauitamakutiat tshetshi utinaman
nete utenat. Ne atusseun ninishtitan e innushkueuiat
etusseiat. Anitshenat innushkueuat uatshi-atussemakau
shash uinuau utinamupanat mitshuapa. Ne peik[u]
katshishe-utshimau-atusset peikuau uetshimau-aimiat
ekue ishimit : « Ne tshinuau etusseiek[u], nishtam tshinuau
tshika uauapatamatishunau mitshuapa tanenua menuatamek[u] kie meshkanaua etamuti tanite menuatamek[u]
tshetshi apiek[u] », nitaitikunan ne katshishe-utshimau-
atusset. Ne atusseun etusseian namaieu tshe ut atatauа-
tsheian nitinniun tshetshi ne ut utinaman mitshuap
utenat. Minuat uetitshipanit tshetshi utshimau-aimiat,
ne katshishe-utshimau-atusset eukuannu essishuet :
« Ne innushkueu eka tshe utinak mitshuapinu utenat apu
tshika ut atusset umenu atusseunnu », issishueu. Nenu
essishuet ninishtutuau nin uet issishuet. Uenashk ekue
itak : « Tshe kanuenitamek[u] tshitatusseunuau, apu
apashtaian mitshuap utenat », nitau. Anitshenat katshishe-utshimau-atusseht ka ui ishi-kushtatshiht nenu ut
atusseunnu, namaieshapan muk[u] nin etutuht, tanishapani
kutaka innua e tutuaht tshetshi ut utinaminiti mitshuapinu nete utenat.

they talked to them, they would constantly contradict themselves. That is why they were funny and that is how they fooled the Innu. But some knew about the civil servants and there were some homes into which they could not go. Despite that, they never got discouraged, they always found a way to speak to them.

Me, for instance, they were never able to come see me in my home, then one day, they gave me a job and I worked for them. This job consisted of, for us, the Innu women, to learn how to take care of our houses in town after the move. During the meetings that we held about our work, the officials from Indian Affairs would make use of that time to talk to me about getting a house in town. We were three doing this work. The Innu women with whom I was working had already, them, gotten houses. One day as we were holding our meeting, one of the civil servants told us: "You who are working, you will be the first to choose your house and which street you would prefer to live on." The fact of having a job is not a reason for me to sell my culture in exchange for a house in town. When the time came to hold another meeting, the same civil servant said: "If an Indian woman does not get a house in town, she will no longer have this job." I understood the reason why he said this. I immediately replied: "Keep your job, I have no use for a house in town!" I was not the only one, apparently, that the civil servants tried to bribe with a job. They did the same thing with other Innu so that they would get a house in town.

Katshi tshishtakaniti mitshuapa nete utenat eshk[u] eka
atapinanut, pitama tshika mishakau Kanetshia[16] mak
kutakat katshishe-utshimau-atusseht anite Uepishtikueiat
tshe ututeht issishuenanu. Nin ekue itenitaman anitshenat
katshishe-utshimau-atusseht nenu tshe mishakaht, kie
peikuan Kanetshia, muk[u] eukuannu tshe ut takushiniht
tshetshi natshi-minuenitahk katshi uieshimaht innua,
katshi manukuaht nete utenat.

Ne ut kaiatapinanut tshitimatshenitakuanipan ka
ishpanit. Ka itashiat ute Tshuan-shakaikanit, kassinu
papeik[u] innu kie kassinu papeik[u] innu-auass, nititeniten,
kassinu auen papeik[u] takuannikupan etenitak anite uteit.
Katshi atapinanut nete utenat, ute Tshuan-shakaikanit
nasht nuniatanat katshishe-utshimau-atusseht, uiesh
kutuasht-tatupishimua apu nita ut uapamitshiht. Mak
uiesh katshi kutuasht-tatupishimua katshi atapinanut
ek[u] eshkuashakaniti mitshuapa ute Tshuan-shakaikanit
nenua innuat uitshuaua ka atapiht nete utenat.

Mak kutak tshekuan, tatupishimua katshi atapiht
innuat nete utenat, nipetuatan Kanetshia eimit anite
kanatutakannit. Eukuannu essishuet : « Anitshenat innuat
ka manukuakaniht nete utenat, uinuau nenu ishi-
natuenitamupanat tshetshi manukuakaniht nete utenat
usham innuat shakuenimuikupanat utinniunuau.
Kie nenu uitshuaua ka tutakanniti eukuannua ishi-
natuenitamupanat tshetshi ishinakutakanniti », issishueu.
Nimashkateniteti pietuk nenu essishuet Kanetshia.
Ka tshitshipannanut e utshimau-aiminanut ute Tshuan-
shakaikanit ne ut ka ui atapinanut, nanitam nitituteti
kie nuash mashten tshishik[u] uetshimau-aiminanut ute
Tshuan-shakaikanit nitishpish shatshuapateti. Apu nita
ut petuk peik[u] innu tshetshi issishuet : « Nin eukuan
uet ui atapian nete utenat usham nishakuenimun ume

When the houses had been built in town, just before the move, it was said that Chrétien[28] was going to come with officials from the Department of Indian Affairs from Québec City. I then thought that the only reason for their visit was to rejoice in having duped the Innu so insidiously after they had moved them to town.

It was pitiful to see how things went during the move. All the Innu from Lake John, each and every adult and each and every youth, everyone must have felt something in their hearts, I believe. After the move to town, we, from Lake John, completely lost sight of the officials from Indian Affairs, we did not see them again for six months. About six months after the move, the houses, here in Lake John, of the Innu who had moved to town, were burnt.

There is another thing. A few months after the Innu had moved to town, we heard Chrétien on the radio. This is what he said: "It is the Indians themselves for whom we built the houses who asked that we build them these houses in town because they were ashamed of their way of life. And it is them who asked that they be built the way they have been." I was surprised to hear Chrétien say that. When we started to hold meetings about the move, here in Lake John, I always attended and I went up until the last meeting. I never heard an Innu say: "Me, the reason why I want to move to town, is because I am ashamed of my Innu way of living." On the other hand, I often saw the officials from Indian Affairs push the Innu to move to town. That

eshinniuian e inniuian » tshetshi issishuet. Anitshenat uin
tapue katshishe-utshimau-atusseht mitshetuau nuapamatiat uinuau natshinepanat innua nete utenat. Nin eukuan
uet issishueian ne katshishe-utshimau-atusset ka ishpish
pet atusseshtuat innua, katshi tutuat tshetshi matshi-
paniat innua ut uin utitenitamun, nete ma aishkat kau
nenua innua eukuannua pemushinatauat. Miam mate ne
Kanetshia nenu essishuet, uin nenu muk[u] ui minupaniti-
shu ek[u] nenua innua ui patashtaueu.

Kanetshia tapuetakue nenu ka issishuet, tshekuanitshe
kashikat uet ishi-mamitunenitamat tshetshi nanatuapatamat kau nitinniunnan ? Kashikat e inniuiat tshetshipaniat kau tshetshi nanatuapatamat nitinnu-inniunnan
namaienu kauapishit utitenitamun, ninan nititeni-
tamunnan. Uesh ma eukuan kauapishit ka ushkuish-
tuimit e inniuiat tshe ishpish inniuiat tshetshi nashamat
kakusseshiu-aitun mak tshetshi apashtaiat kakusseshiu-
aitun mamu kauapishit, nete aishkat tshetshi ushteshitu-
tutshit kauapishit. Kauapishit eukuannu uin utitenitamun.

Kauapishit nashpit apu ui petaman tshetshi uauitamakauian tshetshi ushteshitutuk, nitishpan kauapishit
utinniun. Nishunnuepipuna eshpish peikutau apian ute
Tshuan-shakaikanit, mishta-matshanipan nitshinan kie
kassinu nitaishi-animiuti shetshen mak nitauassimat
shetshen nanushipanat. Kashikat ninishtuten, e inniuian,
kauapishit utinniun eukuan ka matshi-tutakuian. Eukuan
ka ut eka atapian nete utenat. Tanite muk[u] nin ninish-
tuapaten nitinniun, apu tat kauapishit tshetshi anu uin
nishtuapatak nitinnu-inniunnu. Ka tatupipuna apian ute
Tshuan-shakaikanit, niminu-tshishkutamatishuti kauapishit utinniun mak nin e inniuian nitinniun. Eukuan
nitishi-mishketi : anu nin nitinnu-inniun minuapan kie e
mamitunenitamani, uemut eukuan anu niminuateti.

is why I say that since the civil servants have worked
for the Innu, they first find a way so that their ideas
cause trouble among them, and then they say the Innu
are the cause. For instance, if Chrétien said what he
said, it was to get away with it by putting the responsibility on the Innu.

If what Chrétien said was true, why then would we
today be thinking of finding our Innu way of life again?
The fact that we are now beginning to look for our Innu
culture, that is not the White man's idea, it is ours. But it
is the White man who forced us, we the Innu, to be governed by the White administration until we die, and to
live under the White man's regime so that in the future,
the White man would be our brother. That is the White
man's project.

Me, I absolutely do not want to hear that the White
man is my brother, I am fed up with the White man's
way of life. Over the last twenty years that I have lived
here in the same place in Lake John, our house has been
lamentable, I have had all sorts of unnecessary miseries, and my children have been sullied unnecessarily.
Today, I understand that it is the White man's way of
life that caused me harm, me an Innu woman, and that
is why I will not move to town. There is only me who
knows my life, there is no White man who knows my
life as an Innu woman better than I do. Since I have
been living here in Lake John, I have carefully analyzed
the White man's culture as well as my own Innu culture. I have found that my Innu culture was far better
and, if I think about it, it is the one that I prefer.

Ne ut eka ka atapian nete utenat, mitshenipan
tshekuan : ka tatupipuna apian ute Tshuan-shakaikanit,
nitauassimat tapanat etuteht katshishkutamatsheutshuapit kie tapanat etuteht muk[u] anite itetshe kaminnanunit.
Anitshenat nitauassimat ka ituteht nete utenat katshishkutamatsheutshuapit, tekushinitaui ute Tshuan-shakaikanit mitshetuau nitikutiat : « Nimanenimikaunan anite
katshishkutamatsheutshuapit, kakusseshiu-auassat nima-
nenimikunanat, katshishkutamatsheshiht kie uinuau
ekue manenimimiht. » Ek[u] anitshenat nitauassimat etutetaui anite kaminnanunit nete utenat, takuanipan nutim
peikutipishkua nashpit eka uet nipaian eshuapamakau
tshetshi takushiniht. Tekushinitaui ute Tshuan-shakaikanit, nanikutini nuapamau nitauassim nutim shukushiu
kie utashtamik[u] nutim pakupannit : ne nitauassim
kamakunueshiniti utamaukushapan nete utenat. Kauapishit eukuannu ka ishi-matshi-tutuat nitauassima ka itenitak tshimut tshetshi ushteshitutuk.

Kauapishit ka itenitak tshimut tshetshi ushteshitutuk,
nishtam katshishkutamatsheutshuapinu niminikuti.
Kauapishit ka ui tshishkutamuimit utinniun e inniuiat,
miam nishtuait ishinakuannipan ukatshishkutama-
tsheutshuap : peik[u] eukuan kakusseshiu-katshishkutamatsheutshuap, nish[u] eukuan kaminnanut, nisht[u] eukuan
kamakunueshiutshuap. Neunipani mamu akushiutshuap.

Kauapishit mishta-apashtapan iapit nenu akushiutshuapinu ka tshishkutamuimit utinniun. Miam anitshenat
kamakunueshiht ueshikuiataui nitauassima, uemut ekute
akushiutshuapit patukaiakanniti nitauassima. Anitshenat
nitauassimat ueshikuikutaui kamakunueshiniti, eshk[u]
takuannu kutakatshinu ka ui ishi-tshishkutamakutau
kauapishiniti : eukuannu tshetshi natshi-miniht
ishkutuapunu anite kaminnanunit. Nitauassimat

There are many reasons why I did not move to town. Since I have lived in Lake John, some of my children went to school and some only went to the bar. My children who went to school in town often told me, upon their return to Lake John: "We are made fun of in school, the White children laugh at us and the teachers insult us too." As for my children who went to the bar in town, there were nights that I did not sleep at all because I was waiting for them to come home. When they returned to Lake John, sometimes I would see one of them bloodied, his face completely injured: he had been beaten, apparently, by the police officers, over there, in town. That is the harm that the White man has caused my children when he thought to become my brother without my knowledge.

When the White man thought to become my brother without my knowledge, the first thing he gave me was the School. When he wanted to teach us his culture, to us the Innu, his School had three facets: the first was the School Board, the second, the Bar, and the third, the Prison. Along with the Hospital, that makes four.

The White man also made great use of the hospital to teach us his culture. For instance, when the police injure my children, they must go to the hospital. When my children are injured by the police, they are given one more lesson by the White man: to go drink at the bar. That is where my children think of going afterwards. When they leave the bar, it is only to be given, next door, another one of the

eukuannu minuat miamitunenitahk tshetshi ituteht. Nenu
kaminnanunit uet unuitaui, muk^u ashu-pitutsheuat nenu
kutakatshinu ka ishi-tshishkutamakutau kauapishiniti,
eukuannu kamakunueshiutshuapinu. Anite kamakunueshiutshuapit uet unuiti, nanikutini ne nitauassim
ushikuikushapan kamakunueshiniti, eukuannu
akushiutshuapit patukuiakanit. Eukuannu mashten
anite akushiutshuapit uet unuit. Ume eshpaniti,
nin eukuan eshi-utinaman : nitauassim uin e innu-
auassiut eukuannu kiatshitinat ukanuma e innu-auassiut
tshe ishpish inniut tshe eka nita nishtuapatak utinniun
kie tshe ishpish inniut tshe eka nita katshipishkak anite
kakusseshiu-atusseunit. Kauapishit eukuannu muk^u ka
ishi-mamitunenitak tshetshi ishi-matshi-tutuat nitauassima ka itenitak tshetshi ushteshitutuk e inniuian.

Nitauassimat apu minuenitaman tshetshi uapamakau
kashikanit natamik^u meshkanat tshetshi papamuteht.
Kauapishit eukuan uin ka nanuiat nitauassima kie eukuan
uin tshe nanatuapatak tan tshe ishi-unikapauiat nenua
nitauassima. Uesh ma anitshenat nitauassimat kie uinuau
takuannipan utinniunuau kie anu minuanipan anite
innu-mitshuapit ka ut inniuht. Mate innu-mitshuap,
nititeniten nin, apu takuak kutak mitshuap anu tshetshi
minuashit kie anu tshetshi uashkamat. Kie innu-mitshim
apu takuak kutak mitshim anu tshetshi minuat kie anu
tshetshi uashkamat. Ka tatupipuna peikutau apian ute
Tshuan-shakaikanit, tshekuannu anu ka ut mishanit ka
ishi-matshi-tutut kauapishit, eukuannua nitauassima ka
nanuiat mak ka tshitaimut nitinnu-mitshiminu tshetshi
mitshian. Kashikat miamitunenitamani, nimitaten ka
tatupipuna shetshen peikutau apian kie apu anu ui petaman tshetshi uauitamakauian kauapishit utinniun.

White man's lessons: that of the prison. When they
leave the prison, sometimes they have been hurt
by the police so they are brought to the hospital;
and it is the hospital that my children leave in the
end. I myself think that it is in that moment that
my child receives his diploma as a young Innu so
that he will never know, for the rest of his life, his
culture and throughout his life, he will not interfere
in the job market. That is everything that the White
man thought of, how to harm my children, when
he thought of becoming my brother, me, an Innu
woman.

I do not like to see my children loafing around.
It is the White man who ruined them and it is up
to him to find a way to put them back on the right
path. My children also had a culture and it was
preferable for them to live in a tent. In my opinion,
there is no house that is more beautiful and cleaner
than a tent. And there is no better or cleaner food
than Innu food. Over the years that I have lived in
the same place, here in Lake John, the greatest harm
that the White man has done to me has been to ruin
my children and to forbid me from eating my Innu
food. When I think about it today, I regret the years
that I have lived in the same place unnecessarily
and I want even less to hear about the White man's
way of life.

Kie nin e inniuian nipa minueniten tshetshi kanueni-
taman nitinniun. Kie nipa minueniten kie nin e inniuian
eiapit kie eiapit tshetshi tshissenitakushian e inniuian
uesh ma kie nin nimishta-ishpiteniten nitinnu-inniun kie
nimishta-ashinen eshinniuian e inniuian tanite eukuannu
ka ishi-minit Tshishe-manitu tshetshi ishinniuian.

Me too, an Innu woman, I would be happy to keep my culture and to know that I will always be Innu. Me too I have a lot of respect for my Innu life and I am deeply proud of it because that is the life that God gave me.

9

Kauapishit tan tshe ishi-utinimit aishkat ?

Nin eukuan etenitaman : e inniuiat kauapishit piku-
namupan tshimut nitinniunnannu. Nitauassiminanat
kashikanit apu pikutaht anite minashkuat tshetshi
ishinniuht miam ueshkat ka ishinniuiat. Kashikat nitani-
miunan tshetshi ishi-kutshipanitaiat tshetshi ishinniuiat
miam ueshkat ka ishinniuiat. Kashikat namaieute nin
nitinniunit etaian kie namaieute nin nitshit epian. Niti-
shinniun kauapishit utinniun muk^u tapue apu takuak
peikutshishikua tshetshi minuenitaman tanite e inniuian
apu tipenimitishuian, kauapishit nitipenimik^u. Kashikat ume eshinniuiat nititenitakushinan miam peikuan
aueshish. Aueshish nanitam shetshishu kie nanitam
ashuapatam^u tshetshi nipaiakanit. Eukuan miam eshi-
nakushiat kashikat katshi pikunakanit e inniuiat nitinniunnan. Kauapishit eukuan ka tutuimit tshe ishpish
inniuiat nanitam peikutau tshetshi apiat. Kashikat e
inniuian mishta-mueshtatapiani peikutau epian, muk^u
anite uashka nitshit ekute pepamuteian kie nitshisseniten tshe ishpish inniuian, apu nita tshika ut tshi pikuian
katshi tshishtikanikatut kauapishit.

Katshi natuapamimit kauapishit ute nitipenitamun-
nat, kashikat e inniuiat apu tshekuan ishpitenitakushiat
kie apu tshekuan tipenitamat. Nitaueshishiminanat
– innu-aueshishat – kashikat namaieu ninan nitaueshishiminanat, kauapishit nenua utaueshishima ;

9

How will the White man consider us in the future?

I myself think that the White man destroyed our culture without our knowledge. Now our children are incapable of living in the bush the way we used to in the past, it is difficult for us to live the way we did before. Now, it is not within my own culture that I find myself and it is not in my house that I live. I live the White man's life and truly, there is not one day that I am happy because I, who am an Innu woman, I no longer govern myself, it is the White man who governs me. In our way of living today, we are like an animal: the animal who is always afraid and waiting to be killed. This is what our life looks like today now that our Innu culture has been destroyed. It is the White man who made it so that we would be sedentary until the end of our days. Today, me, an Innu woman, when I am too bored with always staying in the same place, it is only nearby my house that I walk and I know that for as long as I live, I will never be able to escape the enclosure that the White man has trapped me in.

After he came to us in our domain, we, the Innu, are no longer worth anything and we no longer govern ourselves. Our animals, the Innu animals, no longer belong to us today, they are the White man's animals; our territory no longer belongs to us, it is

nitassinan kashikat namaieu ninan nitassinan, kauapishit
nenu utassi. Anite nitassinat uin muk^u aituteu nete ua
aitutet kie muk^u anite ua mamanukashut tshi mani-
kashu. Kauapishit kashikanit kassinu anite nitassinat
mamashinaitsheu, kassinu anite minashkuat aiakuash-
kuaim^u mashinaikannu. Eukuan essishuet : « APASHTA-
KANU ASSI » kie « TIPENITAKANU ASSI ». Kauapishit
apu shakuenimut nenu etutak tshetshi mamashinaitshet
kassinu anite minashkuat tshetshi ishi-katshinassimat
innua miam uin tepenitaki assinu ute nutshimit. Kauapishit kashikanit ute nitassinat kassinu eshpish tshissenitak
tshetshi ishi-manenimimit, nitishi-manenimikunan.

Tshekuannitshe kauapishit kashikanit nanitam uet
issishuet : « Innuat nin niminauat kassinu tshekuannu » ?
Kashikat eshinniuiat kauapishit utinniun, mitshetuau
nipetenan essishuet kauapishit : « Innuat mianukua-
kanitaui, eukuan nin nishuniam etusseiani netakass^{17}
e tshishikashuian », issishueu kauapishit. Nititeniten
nin nitassinan tshe ishpish inniunanut nutim eshpishanit tshetshi nanutat kie nitinnu-aueshishiminana
kassinu eishinakushiniti tshetshi nanuiat kauapishit,
apu tshekuan ishpitenitakuak peik^u ka kashkatshat
kakusseshiu-mitshuap kie peikuan shuniau tatuminiau
apu tshekuan ishpitenitakuak. Nin eukuan etenitaman :
apatenitakuakakue e inniuian tshe ishpish inniuian
tshetshi apian anite kakusseshiu-mitshuapit, ushtuin
atut nita nipa minikuti kauapishit tshetshi apian anite
kakusseshiu-mitshuapit.

Mak kauapishit nanitam nipetenan essishuet : « Innuat
uinuau apu ui atusseht ek^u ume ninan etusseiat, netakass
e tshishikashuiat, eukuannu uet inniuht innuat. » Eshk^u
eka ka shenakanit ashini – nenu ka mishkak shashish
innu Tshishennish-Pien shash tshekat nishumitashumi-
tunnuepipuna – ute Tshiuetinit apu ut tat peik^u kauapishit

the White man's territory. In our territory, only he can go wherever he wants, and wherever he wishes to build a house, he can build one. Now he writes things all over our territory, everywhere in the woods he puts up signs that say: PRIVATE PROP- ERTY. The White man is shameless in putting up signs everywhere in the woods so that he can make the Innu believe that he is the owner of the territo- ries, here, inland. Today in our territory, whatever the White man can do to insult us, he does it.

Why does the White man constantly say today: "I am the one who gives everything to the Indians"? Now that we are living the White man's life, we often hear him say: "It is with the taxes that I pay, it is with my money that houses are built for the Indi- ans." I myself believe that an apartment – and even a few million dollars – is not a steep price to pay compared to how the White man has wasted forever all of our land and all of our Innu animals. And I think had it been vital for me, an Innu woman, to live the rest of my days in a White man's house, the White man probably never would have allowed me to live in a White man's house.

We also often hear the White man say inces- santly: "The Indians do not want to work and we are the ones that support them when we work and pay taxes." Before the mine was opened, which was discovered almost two hundred years ago by the Innu Tshishennish-Pien, there were no White work-

ka atusset tanite apu ut takuak kakusseshiu-atusseun kie kassinu kutak tshekuan apu ut takuak : ka ashamitunanut shuniau apu ut takuak, auass-shuniau apu ut takuak, tshishenniu-shuniau apu ut takuak, neshumash kie netakass apu ut takuaki; kie kassinu eishinakuak mishtikushiu-mitshim apu ut takuak, kakusseshiu-atauitshuap apu ut takuak ute Tshiuetinit, akushiutshuap apu ut takuak; innu-assia e apishashiti apu ut takuaki : ume Tshiuetin nutim eshpishat innu-assiunipan tanite ute Tshiuetinit apu ut peikussit kauapishit; kautshimau-aiminanut ka papamitapenanut apu ut takuak : papeik^{u} innu uin uetshit utshishe-utshimamitutatishuipan. Kassinu eishinakuak kamashinatautishunanut miam tshetshi ut uieshimakanit innu ute nitassinat apu nita ut uapatamat : kassinu papeik^{u} innu kanuenitamupan namashukite. Kakusseshiu-katshishkutamatsheutshuap muk^{u} tshiam tshetshi ut amissenakanit innu-auass, ute Tshiuetinit apu nita ut uapatamat : kassinu papeik^{u} innu kautishkuemit utaumau mak ukaumau uin uetshit ishi-atusseshtatishuipan miam katshishkutamatshesht kassinu utauassima. Nanimissiu-ishkuteu-uashtenitamakan apu nita ut uapatamat, pimi ka kutuatshenanut apu nita ut uapatamat ute nitassinat.

Tshekuannitshe ma kauapishit nanitam uet issishuet : « Innuat nin niminauat kassinu tshekuannu » ? Kauapishit apu ut uishamitshit ute nitassinat kie apu ut natuenitamutshit tshetshi petat kassinu eishinakuannit utinniun. Ute Tshiuetinit eshk^{u} eka peik^{u} kauapishit ka tat, kie ninan e inniuiat takuanipan nitinniunnan, kie ninan apu tshekuan nutepaniat, kassinu tshekuan nikanuenitetan. Mitshuapa nikanuenitetan, namaieu netakassa nimanukakutan. Kauapishit ka ui minit peik^{u} kakashkatshanit mitshuapinu, nititenimikutshe : « Tshika mishta-ashineiku... » Kauapishit nitauassima

ers in the North because there was no paid work nor
any of those kinds of things: there was no welfare,
no family allowances, no old age pension, no unem-
ployment insurance, no taxes; there were not all the
White man's kinds of food, no stores, no hospital
either; there were no tiny reserves: the North in all
its extent was a reserve because there were no White
men; meetings that go on endlessly, there were none
of those: each Innu was his own government. We
never saw in our territory all those voting systems
that are set up to fool the Innu: each Innu was on
his own the majority. We never saw, here in the
North, school boards that only confuse the Innu
youth: every family father and family mother acted
as teachers for all their children. Electric light and
heating oil, we had never seen that in our territory.

Why does the White man say constantly: "I am
the one who gives everything to the Indians"? We
did not invite him into our territory, we did not ask
him to bring the things of his culture. Before the
White man came to the North we too, Innu, had a
culture and we were short of nothing, we had everything. We had houses and it is not because of taxes
that they were built for us. When the White man
offered me an apartment, he must have thought
that that would make me proud...After my children were sullied by the White man, no house

e innu-auassiuniti katshi nanuiat, namaieu mitshuap
tshe minuenitamikuian kie namaieu shuniau tanite
nitauassimat namaieu natamik^u tshekuan, namaieu
mitshuap, namaieu shuniau kie nitauassimat namaieu
miam natamik^u tshekuan ka atauatshenanut.

Kauapishit katshi tshimutamuimit nitinniunnannu
kie nitassinannu, kashikanit innu kie innu-auass etusse-
taui anite kakusseshiu-atusseunit muk^u makanipakannu
mak uatshikatashkunu, eukuannu eshi-atusseht. Kauapishit ka utinat nitauassima e innu-auassiuniti tshetshi
kakusseshiu-tshishkutamuat, issishuepan : « Innu-auass
tshika kauapikueshiu, innu-auass tshika natukunishiu,
innu-auass tshika katipaitsheshiu. » Kassinu aissishuepan
kashikanit tshe aishi-atusseniti innu-auassa. Kashikat
nitauassimat shash nishunnuepipuna eshpish ituteht anite
kakusseshiu-katshishkutamatsheutshuapit. Ute nitshit
apu kanuenimak kauapikuesht kie apu kanuenimak
kakashteukupeshkueu kie apu kanuenimak katipaitshesht
kie apu kanuenimak natukunish. Kashikat eukuan muk^u
uiapataman nitauassimat e innu-auassiuht metshi-uaui-
nakaniht anite tipatshimu-mashinaikanit.

Ninapem e inniut anite kakusseshiu-atusseunit atu-
sseu : eukuannu iapit kauapishit nenu utishi-uaueshtaun.
Ne ninapem e inniut nenu e kakusseshiu-atusset tshishikashu netakassinu miam peikuan kauapishit. Tshekuannitshe ma kauapishit nanitam uet ui animishikatuimit
nenu ut e tshishikashut netakassinu etusseti ? Kassinu
tshekuan eishinakuak netakass e tshishikashunanut, uin
nenu kauapishit utinniun. Ninan eshinakuaki tshetshi
mamashikauiat netakass tshashikashuiat, kassinu anite
kie ninan ishinakuan tshetshi mamatueiat tshashikashuiat netakass uesh ma nitinniunnan ka ishinniuiat,
apu peik^u shumanitshish ut tshishikashuiat netakass.

and no amount of money could satisfy me because my children were not just anything, they are not a house, they are not money. My children, they are not something that can be sold.

After the White man stole our culture and our territory, the Innu, young and adult, who were wage-earning, worked pick and shovel. When the White man took my children to give them a White education, he said: "The Indian youth will become a priest, the Indian youth will become a doctor, the Indian youth will become a surveyor."[29] He named all the professions that the young Innu would work as today. It has been twenty years now that my children go to the White man's school. In my home, I do not have a priest, I do not have a nun, I do not have a surveyor, and I do not have a doctor either. Today all that I can see is that my children are denigrated in the newspapers.

My husband is Innu and he has a paid job; that too is a White man's thing. My husband who is Innu and who is a wage earner pays taxes just like the White man. Why does the White man always bother us because he pays taxes when he works? All those taxes that need to be paid, it is his culture. We are the ones who should be upset that we have to always pay taxes and we are the ones who should complain: when we lived the Innu way of life, we never paid one cent in taxes.

Kashikat ninan e inniuiat ishinakuan tshetshi tatue-
tamat kassinu ka pet aishi-uieshimimit kauapishit kie
uemut tshetshi natutuimit, mauat nanitam tshetshi
anuetuimit uiauitamutshiti tan eishi-mamitunenitamat
tshetshi ishi-uaueshitishuiat. Uesh ma kashikat papanu
tshetshi nishtutamat kassinu ka pet aishi-uieshimimit
kauapishit. Kashikat eimiati, kuetshipanitaiati tshetshi
tshishpeuatitishuiat, kauapishit nanitam eukuannu
eshimit : « Tshimin, tshiminukashun ». Ishkutuapui
tshe ishpish inniunanut aua ne nanitam tshe patash-
taukuiat muku ninan e inniuiat ? Ne matshi-manitu-
ishkutuapui apatenitakuakakue, ushtuin atut nita
takuannipan tshetshi minimit kauapishit. Tshipetetau
nitinnu-mitshiminan mishta-apatenitakuanipan tshe
ishpish inniunanut tshetshi ut inniuiat eku tshuapatetau
nitshitaimakaunan innu-aueshish tshetshi mutshit…
Nimitshiminan innu-mitshim ka ishi-mitshishuiat, apu
ut apashtaiat akushiutshuap tanite eukuan nimitshiminan ninatukuikutan. Kie kamakunueshiutshuap apu
ut apashtaiat, kamakunuesht apu nita ut tatshinimit.
Kashikat tapue niminnan kassinu eishinakuak ishkutuapui kie tapue tshekat eshakumitshishikua nipitutshenan
akushiutshuapit ne ut ishkutuapui. Kauapishit apu nenu
mashkatenitak kie apu uauitak anite kanatutakannit
kie anite katshitapatakannit kie apu mashinaitshet anite
tipatshimu-mashinaikanit.

Kauapishit kashikanit issishueu : « Innuat nitaniminikunanat, eukuanat innuat muku iapatshiaht kamakunueshiniti ». Kauapishit apu tapuet nenu essishuet.
Kamakunuesht namaieu ninan nitinniunnan, namaieu
ninan e inniuiat ka ut takushinit kamakunuesht ute
Tshiuetinit. Kamakunuesht ushkat ka takushinit ute
nitassinat, tshekuennua eshinniuniti uitsheuepan ?
Eukuannua kauapishiniti uitsheuepan tshetshi atussesh-

It is us, the Innu, who should lament all the
White man's injustices and he should listen to us
rather than always oppose us when we tell him how
we want to organize ourselves. The day has come
that we understand all of the White man's tricks.
When we speak, when we try to defend ourselves,
he always says to us: "You have been drinking,
you are drunk." Is it really alcohol that will, our
whole lives, keep us down, only us, the Innu? Had
that damn alcohol been vital to us, the White man
would probably never have given it to us to drink.
You have heard that our Innu food was always
essential to us to live and you have seen that we are
forbidden to eat our Innu animals...When we ate
our food, our Innu food, we did not need a hospital
because our food was our medicine. And we did not
need a prison: the police were never concerned with
us. It is true that nowadays we drink all kinds of
alcohol, it is also true that almost every day we have
to go to the hospital because of it. The White man is
not surprised, he does not speak of that on the radio
or on television, he does not write about that in the
newspapers.

The White man says: "The Indians are giving us
a hard time, they are the only ones for whom the
police are useful." The White man does not speak
the truth. The police, that is not our way of life and
it is not because of us, the Innu, that they came to
the North. When the police came for the first time,
with which race did they come? They accompanied
the White man so as to work for him because the

tuat uesh ma uin kauapishit apu tshi inniut eka e kanuenimikut kamakunueshiniti kie apu tshi inniut eka e
kanuenimat kamakunueshiniti.

Kauapishit issishueu : « Innu-auassat nitaniminikunanat, nitshimutamakunanat ». Kauapishit nenu
essishuet, apu nishtutatishut. Nin etenitaman, kauapishit
uin apu nita tshika ut tepi-tshishikuat innu-auassa ka
ishpish mishta-tshimutamuat. Eukuan uin ka tshimutamuat innu-auassa utinniunnu ashit utassinu. Kauapishit
eukuan uin ka tshimutamuimit kie ka pikunak nutim
eshpishanit nitassinannu kie nitaueshishiminana eukuan
uin ka tshimutamuimit. Eshi-nishtutaman nin, ninan e
inniuiat nitaniminikunan kauapishit, ninan nimatshi-tu-
takunan kauapishit kie ninan nitshimutamakunan
kauapishit kie ninan e inniuiat pikunam^u nimatshuni-
shiminannu. Ninan nuakaikunan kauapishit kie ninan
nimamashikunan kauapishit ute nitassinat uesh ma uin
ninatuapamikutan ute nitassinat.

Kauapishit nipetetan peikuau essishuet : « Matshi-
manitu innuat ute Kaiatushkanunit apu tshissenitahk
tan tshe ishinniuht ». Kauapishit nenu essishuet tapueu.
Kauapishit nitshimutamakutan nitinniunnannu kie
nitassinannu, kashikat tapue apu tshissenitamat tan
tshe ishinniuiat. Muk^u issishuetau ne kauapishit ashit
nutim utauassima muk^u peikupipuna kanuenimikuti
innua peik^u kautishkueminiti anite nutshimit kie anite
innu-mitshuapit ek^u nenu umitshim issishuetau muk^u
peikupipuna nashpit apu tshika ut mitshit. Ne kauapishit
ka issishuet « Matshi-manitu-innuat apu tshissenitahk tan
tshe ishinniuht », nititenimau nin ushtuin kie uin atut ut
tshissenitam^u tan tshe ishinniut kie ushtuin tshipa mish-
kam^u e animiut. Uesh ma kauapishit namaienu utinniun
anite minashkuat kie namaienu utinniun innu-mitshuapinu kie namaienu utinniun innu-mitshiminu. Kashikat

White man, he, cannot live if he is not protected by the police and if he does not have police officers.

The White man says: "The young Indians are giving us a hard time, they steal from us." When he says this, he does not understand himself. In my opinion, it is the White man who will never be able to settle his debt with the young Innu because he has stolen so much from them. He is the one who stole from us and destroyed all of our territory, he is the one who stole our animals. The way I see things, it is us, the Innu, who are having a hard time with the White man. It is the White man who has caused us harm, who steals from us and who destroys our property, ours, the Innu. He is the one who irritates us and he is the one who bothers us in our territory because he is the one who came here to find us.

Once we heard the White man say: "The damn savages of Schefferville do not know how to live." The White man speaks the truth when he says this. He stole from us our culture and our territory and today, it is true, we do not know how to live. But let us consider the case of this White man who, with all of his children, would be kept by an Innu family for one year, in the bush in a tent, and let us say that, during that one year, that White man could not eat his own food. I myself think that that White man who said: "The damn savages do not know how to live," he would probably not know how to live either and he would probably find it difficult. The bush, that is not his life, the tent, that is not his life, and the Innu food, that is not his life either. Nowadays, it is the White man who forces us to live his life.

eukuan uin ueshkuishtuimit tshetshi ishinniutshit utinnniun. Tshekuannitshe ma kauapishit kashikanit uet issishuet : « Matshi-manitu-innuat apu tshissenitahk tan tshe ishinniuht » ?

Tshekuannitshe kauapishit kashikanit uet issishuet : « Innuat nitaniminikunanat » kie « Innuat muku eukuanat iapatshiaht kamakunueshiniti » ? Kauapishit kashikanit animinitshiti kie uakashimiti kie uinenimimiti e inniuiat ute nitassinat, uin ishinakuannu tshetshi itshetet ute Tshiuetinit. Uesh ma ninan e inniuiat at ui itsheteiati ute Tshiuetinit nenu uet aieshkushiuinitshit kauapishit kie nenu uet uakashimit kie nenu ut e uinenimimit, apu tshissenitamat tanite nipa itutenan : ekute ute nitassinat etaiat. Kauapishit nipetetan essishuet : « Innuauass metshi-tutak tshika itshetishauakanu ute Kaiatushkanunit ». Kauapishit nenu ka issishuet, eukuan apu ut nishtutamat e inniuiat : ute Kaiatushkanunit innu-auass itshetishauakaniti, tanite tshe itishauakanit ? Innu-auass eukuan uin utassi Tshiuetinnu uesh ma kassinu innu-auass eukuan uinishtam ka tat ute Tshiuetinit eshku eka peiku kauapishit ka takushinit.

Nititeniten nin kashikat namaieu ninan e inniuiat eshinakuak tshiam tshetshi inniuiat ute nitassinat, eukuan uin kauapishit eshinakuannit tshiam tshetshi inniut. Kauapishit namaienu uin tshetshi tipenitak ute nitassinat. Kauapishit eka ui nishtutaki anu uin eshinakuannit tshiam tshetshi inniut, uin kauapishit ishinakuannu tshetshi tshiuet tanite nete ka ututet.

Why does he now say: "The damn savages do not know how to live"?

Why does the White man say: "The Indians are giving us a hard time" and "The police are only useful for the Indians"? If we are giving him such a hard time here in our territory, if he hates us and is disgusted by us, it is the White man who should leave the North. Even if we, the Innu, wanted to leave the North because we bother the White man, because he hates us and is disgusted by us, we do not know where we would go: we are here on our land. We have heard the White man say: "The young Indians who are causing trouble, we are going to clear them away from Schefferville." When the White man said that, we did not understand: if the young Innu are expelled from Schefferville, where would they go? The North is their territory because each young Innu was here first in the North, before the White man came.

I myself believe today that it is not up to us but to the White man to behave here in our territory. It is not up to the White man to govern in our territory. And if the White man does not want to understand that it is up to him to behave, he is the one who should go back to where he came from.

Punipanu aimun

Nin eukuan matshi-manitu innushkueu. Kashikat pietamani eshinikatikauian SAUVAGESSE nimishta-ashinen.
Kauapishit pietuki essishueti nenu aimunnu, nitishi-
nishtuten kauapishit nanitam nuitamak^u tapue eukuan
nin tshitshue innushkueu mak kauapishit nuitamak^u
ninishtam anite minashkuat katshi ut inniuian. Uesh ma
kassinu tshekuan anite minashkuat ka ut inniuimakak
eukuan anu uet minuat inniun. Tshima nanitam petuk
kauapishit tshetshi ishinikashit SAUVAGESSE.

Afterword

I am a damn Savage.[30] I am very proud when, today,
I hear myself being called a Savage. When I hear
the White man say this word, I understand that he
is telling me again and again that I am a real Innu
woman and that it was I who first lived in the bush.
And still, all things that live in the bush, that is
the best life. May the White man always call me a
Savage.

Notes

Book One: *Eukuan nin matshi-manitu innushkueu*

Notes in this section were provided by Jérémie Ambroise, who worked on the revisions and standardization of the original Innu version of *Eukuan nin matshi-manitu innushkueu*, along with translator and linguist José Mailhot and advisory committee members Anne-Marie André, Judith Mestokosho, Céline Bellefleur, and Philomène Grégoire.

1 Tests (from French *les tests*), refers to a competency card.
2 Law (from French *la loi*).
3 Regulation, rule (from French *les règlements*).
4 University (from French *l'université*).
5 Diploma (from French *les diplômes*).
6 Innu (from French *Montagnais*).
7 Pierre Elliott Trudeau, former Prime Minister of Canada (from *Trudeau*).
8 Knights of Columbus (from French *Chevaliers de Colomb*).
9 Madam (from French *madame*).
10 Snowmobile (from Québec French *les skidoo*)
11 Plywood (from Québec French *les plywoods*).
12 Witness (from French *les témoins*).
13 Bologna (from Québec French *balôné*).
14 City council (from French *la ville*).
15 Majority (from French *la majorité*).
16 Jean Chrétien, former prime minister of Canada (from *Chrétien*).
17 Tax (from French *les taxes*).

Notes

Translation of Book One: I Am a Damn Savage

1 As I explain in the Afterword, I have kept the 2015 revision to the word "Innu" instead of the 1976 word "Indian."

2 The French pronoun used here to signify the aforementioned person is "elle," "she," to agree grammatically with "personne." English does not impose the same grammatical constraint as the French, thereby giving me an option: I find it interesting to use "she" here in translation, rather than the generic "he," given that the author is a woman speaking of her experience, but bearing in mind that this is an experience that can extend to any potential writer.

3 The author uses "le Blanc" throughout. I have chosen to use "the White man" for the sake of grammatical clarity, but also to call attention to the paternalistic and gendered aspects of colonialism, especially in cases of land conquest and expropriation. The Innu word, *kauapishit*, translates as "White person, person of the White race" (*Online Innu Dictionary*). In other instances, for example in Chapter 3, when Kapesh deplores how "le Blanc" treated the Innu children, this should be read rather as all-encompassing of settler society, as the Innu word suggests.

4 As I explain in the Afterword, this is one of a few instances in which the author used *Innu Mutania* in 1976, which translates into French as "l'Indien Montagnais." To reflect the 1976 translation, I have used "Montagnais Innu" in these instances (38–39).

5 Bread made with baking powder instead of yeast (footnote added by translator in the 1976 French version).

6 Traditional banquet (original in the French text; footnote added by translator in the 1976 French version).

7 Large rectangular tent with an entrance at each end, where the *makushan* would take place (original in the French text; footnote added by translator in the 1976 French version).

8 Pierre Elliott Trudeau, former Prime Minister of Canada, 1968–79 and 1980–84.

9 I have left this instance of the word "Indian" here because it speaks to the stereotype of the "Hollywood Indian" as seen in films and westerns.

10 This is the second instance of the expression *Mutania*, "les Indiens montagnais" (plural), used in the 1976 version (48–49).

11 Innu community now known as Pessamit (footnote added by proofreader in the 2015 French version).

12 This is the third instance of the word *Mutania Innu*, "Montagnais," used in the 1976 version (53–54).

13 In the 1976 translation, this sentence was translated as "un steamer qui venait à Bersimis de temps à autre" ("a steamer that came to Bersimis from time to time") (55). In light of the 2019 revisions to the French translation ("une goélette venait régulièrement à Bersimis"), I have corrected it.

14 As I explain in the Afterword, I have kept the word "Indian" in instances of direct speech by White people.

15 This is the fourth instance of the word *Mutania*, "les Indiens montagnais," used in the 1976 version (66–67).

16 This is the fifth and last instance of the word *Mutania* used in the 1976 version (77–78). Here it is used to describe the language, *Mutania innu-aimun*, "la langue montagnaise," the Montagnais (Innu) language.

17 The Innu name for the Hamilton River (now Churchill) is *Sheshatshiu-shipu* (footnote added by proofreader in the 2015 French version).

18 In the 1976 French translation, the Innu word *kaminnanut* was translated as "l'hotel" – the hotel. However, in the 2019 revised translation, it has been corrected to "le bar" – the bar.

19 The Indian Act, which passed in 1867, contained a clause that forbade Indians to drink alcohol. This clause was amended in 1963 (footnote added by translator in the 1976 French version).

20 In the 2015 revision, "God" was replaced with "The Creator." The Innu word, *Tshishemanitu* (*tshishe-manitu*, also great spirit), is translated in the *Online Innu Dictionary* as "God," which was the intended meaning, given that the author was Christian. The expression "The Creator" is often used in lieu today to signal the rejection of colonial religions for more traditional beliefs. However, it seemed more appropriate here to leave the original meaning.

21 Meat from a whole caribou that is cut up finely, dried, and carefully wrapped in the subcutaneous tissue, then in the animal's hide. Preparing this type of meat bundle is an art (footnote added by translator in the 1976 French version).

While revising her 1976 French translation, Mailhot noticed that a part was missing. The full French passage, which I have translated in full as well, is "L'Indien ne se voit jamais utiliser un canot d'écorce qu'il a lui-même fabriqué, couvrir son habitation avec de l'écorce de bouleau ou de la peau de caribou et faire du feu directement sur le sol de son habitation. L'Indien ne se voit jamais utiliser un seul jeune arbre pour se fabriquer une lance à caribou et il ne se voit jamais, après avoir tué un beau caribou, faire préparer par la femme indienne un *tamatshipeshikan*." Also, in the original passage, the spelling of *tamatshipeshikan* was *timitshipashikan*.

22 *Shetshipatuan* is the Innu word for this hairstyle (footnote added by reviewer in the 2015 French version).

23 The fir branches with which the floor of the tent is made are replaced periodically. If the camp stays in the same place for a long time, the reserve of fir branches is quickly used up (footnote added by translator in the 1976 French version).

24 In the 1976 French translation, the Innu word *kamanitsheshit* [*kamanu-tshesht*] (186) was translated as "contracteur" – contractor. However, in the 2019 revised translation, it has been corrected to "charpentier" – carpenter.

25 In the 1976 translation, this was translated as "les Indiens qui sont inaptes à travailler" ("the Indians who were unfit to work") (196). In light of the 2019 revisions to the French translation ("les Indiens qui ne sont pas inté-ressés à travailler"), I have corrected it.

26 In the 1976 French translation, this was translated as "Si tu peux t'organiser pour qu'ils soient moins pactés..." ("If you can find a way for them to be less drunk...") (205). In the 2019 revision, it has been changed to "Si tu peux t'organiser pour qu'ils soient moins portés à se paqueter..." ("If you can find a way for them to be less inclined to get drunk..."). I have corrected this here as well, since the change reflects the speaker's opinion that drinking is both a choice and a vice – and only changing that behaviour would see them get their houses built.

27 Today the Assembly of the First Nations of Quebec and Labrador (AFNQL) (footnote added by reviewer in the 2015 French version). As I explain in the Afterword, rather, the Indians of Quebec Association is an "ancestor," or "predecessor," of the AFNQL.

28 Jean Chrétien, former Minister of Indian and Northern Affairs Canada (INAC), 1968–1974. (Renamed in 2015 Indigenous and Northern Affairs Canada, INAC was dissolved in 2017 and replaced with two separate departments, Indigenous Services Canada and Crown-Indigenous Relations and Northern Affairs Canada.)

29 In the 1976 French translation, the Innu word *katipaitsheu* [*katipaitshesht*] (229) was translated as "ingénieur" – engineer. However, in the 2019 revised translation, it has been corrected to "arpenteur" – surveyor.

30 As I explain in the Afterword, the French word "sauvagesse" – used in both the Innu original and in the French translation – is gendered and difficult to render as such in English. Kapesh's use of the French word in the Innu text, however, is interesting and can be read as an attempt to reclaim and reappropriate it, by coupling it with a sense of pride on her part.

Tanite nene etutamin nitassi?

What Have You Done
to My Country?

I

Mishta-shashish, tshishennu tapan anite minashkuat.
Mishta-uinipishiu mak ussima kanuenimeu. Iapit
nenua ussima uinipishinua.

Ne tshishennu, anite etat minashkuat e peikussit,
nenu eshinniut mashkatenitakushu eshpish innishit. Apu
tshekuannu nutepanit, mishtaminupu. Utassi mishta-
minuashinu kie mishta-mishanu, ushipima mitshetuait
anite uinipekut ut uauinupannua. Kie anite etat minashkuat, uin e peikussit pakassitishu.

Anite etat apu tshekuannu nitautshitat. Mitshiminu
apu nitautshitat kie minisha apu nitautshitat. Mitshetuait
eishinakushiniti aueshisha tanua, namesha kie, mitshetuait anite shakaikanissit kie shipit tanua. Kie nenua
minisha mitshetuait eishinakuanniti kassinu anite nitau-
tshinnua shetshen. Eukuannu nenu muk^u eshi-pakassiut kie
tapue minuinniuat ashit ussima, nanitam ussi-mitshiminu
mitshuat. Ne tshishennu namaienu shunianu eshi-pakassiut. Apu nishtuapatak shunianu usham apu nita uapatak. Mishkut tapue nenu utassi nanitam uashkamanu.

Anite etat minashkuat apu tshekuannu anite takuannit
tshetshi matshi-natukunikatakut. Iakushiti, uin uetshit
natukuitishu. Anite assit ekute uet utinak tshekuannu tshe
natukuitishuatshet. Kie nenua passe aueshisha ka taniti
utassit iapit anite ut mishkam^u e minuanit natukunnu.

Ne tshishennu kassinu eishinakushiniti aueshisha
ka ut inniut, kassinu nenua mishta-ishpitenimeu. Apu

I

A very long time ago, there was an old man who lived in the woods. His skin was very dark. He was raising his grandson, who also had very dark skin.

The old man, who was alone in the woods, had a remarkable way of living, it was so ingenious. He lacked nothing, he was very well off. His territory was very beautiful and very big. He had many rivers that flowed into the sea.[1] And in the woods, where he lived, he depended only on himself for his subsistence.

Where he lived, he did not cultivate anything. He did not grow either his food or his fruit. There were several species of animals, there were also several species of fish in the lakes and rivers. As for the fruit, several varieties grew naturally all over the place. Those were his only resources. His grandson and he were in good health. They always ate fresh food. It was not thanks to money that the old man provided for his needs. He did not know about money, he had never seen any. On the other hand, his territory was always clean.

In the woods where he lived, there was nothing that could poison him. When he was ill, he took care of himself. It was from the earth that he took what he needed to cure himself. He could also find good remedies from certain animals in his territory.

The old man had a great respect for all the species of animals upon which he depended to live. He never wasted

nita metuatshet kie apu nita nipaiat shetshen peik[u]
eshinakushiniti aueshisha. Assinu iapit ishpitenitam[u] :
nipinu, ashininu, nekanu, kassinu eishitakuannit
anite assit. Mishtikua apu nita tshimakauat shetshen.
Utshua, shipua, shakaikanissa, shipissa, uin nenu
kassinu uauitam[u] tshe ishinikateniti. Kie nenua ussima
utishinikashunnu, uin nenu mineu.

   Nenua ussima kenuenimat mishta-shuenimeu kie
mamitunenimeu nete nikan. Kassinu tshekuannu
tshishkutamueu e natauti, uitsheueu kie nanitam tipatshi-
mushtueu anite utat tipatshimunnu, miam utauia kie
umushuma utipatshimunnu. Kie uetakussiniti eshk[u] eka
nipaniti, ussima nanitam pitama atanukueu. Ne auass
nanikutini puamu. Ueniti tshietshishepaushiniti ekue
tipatshimushtuat umushuma ka ishi-puamut. Ne tshishennu
uin ekue uitamuat ussima essishuemakannit nenu
upuamunnu. Kie ne auass nanitam tapueu peuamuti.

   Ne tshishennu nenu assinu nutim eshpishanit kassinu
nete aitutaieu nenua ussima tshetshi minu-nishtuapa-
taminiti. Anite etat minashkuat, apu auennua mamashiat
kie apu auennua mamashikut. Uiapamati auennua, eukuannua muk[u] aueshisha uiapamat mak pietaki tshekuannu,
eukuannua muk[u] uishkatshana pietuat e tatuetaminiti
anite uashka uitshit.

   Ne auass mishta-minuateu nenua umushuma kie apu
nita mueshtatak. Minuatam[u], papu kie mamitshetuait
aishi-metueu. Nanikutini uitsheuku umushuma mietueti.
Miam tekuatshinniti ushkat meshkutinniti, shushkua-
teimuat anite mishkumit, umassinuaua muk[u] apashtauat.
Nanikutini shuakueuat. Ne auass apu nita tshiamapit
pitukamit. Ishi-tshishkutamaku umushuma tshetshi eka
tshitimit kie ashit tshetshi eka ishpishit tshetshi matshi-
kaushit. Ne tshishennu mashkatenitakushu eshpish
pikutat tshe aishi-tshishkutamuat nenua ussima.

or killed an animal for no reason, no matter what kind. He also respected the land: the water, the stones, the sand, and everything that can be found on the land. He never cut down a tree unnecessarily. He is the one who gave a name to the mountains and the rivers, to all the lakes and the rivers. He is also the one who gave a name to his grandson.

He loved the grandson for whom he was responsible very much and thought about his future. When he was out hunting, he taught him everything. He took him along and always told him stories about the past, stories from his own father and his grandfather. And in the evening, before his grandson went to sleep, he would always tell him legends. The child dreamed sometimes. When he woke up, in the morning, he would tell his grandfather about his dream and the old man would explain what it meant. Whatever the child dreamt about always happened.

The old man would bring his grandson all over the land so that he would know it perfectly. Where he lived, in the middle of the woods, he did not bother anyone and no one bothered him. The only beings that he would see were the animals and the only noise he would hear were the calls of the jays around his camp.

The child loved his grandfather very much and was never bored. He was well, he laughed. He had all sorts of games. Sometimes his grandfather would go play with him. At the first frosts of autumn, they would skate on the ice in their moccasins. Sometimes, they would go tobogganing. The child never stayed indoors doing nothing. His grandfather taught him not to be lazy and not to find time for being bothersome. It was surprising to see how gifted the old man was at providing such an education to his grandson.

Ne auass apu nita manatuet tanite ne tshishennu apu auat takuannit umanatueun. Muk^u nenu tshekuannu ka apatannit mak nenu tshekuannu ka itenitakuannit tshetshi ut inniuht eukuannu muk^u eishi-mamitunenitak tshetshi ishi-tshishkutamuat nenua ussima. Eishinakushiniti aueshisha kie namesha kie eishinikatakanniti aueshisha kie namesha, kassinu nenu uauitamueu nenua ussima.

The child never swore, the old man did not even know any swear words. The only things he wanted to teach his grandson were useful and necessary things for life. He explained everything he needed to know about the different species of mammals and fish.

II

Ne aueshish eishinakushit kie namesh menushkaminiti
kassinu tshimakateu. Ekᵘ ne uin tshishennu itenitakushu
nanitam nanatuapameu aueshisha e uinnuniti tshetshi
muat, nanitam piminu ui mitshu. Nenua ussima peikuan
etenitakushiniti. Ekue itat ussima :

– Nitshissenimau peikᵘ aueshish apu nita tshimakatet
napinniti, nete tau uinipekut, atshikᵘ ishinikatakanu, iteu.
Tshika itutenan nete uinipekut tshetshi natshi-muakᵘ
atshikᵘ, tshe ishpish ashuapatamakᵘ tshetshi minushit
aueshish kie namesh ute etaiakᵘ, iteu.

Ekue tipatshimushtuat ussima :

– Nananat nutauinanat kie nimushuminanat,
eukuannu tutamupanat uinuau menushkaminiti :
nashipepanat nete uinipekut kie eukuannua atshikua
ishi-pakassiuipanat mak tshiashku-uaua mak tshiashkussa, iteu. Tekushinitaui kau ute nutshimit, petapanat
atshiku-piminu. Kie tshinanu takushiniakui kau ute
minashkuat, tshika petanan atshiku-pimi, iteu.

Ne tshishennu itenitakushipan anite pet utat, tshekuannu katshi issishueti tshetshi tutak, nanitam uemut ui
tutamupan. Nenua ussima tshetshi tshissinuapamikut uet
tutak. Ne auass minuenitamᵘ nenu etikut umushuma.

– Nipa minueniten tshetshi uapataman nete uinipekut
eshkᵘ e inniut nimushum, itenitamᵘ.

Pitshenik shetshishu nenua umushuma tshetshi
nipiniti.

II

When the season came for the snow to melt, all the species of mammals and fish would grow thin. The old man, knowing this, looked for fat animals to feed himself. He always liked to eat fat. His grandson had the same habit.

— I know an animal that is never thin during the summer, the old man told his grandson. He lives by the sea. We call him *atshuk*. We will go to the coast and eat seal until the animals and the fish are good to eat again here.

Then he added:

— That is what our fathers and our grandfathers did at the beginning of summer. They went down to the sea and lived off seal, eggs, and young seagulls. When they returned inland, they brought back seal oil. We too, upon our return to the woods, we will bring some back.

The old man always had one habit: when he said he was going to do something, he always had to do it. By doing so, he wanted his grandson to follow his example. The child, delighted by what his grandfather had said, thought:

— I would be happy to see the sea while my grandfather is still alive.

He had started to worry that his grandfather would die.

– Shash tshishenniu, itenimeu.

Ne tshishennu katshi tshishi-mamitunenitak nenu ua nashipet ekue uaueshtat utush. Ushkuai-utinu ishi-nakuannu utush nenu tshe apashtat tshe nashipet. Katshi uaueshtat utush ekue naushunak shipinu e mishishtikua-nit ekue itat ussima :

— Eukuan ne shipu tshe apashtaiak[u] nuash tshe takushiniak[u] nete uinipekut, iteu. Mishta-shipu ishini-kateu. Nete pessish uinipekut tau namesh, mishishtu. Utshashumek[u] ishinikatakanu. Tshitshue minushiu, pimiu, mishta-uitshitu e muakanit, iteu.

Ne tshishennu eukuannu epushit ashit ussima. Nenu niashipet kassinu etatinniti shakaikana kie kassinu etatinniti kapatakana uauitamueu eishinikateniti nenua ussima nuash ishpish uinipekut. Tekushiniht nete uini-pekut, mishta-minu-tshishikanu kie minupeiashinu. Ne tshishennu ekue aitapit kassinu nete taukam kie nete katak[u] naneu. Nete ishpimit iapit aitapu. Apu tshekuannu uapatak maniteu-tshekuannu, apu auennua taniti kie apu tshekuannu petak tshetshi tatueuetakannit. Eukuannua muk[u] tshiashkua uiapamat kie eukuannua muk[u] pietuat. Ekue itikut ussima :

– Nimushum, tapue minuashu assi kie nekau kie nipi, itiku.

Ekue itat nenua ussima :

– Nititeniten nin eukuan uin Ka Tipenitak uiapamak[u] tshatapatamakui ne assi eshpish minuashit kassinu anite, iteu.

Katshi aitapit kassinu nete katak[u], ne tshishennu ekue manukashut anite naneu nekat. Ekue itat ussima :

– Tshika naneueinan uenapissish, tshika nanatuapamanan atshik[u], iteu.

Ne auass minuenitam[u] nenu etikut umushuma usham minuatam[u] uiapatak kassinu anite naneu eshpish minua-shinit. Ekue itat umushuma :

– He is getting old, he thought.

Having decided to go down to the sea, the old man repaired his birchbark canoe. This is how he travelled to the coast. When the canoe was repaired, he chose a large river and said to his grandson:

– This is the river we will follow; it is called *Mishta-Shipu*. Near the coast, there is a kind of fish, a big fish, that we call *utshashumek*. It is very beautiful, it is fat and very good to eat.

And so the old man sets out on his journey with his grandson. All the way down the river until the ocean, he tells him all the names of all the lakes and portages. Upon their arrival on the coast, the weather is beautiful and the water calm. The old man looks out to sea and up and down the coastline scanning the sky. He does not see anything unusual: there is nobody, no unnecessary noise to be heard. All one can see and hear were the seagulls. So, his grandson says:

– Grandfather, how beautiful, the land, the sand, the water...

And the old man answers:

– Looking at this scenery, I think it is the Creator himself that we are seeing, it is so beautiful.

After contemplating the horizon, the old man sets up camp on the sandy beach.

– We will follow the shoreline for a while in search of seals, says the old man to his grandson.

He is delighted by what his grandfather says, he enjoys admiring the beauty of the shoreline.

– Uenashk uta tshinipi ! Nanatuapamatau atshik^u kie tshiashku-uaua mak tshiashkussat ka ishin, iteu.

Ne tshishennu ekue itat ussima :

– Eka ma shuk^u aiashikuashi ! Tshuapamin eshpish tshishenniuian, nitaieshkushin nin. Tshitshisseniten eshpish pitshat uetuteiak^u, iteu.

Ne tshishennu ekue utinak utush ekue naneueik nenu uinipekunu ashit ussima. Kie tapue uipat uapameu atshikua, mitshetinua, mitshetuait nete ut papekupenua ekue nipaiat peik^u. Apu anu ui nipaiat shetshen, apu ui nanuiat. Katshi nipaiat peik^u tshetshi muat, minuenitam^u ekue tshiueunat uitshit. Ekue itat ussima :

– Eukuan tshe ashteieshkushian uenapissish. Shash takuan tshimitshiminan.

Ekue naikuat nenua atshikua ashit ekue putatak nenu uikuaiatshikunu, ekue pashak tshetshi ashtat nenu pimia-tshikunu tshetshi tshiuetatat nete nutshimit. Katshi muaht nenua atshikua e uinnuniti, e nishiht mishta-mi-nuenitamuat, papuat.

Tatutshishikua katshi nutapiht, minuat kutaka eshi-nakushiniti uinipeku-aueshisha ui mueuat. Ne tshishennu kassinu nete minishtikut aituteu uinipekut. Tshiashku-uaua nanatuapatam^u kie tshiashkussa ui nipaieu tshetshi muat. Nenua tshiashku-uaua meshkak, utinam^u muk^u tshe-tshi mitshit, apu shetshen mautat. Minu-nishtuapatam^u kassinu nenu tshekuannu ka ut inniut. Pineshu eishi-nakushit tau eka matshinanuniti uaua. Ne tshishennu nenu uiapatak, nishtuapatam^u kie apu utinak shetshen. Kie nenua ussima nishtutamunieu tshetshi eka nita utinami-niti nenua uaua eka ka mitshinanuniti. Uiapataki uaua ka mitshinanuniti, nishtuapatam^u nenu shash peneshishunit kie nenu eshk^u eka peneshishunit. Etenitaki tshetshi uti-nak tshetshi mitshit, uauapatam^u nenu eka peneshishunit. Eukuannu uetinak. Nenu peneshishunit, kau ekue ashtat anite utshishtunnit nenua pineshua.

– Quick, hurry up! Let's go look for seals, eggs, and young seagulls, like you taught me!

The old man says to his grandson:

– Stop shouting at me! You can see how old I am. I am tired, me. You know how far we have come.

They get in their canoe and follow the shoreline. Soon enough they spot several seals emerging from the water in different places. They do not want to kill more than they need so as not to waste any. They are satisfied with killing one to eat and bring it back to their camp.

– At last, I will rest a bit, said the old man. We now have something to eat.

After cleaning the seal, they inflate the paunch and dry it so that they can put in it the oil that they want to bring back to their territories. Both are very happy to have eaten fatty seal, and they laugh.

A few days later, wanting to eat another kind of animal that one finds by the sea, the old man travels to the islands along the coast. He searches for eggs and young seagulls to kill. When he finds seagull eggs, he only takes what he can eat, he does not take more unnecessarily. He knows well what he needs to subsist. Among the species of birds, there are some whose eggs one does not eat. When the old man sees those, he does not take them for nothing. Thus, he teaches his grandson to never take the eggs that one does not eat. He knows how to tell which ones are about to hatch from those that are not yet as far along. If he is look-ing for eggs to eat, he chooses freshly laid ones. As for those that have been brooded, he puts those back into the bird's nest.

Minuat ekue tutak uashuakanashkua ekue itutet nete
etaniti utshashumekua. Ekue itat ussima :
– Anutshish tshe tipishkat, tshika uashuanan.
Nipaiakui utshashumek[u], nika pashuau tshetshi
nimauiak[u] kushpiakui.
Ekue uashuaht tepishkanit. Nisht[u] katshi nipaiaht :
– Eukuan tshe ishpish nipaiak[u], tshika ishpannan.
Minekashish tshika muanan utshashumek[u], iteu.
Ne tshishennu katshi ashteieshkushit ekue itat ussima :
– Eukuan tshe tshiueiak[u]. Petshikatshish tshika tshi-
uenan miam tshe ishpish minushit namesh kie kutak
aueshish ka tat nete nutshimit, iteu.
Ua tshiuet kau nete nutshimit, minuat ekue uaueshtat
utush tshetshi eka mamashikut usham pitshanu tshe
itutet. Nenu tshauet kau nete katak[u] nutshimit, iapit
eukuannu Mishta-shipinu e apashtat nuash tekushinit
nete utitaunit. Nenu tshauet, petshikatshish tshiueu tanite
ashit eshakumitshishikua nanatauitishu natamik[u] eishinakushiniti aueshisha. Nenua ussima shash pikutanua e
peikussiniti tshetshi natauniti. Namesha nepaiataui eka
e uinnuniti ekue pimikatuaht nenu atshiku-piminu ka
mautaht anite uikuaiatshikut.
Tekushiniht anite utitaunuat, apishish aieshkushiu ne
tshishennu. Shash mamitunenitam[u] nenu eshpitishit.
Pitshenik ui uaueshtau utatusseun. Ekue itat nenua ussima :
– Niminueniten katshi tshishkutamatan kassinu
tshekuan kie katshi uapatinitan nutim eshpishat tshiti-
penitamunnu eshk[u] e inniuian kie katshi uapatinitan
eishinakushit aueshish nete ka tat uinipekut. Aishkat itu-
teini e peikussin, apu tshika ut animiuin. Tshitshisseniten
shash tshekat tshika peikussin, tshika nakatitin, uemut
nika nipin, tshuapamin shash nimishta-tshishenniun.
Tshitshissenimitin ennishin. Tutamini kassinu miam ka
ishi-tshishkutamatan, ishi-atusseshtatishuini miam ka

Later, he makes a *nigog* and goes to where the salmon are. He tells his grandson:

— This time, we are going to fish with the *nigog* when night falls. If we kill salmon, I will dry it and that will serve as provisions for our trip back inland.

After catching three salmon, the old man says:

— We will stop catching them now, this will suffice. We will have enough to eat for a long time.

After resting, the old man says to his grandson:

— Now we are going to go back home. We will go slowly so as to leave time for the fish and other animals back home to be good to eat again.

Having decided to return inland, he repairs his canoe so as not to have troubles before taking on their long journey. In order to return to the hinterland, he once again travels along the Moisie River that brings him all the way home. He travels without haste because every day he has to hunt for some animal or other to feed himself. His grandson can now hunt on his own. When they catch a fish that is not fat, they pour oil on it, that which they put in the seal's paunch.

Upon their return, the old man feels a bit tired. He starts to think about his old age and decides to put his affairs in order.

— I am happy to have taught you everything, to have shown you the vastness of our domain during my lifetime and to have shown you the different animals that live on the coast. Later, when you will go there on your own, it will not be difficult. You know that you will soon be alone because I am going to have to leave you. I have to die, you can see that I am old. I know that you are sensible. If you do everything the way I taught you, if you work for yourself with as

ishi-tshitapamin ka ishpish minuataman e atusseian, tshe
ishpish inniuin apu nita tshika ut animiuin, iteu. Uesh
ma ute ka ut inniuiak[u], kassinu eshpishat nitipenitamun
eukuan tshin nutim tshe nakatamatan, iteu.

Ne auass nenu etikut umushuma, tshitapameu kie
mashkatenitam[u].

– Apu tshekuannu kanuenitak, itenimeu.

Ekue itat umushuma :

– Tshekuan ne tshe nakatamuin nimushum ? iteu.

Ne tshishennu ekue itat ussima :

– Nitassi nutim eshpishat ashit kassinu eishitakuak :
aueshishat eishinakushiht, nameshat kassinu eishinakushiht, mishtikuat, shipua kassinu etatiki, eukuan
ne tshe ishi-nakatamatan tshekuan. Aianishkat eukuan
nanitam tshe ut inniuin, iteu. Ne aueshish eishinakushit
ka ut inniuiak[u] tshika nipaiau eshpish ui apatshit. Eka uin
manatshi e ui minu-apatshiti uesh ma ne aueshish eukuan
eshinakuak tshinanu tshipakassiunnan. Ume tshekuan
tshe uitamatan eka nita uni-tshissi, iteu. Tshe ishpish inniuin, tshe tutamin miam ka tutaman, tshe ishpitenimat
kassinu eishinakushit aueshish. Eka uin nita pitama me-
tuatshe ua nipaiti kie eka uin nipai shetshen nuash tshetshi
nanuit, iteu, uesh ma nete aianishkat eukuan kie tshin
nanitam tshe ishi-pakassiuin. Mak eka uin nita utin
peik[u] eshinakushit aueshish tshetshi kanuenimat, iteu.
Mak tshe ishpish inniuin, tshe ui nashuin ka ishpish
mishta-kutshipanitaian nanitam tshetshi minu-
pakassitishuian. Tshe mitimein nanitam aianishkat
tshinanu tshimeshkanaminan, iteu.

Ne auass shash tshissenitam[u] tshe nakatikut umushuma,
tshe nipiniti, tshe peikussit anite minashkuat. Muk[u] apu
tshekuannu itenitak.

– Tapue apu tshekuan nutepanian, shash kassinu
tshekuannu nitshishkutamakuti nimushum, itenitam[u].

much love for your task as you saw me do, you will never in your life have any hardship. Since it is here that we lived, you and me, it is to you that I will leave all that I have.

The child looks at his grandfather, surprised.

– He does not own anything, he thought.
He says to his grandfather:
– What will you leave me, grandfather?
And the old man responds:
– The whole of my territory with everything upon it. All the kinds of animals, the kinds of fish, the trees, all the rivers, that is what I will leave you as inheritance. From generation to generation, it is on this that you will depend forever to live. You will kill, as long as it is necessary, all the species of animals on which we have lived, you and me. Do not spare them if it is for your own reasonable use, because you know that that is our means of existence. Never forget what I am going to tell you: Throughout your life, you will do as I did: you will respect all the species of animals. Never make them suffer before killing them and never go so far as to waste them by killing them for no reason because you too, for generations to come, it is on them that you will depend to live. And also, never catch an animal to keep it in captivity, no matter what kind. For all of your life, you will try to follow my example: I have tried hard to be self-sufficient. In the times to come, you will follow the path that we have traced, you and me.

The child knows that his grandfather is going to leave him. He knows he is going to die. He will be alone in the woods. But he is not worried.

– I truly have everything that I need, he thought, my grandfather taught me everything.

III

Katshi nipiniti umushuma, ne auass ekue puamut. Eukuannu eshi-puamut :

— E papamuteian minashkuat, e natauian,
ninatshishkuauat auenitshenat. Uapishiuat mak kassinu
etashiht ishinakushuat miam eka ennishitaui, mishta-
utshepiuat kie e pimutetaui mishta-tshishipanuat. Kassinu
etashiht mishta-tshishkueienitakushuat, ishi-puamu.

Piekupanit papu.

— Kauitenitakushiht nipuatauat, itenitam[u].

Kutshipanitau e peikussit tshetshi nishtutak upuamun.

— Nasht nika utitik[u] Atshen, eshi-puamuian...,
itenitam[u].

Nenu katshi puamut, apu minekash tapue takushinnua
maniteua, uapishinua mak petanua tshekuannu tshetshi
atauatsheniti. Enut uiapamat maniteua, apu kushtat.

— Eukuan ne peik[u] ka puatak, e uitenitakushiht auenitshenat, itenitam[u].

Tshimut ekue nakatuapamat eitiniti muk[u] apu ui
manenimat kie apu ui matshi-tutuat.

— Kau tshika tshiueu..., itenimeu.

Tshiam ekue pushukatat. Ne kauitenitakusht pushukatikut nenua auassa mishta-minuenitam[u], mishta-
tshishkueienitakushu. Mishta-utsheshtiapiu usham
nenu mamitunenitam[u] ka ishi-petat tshekuannu tshetshi
atauatshet. Katshi pushukatikut nenua auassa, uenashk
ekue uapatiniat nishtam passikannu mak mukumannu

III

After the death of his grandfather, the child has a dream:

He is walking through the forest to hunt, he meets people. They are white and they all look ridiculous. They are in a great hurry, they walk quickly and all look very excited.

When he awakens, he smiles.

– I dreamt about Polichinelles.

He tries on his own to understand the meaning of the dream:

– *Atshen* is surely going to come this way..., he thinks.

Not long after, a stranger with white skin indeed arrives, carrying goods. This is the first time that the child sees a stranger, but he is not afraid of him.

– It is one of the Polichinelles that I dreamt of, he tells himself.

Casually, he observes his doings but he does not intend to offend him or to harm him.

– He will leave again..., he thinks.

So he shakes his hand politely. The Polichinelle is delighted and excited to have his hand shaken by the child. He is very nervous because he is thinking about what he has brought to sell. Without delay, he shows him a gun, then a long knife with a wide blade. The

tshinuapishkanu mak anakashkapishkanu. Ne kauitenitakusht kie ne auass e nishiht tapishkut animiuat tshetshi
nishtutatuht e aimituht. Ashit utitshiuaua apashtauat,
eishi-uashteimatuht tshetshi nishtutatuht ua aimituht
kie kutshipanitauat e nishiht tshetshi tshishkutamatuht
utaimunuaua.

   Ne auass uiapatak nenu passikannu kie mukumannu
ekue papit, mushtuenitam^u tshetshi kanuenitak. Ne kauitenitakusht uiapamat nenua auassa piapiniti, anu tshishkueienitakushu ekue itat :

   – Minini tat^u shuniau-aueshishat, tshika minitin ume
passikan. Peikuan ume mukuman, pikutaini tshetshi
minin tat^u uapishtanat, tshika minitin, iteu.

   Ne auass apu anuetuat nenu etikut tanite eukuannu
ushkat tshashikashut tshekuannu ekue minat tat^u shuniau-
aueshisha tshetshi minikut peik^u passikannu mak peik^u
mukumannu. Ne kauitenitakusht katshi minikut nenua
auassa tat^u shuniau-aueshisha, ekue mishta-papit ekue
itenitak :

   – Apu nita tshika ut tshiueian ute katshi takushinian.
Ekute ute tshe ut uenutishian, itenitam^u.

   Ne auass katshi tshishikashut nenu upassikan kie umu-
kuman, ekue tshitapatak tshetshi uitak tshe ishinikatak.
Mekuat e uauapatak, minuat kutaka kauitenitakushiniti
takushinnua. Iapit uapishinua kie iapit tshishkueienita-
kushinua muk^u iapit apu kushtat, iapit tshimut nakatua-
pameu eitiniti. Peikuan apu ui manenimat kie apu ui
matshi-tutuat.

   – Tshika tshiueu uipat kau…, itenimeu.

   Tshiam ekue pushukatat. Ne kauitenitakusht epushukatikut nenua auassa, tapue tshishkueienitakushu,
mishta-minekash aiatshipitamueu utitshinu ekue itat :

   – Nikuss, tapue tshiminupin ute etain minashkuat.
Minuashu kie mishau tshitassi, iteu. Apu ui mamashitan.

Polichinelle and the child both have trouble understanding each other as well. In order to make sense of
their words, they each make gestures with their hands
and each tries to teach his language to the other.

Seeing the gun and the knife, the child smiles, he
would like to possess them. Seeing his smile, the Polichinelle gets even more excited.

– If you give me this many pelts, he tells him, I will
give you this gun. It is the same for this knife, I will give
it to you if you can bring me this many marten pelts.
The child does not say no to this proposal, it is the
first time that he pays for something. So he gives him
a certain amount of pelts so that the other will give
him a gun and a knife. After receiving the pelts from
the child, the Polichinelle bursts out laughing.

– Now that I have come here, I will never go away,
this is where I will make my fortune, he thinks.
The child looks at his gun and his knife atten-
tively to give them a name. While he examines them,
another Polichinelle arrives. This one is white too,
and he is all excited as well. Once again, the child is
not afraid and he watches him without him knowing. Likewise, he does not intend to offend or to harm
him.
– He will go away soon..., he thinks.
And he shakes his hand without a second thought.
The Polichinelle is very excited to have his hand shaken
by the child, he shakes it for a long time and says:
– My son, you are really well off here in the woods.
Your land is beautiful and big, I do not want to disturb

Nitakushin tshetshi tshishkutamatan aiamieun mak tshitishinikashun nika tuten. Tshika ishinikatitin miam ninan kie eukuan nanitam tshe ishinikashuin aianishkat, iteu. Ushkat e tshitshipaniak[u], nishtam tshin tshika tshishkutamun tshitaimun tshetshi tshishkutamatan aiamieun kie aiamieu-mashinaikan eshi-aimin, muk[u] uenapissish tshetshi apashtain, iteu. Aishkat kau ninan eshi-aimiat tshika ishi-tshishkutamatin aiamieun kie peikuan ne aiamieu-mashinaikan. Minuat nete katak[u] aianishkat, kau minuat tshe ishi-tshishkutamatan aiamieun eshi-aimin. Eka uin mashkatenita kie eka uin uitenita nikuss, eka uin ne ut ui pikuna tshishtikuan tatuau tshe mishkutunaman tshitaimun, iteu.

Ne auass tapuetueu etikut nenua kauitenitakushiniti muk[u] tshimut mashkatenimeu kie tshimut shetshiku kie ashit shash uitenimeu.

– Apu innishit nenu essishuet..., itenimeu.

Ekue tshishkutamuat nishtam nenu uin utaimun tshetshi tshishkutamakut aiamieunnu eshi-aimit mak aiamieu-mashinaikannu. Katshi tshishkutamatishut aia-mieunnu eshi-aimit, minuenitam[u] kie tapuetam[u] mak mishta-ishpitenitam[u]. Kie nenu aiamieu-mashinaikannu katshi nishtuapatak eshi-aimit, nanitam tshitapatam[u] ashit nanitam nikamu aiamieu-nikamuna. Eshi-natshish-kaki tshetshi animiut, eukuannu aiamieunnu nanitam etishimut tanite mishta-shutshenitam[u] aiamieunnu. Anu shutshenimu kassinu tshekuannu ua tutaki.

Ne kauitenitakusht mashten ekue itat nenua auassa :

– Tshe ishpish inniunanut, iapit apu nita anu tshin tshika ut shutshenimitan ne ut tshitaimun. Iapit nin nanitam nika takuaimaten ne tshitaimun, iteu.

Ne auass nenu etikut, apu tshekuannu itenitak.

you. I have come here to teach you about religion and
to make up a name for you. I will give you a name like
ours. This is the one that you will pass on from generation to generation. To start, you will first teach me
your language so that I can teach you the prayers and
the missal in your own language. But that will only
serve you for a short amount of time. Later, it is in our
own language that I will teach them to you. Then, in
a distant future, I will teach you about religion again
in your own language. Do not be surprised and do not
laugh, my son. I will change your language a certain
amount of times but do not rack your brain over it.

The child approves of what the Polichinelle says
but, inwardly, he is surprised and afraid. Otherwise,
he finds him amusing.

– He is not very smart to say such things…, he
muses.

First, the child teaches him his language so that
the other can teach him the prayers and missal in that
language. After he has learned the prayers, the child
is happy, he is a believer and he has a lot of respect
for religion. Now that he knows the missal in his language, he reads it incessantly and sings hymns constantly. When he encounters difficulties, he turns to
prayer in which he has great faith. He is surer of himself in everything he undertakes.

Upon leaving him the Polichinelle tells the child:

– As long as the world exists, it will never be you
that I trust the most when it comes to your language.
Anyway, it is I who will always govern it.

The child remains indifferent to these words. He
does not respond.

– Apu tapuet. Apu tshika ut tat ute, tshika tshiueu…, itenimeu.

Apu tshekuannu itat.

Ne auass katshi natshishkuat umenua kauitenitakushiniti, minuat uapameu kutaka auennua pietashtamuteniti. Petanua miutinu, mishta-mishanu. Uiapamat kutaka auennua netuapamikut, iapit tshiam ekue natu-natshishkuat, tshiam ekue pushukatat.

– Kau put tshika tshiueu…, itenimeu.

Ne kauitenitakusht katshi pushukatikut nenua auassa, ekue minat nenu tshekuannu ka petat ekue itat :

– Umenu matshunishinu mak mitshiminu tshititishaimak^u nutshimaminan, iteu.

Ne auass mishta-minuenitam^u kie pakuatam^u tshetshi uapatak nenu tshekuannu ka itishaimakut nenua utshimau-kauitenitakushiniti. Nishtam nenu matshunishinu eukuannu uiauapatak ekue mishkak uapuiannu, uapinuanu mak mishta-kauekannu. Mak ekue mishkak massina, makununua, kashteuanua mak mishta-kanuapekannua. Minuat nenu mitshiminu ekue uauapatak. Mishkueu shaieua mak utamakan-kukusha.

Ne auass nenu katshi uauapatak, ui shakuenimu mak ui tshishuapu tshimut. Muk^u apu tshekuannu issishuet.

– Nui manenimik^u, akushunnu mak uinnakushunnu petau, itenimeu.

Ekue tutak ishkutenu e mishanit ekue uepimitak nenu uapuiannu anite ishkutet kie nenua massina. Ekue utinak nenua utamakan-kukusha ekue akutat anite mishtikut, uishkatshana ashameu. Nenua shaieua ekue kuanikupitat anite assit, anikutshasha tshetshi muaniti.

Ne auass eshk^u mishta-minuatam^u anite etat minashkuat kie eshk^u nanitam natau. Pitshenik uakaiku nenua kauitenitakushiniti.

– He is lying. He will not stay here, he will go away..., he thinks.

He does not say anything.

After meeting that last Polichinelle, the child sees another figure coming towards him. This one is carrying a very big package. Once again the child goes to meet him and politely shakes his hand.

– Maybe he will go away again..., he tells himself.

After their handshake, the Polichinelle gives the child what he has brought and tells him:

– Here are clothes and food that our master sends you.

The child is very happy and impatient to see what the master of the Polichinelles has sent him. First he examines the clothes. There is a grey blanket, very rough, and a pair of black boots, very tall. Next, he examines the food: he finds beans and pork cheeks.

The child is embarrassed and angry. But he does not say a word.

– He wants to make fun of me. He brings me filth and sickness, he thinks.

So he lights a big fire and throws in the blanket and the boots. He takes the cheeks and suspends them from a tree branch, offering them to the jays. Then, he spreads the beans on the ground so that the squirrels can eat them.

The child still feels very well in the woods and continues to hunt. However, he is starting to become annoyed by all these Polichinelles.

– Shash nimamashikuat mak aiat apu innishiht,
itenimeu.

Katshi ishkuashak nenua matshunisha ka petakanniti,
minuat kutaka kauitenitakushiniti natuapamiku. At nenu
e uakaikut, tshiam ekue pushukatat. Apu tshissenimat tan
eshi-atusseniti. Ne kauitenitakusht epushukatikut nenua
auassa ekue itat :

– Eukuan nin tekushinian tshetshi natukuitan kie
eukuan nin nanitam aianishkat tshe natukuitan. Tshika
punitan e natukuitishuin mak nenua tshinatukunima
kassinu eishinakuaki tshika uepinen. Nete aishkat ninan
nenua nika atauatshenan kassinu anite natukunitshuapit,
iteu.

Ne auass tapuetam[u] nenu etikut kie tapue mishta-
shutshenimeu. Ekue itenitak tshetshi punitat nenu uin
uetshit ka natukuitishut kie nenua natukuna ka ishi-
kanuenitak nutim uepinam[u].

Ne auass mashkatenitam[u] nenu eitashumikut kauitenitakushiniti ekue itenitak :

– Tshekuannitshe etenitakushiht anitshenat tat[u] natua-
pamiht maniteuat ? Kassinu natamik[u] ishi-aimuat…,
itenitam[u].

Eshpish mamitunenimat, tshek ekue puamut. Eukuannu
eshi-puamut :

Nitamatshuen utshu, mishta-makatinau, ekue aitapian
nete katak[u]. Eshpish aitapian, tshek ekue petaman
tshekuan, anite ishpimit tatueuepanu. Ekue aitapian kassinu nete ishpimit. Tapue nuapamau pineshu, pet papanu,
mishta-mishishtu, uiesh miam shaputuan ishpishtitshe.
Nete itetshe uinipekut utshipanu. Ekue uapamak teueut
apu katak[u] etaian. Ashit ekue uapataman uashka etaian
mitshetuait uet uashashkutet, ishi-puamu. Eshpish aitapian
anite takutauat, tshek ekue utishit tshishennu, mishta-
tshishenniu. Ishi-aimu miam eshi-aimian ekue ishit :

– They are bothering me, and, they are being more and more stupid.

The child is visited by yet another Polichinelle. Although this one bothers him, he politely shakes his hand and wonders what kind of work he does. When he shakes his hand, the Polichinelle introduces himself:

– I am the one who has come to take care of you. It will always be me who will heal you henceforth. You will cease to do so yourself. You will get rid of your different medicines. From now on, it is we who will sell them in pharmacies.

The child approves of what the Polichinelle says and he trusts him greatly. He decides to no longer heal himself and throws away all the remedies that he possesses.

The child is surprised by the things that he is ordered to do.

– What is up with all these strangers coming to see me? They all talk such nonsense..., he thinks.

From all this thinking about them, he falls asleep and has a dream.

He climbs up a very high mountain and scans the horizon. He hears a sound coming from the sky. He looks everywhere and sees, coming towards him, an enormous bird the size of a *shaputuan*. The bird lands next to the child amid gleams of fire. Suddenly, an old man approaches and speaks to him in his language: "Here where you are living, in the middle of the woods, all the land will soon be named in a foreign language."

« Ute etain minashkuat, apu tshika ut minekash, nutim
eshpishat assi kutak eshi-aiminanut tshika ishinikateu »,
nitik⁽ᵘ⁾ ne tshishennu, ishi-puamu.

Ne auass kushtatshikushu nenu eshi-puamut. Uenit
tshietshishepaushinit, minekash mamitunenitam⁽ᵘ⁾
nenu upuamun. Kutshipanitau tshetshi nishtutak.
Tshissenitam⁽ᵘ⁾ iapit tshe uapatak upuamun, nanitam
tapueu peuamuti. Muk⁽ᵘ⁾ apu nishtutak e peikussit
puamunnu.

Tapue apu minekash e papamutet minashkuat, tshek
petam⁽ᵘ⁾ tshekuannu tetueuepannit. Ekue aitapit anite
ishpimit ekue uapamat upashtamakana piapanniti, nete
itetshe uinipekut utshipannua ekue tueuniti pessish etat.
Uapameu mitshetinua kauitenitakushiniti uet kapaniti,
passe petanua makanipakana mak uatshikatashkua.
Uiapamat uieshami-mitshetiniti tekushinniti, apu ui
natuapamat tshetshi pushukatat, shash apu minunuat
eshi-takushinniti. Ne upashtamakan katshi tueut anite
minashkuat, apu muk⁽ᵘ⁾ peikuau papanit kie aiat mami-
shishtuat piapaniht. Eukuanat pietautaht mitshetuait
eishinakuanniti atusseuakana. Ne auass mashkatenitam⁽ᵘ⁾
uiapatak nenu tshekuannu eishinakuannit pietautakannit.

– Tshekuannitshe ua tutahk ute…? itenimeu.

Ashit ashuapameu tshetshi aimikut. Apu natuapamikut tshetshi pushukatikut kie apu nashpit aimikut. Ne
peik⁽ᵘ⁾ kauitenitakusht ka petautat atusseuakana ekue
natuapamat nenua auassa ekue itat :

– Tshimikai nimitiminana, nui apashtanan mita, iteu.

Ne auass mashkatenitam⁽ᵘ⁾ nenu etikut.

– Atut tshika ut tshiueuat, ui apitshenat ute…,
itenimeu.

Muk⁽ᵘ⁾ iapit tshitimatshenimeu.

When he wakes up, the next morning, he thinks about it for a long time. He tries to understand. No matter what, he knows that his nightmare will come true. His dreams are always true. But on his own, he does not understand its meaning.

Indeed, shortly after, while walking in the woods, the child hears a strange sound. He looks up at the sky and sees a plane arriving from the sea that lands near him. He sees several Polichinelles get off the plane. Some are carrying shovels and pickaxes. Seeing so many arrive at once, he does not dare go close enough to shake their hands. It displeases him to see them appear like that. After landing in the woods, the plane makes other trips. Bigger and bigger ones arrive carrying all sorts of different machines. The child is stunned.

– What can they be planning to do here...? he wonders.
And he waits for them to come speak to him. One of the Polichinelles approaches the child and tells him:

– Cut us some firewood. We need it.
The child finds it strange to be asked that.
– Maybe in fact they will not leave, they must want to stay here..., he thinks.
Nevertheless, he pities them.

– Tapue nuapamauat, uinuau apu pikutaht ute minashkuat, itenimeu.

Ekue tutamuat umitiminua.

Anitshenat kauitenitakushiht mashten ka takushiniht, katshi uapatahk anite e apiniti nenua auassa, mushtena-mueuat utassinu.

– Tshima eka tat ute uin..., itenimeuat nenua auassa.

Kie shash apu nashpit apatenimaht. Muk^u uinuau nenu etashiht mamu ekue aimituht tshekuannu tshe tutahk. Ne kauitenitakusht peik^u ne nishtam eimit ekue issishuet :

– Ume anutshish tshe tshitshipaniak^u e atusseiak^u, nishtuait tshika ishi-atussenanu : passe shash tshika tshitshipanuat tshetshi munaihk utshua mak passe tshika tutamuat ishkuteutapan-meshkananu mak passe tshika tutamuat mitshuapinu anite tshetshi kanuenimakanit ne auass tshetshi eka mamashitak^u tshe ishpish atusseiak^u, iteu.

Minuat ekue issishuet :

– Tshishtaiakui ne ishkuteutapan-meshkanau, tshe ishpanit ishkuteutapan nete ka tat ne auass, tshe autaiak^u utshua. Papanitaiakui nete uinipekut, minuat tshe pushtaiak^u pineshautit, tshe atauatsheiak^u nete uiesh aka-meu ka utshipaniak^u, issishueu.

Ne kauitenitakusht ka minat nenua auassa utamakan-kukusha mak massina e kanuapekanniti mishta-pakuatam^u uenashk tshetshi ishpannit nenu eshi-uauitahk. Tapue nasht akushu kie shash utsheshtiapiu nenu ut ekue issishuet :

– Nika tuten uenashk etenitaman.

Ekue natuapamat nenua auassa ekue utshipitat ekue uepimitat nete ka ututet meshkananu, kauitenitakushiniti umeshkanaminu. Ne utshimau-kauitenitakusht mishta-minuenitam^u ekue issishuet :

– I can see that they do not know how to manage in the woods, he tells himself.

And he cuts them their firewood.

After seeing the place where the child lives, the last Polichinelles to arrive begin to covet his territory.

– If only he was not here..., they say to themselves, referring to the child.

And yet, they pay absolutely no attention to him. They speak of their projects strictly between themselves.

– Now, we will begin the work. We will separate into three groups: one group will dig in the mountains, one group will build a railway, and the third will erect a building where the child will be kept so that he does not bother us during the work.

And then they say:

– When we have finished the railway and a train can go to the child's land, we will transport the mountains. When we reach the coast, we will load them on a big ship and we will sell them somewhere on the other side of the ocean, there where we come from.

The Polichinelle who had given the pork cheeks and the boots to the child is impatient to see this project carried out without delay. It makes him so nervous, it literally makes him ill.

– I will, without delay, do what I have in mind! he claims.

He goes over to the child, catches him, and hurries him along on the path that he himself has just walked, the path of the Polichinelles. The Polichinelle-boss is very satisfied and says:

– Tshe ishpish inniunanut, nanitam nika tshipain nitukaia tshetshi eka nita petaman ne tipatshimun, ne auass uin nishtam katshi tat ute minashkuat, issishueu.

Ekue tutahk nikamunnu ekue nikamuht kassinu etashiht :

– U-ka-na-tau a-ia-nish-kat nu-ta-ui-nanat u-ta-ssi-uau…, ishi-nikamuat, mishta-minuatamuat.

– I will cover my ears until the end of time so that I will never hear someone say that it was this child who, the first, was here in the woods.

The Polichinelles then compose a hymn and all sing in chorus:

– O – Ca – na – da – our – home – and – na – tive – land..., they sing with great delight.

IV

Ne auass uin katshi uepimitakanit nete kauitenitakushiniti umeshkanaminit, ekuan etapit. Tshitapameu nenua
kauitenitakushiniti nekamuniti.

– Tshekuannitshe eshpish mishta-tshishkueiapatahk...?
itenimeu.

Anitshenat kauitenitakushiht katshi puniht e nikamuht, mamitunenitamuat, kushpinenimeuat nenua
auassa tshetshi kau tshiueniti nete ka taniti. Ne kauitenitakusht ka minat nenua auassa massina e kakanuapekan-
niti mak utamakan-kukusha ekue natuapamat ekue itat :

– Matshi tshitute nete ka ututeiat, mitime
nimeshkanaminan. Tshika minuaten kie apu tshika ut
animiuin kie apu tshekuan tshika ut nutepanin. Kassinu
tshekuan tshika minitinan shetshen, nuash shuniau tshika
minitinan, iteu. Kie tshika tshishkutamatinan anite ninan
nikatshishkutamatsheutshuapinat tshetshi ishinniuin
miam ninan kie tshetshi ishi-aimin miam ninan, iteu. Kie
nanitam tshika tauat auenitshenat tshe uitsheushkau, tshe
kanuenimishkau. Tshe ishpish mitimein nimeshkanaminan, nanitam tshika natshishkuauat kutakat auenitshenat
miam ume ninan etenitakushiat, iteu.

Ne auass ekue tshitutet. Tanua uatsheukut kauitenitakushiniti niakatuenimikut tshetshi eka nita ishi-kutshipa-
nitat tshetshi kau tshiuet.

Ne auass nenu tshetutet, apu minekash pimutet ekue
uapatak mitshuapinu tshematenit, mishta-mishanu. Ekue
itat nenua kauitenitakushiniti ka uitsheukut :

IV

Having been made to fall into the path of the Polichinelles, the child remains seated there, watching them
sing.

– What are they so excited about...? he wonders.

Once their song is finished, the Polichinelles start
to think. They worry that the child will return to
the place he came from. The Polichinelle who gave
him the boots and the pork cheeks goes over to him,
shouting:

– Go on, go away to where we have come from,
follow our path! You will like it, you will not have
any troubles, and you will want for nothing. We will
give you everything for free, we will even go so far as
to give you money. We will educate you in our own
school so that you can live like us and speak like us.
There will always be people to accompany you and
keep you. As long as you follow our path, you will
constantly meet more of our kind.

And so the child sets off. A Polichinelle accompa-
nies him and watches over him so that he does not
attempt to retrace his steps.

At a short distance from his starting point, the
child sees a big house.

– Tsheku-mitshuap ne ? iteu.

Kauitenitakusht ekue itat nenua auassa :

– Eukuan an nikatshishkutamatsheutshuapinan.

Ekute anite tshe kanuenimikauin uenapissish. Tshika shatshuapamitin nanikutini, tshe uitamuin animiuini.

Ekue minat etashtenit mitshuapinu anite tshe natua-pamikut ui uapamikuti.

Ne kauitenitakusht ekue pitukaiat nenua auassa anite ukatshishkutamatsheutshuapuat. Ekue itat nenua kutaka kauitenitakushiniti etaniti anite pitukamit :

– Ue auass, nimishkuatan nete minashkuat, iteu. Nipeshuau ute tshetshi kanuenimek[u] uenapissish tshetshi eka mamashitat nenu tshe ishpish atussenanunit nete ka tat minashkuat, iteu.

Ekue uauitamuat tshe ishi-tutuakanniti nenua auassa tshe kanuenimakanniti. Minekashish aimieu :

– Ue auass tshika uitamatinau tshe tutuek[u] tshe ish-pish kanuenimek[u] ute pitukamit. Uenapissish tshika maminuashiauau tshetshi shatshitak[u] kie tshetshi minu-atak nenu peikutau pitukamit tshe kanuenimek[u] kie tshetshi eka nita ishi-mamitunenitak tshetshi kau tshiuet nete ka tat minashkuat, iteu. Muk[u] ushkat kassinu tshekuannu tshika minauau shetshen. Tshika itasha-mauau miam tshinanu tshetshi uni-tshissitutak umitshim. Tshika ishi-tshishuashpitauau miam tshinanu eshi-tshishuashpishuiak[u] tshetshi uni-tshissitutak ka ishi-tshi-shuashpishut, iteu. Ashit tshika tshishkutamuauau miam tshinanu eshi-tshishkutamatishuiak[u]. Muk[u] uemut tshika nakatuenimauau akua ueshami-pikutati nenu tshe ishi-tshishkutamuek[u] uesh ma ne auass apu nishtuapamak[u], put anu uin tshipa tshi minuanu ushtikuan mak tshinanu, iteu. Ueshami-pikutati nenu tshinanu eshi-tshishkutamatishuiak[u], nete aishkat nanitam tshika uakaikunan, tshika nanatuenitamakunan pakassiunnu

– What is that, that house? he asks the Polichinelle.

The Polichinelle says to the child:

– That is our school, that is where you will be kept for a certain time. I will come see you sometimes and you will tell me if you are having any problems.

He gives him an address where he can find him if he wants to see him.

The Polichinelle brings the child to the school. He says to the Polichinelle inside:

– Here is a child that we found in the woods. I have brought him here for you to keep him. We must avoid that he bothers us as long as there will be a construction site in the woods, there where he was.

Then he explains to him at length how to treat the child left in his care:

– For some time, you will pamper him so that he likes us and appreciates that you keep him confined indoors and never thinks about returning to where he used to live. In the beginning only, you will give him everything for free. You will feed him like us so that he forgets his own food. You will clothe him like us so that he forgets his own ways of dressing. You will provide him with the same education as us. But at all costs you will have to make sure that he does not perform too well in his studies because we do not know this child. It may be that he is perhaps more intelligent than us. If he performs too well in the same kind of studies that we do, he will not cease to bother us later on, and he will demand to make a living the same way we do. During some time, you will teach him about sports to distract him. There too, you will have to keep an eye on him: make sure that he never outperforms us. I have one last thing to tell you: make sure

miam tshinanu eshi-pakassiuiak[u], iteu. Mak metueunnu
eishinakuannit uenapissish tshika tshishkutamuauau tshetshi eka mueshtatak. Muk[u] iapit uemut tshika nakatuenimauau akua anu uin pikutati metueunnu mak tshinanu,
iteu. Mak kutak tshekuan mashten tshe uitamatikut. Ne
auass tshe kanuenimek[u] tshika ishi-atusseshtuauau nete
aishkat tshetshi eka nita anu uin ishpakushit mak tshinanu. Ekuan, tshima minupaniek[u], iteu.

Ne kauitenitakusht uetinat nenua auassa tshetshi kanuenimat, nishtam ekue mannamuat ka ishi-tshishuash-
pishuniti ekue minat matshunisha mak mishtikushiussina
tshetshi tshikamutaniti. Ne auass katshi tshishuashpitakanit
miam kauitenitakushiniti eshi-tshishuashpishuniti, apu
nakanauit, shakuenimu. Nenua mishtikushiussina ushkat
tshekamutat, nukushu apu minushkakut : e pimuteti
mishta-papituteshtau. Kie nenu mitshiminu eishinakuannit eshamikut nenua kauitenitakushiniti, apu minuatak
tshetshi mitshit. Nenu nanitam mamitunenitam[u] atiku-
uiashinu mak nutshimiu-namesha. Nanitam shiuenu. Ne
kauitenitakusht ka kanuenimat nenua auassa, uin mak
nenua uitshi-kauitenitakushiniti mitshuat uishautiku-
uiashinu e minuanit. Nenua auassa muk[u] utatshishi-kuku-
sha nishuait eshinakushiniti mak ka nutamashkuannit
uiashinu, eukuannu nanitam peikutau eshamat. Nenua
auassa tshissenimeuat kie uapameuat eka menuataminiti
nenu umitshimuau. Minuat tapue nenu e ishkushtahk
mitshiminu apu ui uepinahk, eukuannu ashit eshamaht.

Ne kauitenitakusht ka kanuenimat nenua auassa uipat
tshissenimeu eshpish innishiniti nenu eishi-tshishkutamuat.
Tshimut mamash ekue tshishkutamuat. Tshek ekue ui
tutuat tshetshi uakataminiti nenu katshishkutamatuna-
nunit kie tshetshi shakuenimuniti. Apu minu-tshishuashpi-
tat ashit mamishaimueu umatshunishiminua. Nanikutini
ekue utinak shikaunissinu ekue shikauiat ekue itat :

that the child in your custody may never surpass us some day. That is all. I wish you good luck.

The Polichinelle with whom the child was left starts by removing his clothes. He gives him other ones and he makes him put on stiff shoes. The child who has now been dressed up in the way of the Polichinelles is not used to these clothes. He is uncomfortable. It is the first time that he has shoes on, and this does not feel right to him: he walks pigeon-toed. He does not like to eat the kind of food that the Polichinelles give him. He thinks constantly about caribou meat and fish from the lakes. He is hungry all the time. The child's guardian and his colleague-Polichinelles, they eat good beef. As for the child, they always serve him the same thing: two kinds of sausage and baloney. They know it, they see it, that the child does not like their food. Furthermore, they also give him the leftovers that they do not want to throw away.

The Polichinelle who takes care of the child soon realizes how well the child is doing in his studies. And so, very casually, he starts to teach him poorly. He makes sure that the child hates studying and feels ashamed: he no longer dresses him properly and patches up his clothes. Sometimes he combs through his hair and says:

– Tshutikumin, iteu.

Ne auass, eshpish tat anite kauitenitakushiu-
katshishkutamatsheutshuapit, tshek uapatam[u] umassina
nete nikan shepannua, shatshitinnua ushita. Ekue
uapatiniat nenua ka kanuenimikut ekue itat :

– Tautu, shiuenu nimassin, iteu.

Ne auass tshek eshpish mueshtatak nenu ut peikutau
pitukamit e kanuenimikut kauitenitakushiniti, tshek ekue
itenitak tshetshi unuit anite ut katshishkutamatsheutshuapit. Shash uakateu nenua kenuenimikut, matenitam[u]
kassinu nenu eitutakut. Ne kauitenitakusht tshessenimat
nenua auassa eka menuataminiti anite, ekue itat :

– Matshi uenashk unui, itenitamini tshetshi unuin,
iteu.

Ne auass uin apu ishpitishit tshetshi mamitunenimiti-
shut nete nikan, eka taniti auennua tshetshi uauitshikut,
ekue unuit. Uenuit anite ut katshishkutamatsheutshuapit,
tapue shash mishta-ait itenitakushu kie shash apu ishpish
minuinniut, apu ishpish shutshishit miam ueshkat. Nenua
umassina eshk[u] shepannua nete nikan, eshk[u] shatshitinnua ushita. Kie tapue shash pitshenik unitau utaimun kie
nenu aiamieunnu eshi-aimit ka ishi-tshishkutamakut
nenua kauitenitakushiniti pitshenik unitau.

Katshi unuit anite ut katshishkutamatsheutshuapit :

– Ushtuin nika animiun, itenitam[u]. Nika nanatuapa-
mau kauitenitakusht ka minit utamakan-kukusha mak
uapuiannu.

Ekue itutet nenu ka minikut etashtenit anite e apiniti.
Patutshet, apu taniti muk[u] tanua kutaka kauitenitakushiniti ekue minikut nete minuat etashtenit mitshuapinu
tshe itutet. Ekue itutet nete etishaukut nenua kauitenitakushiniti. Patutshet nenu mitshuapinu, iapit namaieute

– You have lice.

The child, who has been at the Polichinelles' school for some time now, one day notices that the tip of one of his shoes has come undone; his toes poke out. He shows it to his guardian and says:

– My shoe is hungry, he is opening his mouth.

Feeling more and more bored, the child thinks about leaving the school. He has come to hate the one who keeps him, he is aware of how he is being treated. When the Polichinelle finds out that the child is not happy to be there, he tells him:

– Leave immediately from here if that is what you want.

The child is not yet old enough to think about his future and there is no one to help him. He leaves. He has become very different from who he was before, his health is not so good, he is not as strong as he used to be. The tip of his shoe is still open and his toes still poke out. He has started to forget his language and he has slowly forgotten the prayers that one of the Polichinelles had taught him.

Once he has left the school, the child thinks to himself:

– Maybe I do have some problems. I am going to look for the Polichinelle who gave me the pork cheeks and the blanket.

He goes to the address that the Polichinelle had given him but does not find him there. He is given the address of another house. So he goes there but does not find him there either. A third Polichinelle gives him a phone number for the place where the

etaniti, muku tanua kutaka kauitenitakushiniti. Ekue
minikut etashtenit kaiminanunit nete etaniti nenua ua
uapamat. Ne auass uenashk ekue matuetitat nenu etashtenit ekue itikut nenua uetinaminiti kaiminanunit :

– Ushkat ka itutein mitshuap, ekute etat anutshish,
itiku.

Shash mishta-kataku ituteu, shash patshitenimu.

– Apu minuat tshika ut kau tshiueian, shash ishpannu
eshpish papami-nashauk, itenitamu.

Ekue puniat. Apu tshi uapamat kie shash apu
apatenimat.

– Peikuan at uapamaki, muku tshiam nipa
katshinassimiku, itenimeu.

Ekue tshitutet. Iapit tanua kauitenitakushiniti uiauui-
tshikut tshetshi eka nita ishi-mamitunenitak tshetshi kau
tshiuet nete ka ututet.

Ne auass eshpish pimutet ekue uapatak atauitshuapinu
tshematenit. Mishta-minuenitamu.

– Nika natshi-aian nimassina, itenitamu.

Patutshet nenu atauitshuapinu, uapameu kauitenitakushiniti anite pitukamit, mitshetinua niatshi-ataueniti,
ekue nanatuapatak umassina. Katshi mishkak massina e
minuatak kie tiepishkak, kie uin ekue itutet nete katshi-
shikashunanunit tshetshi tshishikashut umassina mamu
kauitenitakushiniti. Ne kauitenitakushiu-ataunnish
apu tshitapamat nenua auassa. Kassinu etashiniti katshi
pimipaniat uitshi-kauitenitakushiniti, nete mashten ekue
pimipaniat nenua auassa. Manikut nenua auassa shunianu,
mishta-minuenitamu ekue itat :

– Tshinashkumitin kie tshin, iteu.

Ne auass katshi unuit anite ut atauitshuapit, tshishuapu
nenu ka tutakut kauitenitakushiu-ataunnisha. Ekue mannak nenua umassina ka shepanniti ekue uepimitak nete
kataku ekue issishuet :

man he is looking for should be. The child dials hast-
ily the number and someone answers:

— At this time, he is in the first house where you
went.

The child has already travelled very far, he lacks
courage.

— I am not going back there once again, he tells
himself. I have chased after him long enough.

So he gives up. He has not been able to find him
and he no longer really wants to.

— And even if I saw him, he would only lie.

He gets going again, still followed by a Polichinelle
who is there to make sure he does not think about
going back to the place he came from.

Along the way, the child sees a store. He is
delighted.

— I am going to buy myself some shoes, he thinks.

As he enters the store, he sees several Polichinelles
inside doing their shopping. He looks for shoes.
When he has found some that he likes and that are
the right size, he goes over to the cashier to pay for
them. The Polichinelle-clerk does not look at the
child. He serves him last, after all his Polichinelle
friends. He is happy to take his money and says:

— Thanks to you too.

As he leaves the store, the child is angered by the
way the Polichinelle-clerk treated him. He takes off
his old shoes and throws them away, saying:

– Matshi-manitu-kauitenitakushiht umenua umassinuaua ! issishueu.

Katshi tshikamutat nenua ushkassina, minuat ekue
tshitutet. Shash mueshtatam^u, mamitunenitam^u nete ka
ututet. Nanikutini apashapu kie shash tshissenitam^u apu
nita tshika ut kau tshi tshiuet kie shash pitshenik aieshkushiu, apu shapishit.

Eshpish pimutet, tshek ekue uapatak akushiutshuapinu
tshematenit.
– Nika pitutshen, nitakushinatshe, itenitam^u.
Patutshet nenu akushiutshuapinu, uapameu kauitenitakushiniti, mishta-mitshetinua anite pitukamit. Kie uin
ekue natuapamat nenua kauitenitakushiu-kamashinata-
uaniti auennua tshe ishi-pitutsheniti ekue itat :
– Natukunish nui uapamau, iteu.
Ne ka mashinataitshet kauitenitakusht ekue utinamuat
nenua auassa utishinikashunnu ekue itat :
– Neu tshi pimipanitaui, eukuan tshin tshe ut
pimipanin, tshe uapamat natukunish, iteu.
Ne auass ekue ashuapatak kie uin anite ka ashuapa-
takannit mamu kauitenitakushiniti. Tshitapameu eishi-
pitutsheniti anite natukunisha. Ne auass nenu eshinniut e
peikussit, etati anite e mitshetiniti nenua kauitenitakushiniti, apu shuk^u minuinniut, shakuenimu. Uapamitishu
mishta-ait etenitakushit kie mishta-ait eshinakushit mak
nenua kauitenitakushiniti kie ashit uapameu passe utash-
tamikut manenimiku kie uaushinaku. Uiapamat neu
katshi pimipanniti, mishta-minuenitam^u.
– Eukuan nin tshe ut pimipanian, tshe uapamak
natukunish, itenitam^u.
Ekue uemashkakut kutaka kauitenitakushiniti patutshe-
niti anite natukunisha. Ne auass minuat ekue ashuapamat

— So much for the damned Polichinelles' shoes! he says.

He puts on his new shoes and starts walking again. He is sad, he thinks about the place where he came from. Sometimes he glances backwards, he knows he can never return. He starts to feel tired, he no longer has any strength.

On the way, he sees a hospital.

— I am going to go in, he thinks to himself, I must be ill.

As he enters the hospital, he sees there are several Polichinelles inside. Like the others, he goes up to the receptionist and says:

— I would like to see the doctor.

The Polichinelle-secretary writes down his name and says:

— There are four people before you, then it will be your turn to see the doctor.

Like the others, the child waits in the waiting room. He looks at the people going into the doctor's office. He, who lives in solitary, does not feel very comfortable in his skin. He is uncomfortable being alongside so many Polichinelles. He realizes that he is very different from them, in his behaviour and his appearance. Some make fun of him and laugh in his face. He is glad when the four Polichinelles before him have gone through. He says to himself:

— It will now be my turn to see the doctor.

Just then, he is passed over by a Polichinelle who slips into the doctor's office. He waits until that one leaves. As

tshetshi unuiniti nenua ka uemashkakut. Uenuiniti anite
ut natukunisha, shash minuat kutak kauitenitakusht ekue
pitutepatat anite. Ne auass eshk^u apu patshitenimut.

– Unuiti ne, nasht eukuan nin tshe pitutsheian,
itenitam^u.

Ne kauitenitakusht uenuit anite ut natukunisha, shash
minuat kutak ekue pitutepatat, kuetatishkueu nenua
auassa. Ne auass eukuannu petshitenimut. Aieshkushiu
kie shakuenimu. Ashit mashkatenimeu nenu etutakut
ekue unuit anite ut akushiutshuapit. Uin e peikussit apu
tshi uapamat natukunisha. Katshi unuit ekue apit anite
unuitimit, ashteieshkushiu. Ashit mamitunenimeu nenua
kauitenitakushiniti ka tutakut.

– Muk^u uinuau nanitam apatenimitishuat kie tapue
muk^u uinuau uauitshituat, itenimeu.

Tshek ekue pashikut ekue tshitutet minuat. Iapit
eukuannu meshkananu metimet, kauitenitakushiniti
umeshkanaminu. Shash apu shuk^u minuatak nenu
meshkananu metimet.

– Usham aiat nitanimiun kie aiat nimanenimikuat
kauitenitakushiht, itenitam^u.

Nenu eshi-mamitunenitak, aiat patshitenimu. Pitshenik apu ishpish shutshenimitishut miam ueshkat ka
ishpish shutshenimitishut, e peikussit kassinu tshekuannu
etutaki.

– Tapue anu nin nimanenitakushinatshe mak
kauitenitakushiht, itenitam^u.

Tshek eshpish pimutet, ekue uapamat kutaka kauitenitakushiniti pietashtamuteniti tshe natshishkuat, ekue itikut :

– Nika uauapaten tshipita, itiku.

Tapuetueu nenu etikut. Ne kauitenitakusht katshi uaua-
patamuat uipitinua, mishta-tshishuapu ekue itat :

he exits the doctor's office, another Polichinelle rushes in. The child does not despair yet.

– When that one leaves, it has to be my turn to go in, he tells himself.

When the Polichinelle leaves, once again, another one rushes in in front of the child. In that moment, he loses courage. He is tired and humiliated. In addition, he is surprised that they would do this to him. So he leaves the hospital. He is the only one who was not able to see the doctor. Outside, he sits down. He rests as he thinks about the way the Polichinelles have treated him. He says to himself:

– They only give importance to themselves, and they protect each other constantly.

He gets up and starts walking again. He is still following the same path, that of the Polichinelles. It no longer pleases him very much.

– I am having more and more trouble and the Polichinelles are making fun of me.

The more he thinks about it, the more he feels discouraged. He starts to have less and less confidence in himself in everything that he attempts.

– I must be even more contemptible than the Polichinelles, he tells himself.

Along the way, he sees a Polichinelle approaching who says to him:

– I will examine your teeth.

The child agrees. After he has examined him, the Polichinelle is very angry.

– Nika manipiten kassinu etatiki tshipita kie nika
tuten kutaka tshipita. Nika ishinakutan miam tshitshue
mipita. Natamik[u] tshekuan nika apashtan muk[u] eka
uin uinenita uesh ma eukuan ume ushkat kie namaieu
mashten, iteu.

Ne auass katshi tshikamutatinikut kauitenitakushiniti
nenua mipita ka tutaminiti, tapue uinenitam[u] ekue tshitutet minuat. Ashit mamitunenitam[u] nenua uipita ekue
itenitak :

– Tapue kie nin shash kassinu nika ishi-uinnakushin
eshi-uinnakushiht anitshenat matshi-manitu-kauitenitakushiht. Ka peikussian minashkuat nimishta-
uashkamishiti, itenitam[u].

Ne auass eshpish pimutet ekue uapamat minuat kutaka
pietashtamuteniti kauitenitakushiniti tshe natshishkuat
ekue itikut :

– Nika uauapaten tshissishikua.

Tapuetueu nenu etikut. Ne kauitenitakusht ekue uaua-
patamuat ussishikunua ekue itat :

– Tshika unitan tshissishikua, iteu. Nanimissiu-
uashtenimakan tshitutakun mak kamataupikutakanit
mak katshitapatakanit, iteu. Umenua ussishikukauna tshe
minitan, tshika tshikamutan eka ui unitaini tshissishikua,
iteu.

Ne auass ekue tshikamutat inishat nenua ussishikukauna ekue kutshipanitat nete katak[u] tshetshi uapa-
tamuatshet. Miam tushkapatshikan ui itapashtau nenua
ussishikukauna. Apu anu tshi uapatak nete katak[u] ekue
mannak nenua ussishikukauna ekue pitaik anite
ukassipitakanit. Ekue tshiuekapaut minuat nete ka ututet. Shash tshitshue patshitenimu kie mueshtatam[u]. Iapit
inishat ekue tshitutet. Iapit eukuannu peikutau meshkananu miamitimet.

– I am going to pull all of your teeth out and I am going to make you new ones that will look like real teeth. I am going to use a special product but do not get ill, because if it is the first time, it will not be the last.

After the Polichinelle has put in the new teeth that he made, indeed the child feels nauseous. As he gets going again, he thinks about his teeth and says to himself:

– Now I am going to be as full of filth as those damn Polichinelles. Me who was so clean when I lived alone in the woods.

Further along, another Polichinelle comes up to him and says:

– I am going to examine your eyes.
The child agrees and the Polichinelle examines him:
– You are going to lose your sight. It is because of electric light, cinema, and television. You will always have to wear glasses that I will give to you if you do not want to go blind.

The child puts on his glasses half-heartedly and tries to look at the horizon. He wants them to work like binoculars. But he does not see any better. He takes them off and puts them in his pocket. He turns once again to look back in the direction he came from. He now feels very depressed and is filled with sadness. He continues walking anyway, regretfully, still following the same path.

Eshpish pimutet tshek shiuenu. Mamitunenitam[u] umitshim ueshkat ka ishi-mitshishut. Tshissenitam[u] apishish anite upimeshkanau minashkuat tshi itutet :

— Uemut nipa mishken nimitshim, itenitam[u].

Muk[u] tanua kauitenitakushiniti nanitam niakatua-pamikut akua apishish minashkuat tshetshi itutet. Ne kauitenitakusht uatsheuat nenua auassa muk[u] nanitam kukuetshimeu eishinakushiniti kie eishinikatakanniti aueshisha kie namesha kie ashit kukuetshimeu tsheku-shishipa kie tsheku-namesha anu uet minushiniti. Ne auass uin ashineu nenu eishi-kukuetshimikut ekue uauita-muat kassinu nenu tshekuannu ua ishi-tshissenitaminiti.

Ne auass eshpish pimutet, shash minuat ekue natshish-kuat kutaka kauitenitakushiniti. Apu auat ui natshika-paut. Shash uakaiku nenu nanitam e natshishkuat kauitenitakushiniti. Ekue nakanikut ekue itikut :

— Tshika nanatu-tshissenimitin, nika utinen tshimik[u] tshetshi tshissenimitan tsheku-mitshim tshe minitan tshetshi mitshin, itiku.

Ne auass ekue itenitak :

— Anitshenat kauitenitakushiht kassinu eissishueht nanitam ninatutuatiat kie iapit nika tapuetuau nenu eshit, itenimeu.

Ne kauitenitakusht katshi utinamuat nenu umikunu, ekue minat mashinaikanuiannu ekue itat :

— Tshe ishpish inniuin, apu nita tshika ut tshi mut namesh, iteu. Muti namesh, tshika akushin kie ma tshika nipin, iteu.

Ne auass nenu etikut mishta-shetshishu.

— Tshekuan ek[u] ume nin tshe mitshian . . . ? itenitam[u]. Ekue tshitutet enuet iapit minuat.

Apu minekash pimutet, uapameu minuat kutaka petashtamutenua kauitenitakushiniti. Ne kauitenita-

After walking for so long, he is hungry. He thinks about the food that he used to eat. If he could just go into the forest alongside the road, he thinks:

— Surely I will find some food.

But a Polichinelle is constantly watching him in case he ventures into the woods. The Polichinelle accompanying him keeps asking him questions about the aspects and names of mammals and fish; he wants to know which is the best waterfowl and the best fish. The child, him, is proud to be questioned this way and tells him everything he wants to know.

Along the way, the child meets yet another Polichinelle. He does not even want to stop, it annoys him to be constantly meeting Polichinelles. But the latter stops him:

— I am going to conduct an analysis, I am going to draw some of your blood to know what kind of food I will be able to let you eat.

The child thinks to himself:

— Whatever they may think, I have always listened to the Polichinelles and I will agree to what this one is asking me to do as well.

After taking the sample, the Polichinelle gives the child a piece of paper:

— For the rest of your life, you can no longer eat fish. If you eat any, you will get sick or you might die.

The child is frightened.

— But what am I going to eat then...? he wonders.

And he sets off once again, nonetheless.

He has only walked a short distance when he happens upon yet another Polichinelle coming towards

kusht pieshuapamat nenua auassa, mishta-minuenitakushikashu ekue itat :

– Kuei ! Kuei ! iteu.

Ne auass kie uin mishta-minuenitakushikashu ekue
itat kie uin :

– Kuei ! Kuei ! iteu.

Ne kauitenitakusht katshi pushukatikut nenua auassa
ekue itat :

– Tshekuan eshinakushin ? Tshimishta-aieshkushiu-
nakushin mak tshipatshitenimunakushin, iteu. Tshika
minitin tatuputai ishkutuapui tshetshi uni-tshissin e
mueshtatamin ashit tshetshi ashteieshkushin, iteu.

Ne auass tapuetam^u ekue utinak tatuputai nenu ishkutuapunu ekue minit. Tapue tatuputai katshi minit,
mishta-minuenitam^u kie shash uni-tshissu nenu ka
mueshtatak nete ka ututet. Kie nenu apishish uni-tshissu
eshpish manenimikut kauitenitakushiniti. Shash minu-
kashu kie aiat ui minu ishkutuapunu kie tshek tshishuapu,
manatueu. Kie uin aishi-manatueu eishi-manatueniti
nenua kauitenitakushiniti. Ekue tshitutet minuat iapit,
eshk^u nanatuapatam^u tshetshi minit. Shash apu tshekuannu mamitunenitak.

Ne auass nenu tshetutet e minukashut, uenapissish pimu-
teu, minuat kutaka kauitenitakushiniti uapameu pietashtamuteniti. Passikannu tshikamutanua anite uianit mak
utamaikanashkunu takunaminua. Ne kauitenitakusht uiapamat nenua auassa menukashuniti, mishta-minuenitam^u.

– Tshessinat nika makunau, itenimeu.

Pitama ekue passitshet anite ishpimit tshetshi kushta-
tshiat ekue utshipitat ekue ututamuat anite utashtamikunit ekue itat :

– Kamakunueshiutshuapit tshika natshi-nipan, iteu.

Ne auass ekue itat nenua kauitenitakushiniti :

him. Approaching the child, the Polichinelle tries to be very friendly:

– Hello! Hello! he says.

The child tries to be friendly as well and answers:

– Hello! Hello!

After shaking the child's hand, the Polichinelle says to him:

– What is wrong with you? You look very tired and depressed. I am going to give you a couple of bottles of alcohol to make you forget your troubles. And it will make you feel more relaxed as well.

The child agrees. He takes the bottles of alcohol and drinks. Indeed, after having a drink, he feels happier, he has forgotten that he missed the place he came from. He has also forgotten a little about how offended he felt by the Polichinelles. He ends up getting drunk and wanting to drink more and more. Soon enough, he gets angry and starts to swear. He uses the same swear words as the Polichinelles. He starts walking again, looking for more alcohol to drink. He no longer thinks about anything else.

The child continues his journey, drunk. He has only walked a short distance when another Polichinelle shows up. This one is carrying a gun and holding a club in his hand. The Polichinelle is very happy to find the child in a drunken state.

– I will arrest him for sure, he says to himself.

First he fires a shot in the air to scare him then he pulls him abruptly towards him and punches him in the face repeatedly, saying:

– You are going to sleep it off in prison.

The child answers:

– Tshekuan uet ui pitukain anite tshikukush-
mitshuapuat muk^u e minukashuian ? Apu tshekuan
ishi-matshi-tutaman, iteu.

Ekue itikut :

– Tshitshissenimitin apu tshekuan ishi-matshi-tutamin
muk^u ume nin uiapamin eshi-tshishuashpishuian, eukuan
eshinakuak nitatusseun, tshetshi pitukaitan kamakunueshiutshuapit, iteu.

Ne auass uenuit anite ut kamakunueshiutshuapit, ekue
tshitutet minuat. Shash apu minukashut muk^u akushu
ushtikuan mak anu mueshtatam^u nete ka ututet. Iapit
nanitam apashapu kie shash petam^u tipatshimunnu eish-
pannit nete ka ututet minashkuat.

Tshek eshpish pimutet meshkananu, ekue natshishkuat
minuat kutaka kauitenitakushiniti. Ekue itikut :

– Anutshish tshika uaueshitin. Tshika tuten katapuenanut miam peikuan ninan tshetshi tipatshimushtuin
tshekuan ka tutamin ka minukashuin, iteu.

Ne auass ekue mamitunenitak nenu etikut ekue
itenitak :

– Tapue nika tutakuat anitshenat kauitenitakushiht,
nipiani, tshetshi ituteian atamashkamikut..., itenitam^u.

Ekue itat :

– Apu tshi tapuetatan tshetshi tutaman katapuenanut.
Eshi-mashinataiman anite pet utat eitutuiek^u kie
eitenitakushiek^u, at peikutshishemitashumitannu tatuau
tutamani katapuenanut, nasht e tapueian, niminu-tshi-
sseniten atut nita nipa kanieun. Uemut nanitam tshin
tshika kanieuitishun. Apu nita uapamitan peik^u tshekuan
etutamini tshetshi apashtain kakuishkupanit. Tanite nene
etutamin kakuishkupanit ka petain ute ? Tshimatushtueiti
a nene anite kauepinashunanut, nenua ka tutamin
tshikauepinashunanima kassinu anite katshi takushinin
ute ? iteu.

– Why do you want to send me to your pigsty when all I am is drunk? I did not do anything wrong.

The Polichinelle replies:
– I know that you did not do anything wrong. But you can see my uniform, my job is to put you in prison.

When he leaves the prison, the child sets off once again. He has sobered up but his head hurts and he misses more than ever the place he came from. He looks back constantly. He has heard things, about what is going on back home, in the woods.

Along the way, he meets another Polichinelle who tells him:
– Now I am going to judge you. As we do, you will take an oath and tell me what you did while you were drunk.

The child thinks about this and says to himself:

– Truly, these Polichinelles are going to send me to hell when I die…, he thinks.

He says:
– I cannot take an oath, he answers. From what I have seen of your doings towards me and your behaviour thus far, even if I took a thousand oaths and told you the absolute truth, I know very well that I would never win my case. Obviously, you will always let yourself win. Never, in all of your actions, have I seen you act justly. What have you done with the justice that you brought here? Did you toss it into the fire or in one of those rubbish dumps that you have created all over the place since your arrival?

Ne kauitenitakusht etikut nenua auassa, mishta-
tshishuapu ashit mishta-tshishkueienitakushu. Ekue
natuapamat ekue utinamuat utitshinu ekue ashtauat anite
takut aiamieu-mashinaikanit ekue itat :

— Tshitititin tshetshi tutamin katapuenanut kie uemut
tshika tuten ! iteu.

Ne auass aiat mashkatenimeu nenua kauitenitakushiniti e uapamat eitiniti kie e petuat eissishueniti. Shash apu
mishkuat peik^u tshetshi shutshenimat.

— Nin nipeikussin. Anitshenat etashiht
kauitenitakushiht namaieute tshe mishkuk auen tshetshi
tshishpeuashit, itenitam^u.

Aiat shetshishu, aiat patshitenimu.

— Tan ititshenat kassinu etashiht…? Tshinikuanipan-
nitsheni ushtikuanuaua, itenimeu.

Ne auass minuat enuet ekue tshitutet. Iapit eukuannu
meshkananu metimet. Shash nashpit apu tshissenitak
tanite etat kie shash apu nishtuapamitishut kie shash apu
pikutat tshetshi ishi-aimit ka ishi-aimit. Kie shash apu
auat pikutat muk^u tshetshi tshipaiatikukashut eshi-aimit.

Apu katak^u itutet, uapameu kauitenitakushiniti
pietashtamuteniti, mitshetinua tshe natshishkuat. Passe
takunaminua tshekuannu. Anitshenat kauitenitakushiht
uiapamaht maniteu-auassa pietashtamuteniti, shash
mishta-tshishkueienitakushuat ekue utinahk nenua
utakunikanuaua eshk^u eka utitaht ekue akunaht. Ne auass
uiapamat nenu etutakut :

— Tshekuannitshe etutuht…? itenimeu.

Mishta-shetshishu.

259 WHAT HAVE YOU DONE TO MY COUNTRY?

The Polichinelle, angry and irritated by the child's words, approaches the child, grabs his hand, and places it on the Bible and says:

– I tell you to take an oath and you will do it no matter what!

The child is more and more stunned by the doings and statements of the Polichinelles. There is not one of them left that he can trust.

– I am on my own. And it is not among the Polichinelles that I will find someone to defend me.

He is more and more afraid, he feels more and more discouraged.

– But what is wrong with them all...? Something is not quite right in their heads.

Nonetheless he continues to follow the same path. He can no longer speak his language. He is no longer able to make the sign of the cross in his language either.

He has not gone far before more Polichinelles approach him. Some of them are carrying something in their hands. Seeing a strange child coming towards them, they get very excited. They grab their cameras and start to film him.

– What on earth are they doing to me...? the child wonders, seeing them act this way.

He is very scared.

– Tapue shash nika nipaikuat kauitenitakushiht, nui passukuat, itenimeu.

Iapit inishat ekue natuapamat ekue pushukatat kassinu etashiniti. Ekue itikut :

– Ma tshipa tshi uapatininan ueshkat ka ishinniuin eshk[u] minashkuat ka tain ? itiku. Nipa kanuenitenan tshitinniun anite kamatau-pikutakanit mak anite katshitapatakanit tshetshi tshitapatahk natamik[u] eishinniuht. Kie ma tshin nete aishkat aianishkat mueshtatamini tshitinniun, ekute tshe uapatamin anite katshitapatakanit mak anite kamatau-pikutakanit ueshkat ka ishinniuin, itiku.

Ne auass tapuetueu nenu etikut. Kutshipanitau tshetshi tutak miam ueshkat ka ishinniut. Apu tshi tutak usham shash ueshami-mitshetinua kauitenitakushiniti, shash nutim uashka tanua.

Nenu meshkananu ka mitimet ekuan eshkuapekannit, apu takuannit anite minuat tshetshi ishi-tshitutet kie shash nashpit apu nishtuapatak nete ka ututet. Eukuannu metenitak nasht tshetimatshishit. Mishta-mamitunenitam[u]. Tshissenitam[u] anite etat, uin shash apu tshekuannu kanuenitak tshetshi ut pakassiut aianishkat. Kie uin shash uauanenitam[u]. Mashten ekue tshiuekapaut nete ka ututet. Uapatam[u] shash nutim pikunikannu nete ka ut inniut. Uapatam[u] mitshet utshua mamishi-pakuneianua. Nasht patshitenimu ekue issishuet :

– Nitassi nana eshapan, issishueu.

– The time has come, the Polichinelles are going to kill me, they want to shoot me, he thinks.

He goes towards them anyway, half-heartedly, and shakes each of their hands. They ask him:

– Could you show us how you used to live when you were in the woods? We will preserve your way of living through cinema and television so that other nations can watch it. Or, when you yourself, in generations to come, miss your culture, well you will be able to see on television and in the cinema how you used to live.

The child lets himself be persuaded. He tries to do as he used to, but he is not able because there are too many Polichinelles, they are everywhere.

He has now come to the end of the path that he has been following. He can no longer move forward and he no longer knows the place he came from. He realizes then that he is truly miserable. He thinks for a long time. He knows, now, that he has no way to exist in the future. He starts to feel nervous himself. One last time, he looks back in the direction from which he came. He sees that everything has been destroyed, where he used to live, there are large holes in several of the mountains. Completely demoralized, he says:

– So that is what they have done to my country…[2]

V

Ne kauitenitakusht ka minat nenua auassa utamakan-
kukusha mak massina e kanuapekanniti, uiapamat nasht
petshitenimuniti, ui shetshishu ashit ui kashu.

– Tshima eka nita petakuak ume tipatshimun…,
itenitam^u.

Ekue natuapamat nenua auassa ekue itat :

– Mushtuenitamini tshetshi tshiuein kau nete ka
ututein, tshe tshiuein. Kie ma nin a kau tshika tshiuetai-
tin ? iteu.

Ne auass nenu etikut, eukuannu menupannit tshetshi
aimiat kie enut tshitshue tshe aimit. Apu tshekuannu
kushtak uetitshipannit tshetshi aimit. Ekue itat nenua
kauitenitakushiniti :

– Tshitshishkueiapaten a tshin ne essishuein ? Nin
apu nishtuapataman nete ka ututeian. Aua tshin tshipa
nishtuapaten ? iteu. Ka uishamiek^u tshetshi uitsheutikut, tshimishta-ushkuishtutau kie tshuitsheutitau.
Muk^u ka ishpish uitshimakanitutuiek^u, takuanipan
nanikutini e mishta-mashkatenimitikut kie nanikutini
nasht tshekat tshitututau tshetshi patshitenimuian kie
nanikutini tshimishta-uitenimititau ka aitutuiek^u kie ka
ishi-katshinassimiek^u. Mak kutak tshekuan. Ka ishpish
uitsheutikut, kassinu tshekuan etutamekui, nin nanitam
utat nuaututeti. « Apu tshissenitak » a, tshititenimitau ?
Niminu-tshisseniteti muk^u apu ut ui uapatinitikut kie apu
ut aimitikut. Peikuan tshitshissenimititau ka ut tutuiek^u

V

Seeing the child completely demoralized, the Polichinelle who had given him the pork cheeks and the boots
starts to worry and wants to get out of this mess.

– Hopefully no one will ever know this story…, he
says to himself.

So he goes towards the child and says:

– If you would like to go back to where you came
from, all you have to do is go back, or would you
rather that I take you back there myself?

What the Polichinelle says to the child gives him the
chance to finally speak up. It is the first time that he
will speak to him truly. He is not afraid when the time
comes for him to speak up. He says to the Polichinelle:

– Are you crazy, you, telling me something like
that? I do not even know myself where I come from.
Are you supposed to know? When you asked me to
join you, you forced me, roughly, and I went with you.
But since you have been my neighbours, you have
sometimes shocked me; at times, you almost managed to discourage me for good and at other times,
your doings and your lies towards me really made me
laugh. During this whole time that I have been with
you, in all that you have done, I have always been the
one to stay behind. You think I did not know? I knew
it very well but I did not want you to see it and I did
not say anything. This does not mean that I did not

mukᵘ ne e uinipishian. Nipashta-tuten a ne e uinipishian?
iteu. Tshinuau tapue tshuapishinau kie tshiminushinau
ussit e tshitapamikauiekᵘ. Mukᵘ eshi-nishtuapamitikut,
mitshenipan tshekuan ka tutamekᵘ atamit anu e kashteuat
mak ume nin eshpish uinipishian, iteu.

Anutshish uiapamin eshpish tshitimatshishian, mukᵘ
tshiam tshui kashun, tshui tshinipin tshetshi tshiue-
tishauin kau nete ka ututeian. Tshekuan ne? Takuan a
tshekuan anite minuat miamitunenitamin? iteu. Anutshish tshishat tshika uitamatin etenitaman. Tshiueiani kie
peikuan eka tshiueiani nete ka ututeian, animiuiani tshin
ut, uemut tshin nanitam tshika teputepuatitin, nanitam
tshe aieshkuishtuin kie nanitam tshe ui ishpishin. Eka uin
nita kashushtui ua uapamitani, ua apatshitani. Mak tshe
ishpish inniuian aianishkat, eka uin nita mueshtatshi nin
ut, uesh ma ueshkat nete minashkuat ka ishi-pakassiuian,
apu nita ut nanatu-pakushitan tshekuan, iteu.

Mak ume tshe ishi-uitamatan, eka nita uni-tshissi. Tshe
ishpish atusseshtuin nete nikan, eka uin nita minuat tuta
tshekuan nin ut eka kukuetshimin kie eka tapuetaman.
Ui kukuetshimini tshekuan, ui mashinaimuini, eshi-
aimian tshe ishi-mashinaimuin tshetshi minu-nishtutatan.
Mak kutak tshekuan. Eka uin nita ashu-patshitini tshimut
eshkᵘ eka kukuetshimin kie eshkᵘ eka tapuetaman, iteu.
Mak eshkᵘ eka tshissenitaman tanite tshe ituteian kie tan
tshe ishi-pakassiuian, ashuapami, eka ui tshinipi. Pitama
nika minu-mamituneniten uesh ma namaieu e apishashit
kie namaieu natamikᵘ tshekuan. Mak ma tshipa tshi min
tshetshi ashteieshkushian uenapissish? Anumat nitaieshkushin. Tshitshisseniteti ka ishpish tshi takushiniekᵘ
ute, namaieu nana inniun nin ka ishinniuian. Nanitam
nikushtatshiti. Matshishuiani, apu peikuau ut minu-
mitshishuian. Minuat ma ka tutuiekᵘ, ka tshitaimuiekᵘ

know that you were treating me this way only because of my skin colour. Is it a sin to have dark skin? You, it is true, you are white, you are beautiful to look at from the outside. But knowing you as I do now, many of your actions are actually much darker than my skin is.

Now that you see how miserable I am, you simply want to slip away, you want to send me back to where I came from as quickly as possible. What does this mean? Do you once again have something else in store? Let me tell you right now what I think. Whether I go back or not to where I came from, if I find myself in trouble, be assured that it is at you that I will yell. Be assured to always see me, and make yourself available, do not ever hide from me if I want to see you, if I need you. In the future, and until I die, do not ever grow tired of me. Because before, when I was leading my life in the woods, I never asked you for anything.

Never forget what I am going to tell you. When you will work for me in the future, do not undertake anything that has to do with me without asking me first and without me agreeing to it. If you want to ask me questions, if you want to send me letters, you will write to me in my language so that I will understand you properly. And there is another thing. Do not ever transfer me from one jurisdiction to another without telling me, without asking me, and without me agreeing to it. As long as I will not know in which direction I am going or how I am going to live, wait for me, and do not be in a hurry. I will first have to think about this because it is no small thing, it is not just anything. And, could you not let me rest a little? I am tired. Since your arrival here, this is no way of living. I have always been very afraid. And when it comes to food, I have not had one decent meal, because

nin nimitshim tshetshi mitshian, ka ashamiekᵘ inishat mitshim eka menuataman tshetshi mitshian, iteu.

Peikushu mukᵘ tshekuan tshe tshi uitamatan eshi-uapamitishuian nete nikan. Tshe ishpish inniunanut, nitshisseniten apu nita tshika ut uni-tshissitaman ka ishinniuian. Nanitam aianishkat tshika petun tshe uauitaman, iteu. Kie nitshisseniten, ishinniuiani miam tshin eshinniuin, apu nita tshika ut ishi-minuenitaman miam ueshkat kie apu nita tshika ut ishi-minuinniuian miam ueshkat. Nanitam nika akushin kie nuash eukuan tshe ut mishta-uipat nipian aianishkat, iteu.

Kie tshin tshika takuan tshetshi mamitunenitamin ne ut, uesh ma namaieu e apishashit tshekuan ka tutamin, ka utinamin nutim ka ishi-pakassiuian. Kie ma shash a uipat tshimamituneniteti? Tshitaieshkushtati a nipakassiun eshkᵘ eka utinamin tshimut kie eshkᵘ eka nanutain nutim eshpishat nitassi? Tshititeniteti a mishkut tshetshi minin anu e minuat pakassiun? iteu.

Ushkat ka takushinin ute, tshekuan tshipetati? Tshipetati a tshuenutishiun? Mauat tshia? Ka ishi-uapamitan nin, mukᵘ mashkushiu-nushkuauat mak utamakan-kukusha, eukuan mukᵘ tshekuan tshipetati. Mak tshekuan ka ut takushinin ute eka ut uishamitan? Tshin tshui mishta-apatshiti, tshia? Mukᵘ iapit tshui kashuti mak tshui katshinati. Eukuan ka ut eka tshekuan ishi-uauitamuin ka takushinin. Anu tshiminueniteti tshetshi tshimutamuin mukᵘ ne ut e ui ishi-uinitishuin UEPISHTIKUEIAUNNU. Tshititeniten a tshetshi katshinassimin? Tshe ishpish assiut, at eka nita tshipaimini tshitun eishi-teputepuein kassinu anite kanatutakanit kie anite katshitapatakanit, eishi-uinitishuin UEPISHTIKUEIAUNNU, nin apu nita tshika ut natutatan kie apu nita tshika ut tapuetatan. Katshi takushinin ute, eukuan ne mukᵘ ka ut ushkuishtuin tshetshi uitshinniututatan kie ka ut ui amisseuin ashit nin

another one of your actions has been to forbid me my
own food and to force me to eat food that I did not like.

There is only one thing that I can say to you with
regard to how I see myself in the future. I know that
as long as the earth exists, I will never forget the way
I lived and you will hear me speak about it forever. I
know that if I live the way you do, I will never be as
happy as I was before and I will never be as healthy as I
was before. I will always be sick, and because of that, I
will die very young in the generations to come.

You too, you will have to think about all of this
because it is no small thing to have taken away all my
means of existence. Or, have you already been thinking about this for some time? Did you offer me another
livelihood before taking mine away without my knowledge and ruining my territory? Had you thought about
finding me another way to subsist?

Listen still to what I have to say to you: the first time
you came here, what did you bring? Did you bring your
wealth?? No, right? From what I saw, me, you did not
bring anything more than gruel and pork cheeks. For
what reason did you come here, when you were not
invited? You are the one who needed me, right? Once
again, you wanted to hide and to lie. That is why you
did not tell me about anything when you arrived. You
preferred to rob me, if only so that you could call yourself QUEBECOIS. Do you think you can fool me? Even
if, until the end of time, you never shut up and continue to yell all over the place, on the radio and on television, that you are called QUEBECOIS, I will never
agree with you. After your arrival, if you forced me to
be your fellow citizen, if you tried to mingle with me,
and if you tried to change my name, it is only so that

kie ka ut mishkutunamin nitishinikashun : tshe ishpish
inniunanut muk[u] tshin nanitam tshetshi petakuak tshitishinikashun nutim ute uashka.

   Ueshkat ka takushinin, tanite tshututeti ? Tshitshisseniten a tanite ka ututein ? Tshika uitamatin kuishk[u].
Nete akameu tshututeti. Eukuan tshin maniteu aka-
meu ka utshipanit, iteu. Ashit ushkat ka takushinin,
tshimishta-tshitimauti. Anutshish tanite uetinamin
uenutishiun ? Ekute nitassit uet uenutishin ek[u] nin anutshish nitshitimaun tshin ut, iteu.

   Mak kutak tshekuan tshe uitamatan. Katshi utinamin
nutim eshpishat nipakassiun, ma tshipa tshi pun ashit e
uiashian nanitam e ui pakassitishuatshein aianishkat ?
Tshuapamin, namaieu nin mishtik[u] ka tshimakauakanit,
mashinaikanuian ka tutakanit tshetshi atauatshenanut,
mak namaieu nin ashini ka munaikanit tshetshi atauatshenanut, iteu. Kie nin nitinniun, miam tshin.

   Mak kutak tshekuan mashten tshe uitamatan. Ma
tshipa tshi punin e itenimin « apu innishit » ? Tshitshisseniteti a, auen ka itenimat auennua « apu innishit », uin
nenu nutepanu innishunnu ? iteu.

   Ne auass ekue punit e aimit. Tapue mishta-tshishuapu
nenu metenitak eshpish mishta-unitat tshekuannu.
Utassi nutim eshpishanit ashit kassinu eishinakuannit
utinniun, nuash utaimun, nutim nana unitau. Kie shash
tshissenitam[u] nenu tshe ishpish inniut aianishkat, nanitam iapit inishat tshe uitshi-metuemat, tshe uitshi-
tshishkueiapatamumat nenua kauitenitakushikashuniti.

your name would be the only one that could be heard, everywhere, indefinitely.

When you came here the first time, where were you coming from? Do you know where you were coming from? I will tell you frankly. You came from over there, the other side of the ocean. You are an immigrant. When you came here the first time, you were very poor. And now, from whence do you get your riches? Well, it is with my land that you have gotten rich and it is now I who am poor because of you.

I am going to tell you one more thing. Now that you have taken everything that I had to live on, could you in the future stop exploiting me also as a person? You see, I am not a tree to be cut down and made into paper or ore to extract and sell. I am a human being, me too, like you.

I have one last thing to say to you. Will you do me the honour and stop believing that I am not intelligent? Did you know that it is he who thinks that others are stupid who lacks intelligence?

And so the child stopped speaking. He was very angry when he realized the importance of the things that he had lost. He had lost his entire territory, all of the aspects of his culture, and even his language. And he knew that in the future, and until his death, he would have to continue, like it or not, to play the fool with the Polichinelles and to play along with their games.

Glossary

Atshen: Cannibal giant.

Atshuk: Seal.

Black boots, very tall: Army boots.

Mishta-Shipu: Literally Great River (Grande Rivière);
    Innu name for the Moisie River, north coast.

Nigog: Salmon trident, spear.

Polichinelle, Polichinelles (pl.): The term *Kauitenitakushit* used
    by the author does not have an equivalent in French (or in
    English). It literally means "those who are comical," and
    refers to comic book characters or to characters in Charlot
    (Charlie Chaplin) silent movies.

Shaputuan: Large tent with two entrances and several fires.

Utshashumek: Salmon.

Notes

Translation of Book Two: *What Have You Done to My Country?*

1 In the 1979 French version, this sentence was mistakenly printed "Il y avait plusieurs rivières qui se jettaient dans la mer" (9), which translates as "there were many rivers that flowed into the sea." However, José Mailhot told me that the correct French version should have been "Il avait plusieurs rivières" – "he [the old man] had many rivers." This is a crucial difference in terms of land stewardship and territorial claims. In my translation, I have thus corrected it.

2 In the 1979 French translation, this sentence was translated as "Qu'as-tu fait de mon pays?" ("What have you done to my country?"). However, José Mailhot has stated that the proper translation is, in fact, "Voilà donc ce qu'ils ont fait de mon pays…" ("So that is what they have done to my country…"). Indeed, the Innu sentence, *Nitassi nana eshapan* (Kapesh 2004: 60) is an affirmative sentence, and not a question; it is furthermore translated in the *Online Innu Dictionary* as: "That is what has become of my country" ("Voilà ce qu'est devenu mon pays"). This important correction to the original translation will be made in the forthcoming new edition of *Tanite nene etutamin nitassi? – Qu'as-tu fait de mon pays?* by Mémoire d'encrier in 2020. I have thus corrected it here as well.

TRANSLATOR'S NOTE

The English translations presented here stem primarily from the 1976 and 1979 French versions of Kapesh's works. Her recently republished first book, *Eukuan nin matshi-manitu innushkueu – Je suis une maudite sauvagesse* (2019), saw several crucial revisions made to both the Innu version and the French version. First, the Innu text was entirely revised and the spelling corrected in accordance with the publishing policy of Tshakapesh Institute. This important update, which both reflects contemporary usage and will serve Innu language education, was undertaken by Jérémie Ambroise, Innu language advisor at Tshakapesh Institute, and José Mailhot, Innu linguist and translator of the original French version, with the help of an advisory committee made up of Innu speakers Anne-Marie André, Judith Mestokosho, Céline Belle-fleur, and Philomène Grégoire. Second, as Mailhot explains in her own translator's note (qtd. in Kapesh 2019: 205–206), several revisions to the French text were necessary. I was careful to bear in mind all of these revisions and to apply them to my English translation where they had any incidence on meaning. As such, this project was not a straightforward, traditional translation: it was a process that involved the original French translator, who worked very closely over many years with the author on the first bilingual edition, as well as Innu language experts, who worked to update and reflect the changes to the language over the course of the years since its original publication. It is also not straightforward and traditional in the sense that I worked from the French versions, rather than the Innu versions, for I do not speak, or read, Innu. However, the process through which the French versions came to be – a close collaboration between Kapesh and Mailhot over many years – gave me the assurance that working from them was almost (but of course, never entirely) as acceptable as translating from the original Innu. Also, both Mailhot and Ambroise were extremely helpful and generous in their explanations and answers to my questions about the revisions along the way. Finally, it is safe to say that the original French translation did establish its own cultural cache, independent of the Innu; and as such, given the longevity of its life in print, the involvement of the author in the original translation process, and now, the continued interest in making Kapesh's work even more broadly accessible, working from the French versions was warranted. Ultimately, as I explain in more detail in the Afterword, what truly mattered to me in this project was to make these groundbreaking texts available to as many readers and language learners as possible, while also being as true to and respectful of the original text as possible.

Sarah Henzi
November 2019

RECOVERING AND
RECONTEXTUALIZING
AN ANTANE KAPESH:
TRANSLATOR'S AFTERWORD

by Sarah Henzi

"Tshitshipanu aimun" are the opening words of *Eukuan nin matshi-manitu innushkueu – Je suis une maudite sauvagesse* (*I Am a Damn Savage*), Innu writer An Antane Kapesh's 1976 bilingual memoir.[1] *Tshitshipanu* signals a beginning, a departure, and *aimun* can mean a word, a statement, language, speech, and/or an opinion expressed orally.[2] In her preface to *Eukuan nin matshi-manitu innushkueu – Je suis une maudite sauvagesse*, Kapesh writes: "In my book, there is no White voice. When I thought about writing to defend myself and to defend the culture of my children, I had to first think carefully because I knew that writing was not a part of my culture… [But] after having made…the decision to write, this is what I came to understand: any person who wishes to accomplish something will encounter difficulties but nonetheless, she should never get discouraged."[3] *Eukuan nin matshi-manitu innushkueu – Je suis une maudite sauvagesse* is thus a point of many beginnings: of language, of writing, of taking voice, of speaking up, of speaking against – there is no more room for the colonizer's voice.

Eukuan nin matshi-manitu innushkueu – Je suis une maudite sauvagesse is a crucial text, and not only for the writer's perspective on colonial history, the turmoils of which (forced relocation, residential schools, assimilation) she lived through and witnessed; it also signals the (re)beginnings of Indigenous writing in Québec, in the same way that Maria Campbell's *Halfbreed* is referred to as the "rebirth of Indigenous writing in Canada" (Pivato n.p.).[4] An Antane Kapesh is the first Indigenous woman to publish in French;[5] not only does she offer her readers a specifically Innu perspective on the colonial history of Québec, but she reinscribes both her voice as an Indigenous woman that we are compelled to listen to – it is important to remember that this publication comes before the 1985 amendments to the Indian Act – and the voices of her family and ancestors. To this end, she relies on stories and testimonies of her family members – her husband, her father, her mother, her grandparents, and even great-grandparents – that are not only inserted into the text, but act as authoritative voices, at times taking over the narrative and, ultimately, rectifying what stories have been told, how, and by whom.

Similar to the United States, resistance movements and activism fuelled Indigenous cultural production across Canada, and the 1970s are marked by the seminal works of several Indigenous women: Métis writer Maria Campbell's *Halfbreed* (1973), Cree writer Jane Willis (now Pachano)'s *Geniesh: An Indian Girlhood* (1973), Stó:lō author Lee Maracle's *Bobbi Lee: Indian Rebel* (1975), and Inuit writer Mini Aodla Freeman's *Life Among the Qallunaat* (1978). The political climate in Québec as well, from the Quiet Revolution to the October Crisis, is an important factor in the genesis of Kapesh's literary work, which, in turn, must be understood as complementary to and an extension of her own activism and political work, which I discuss further below. Ultimately, what all of these works by Indigenous women have in common is an underlying critique of how different forms of oppression converge, and the effects they have had on Indigenous peoples for decades. In stating how settler society will eventually have to take responsibility and recognize its faults, and accept that, indeed, the Innu – as well as all the other nations – are not going anywhere, An Antane Kapesh's work radically changed both the literary and political scenes in Québec.

Notes Towards a Translation, Part 1

When I moved to Montréal in 2004 to pursue my doctoral studies, I happened upon An Antane Kapesh's two books in a second-hand bookstore. Little did I know, at the time, how precious that was; both had been out of print for years, and it would take several more years until their republication. Little did I realize, too, how lucky I was, a grad student in an English program wanting to work on Indigenous literatures, to be able to read across colonial languages and include francophone texts in my research. It took moving to Vancouver in 2013 to understand how these texts needed to be made accessible to anglophone readers, so as to complement and enrich the field of Indigenous literary studies, as it was and is being studied, developed, and institutionalized: the language barrier needed to be transcended. And in fact, over the last few years, a number of texts written by francophone Indigenous authors have been appearing in translation, such as Rita Mestokosho's *How I See Life Grandmother – Eshi uapataman Nukum* (2011);[6] Joséphine Bacon's *Message Sticks – Tshissinuatshitakana* (2013)[7] and *A Tea in the Tundra – Nipishapui Nete Mushuat* (2017);[8] Naomi Fontaine's *Kuessipan* (2013);[9] Natasha Kanapé Fontaine's *Do Not Enter My Soul in Your Shoes* (2015), *Assi Manifesto* (2016), and *Blueberries and Apricots* (2018);[10] and Virginia Pésémapéo Bordeleau's *Winter Child* (2017),[11] to name a select few – and as I write this, many other translation projects are underway. Similarly, several works, both creative and theoretical, have been and are being translated from English into French, including those by writers such as Marilyn Dumont, Katherena Vermette, Rita Joe, Eden Robinson, Drew Hayden Taylor, Leanne Betasamosake Simpson, Glen Coulthard, and Taiaiake Alfred. As noted by French-Maliseet scholar Michèle Lacombe, "while French-English language barriers are difficult to overcome at gatherings, the work of translation cannot help but facilitate dialogue between Indigenous poets in Canada" (161). Indeed, the new availability of such a wide range of texts in translation is enabling a much-needed dialogue between writers and scholars that moves beyond and across linguistic barriers, gesturing towards what can be thought of, now, as a truly transnational corpus.[12]

An Antane Kapesh's two books had been out of print for decades. Their republication in 2015 by the Saguenay Native Friendship Centre rekindled my desire to see them in translation.[13] This project thus began "officially" in June 2016, when I was able to speak with David Sioui, who spearheaded the project to republish the two texts at the Friendship Centre. The next and most important step – indeed, its importance has remained foremost ever since – was to get the consent of the family for the translation project, even if the legal copyright holder was the Friendship Centre.[14] In *Elements of Indigenous Style: A Guide for Writing By and About Indigenous Peoples*, Opsakwayak Cree publisher and writer Greg Younging lists twenty-two principles that should be kept in mind when working with Indigenous texts. While this essential work was only released in February 2018, I take note of several of the principles that I deem guided my own process: namely, principle 6, collaboration; principle 8, consent; and principle 9, trust. Importantly, in principle 6, Younging notes: "Take the necessary time. That [collaboration] takes time. Do your best to take the time" (31). Many subsequent steps have taken place, and have taken time, since June 2016. Each of them has only made this project stronger.

In this field of work, questions of positionality always arise. Should they not, then the work we attempt to do, as settler scholars, should be called into question. Undertaking the translation of two Innu texts, as a settler scholar, and translating from the French (which is also a translation) into English, thus attempting to work through "the pitfalls of moving from one colonial language to another" (Moyes 90), was admittedly daunting but, as I state in the Translator's Note, warranted. As such, I attempt to ground my process in the theoretical considerations of Lacombe, again, who writes that "translation undertaken by Innu poets themselves, while preferable, is not always possible, and in any case, their priorities as writers may lie elsewhere" and that "academics (especially those who, like me, do not speak an Indigenous language) can play a useful role in promoting the work of translation" (161); of Renate Eigenbrod, who, in *Travelling Knowledges*, writes about being "a facilitator for the discussion of [Indigenous] literatures" (8), albeit from "a positionality of non-authority" (143);[15] and of Daniel Heath Justice, who reminds us that an ethical relationship (and I read here the act of translation as an example of an ethical relationship) "requires respect, attentiveness, intellectual rigor, and no small amount of moral courage" (2004: 9). I thus proceed in the attempt to be useful, ethical, respectful, responsible, non-authoritative, and facilitating.

The Life of An Antane Kapesh

An Antane Kapesh was born in 1926 near Fort Chimo (now known as Kuujjuaq), married in 1942, and lived a traditional, nomadic life (across a territory that spanned from the Moisie River to Kuujjuaq) until 1953, when she and her family were relocated to Malioténam (also known as Mani-utenam), a reserve near Sept-Îles created in 1949, with its own residential school, which was in operation from 1952 to 1971.[16] The reserve had been established "to relocate both the bands living in Sept-Îles and the Innu living in Moisie to this site in order to facilitate their integration in the agglomeration of the city of Sept-Îles...The new Indian Act (1952) [*sic*; 1951] forced the federal government to implement housing, health, education and social security programs, thus providing incentives for the Innu to leave their land and move away from their traditional activities" (Picard 13). These "incentives" – or, as per the Truth and Reconciliation Commission report, "a program of forced removal" – forced the Innu to slowly adopt a sedentary lifestyle, while also making way for "opening up to non-Aboriginal settlers the land occupied by the original reserve created in 1906 (Uashat) [which,] by the post-war years, occupied prime real estate in the heart of Sept-Îles" (Truth and Reconciliation Commission 2015a: 41). Chapter 3 of An Antane Kapesh's first book, *Eukuan nin matshi-manitu innushkueu – Je suis une maudite sauvagesse*, describes this move down to the reserve as a clever ruse: "When he wanted to go out onto our lands, inland, the White man made our eyes shimmer with all the goods of his own settlement on the coast; it is along the coastline that he built our houses, that is where he built our school."[17] Along with the idea of settlement came that of having to earn a living. Following the official establishment of Schefferville in 1955 (the first permanent prospecting infrastructure had been established in 1947),[18] 510 kilometres away back inland, people returned to the area; Kapesh writes, "in 1956, we left the houses that had been built for us in Sept-Îles, on the coast, and we went back to our territories."[19] Chapter 8 describes how while the Innu who returned to Schefferville "thought that Iron Ore would be friendly towards [them] and take pity on [them], given that they were going to destroy [their] hunting territories and make a big profit from them,"[20] instead they were quickly relocated (by June 1956) to Lake John, 3.5 kilometres away from the town. Then, "about ten years after we were moved to Lake John," writes Kapesh, "there was talk to move us back to where we had been evicted from."[21] The proposed place to which they would be moved back is described by Kapesh as such: "The parcel of land that they thought to give us in town was the dirtiest part and was very small, which would have meant even less space than before...After he has dirtied a place, it is in that place that the White man always tries to build houses for the Innu." It is worth noting that the status of the "Schefferville Innu,"[22] who were linked to their original bands of Uashat and Mani-utenam, was not recognized by the federal government until 1968. With this recognition as an autonomous band came the "gift" of land at Pearce Point, on the outskirts of Schefferville, now known as the Matimekush reserve (Picard 13). It is this piece of land that Kapesh was so critical of, but to which most residents of Lake John had moved by 1972, following pressure tactics, which she carefully describes in Chapter 8. The timeframe of all these events is important, because they coincide with An Antane Kapesh's involvement in politics: she notes, "I was part of the Band Council for four years. I was first councilperson during two years and during another two years [1965–1967], I was Band Chief"[23];

"I began to take care of my own business with help from the Indi- ans of Quebec Association"[24] (which was founded in the fall of 1965).[25] Finally, the "dissident families" – as stated on the website of the Matimekush-Lac John community[26] – who refused to move stayed in Lake John. An Antane Kapesh left Lake John in 1976 and returned to Sept-Îles.

Two Groundbreaking Works[27]

Eukuan nin matshi-manitu innushkueu – Je suis une maudite sau- vagesse was published in a single, bilingual Innu-French edition, something that was unheard of in 1976. A subsequent re-edition of the text in 1982 by the Parisian feminist publishing house Éditions des Femmes was in French only.[28] An Antane Kapesh's second book, *Tanite nene etutamin nitassi? – Qu'as-tu fait de mon pays? (What Have you Done to my Country?)* was published in 1979 in French and in Innu, though separately, by the now-defunct Éditions impossibles.[29] In 1981, it was adapted into a play (by Kapesh and José Mailhot) and performed at the Théâtre Denise- Pelletier, in Montréal, from November 12 to December 7, 1981 (Kapesh came from Sept-Îles to attend the premiere).[30] It is worth noting that the Innu versions of both texts reflect "the point at which the process of normalizing the spelling was" (Mailhot 2018), respectively in 1976 and 1979. This process has continued over decades, in large part in order to facilitate the teaching of the language in schools.[31] *Tanite nene etutamin nitassi? – Qu'as- tu fait de mon pays?* was thus "standardized" and included in a 1998 textbook[32] for the Innu Language and Culture program taught at the Cégep[33] of Sept-Îles and, later on, published by the Institut culturel éducatif montagnais (known today as Institut Tshakapesh[34]) in 2004, shortly before the author's passing.[35] Thus, so that this volume may reach the most readers, and be used as a teaching tool, it is the 2004 version of *Tanite nene etutamin nitassi? – Qu'as-tu fait de mon pays?* that is included. At the onset of this project, *Eukuan nin matshi-manitu innushkueu – Je suis une mau- dite sauvagesse*, however, had never undergone the same process. For this English version, as well as for the recently released 2019

French version by Mémoire d'encrier, the 1976 text was entirely revised and the spelling corrected in accordance with the publishing policy of Tshakapesh Institute, which, from 1989 to 1997, oversaw and funded the process of standardizing the spelling of the Innu language. This important update was undertaken by Jérémie Ambroise, Innu language advisor at Tshakapesh Institute, and José Mailhot, translator of the original French version and Innu linguist, with the help of an advisory committee made up of Innu speakers Anne-Marie André, Judith Mestokosho, Céline Bellefleur, and Philomène Grégoire; text input from the published version was done by Marguerite MacKenzie.

As indicated above, both texts were republished in 2015, in bilingual Innu-French editions by the Saguenay Native Friendship Centre. I believe it is important to emphasize that it was a Friendship Centre, and not an established publishing house, that enabled these texts to resurface after decades of being out of print. The impetus for the republication, David Sioui told me, came in large part because of Idle No More, and a desire among the younger generation to see new material and new models.[36] As a result, the reappearance of and relatively easy access to these new editions caused quite a stir; not only are they being used more and more in classes across Québec (in high schools and in universities), but articles are being published, and students are making them primary texts in their graduate research projects. Moreover, several established publishing houses quickly showed a keen interest in taking over the project – including the original publisher of *Eukuan nin matshi-manitu innushkueu – Je suis une maudite sauvagesse*, Leméac, who despite holding the copyright for almost thirty years, never republished it (the rights were reverted back to the family after the author's death in 2004). One explanation for this lack of republication (in Québec, at least, since it was republished in France), as reported by Italian scholar Maurizio Gatti, and according to Cree-Algonquin author Bernard Assiniwi, who at the time of Kapesh's publication had been in charge of Leméac's special series "Ni-T'Chawama/Mon ami mon frère" devoted to Indigenous peoples (1972–1976;

"Bernard Assiniwi" n.p.), was that *Eukuan nin matshi-manitu innushkueu – Je suis une maudite sauvagesse* brought on "negative reactions" from the public, and the publishers received several letters from "outraged readers," compelling Assiniwi to discontinue his series "rather than publish modified texts so as not to displease Québécois readers" (Gatti 2006: 160). If one looks at the different press releases, however, the reviews note that "this is a true and hard book, capable of wakening up those good souls that have fallen asleep due to materialist notions of progress and development" (Martel),[37] it is "a terrible indictment, that all Québécois...should read" (Piazza),[38] and it provides a "flagrant illustration of the dispossession that the Indians are victims of and of the notorious cretinism of the average White man...[and] what the White man has done and continues to do to the Indians is really trashy" (Lebrun).[39] Its "language is simple, direct, without false sentimentality, but grounded in a great wisdom and a long reflection" (Rowan),[40] but there are also "those words that taste of blood, that burn the eyes and that would like to engender violence rather than vain revolt" (Boudreau 1981)[41]: indeed, most reviewers include excerpts from the book in their review, excerpts that compel their readers to "reread [those words] several times before being convinced of their reality...words that one hates to read and that one would like to see disappear forever" (Boudreau 1981).[42] Boudreau's review, for instance, works around the rather graphic passages in *Eukuan nin matshi-manitu innushkueu – Je suis une maudite sauvagesse* (Chapter 6) that speak of police brutality: "After [my son] was admitted to hospital, I thought to go see the chief of police to tell him that two of the city's officers had injured my son...I told him: 'Did you hear about what happened last night? Apparently two officers injured my son.' The chief of police told me: 'I heard about it.' Then he added: 'If your son was injured by police officers, it cannot have been by my men, it must have been by RCMP officers.' The chief of police then told me: 'When the officers injured your boy, you are lucky I was not there, he would be dead!' Then he showed me a gun and said: 'It is with this gun that I would have shot your boy and I would have shot him in the head.'"[43] The inclusion of this passage, both in the text and in reviews is, to say the least, rather remarkable, since it is no secret that several texts written and published during that time were censored – most noteworthy, Maria Campbell's *Halfbreed*, whose publishers made her remove several elements from her original manuscript. The original manuscript[44] of *Eukuan nin matshi-manitu innushkueu – Je suis une maudite sauvagesse* underwent no such editorial censorship (Mailhot 2018).

Education and Assimilation

The question of language and cultural revitalization is paramount to the author. The bilingual formats in which both texts were published were meant to reach the members of her community and instill a desire for resistance and to fight back, but also the broader Québécois audience, as a testimonial account of what was going on within communities. On the one hand, An Antane Kapesh wrote to preserve and share her culture, experience, and knowledge, all of which were disappearing at an alarming rate because many Elders were aged or dying (an aspect that resonates with the loss of the grandfather figure in her second book), or no longer able to speak with their children due to the loss of language (in Chapter 3 of her first book, she writes: "when I speak Innu to my children, they do not understand me, and when they speak to me, I do not understand them well because already, my children can barely speak Innu today"[45]). On the other hand, Kapesh wanted to publicly denounce the conditions in which she and the Innu were made to live, and to address the changes she was witnessing due to land dispossession and education through both the residential and public school systems.

In both of her texts, Kapesh gives a scathing report of the impact of "L'éducation blanche," the White man's education – and this includes not only residential schools[46] but also the provincial education system. Indeed, as per the 1951 amendments to the Indian Act, the federal government was "allow[ed] to enter into agreements with provincial governments and school boards to have First Nations students educated in public schools" (Truth and Reconciliation Commission 2015b: 68). However, this "integration policy" soon revealed to be "not only ill-conceived but actually harmful...[because] students were subjected to an education that demeaned their history [a 1968 survey pointed out that in some schoolbooks, the words *squaw* and *redskin* were used]...and did not even recognize them or their families as citizens" (Indigenous peoples in Canada were not granted the right to vote and therefore act as citizens until 1960) (Truth and Reconciliation Commission 2015b: 75–78). Indeed, in Chapter 3 of *Eukuan nin matshi-manitu innushkueu – Je suis une maudite sauvagesse*, Kapesh points out that they were not told, or consulted, when the children were moved to the provincial system, and she laments how both the White children and teachers picked on and insulted them repeatedly. Throughout the text, she repeats that what worries her the most is that the White man "ruined" her children,[47] and what hurts her the most is that the White man "has no regrets today about our children."[48]

Indeed, Kapesh finds especially deplorable the tactics that were used to convince parents to send their children to school. She reports that when they were told a school was being built, "we were told all sorts of good things and we were shown all kinds of nice things. This was done in the beginning, but only so as not to displease us."[49] Parents were told that sending their children to school would enable them to continue their lifestyle on the land without being "burdened" by their children, which Kapesh considers absurd, because the Innu were "used to always taking care of [their] children [themselves] in the bush."[50] Children were thus made to be seen as a nuisance, and as the reason why parents would eventually be held back from practising their culture. Kapesh adds, "We tried to live like before, to go out onto the land anyway, as we were told. But that did not suit us for long because we are not used to, we Innu, each family living apart from their children. The Innu could therefore no longer go out onto the land ten months at a time because his children were being kept as boarders. Of course he wanted to see them and to check how they were being taken care of, if they were being treated well or not. And it is for this reason, I believe, that the Innu then thought about getting him too a job."[51] According to Kapesh, then, it is the mandatory education of children that generated the parents' eventual, and passively enforced, settlement.

In a 1979 interview with Clément Trudel, Kapesh points to the feelings of "boredom" and "being fenced in" that she witnessed among members of her community as symptomatic of the impact of the loss of land and resources, and the confinement to reserve life: "[and] despite that felt boredom, we are obliged to stay inside the fence" (qtd. in Trudel).[52] That said, the publication of her two books can be seen as her refusal to partake in such a system – while the closing words of the child protagonist in *Tanite nene etutamin nitassi? – Qu'as-tu fait de mon pays?* are "and he knew that in the future, and until his death, he would have to continue, like it or not, to play the fool with the Polichinelles and to play along with their games,"[53] Kapesh's own words at a press conference, held at the National Assembly in Québec City on November 21, 1979, following the publication of her second book, say something else: "If we do not stop playing with you, I think that we will not be able to pull through...We will never be able to do anything with you Whites" (qtd. in Falardeau).[54] She adds, "I no longer want to be called Québécoise because I belong to the Indian [Innu] nation and what is most important to me is to preserve my language, my territory and my culture" (qtd. in Falardeau).[55] Similar affirmations can be found in both her works: in the afterword of *Eukuan nin matshi-manitu innushkueu – Je suis une maudite sauvagesse*, Kapesh states, "I am a damn Savage. I am very proud when, today, I hear myself being called a Savage. When I hear the White man say this word, I understand that he is telling me again and again that I am a real Innu woman and that it was I who first lived in the bush"[56]; and, in *Tanite nene etutamin nitassi? – Qu'as-tu fait de mon pays?* the child protagonist makes it clear that while the Polichinelles want to call themselves Québécois, he "will never agree with [them]."[57] Thus, the issue of voice is, here, paramount – as noted by Cherokee scholar Daniel Heath Justice, "Given the fact that most of settler North America has consistently been either willfully or circumstantially deaf to the words and perspectives of Indigenous peoples throughout colonial history, it is hardly surprising that the issue of voice is both profoundly personal as well as political in Indigenous writing and oratory today" (116) – Kapesh reclaims voice, history, and agency, as an Indigenous woman, as a writer, and as a political person.

The narrative of *Tanite nene etutamin nitassi? – Qu'as-tu fait de mon pays?* is carefully constructed around the child protagonist gradually losing his voice, in addition to his language, culture, and land: the number of direct speech quotations by the boy become fewer and fewer, while those of the Polichinelles increase, until the narrative is mostly theirs. By the end of Section IV, the boy "can no longer move forward and he no longer knows the place he came from...He knows, now, that he has no way to exist in the future."[58] I read this as reflective of Kapesh's words above, on feeling "fenced in" and trapped, but she – and more importantly, the boy – takes over the narrative once again in the final section (Section V). Kapesh gives him a final, resilient outcry, as he confronts and warns the Polichinelles: "Now that you see how miserable I am, you simply want to slip away, you want to send me back to where I came from as quickly as possible. What does this mean? Do you once again have something else in store? Let me tell you right now what I think. Whether I go back or not to where I came from, if I find myself in trouble, be assured that it is at you that I will yell. Be assured to always see me, and make yourself available, do not ever hide from me if I want to see you, if I need you. In the future, and until I die, do not ever grow tired of me."[59] The book ends with a clear message: that despite all the harm done, and although they may still need to play along – "jouer à leurs polichinelleries" – the Innu are not going anywhere, and the colonizers will be held accountable for their actions. Most importantly, Kapesh invites her readers to reflect on how that accountability may be achieved, and it is not up to her to explain, or to ask for anything – "it is [them] who need to understand" (qtd. in Falardeau).[60] After all, Kapesh already did the writing – as reported by Raymond Giroux, who attended the press conference as well, Kapesh said "if the Whites cannot understand her book, then she will not write any others" (Giroux).[61]

Although she did not write another book, today Kapesh's literary legacy is referred to and acknowledged by several generations of contemporary writers and filmmakers, whose works – of which many are bilingual as well – are gaining national and international attention, in large part thanks to their translations. Retracing the steps of Kapesh's life, from living on the land to being relocated to a reserve, to then moving back into the interior, and being relocated once more; from the impacts of the schooling system to the appropriation of land stewardship and destruction of wildlife and plants; from police brutality to racial profiling; and from media misrepresentation to, finally, the publication of *Eukuan nin matshi-manitu innushkueu – Je suis une maudite sauvagesse* – a book that took five years to write – all attest to how, and why, Kapesh's work needs to be not only recovered, but celebrated, and recontextualized as a keystone in the production of Indigenous writing. An Antane Kapesh offers a rewriting of colonial history, an Innu "auto-histoire," to borrow from Wendat historian Georges Sioui – one that reinserts the stories from her father and other Elders as correctives to the narratives produced by the priests and politicians; one that gestures towards the debates around sovereignty in Québec as potential fuel to think in terms of an Innu sovereignty; one that discredits the colonial institutions of education, law, and health care; and last but by far not least, one that calls for the revitalization and the reaffirmation of *Innu-aimun*.

Notes Towards a Translation, Part 2

Lastly, I wanted to share a few "technical" translation afterthoughts and decisions. As indicated above, this was a daunting project, one that necessitated that I make certain decisions, which

I would like to put forward here. Reminiscent of Renate Eigenbrod's idea of a position of "non-authority," this is a gesture to invite conversations on how the process of translation is a very personal, intimate, and subjective act, and thus, I am aware that other possibilities may well exist. With this in mind, I will start with the decision regarding which versions to use for my translations, and move along from there, since all of these choices are, in a way, intertwined.

As stated above, both texts were republished in 2015 by the Saguenay Native Friendship Centre, and both underwent linguistic French and Innu revisions by Geneviève Shanipiap McKenzie-Siouï, as noted on the copyright pages. For the purpose of this translation project, I chose to use the original 1976 and 1979 French versions for two reasons: the first is that José Mailhot worked very closely with An Antane Kapesh when she was doing her own translation into French, and the second is that upon close reading, some of the revisions in the 2015 versions, albeit very minor, do change how the text may be read. For instance, at the beginning of Chapter 3, the 1976 version reads as such: "C'est à cette époque que nous avons vu pour de vrai des fonctionnaires [des Affaires indiennes] pour la première fois et c'était la première fois que nous les entendions *parler aux* Indiens" (69; emphasis mine). The 2015 version reads: "C'est à cette époque que nous avons vu pour de vrai des fonctionnaires pour la première fois et c'était la première fois que nous les entendions *discuter avec* les Innu" (107; emphasis mine). "Parler à," in English, is to speak to, whereas "discuter avec" is to speak with – this, to me, is a crucial difference, one that changes the power dynamics at play between the interlocutors; and in effect, the Innu verb that is used, *aimieu*, translates as "s/he talks/speaks *to* him" (*Online Innu Dictionary*; emphasis mine). Finally, because of the extensive revision work that went into the Innu text in 2019, Mailhot also re-examined her original French translation, and made some small, but significant, changes[62]; these she communicated to me and I have included those that affected the English translation. A noteworthy change, for instance, throughout

Chapter 5, is the Innu word *kaminnanut*, which had been translated as "l'hotel" – the hotel – in the 1976 version. However, in the 2019 revised translation, it has been corrected to "le bar" – the bar.

Other revisions in the 2015 version of *Eukuan nin matshimanitu innushkueu – Je suis une maudite sauvagesse* did give me cause for considerable reflection; two, in particular, are noteworthy. First, unlike the original 1976 version in which the Innu and French versions were presented in an immediate alternate fashion (left page in Innu, right page in French), the 2015 republication presents the Innu text first, in full, followed by the French text, in full. On the one hand, the alternate presentation has the effect of keeping the Innu language present throughout the reading; but, on the other hand, holding a functional opposite-page translation over the course of an entire book – or rather, two books – is impractical. In effect, while the facing-page translation in the 1976 version was set up so that readers could follow along, the grammar of the languages is very different, so sentences in Innu tend to be longer. Thus, while at the beginning of each chapter, the two languages largely correspond on the facing pages, by the end of the chapter, the Innu text extends about a page or two longer than the French text. Initially, I worried that since English sentences are shorter than French ones, such a discrepancy would only be exacerbated. I also felt that such an editorial choice – of placing first the Innu text, and then the translation – would better reflect my wish to give central place to the original text and authorial voice; it is for this same reason that I chose an afterword, rather than a preface. However, after careful consideration and consultation with various people – scholars, teachers, language learners, and editors – it became clear that the original layout, chosen for the 1976 publication, was the better one for this edition as well. First, for language learners, being able to follow the text easily in both languages is imperative. Second, as Kapesh writes in her epigraph: "I would be happy to see other Innu people writing, in the Innu language."[63] If the text – and its layout – was meant to serve as a pedagogical tool to promote language education and, by extension, creative writing, then this intention and choice had to be respected as well.

Second, in the 2015 republication, the word "Indien" (Indian) was replaced with "Innu." In the Innu version of the text, Kapesh uses the word *Innu* (except in four instances where she uses *Innu Mutania*, "Montagnais"[64]), which translates first as "human being," but also as "Innu, First Nations person" (*Online Innu Dictionary*). Of course, the word "Indian" was common in the 1970s, but it seemed far too inappropriate to use throughout in a contemporary translation; thus I maintained that revision, and used the word "Innu," in the hopes that it would reflect better how the author referred to herself and to her people. However, in instances of direct speech by a White person, I did leave the word "Indian," so as to reflect the inherent violence and racism in those interjections; in other places, the French word "sauvage" is used in both versions, which translates as "savage" – these I left as well, for the same reasons. Of note, too, is that the original French title uses the word "sauvagesse" – a very gendered (the female version of "sauvage") and racist term that cannot be rendered as such in English ("savage" thus being the best to be found). It is a term, however, that Kapesh attempts to reclaim by using it also in her afterword (Kapesh 1976: 240). Interestingly, in *Tanite nene etutamin nitassi? – Qu'as-tu fait de mon pays?*, none of these words – Innu, Indian, savage – are used. The only clear indication in the French text that this is an Innu text (apart from the fact that the author is Innu) is the use of Innu terms, the definitions of which can be found at the end in a glossary. As noted above, the White people are referred to as "Polichinelles," in Innu *Kauitenitakushit*, which does not have an actual equivalent, but loosely means "those who are comical" (Kapesh 1979: 83).

The style of An Antane Kapesh's writing is direct and to the point. As noted by friends and colleagues who read my first drafts,[65] I attempted to follow Kapesh's style, for instance by allowing run-on sentences, or phrasing a sentence in the passive voice rather than in the active. I also attempted to stay as close as possible to word choice; for instance, in the opening section of *Tanite nene etutamin nitassi?* – *Qu'as-tu fait de mon pays?*, I translated "[le vieux] ne dépendait que de lui-même pour subsister" (Kapesh 1979: 9) as "[the old man] depended only on himself for his subsistence." I was suggested instead "[the old man] depended only on himself to survive," and while "survive" and "subsist" are synonyms, the French word is "subsister" and not "survivre." Thinking about the specificities of word choice entails thinking about the (possible) meaning(s) the author wanted to convey as well, even more so given that I am working with a translation and not the original text. Another notable example, which was also pointed out by one of my proofreaders, was the "outhouse" that Kapesh and her husband purchased in 1956, whereas the Innu who purchased structures before them had bought "shacks" (Kapesh writes that there were "no more little shacks left, all that [was] left [was] a small outhouse"[66]). In the French version, the word "bécosse" is a Quebecism from the English word "backhouse"; the Innu word, *mishiutshuap*, literally means "where one defecates," which is both used for an indoor washroom and an outdoor structure, i.e., an outhouse. Thus, indeed, that is the structure that Kapesh and her husband purchased, for one hundred dollars, and to which they added extensions to build their house.

A final, important, word-related brainteaser was the expression "dans le bois," which I often translated as "in the woods" or "in the bush," but which can also mean more broadly "on the land." Equally the expression "à l'intérieur des terres," I translated as "inland," "in the interior," "upon the land," or "in the territories." These different options highlight the difficulties of working between colonial (and very limited) languages, on the one hand, and the impossibility at times of truly reflecting the original meaning, which, in land-based languages like *Innu-aimun*, may offer up to a dozen translations, depending on the context. Innu poet Joséphine Bacon, for instance, says that we need to conceive of land as "an intransitive verb" and, as noted by Daniel Chartier, "the French word is dull in the face of the grandeur of this concept" (180).[67] Likewise, to conceive of land as "storied," "routed," and "rooted," as suggested by Mishuana Goeman, is to understand land as "a salient term and concept that weaves people together around common understandings and experiences" (Goeman 72). Thus, in my act of translation, it is not just about depicting a space or place; rather, it is about narrating the relationship between people belonging and moving on and through that space or place – as well as being prevented from doing so – and the histories that are tied within those movements.

This, finally, leads me back to an expression used by Michèle Lacombe: "words that walk…in [and across] referential, metaphorical, translated, spoken dialogical languages" (160). Translation is thinking about the walking of words, how they change and influence each other, the sentence, the paragraph; how they guide one's reading, one's attempt at understanding the author's thoughts, desires, fears, musings, ravings, and unravellings. Translation is about attempting to bring together all these different languages, and mobilizing these affects into (and across) a literary landscape as conceived of and created by the writer. Unlike some of the other scholars I have cited here, who are fortunate in that they can speak and/or collaborate with the poets they are translating[68] – whether extensively or not – I am aware that the writer whom I am translating is no longer here. In recent years, the loss of women mentors and intellectuals, such as Renate Eigenbrod and Jo-Ann Episkenew, has prompted a strong desire to honour and uphold their teachings through, among others, mentorship activities and workshops[69] – essentially, growing and building up the community that they were key in establishing, here, in lands claimed by Canada. With this project, I have wanted to honour, uphold, and promote the work of another woman, who also greatly contributed to establishing the field, but whose writing has yet to receive the attention it deserves, and to inspire more writers and scholars, beyond Québec. As I have attempted to navigate An Antane Kapesh's own "words that walk," amid the different languages at play, I hope to have done justice to her teachings and to her landscapes – territorial and philosophical.

Notes

1 The original spelling of the title, in 1976, was *Eukuan nin matshimanitu innu-iskueu*.

2 *Online Innu Dictionary*. Both definitions retrieved July 1, 2019.

3 "Dans mon livre, il n'y a pas de parole de Blanc. Quand j'ai songé à écrire pour me défendre et pour défendre la culture de mes enfants, j'ai d'abord bien réfléchi car je savais qu'il ne fait pas partie de ma culture d'écrire... [Mais] après avoir une fois pour toutes pris... la décision d'écrire, voici ce que j'ai compris: toute personne qui songe à accomplir quelque chose rencontrera des difficultés mais en dépit de cela, elle ne devra jamais se décourager" (Kapesh 1976: 9).

4 I want to emphasize the "re-" here, because of course there was literature before, different kinds of literature, but then there was also what Canadian literary critic William H. New refers to as a "hiatus" (370) – an interruption, one that can be explained by residential schools and other assimilative policies.

5 In his crucial 2004 (expanded 2009) anthology, *Littérature amérindienne du Québec: Écrits de langue française*, an anthology devoted to Indigenous literatures of Québec in French (and the first such text since Diane Boudreau's 1993 *Histoire de la littérature amérindienne au Québec: oralité et écriture*), Maurizio Gatti did not include the works of An Antane Kapesh. Gatti explains this purposeful omission in his introduction, as due to their status of "translations": the francophone texts, he notes, to which we have access are translations, and thereby "linguistic adaptations and changes are inevitable... To read *Je suis une maudite sauvagesse* in French is to read An Antane Kapesh through the translator José Mailhot" ("Quand un texte est traduit d'une langue à une autre par une personne qui n'est pas l'auteur originel, des adaptations et des changements linguistiques sont inévitables. Ainsi, on lira une réécriture du traducteur, mais qui ne peut plus être considérée au même titre que le texte source. Lire *Je suis une maudite sauvagesse en français*, c'est lire An Antane-Kapesh à travers José Mailhot. Quoique la traduction soit fidèle et compétente, elle demeure une traduction" [18–19]). That said, in his subsequent book *Être écrivain amérindien au Québec*, Gatti does state that An Antane Kapesh became a model of (and for) Innu writing, "a literary reference for many" (149). Indeed, in the 2017 anthology *Tracer un chemin: Meshkanatsheu / Écrits des Premiers Peuples*, the co-authors not only (re)list her, but also refer to her as "the first Indigenous woman in Canada to publish works in French" (Létourneau, Fontaine, and Dezutter 164).

6 Mestokosho's *Eshi uapataman Nukum – Comment je perçois la vie, Grand-mère* was first published in French in 1995 by Éditions Piekuakami; she is credited "as the first Innu poet to publish a collection in Québec" (Gatti 2004: 224). Mestokosho's book, like Kapesh's, was also out of print for many years, until it was republished in both bilingual (French-Innu, 2010)

and trilingual (English-French-Innu, 2011; English translation by Sue Rose) editions by Beijbom Books (Sweden). Additionally, they published a trilingual Swedish-French-Innu version in 2010.

7 Translated by Phyllis Aronoff (original title: *Bâtons à message – Tshissinua-tshitakana*, Mémoire d'encrier, 2009).

8 Translated by Donald Winkler (original title: *Un thé dans la toundra – Nip-ishapui nete mushuat*, Mémoire d'encrier, 2013).

9 Translated by David Homel (original title: *Kuessipan. À toi*, Mémoire d'encrier, 2011).

10 All three were translated by Howard Scott (original titles, all published by Mémoire d'encrier: *N'entre pas dans mon âme avec tes chaussures* [2012], *Manifeste Assi* [2014], *Bleuets et abricots* [2016]).

11 Translated by Susan Ouriou and Christelle Morelli (original title: *L'enfant hiver*, Mémoire d'encrier, 2014).

12 See Henzi: "Un nouveau souffle vient agrémenter les corpus anglophones et francophones de la littérature autochtone – et ce grâce à la traduc-tion...Ainsi, un nouveau dialogue au-delà des frontières linguistiques s'établit enfin, et les intéressés de la littérature autochtone ont accès à un véritable corpus transnational" (n.p.).

13 In 2013, I wrote to translator and linguist specialist José Mailhot to ask if she knew whether the rights were still held by the two publishing houses, Leméac and Éditions impossibles. While Leméac confirmed the rights had been returned to the family upon the author's passing, it was more difficult to get information from Éditions impossibles, since it appears they ceased their activities in 1981.

14 In January 2019, the rights were reverted back to the family so that they could enter into a new publishing agreement with Montréal-based pub-lisher Mémoire d'encrier.

15 Eigenbrod, in speaking about a "positionality of non-authority," is also thinking in terms of the need of "teamwork," and that "Indigenous lan-guage speakers need to be involved" (143). I am lucky in this respect for in this project, I had two language speakers with whom I could consult: José Mailhot, who did the translation and revision of the two original texts (1976 and 1979), and Jérémie Ambroise, Innu language advisor at Tshakapesh Institute.

16 "The Maliotenam school opened in September 1952. It functioned as a combined residential and day school, with 273 students in grades One to Seven. Of these, 168 lived at the school, even though its official capacity was 150. By January 1953, approximately 190 students were boarders and applications for eleven more were under consideration.

"The number fell to 160 during the 1953–54 academic year, largely as a result of Indian Affairs' awareness that the school had been overcrowded since its opening...Maliotenam (Sept-Îles) closed in 1971" (Truth and Reconciliation Commission 2015a: 42–46).

17 "Quand il a voulu s'en aller sur nos terres, à l'intérieur, le Blanc a fait miroiter à nos yeux tous les avantages de son propre établissement au bord de la mer; c'est vers la côte qu'il a construit nos maisons, c'est là qu'il a construit notre école" (Kapesh 1976: 75).

18 See "Then and Now," Ville de Schefferville, 2014.

19 "En 1956, nous avons quitté les maisons qu'on avait construites pour nous à Sept-Îles, au bord de la mer, et nous sommes retournés sur nos terres" (Kapesh 1976: 185).

20 "Nous avions pensé que l'*Iron Ore* serait amicale envers nous et nous prendrait en pitié, elle qui allait détruire nos terrains de chasse et qui allait en tirer de gros profits" (Kapesh 1976: 185).

21 "Une dizaine d'années après être déménagés au Lac John...on commençait alors à nous parler de redéménager là d'où on nous avait délogés" (Kapesh 1976: 197).

22 "Le terrain qu'on envisageait nous donner en ville constituait la partie la plus sale et n'était qu'une petite pointe, ce qui nous ferait encore moins de terrain qu'auparavant...Après avoir sali un endroit c'est à cet endroit que le Blanc cherche ensuite à construire des maisons pour les Indiens [Innus]" (Kapesh 1976: 197).

23 "J'ai fait partie du Conseil de Bande pendant quatre ans. J'ai été premier conseiller pendant deux ans et pendant deux autres années [1965–1967], j'ai été Chef de Bande" (Kapesh 1976: 199).

24 "J'ai commencé à m'occuper de mes propres affaires du côté de l'Association des Indiens du Québec" (Kapesh 1976: 207).

25 In the 2015 revised version of Kapesh's text, Geneviève McKenzie-Sioui added a footnote indicating that the Association des Indiens du Québec, the Indians of Québec Association (IQA), was "today known as the Assembly of the First Nations of Quebec and Labrador (AFNQL)" (146). The AFNQL was founded in May 1985, but it does refer to the IQA as "definitely" its "ancestor or predecessor" (AFNQL, "About us"). The IQA, following an attempt at "internal reorganization" in 1976–1977, ceased its activities in 1977 (Turcotte 51, 131–132). It was succeeded by the Confédération des Indiens du Québec (CIQ), the Indians of Québec Confederation (Turcotte 51, 132). There is little information on this latter organization, but it appears they were still active in 1981 (LaRochelle 60).

26 "Au début des années 1970 quelques familles dissidentes avaient refusé d'emménager à la nouvelle réserve et décidaient de rester au Lac John" (see "Histoire," Conseil de la Nation Innu Matimekush-Lac John).

27 In addition to the two books discussed here, An Antane Kapesh published short stories for children (*Uniam mak shaian utipatshimunissimuau*, Montreal, ministère de l'Éducation, Service général des moyens d'enseignement, 1978), two series of "Stories in Montagnais" (« Petites histoires montagnaises », *Rencontre*, SAA, vol. IV, no. 3, 1983, pp. 14–15 and « Petites histoires montagnaises II », *Rencontre*, SAA, vol. IV, no. 4, 1983, pp. 8–9), and

an article (« Ces terres dont nous avions nommé chaque ruisseau », *Recherches amérindiennes au Québec*, vol. V, no. 2, 1975, pp. 2–3).

28 The objective of Éditions des Femmes, founded in 1973, was "more political than editorial" (Fouque n.p.). Co-founder Antoinette Fouque notes: "The desire that motivated the birth of éditions *des femmes* was more political than editorial: through the publishing house, it is the liberation of women that must be lead forward. It was open to all initiatives of struggle, individual or collective struggles, and in any domain whatsoever" ("Le désir qui a motivé la naissance des éditions des femmes est davantage politique qu'éditorial: à travers la maison d'édition, c'est la libération des femmes qu'il s'agit de faire avancer. Elle était ouverte à toutes les démarches de lutte, luttes individuelles ou collectives, et dans quelque champ que ce soit."). Given the audience (France) and the direction of the press, it is understandable that publishing the text alongside its Innu original version was likely not as important – that would have been an editorial decision, one that Leméac did make with the 1976 bilingual edition (another note on editorial decisions: the photo on the cover of the 1982 version is not of An Antane Kapesh [it is unclear, in fact, who that person is], whereas the photo on the cover of the 1976 version is of the author). In terms of content, however, it is clear that Kapesh's text must have spoken to the editors in terms of struggle, both individual and collective. Finally, the mission of the press to promote women's writing – "faire découvrir les écrits, la pensée des femmes" – also made Kapesh's text a prime candidate.

29 The original spelling of the title, in 1979, was *Tante nana etutamin nitassi?*

30 Robert Lévesque's article in *Le Devoir* (November 14, 1981) provides interesting elements on the play's production, most notably how the director, Jean-Luc Bastien, went to great lengths to do justice to the "Montagnais humour" and to An Antane Kapesh's voice. This humour, however, was not perceived as such by another critic, Jacques Larue-Langlois, who condemns the production as being too moralizing and childish. Likewise, Martial Dassylva is extremely critical not only of the production, but of the text itself, which he sees as "a Manichean discourse of hate, a trial and an indictment without nuances."

31 The release of a report in 1997, *Pour une orthographe unique de la langue innue* (Mailhot 1997), followed by a pan-dialectical dictionary in 2013 have greatly helped establish spelling conventions. See Mailhot, MacKenzie, and Junker, *Online Innu Dictionary* (2013). For more information on the overall project, see innu-aimun.ca.

32 Tanite nana etutamin nitassi? (An Antane Kapesh). *Ka tshitapatakanit mashinaikan, tshetshi apashtakanit Uashau-nessheshepit – Manuel de lecture destiné aux* étudiants *du CEGEP de Sept-Iles*. Institut culturel et éducatif montagnais 1998: 57–86.

33 Common acronym for Collège d'enseignement général et professionnel. In Québec, these are pre-university general and vocational colleges.

34 Founded in 1978, the Institut éducatif culturel atikamekw montagnais (IECAM, Atikamekw Montagnais Educational and Cultural Institute) became, in 1990, the Institut culturel éducatif montagnais (ICEM, Montagnais Cultural and Educational Institute), following the dissolution of the Conseil atikamekw montagnais (Atikamekw Montagnais Council, a political association that sought to defend the rights of Atikamekw and Innu [Montagnais] First Nations). In 2009, the board approved a new name, Institut Tshakapesh (Tshakapesh Institute) and a new logo ("Institut Tshakapesh" n.d.).

35 An Antane Kapesh passed away on November 13, 2004. I am grateful to José Mailhot for explaining and confirming these moments in the publication history of Kapesh's works.

36 See also "Réédition d'un classique, *Je suis une maudite sauvagesse*, maintenant disponible à Saguenay." Interview with Caroline Nepton Hotte, *Soirée boréale*, Radio-Canada, December 2, 2015.

37 "Voici donc un livre franc et dur, capable de réveiller les bonnes consciences endormies par les notions matérialistes de progrès et de développement."

38 "un terrible réquisitoire, que tout Québécois… devrait lire."

39 "l'illustration flagrante de la dépossession dont sont victimes les Indiens et du crétinisme notoire du Blanc moyen… [et] de ce que l'homme blanc a fait et continue de faire aux Indiens est une belle saloperie."

40 "une langue simple, directe, exempte de fausse sentimentalité, mais appuyée sur une grande sagesse et une longue réflexion."

41 "ces mots au goût de sang qui brûlent les yeux et qui voudraient engendrer violence plutôt que révolte impuissante."

42 "ces mots que l'on relit plusieurs fois avant d'être convaincu de leur réalité… ces mots que l'on déteste lire et que l'on voudrait voir disparaître à tout jamais."

43 "Après son admission à l'hôpital, j'ai pensé aller voir le chef de police pour lui dire que deux policiers de la ville avait blessé mon fils… Je lui dis : « Avez-vous entendu parler de ce qui s'est passé cette nuit? Apparemment deux policiers ont blessé mon fils. » Le chef de police me dit : « J'en ai entendu parler. » Puis il ajoute : « Si ton fils a été blessé par des policiers, ce ne doit pas être par mes hommes à moi, ce doit être par des policiers de la Gendarmerie Royale. » Le chef de police me dit ensuite : « Quand les policiers ont blessé ton gars, une chance que je n'étais pas là moi, il serait mort! » Puis il m'a montré un pistolet et m'a dit : « C'est avec ce pistolet que j'aurais tiré sur ton garçon et c'est dans la tête que j'aurais tiré. »" (Kapesh 1976: 139–141).

44 See Deanna Reder and Alix Shield's important article "'I write this for all of you': Recovering the Unpublished RCMP 'Incident' in Maria Campbell's *Halfbreed* (1973)," *Canadian Literature* 237, 2019: 13–25 (published online May 29, 2018).

45   "Quand je parle montagnais [Innu] à mes enfants, ils ne me comprennent pas et quand eux me parlent, je ne les comprends pas bien parce que déjà, mes enfants sont à peine capables de parler indien [Innu] aujourd'hui" (Kapesh 1976: 93).

46   In Québec, the residential school system did not reach the same proportions as it did in other provinces; there were only ten schools (twelve, if you count the three locations at Fort George), and most were not in operation for more than fifteen to twenty years. See Truth and Reconciliation Commission 2015a: 40–46.

47   "Je m'en inquiéterai toute ma vie, c'est que le Blanc ait gâché mes enfants" (Kapesh 1976: 81).

48   "le Blanc aujourd'hui n'a aucun regret concernant nos enfants" (Kapesh 1979: 83). While Kapesh, as noted earlier, uses "le Blanc" throughout her text – which translates grammatically as "the White man" – it should here be understood to signify rather, as does the Innu word *kauapishit* from which it is translated, the more encompassing "White person, person of the White race" (*Online Innu Dictionary*). It is imperative to keep in mind that Kapesh's testimony is one that critiques settler society and its numerous assimilation policies *at large*. The switch to "Polichinelles" in lieu of "le Blanc" in the second book somewhat removes/corrects this imposed gendered aspect.

49   "on nous a dit toutes sortes de bonnes choses et on nous a montré toutes sortes de belles choses. On a procédé de cette façon au début, seulement pour ne pas nous mécontenter" (Kapesh 1976: 67).

50   "l'Indien [Innu], lui qui avait toujours l'habitude de prendre soin lui-même de ses enfants dans le bois" (Kapesh 1976: 73).

51   "Nous avons essayé de vivre comme autrefois, de monter dans le bois malgré tout, comme on nous l'avait dit. Mais cela ne nous a pas convenu bien longtemps parce que nous ne sommes pas habitués, nous Indiens [Innu], à ce que chaque famille vive séparée de ses enfants. L'Indien ne pouvait donc plus monter dix mois dans le bois parce que ses enfants étaient gardés pensionnaires. Il voulait évidemment les voir et savoir de quelle façon on s'en occupait, savoir si on les traitait bien ou non. Et c'est pour cette raison, à mon avis, que l'Indien a alors songé à prendre lui aussi un emploi" (Kapesh 1976: 73).

52   "Les Indiens que je connais ressentent beaucoup d'ennui. Ils se sentent clôturés... Malgré l'ennui ressenti, on est obligé de demeurer à l'intérieur de la clôture."

53   "Et il savait alors qu'à l'avenir, et jusqu'à sa mort, il devrait continuer, bon gré mal gré, à faire le fou avec les Polichinelles et à jouer à leurs polichinelleries" (Kapesh 1979: 81). *Polichinelle* is the French word for Pulcinella, a character from the Commedia dell'arte (Punchinello in English). It also refers to a puppet. The Innu word, *Kauitenitakushit*, does not have an actual equivalent, but loosely means "those who are comical" (see Glossary in Kapesh 1979: 83).

54 "Si nous n'arrêtons pas de jouer avec vous autres, je pense que nous n'arriverons pas à nous en tirer...On ne pourra jamais rien faire avec vous autres les Blancs."

55 "Je ne veux plus qu'on m'appelle Québécoise parce que j'appartiens à la nation Indienne et que ce qui est le plus important pour moi est de conserver ma langue, mon territoire et ma culture."

56 "Je suis une maudite Sauvagesse. Je suis très fière quand, aujourd'hui, je m'entends traiter de Sauvagesse. Quand j'entends le Blanc prononcer ce mot, je comprends qu'il me redit sans cesse que je suis une vraie Indienne et que c'est moi la première à avoir vécu dans le bois" (Kapesh 1976: 241).

57 "Même si, jusqu'à la fin des temps, tu ne fermes pas le bec et que tu continues à crier partout, à la radio et à la télévision, que tu te nommes QUÉBÉCOIS, jamais je ne serai d'accord avec toi" (Kapesh 1979: 79).

58 "Il ne peut plus avancer et il ne connaît plus du tout l'endroit d'où il est parti [...] Il sait que, rendu là, il n'a plus aucun moyen d'existence pour l'avenir" (Kapesh 1979: 71).

59 "À présent que tu vois à quel point je suis misérable, tu veux tout simplement te défiler, tu veux me renvoyer au plus vite là d'où je viens. Qu'est-ce que ça signifie? As-tu encore une fois quelque chose derrière la tête? Je vais te dire dès maintenant ce que je pense. Que je retourne ou non là d'où je viens, si j'ai de la misère à cause de toi, tu peux être sûr que c'est après toi que je vais crier sans arrêt. Attends-toi toujours à me voir et sois toujours disponible, ne te cache jamais de moi si je veux te voir, si j'ai besoin de toi. À l'avenir, et jusqu'à la fin de mes jours, ne te lasse jamais de moi" (Kapesh 1979: 77).

60 "Je n'ai rien à lui [le Ministre Laurin] demander, c'est à lui de comprendre." Falardeau's report of the press conference at the National Assembly adds that "all the answers are in her book." An Antane Kapesh's answer reminds me of Ruby Slipperjack's response to Hartmut Lutz, who wanted to know if there was any political meaning in what she was saying (in relation to her 1987 novel, *Honour the Sun*): "Well, it says, 'this is how I feel,' 'this is what I am feeling,' 'this is what is happening around me' and 'this is how I am reacting,' 'this is how I am dealing with the situation.' That is where it stops. I cannot tell you why this and this and that happens, you figure that out yourself. Who am I to tell you something? It is there for you to see" (Lutz 209). Dian Million remarks that a crucial difference here is between "feel" and "see": "She [Slipperjack] is not interested in how he [Lutz] may position what he 'sees,' since it is not her concern. Her concern is that Lutz keeps in mind the way a child perceives, 'remind you...of that person you once were' (209). This immediately transgresses the way Western knowledge works and the way most academics operate, but she shows what she knows, and what she knows is what it feels like to be an Ojibwa child caught in circumstances that they (her community) and she do not analyze or position to the seemingly obvious 'truths' that people who

write in a Western academic mode think they readily 'see.' What she feels are her frames and no two of us can 'see' them distinctly the same way; thus, feelings are theory, important projections about what is happening in our lives" (Million 61). Indeed, Kapesh states at the press conference, "This book describes my thoughts" ("Ce livre décrit ma pensée"; qtd. in Falardeau).

61   "Mme Kapesh a dit, en conférence de presse, que si les Blancs n'arrivent pas à comprendre son livre, elle n'en fera pas d'autres."

62   These revisions of the French text were done in anticipation of the 2019 bilingual edition of *Eukuan nin matshi-manitu innushkueu – Je suis une maudite sauvagesse* by the Montréal-based publisher Mémoire d'encrier.

63   "Et je serais heureuse de voir d'autres Indiens écrire, en langue indienne" (Kapesh 1976:7).

64   See Kapesh 1976: 38, 48, 54, 66, and 78 (this last instance refers to *Mutania innu-aimun*, the Montagnais language). "Montagnais" (French for "people of the mountain") is an older term that is hardly used anymore, but was common in the 1970s in Québec.

65   I am extremely grateful to Deanna Reder, Richard Cassidy, and Marie Leconte for taking the time to read and comment on these first drafts.

66   "Il ne reste plus du tout de petits shacks, il ne reste qu'une bécosse" (Kapesh 1976: 189).

67   "En français, les Innus parlent du territoire : aller dans le territoire, partir dans le territoire, chasser dans le territoire, trouver la paix dans le territoire. Le mot français reste fade devant la grandeur du concept."

68   Lacombe with Rita Mestokosho and Joséphine Bacon, and Moyes with Natasha Kanapé Fontaine.

69   For instance, at each of the Gatherings of the Indigenous Literary Studies Association (ILSA), a Renate Eigenbrod Mentorship Lunch is held, during which young and emerging scholars are paired with more established members to discuss their research projects and aspirations.

BIBLIOGRAPHY

"About us." Assembly of the First Nations of Quebec and Labrador, 2017–2018, http://apnql.com/en/about-us/. Accessed July 1, 2019.

"Bernard Assiniwi." *Terres en vues – Land inSights*, 2014, https://www.nativelynx.qc.ca/en/literature/bernard-assiniwi/. Accessed July 1, 2019.

Boudreau, Diane. *Histoire de la littérature amérindienne au Québec: oralité et écriture*. Montréal: L'Hexagone, 1993.

Boudreau, Diane. "Je suis une maudite sauvagesse de An Kapesh." *Le Grimoire*, vol. 4, no. 7, 1981: 5.

Chartier, Daniel. "La réception critique des littératures autochtones. *Kuessipan* de Naomi Fontaine." *À la carte: Le roman québécois (2010–2015)*, edited by Gilles Dupuis and Klaus-Dieter Ertler. Frankfurt am Main: Peter Lang, 2017: 167–184.

Dassylva, Martial. "Un texte dramatique qui n'en est pas un." *La Presse*, November 1981: B9.

Eigenbrod, Renate. *Travelling Knowledges: Repositioning the Im/Migrant Reader of Aboriginal Literatures in Canada*. Winnipeg: University of Manitoba Press, 2005.

Falardeau, Louis. "An Antane Kapesh à Québec: « Les Blancs n'ont pas à nous dire comment vivre »." *La Presse*, November 22, 1979: D19.

Fouque, Antoinette. "Les editions *des femmes*." *Desfemmes.fr*, 1991 (updated 2014), https://www.desfemmes.fr/historique/. Accessed July 1, 2019.

Gatti, Maurizio. *Être écrivain amérindien au Québec: Indianité et création littéraire*. Montréal: Hurtubise, 2006.

Gatti, Maurizio. *Littérature amérindienne du Québec: Écrits de langue française*. Montréal: Hurtubise, 2004 [Montréal: Boréal, 2009].

Giroux, Raymond. "Je ne veux plus qu'on m'appelle Québécoise." *Le Soleil*, November 22, 1979: B7.

Goeman, Mishuana. "Land As Life: Unsettling the Logics of Containment." *Native Studies Keywords*, edited by Stephanie Nohelani Teves, Andrea Smith, and Michelle H. Raheja. Tucson: University of Arizona Press, 2015: 71–89.

Henzi, Sarah. "Littératures autochtones et traduction." *Canadian Literature*, September 12, 2017, https://canlit.ca/litteratures-autochtones-et-traduction/. Accessed July 1, 2019.

"Histoire." Conseil de la Nation Innu Matimekush-Lac John, 2017, http://matimekush.com/histoire. Accessed July 1, 2019.

Indigenous and Northern Affairs Canada. "Quebec Region Module." *Aboriginal Awareness Training Program*, 1996: 1–16, http://publications.gc.ca/collections/collection_2018/aanc-inac/R5-617-1996-7-eng.pdf. Accessed July 1, 2019.

"Innu Language Website." *Innu-aimun.ca*, 2005–2019, https://www.innu-aimun.ca/. Accessed July 1, 2019.

"Institut Tshakapesh." *Tshakapesh.ca*, 2013, www.tshakapesh.ca/fr/institut-tshakapesh_14/. Accessed July 1, 2019.

Justice, Daniel Heath. "Conjuring Marks: Furthering Indigenous Empowerment through Literature." *American Indian Quarterly*, vol. 28, no. 1–2, 2004: 2–11.

Justice, Daniel Heath. "Significant Spaces Between: Making Room for Silence." *Or Words to that Effect: Orality and the Writing of Literary History*, edited by F. Daniel and J. Chamberlin. Amsterdam: John Benjamins, 2016: 115–125.

Kapesh, An Antane. "Ces terres dont nous avions nommé chaque ruisseau." *Recherches amérindiennes au Québec*, vol. V, no. 2, 1975: 2–3.

Kapesh, An Antane. *Eukuan nin matshimanitu innu-iskueu – Je suis une maudite sauvagesse*. Montréal: Leméac, 1976.

Kapesh, An Antane. *Eukuan nin matshimanitu innu-ishkueu – Je suis une maudite sauvagesse*. Chicoutimi: Éditions du CAAS, 2015.

Kapesh, An Antane. *Eukuan nin matshi-manitu Innushkueu / Je suis une maudite Sauvagesse*. Montréal: Mémoire d'encrier, 2019.

Kapesh, An Antane. "Petites histoires montagnaises." *Rencontre*, SAA, vol. IV, no. 3, 1983: 8–9, 14–15.

Kapesh, An Antane. *Qu'as-tu fait de mon pays?* Montréal: Éditions impossibles, 1979.

Kapesh, An Antane. "Tanite nana etutamin nitassi?" *Ka tshitapatakanit mashinaikan, tshetshi apashtakanit Uashau-nesseshepit – Manuel de lecture destiné aux* étudiants *du CEGEP de Sept-Iles*. Sept-Îles: Institut culturel et éducatif montagnais, 1998: 57–86.

Kapesh, An Antane. *Tanite nana etutamin nitassi? – Qu'as-tu fait de mon pays?* Chicoutimi: Éditions du CAAS, 2015.

Kapesh, An Antane. *Tanite nene etutamin nitassi?* Sept-Îles: Innu-aitunnu mak innu-katshishkutamatinanut (ICEM), 2004.

Kapesh, An Antane. *Tante nana etutamin nitassi?* Montréal: Éditions impossibles, 1979.

Kapesh, An Antane. *Uniam mak shaian utipatshimunissimuau*. Montréal: Ministère de l'Éducation, Service général des moyens d'enseignement, 1978.

Lacombe, Michèle. "'Pimuteuat/Ils marchent/They Walk': A Few Observations on Indigenous Poetry and Poetics in French." *Indigenous Poetics in Canada*, edited by Neal McLeod. Waterloo: Wilfrid Laurier University Press, 2014: 159–182.

LaRochelle, Réal. "Un cinéma de défense des droits des Autochtones." *Copie Zéro*, no. 11, October 1981: 60–66.

Larue-Langlois, Jacques. "Deux fois le racisme." *Le Devoir*, November 24, 1981: 14.

Lebrun, Paule. "Je suis une maudite sauvagesse." *Châtelaine*, January 1977: 10.

Létourneau, Jean-François, Naomi Fontaine, and Olivier Dezutter, editors. *Tracer un chemin – Meshkanatsheu*. Wendake: Hannenorak, 2017.

Lévesque, Robert. "An Antane Kapesh *'Qu'as-tu fait de mon pays?'*" *Le Devoir*, November 14, 1981: 32.

Lutz, Hartmut, editor. *Approaches: Essays in Native North American Studies and Literatures*. Augsburg: Wissner, 2002.

Mailhot, José. "Correspondances personnelles." Email correspondence, March 26–April 10, 2018.

Mailhot, José. *Pour une orthographe unique de la langue innue*. Sept-Îles: Institut culturel et éducatif montagnais, June 1997.

Mailhot, José, Marguerite MacKenzie, and Marie-Odile Junker. *Online Innu Dictionary*, 2013, http://www.innu-aimun.ca/dictionary. Accessed July 1, 2019.

Martel, Réginald. "La colère froide du 'bon Sauvage.'" *La Presse*, September 18, 1976.

Million, Dian. "Felt Theory: An Indigenous Feminist Approach to Affect and History." *Wicazo Sa Review*, vol. 24, no. 2, Fall 2009: 53–76.

Moyes, Lianne. "Listening to 'Mes lames de tannage': Notes toward a Translation." *Canadian Literature*, vol. 230–231, Autumn/Winter 2016: 86–105.

Nepton Hotte, Caroline. "Réédition d'un classique, *Je suis une maudite sauvagesse*, maintenant disponible à Saguenay." *Soirée boréale*, Radio-Canada, December 2, 2015.

New, William H. *Encyclopedia of Literature in Canada*. Toronto: University of Toronto Press, 2002.

Online Innu Dictionary, 2013, http://www.innu-aimun.ca/dictionary/Words. All words last accessed July 2019.

Piazza, François. "Je suis une maudite sauvagesse." *Le Dimanche*, November 21, 1976.

Picard, Raphael. "Study on Land and Resource Use by the Innu and Naskapi, Howse Property Iron Ore Project, Howse Minerals Limited." *Canadian Environmental Assessment Agency*, December 2014, https://www.ceaa.gc.ca/050/documents/p80067/114011E.pdf. Accessed July 1, 2019.

Pivato, Joseph J. "Maria Campbell." *English-Canadian Writers*, 2009 (updated February 12, 2015), http://canadian-writers.athabascau.ca/english/writers/mcampbell/mcampbell.php. Accessed July 1, 2019.

Reder, Deanna, and Alix Shield. "'I write this for all of you': Recovering the Unpublished RCMP 'Incident' in Maria Campbell's Halfbreed (1973)." *Canadian Literature,* vol. 237, 2019: 13–25 (published online May 29, 2018).

Rowan, Renée. "Je suis une maudite innu-iskueu." *Le Devoir*, January 10, 1977: 12.

"Then and now," Ville de Schefferville, 2014, http://www.ville-schefferville.ca/decouvrir-schefferville/histoire.html. Accessed July 1, 2019.

Trudel, Clément. "Une Mère Courage montagnaise." *Le Devoir*, November 22, 1979: 18.

Truth and Reconciliation Commission. *The Final Report of the Truth and Reconciliation Commission of Canada: Canada's Residential Schools: The History, Part 2 – 1939 to 2000.* Montréal: McGill-Queen's University Press, 2015a.

Truth and Reconciliation Commission. *Honouring the Truth, Reconciling for the Future: Summary of the Final Report of the Truth and Reconciliation Commission of Canada.* Toronto: Lorimer, 2015b.

Turcotte, Yanick. *L'Association des Indiens du Québec (1965–1977) et le militantisme autochtone dans le Québec des années 1960–1970.* Master of Arts Thesis, Université de Montréal, January 2018, https://papyrus.bib.umontreal .ca/xmlui/bitstream/handle/1866/20154/Turcotte_Yanick_2018_memoire .pdf?sequence=2&isAllowed=y. Accessed July 1, 2019.

Younging, Greg. *Elements of Indigenous Style: A Guide for Writing By and About Indigenous Peoples.* Edmonton: Brush Education, 2018.

ACKNOWLEDGEMENTS

I would like to acknowledge and thank, from the bottom of my heart, the following people for being a part of this project and making it happen:

John André, for his support and trust in this project, and for providing the beautiful photo of An Antane Kapesh,

Josie-Ann Bonneau, for her extensive work in getting this project approved by the Board of the Saguenay Native Friendship Centre, for her support and trust in this project,

Roger Kupaniesh Dominique, for providing the beautiful artwork for the cover,

Jérémie Ambroise, José Mailhot, and the advisory committee (Anne-Marie André, Judith Mestokosho, Céline Bellefleur, and Philomène Grégoire), for their amazing work and dedication in revising and standardizing the Innu version of *Eukuan nin matshi-manitu innushkueu*,

Jérémie Ambroise, for his help, guidance, patience, and enthusiasm in the project,

José Mailhot, for her feedback and explanations, and insight into the original French translations,

Marguerite MacKenzie, for her guidance and enthusiasm in the project,

Deanna Reder, for her guidance, feedback, and unfailing belief in this project, and for helping me bring it to Wilfrid Laurier UP,

Siobhan McMenemy, for her advice, patience, guidance, help in navigating the publishing rollercoaster, and belief in this project,

Lisa Quinn, and the team at Wilfrid Laurier UP, for all the logistics involved, and for giving this work its English home,

Marie Leconte and Richard Cassidy, for reading over the first versions of the translations, and for their feedback,

Lianne Moyes, for reading over the first version of the Afterword, and for her continuous support and advice, and our many, many conversations about this project,

…and all my friends, family, mentors, and colleagues who supported this project since its inception in so many different ways. The end result is so much better thanks to all of you.

Books in the Indigenous Studies Series

Blockades and Resistance: Studies in Actions of Peace and the Temagami Blockades of 1988–89 / Bruce W. Hodgins, Ute Lischke, and David T. McNab, editors / 2003 / xii + 276 pp. / illus. / ISBN 978-0-88920-381-5

Indian Country: Essays on Contemporary Native Culture / Gail Guthrie Valaskakis / 2005 / x + 293 pp. / illus. / ISBN 978-0-88920-479-9

Walking a Tightrope: Aboriginal People and Their Representations / Ute Lischke and David T. McNab, editors / 2005 / xix + 377 pp. / illus. / ISBN 978-0-88920-484-3

The Long Journey of a Forgotten People: Métis Identities and Family Histories / Ute Lischke and David T. McNab, editors / 2007 / viii + 386 pp. / illus. / ISBN 978-0-88920-523-9

Words of the Huron / John L. Steckley / 2007 / xvii + 259 pp. / ISBN 978-0-88920-516-1

Essential Song: Three Decades of Northern Cree Music / Lynn Whidden / 2007 / xvi + 176 pp. / illus., musical examples, audio CD / ISBN 978-0-88920-459-1

From the Iron House: Imprisonment in First Nations Writing / Deena Rymhs / 2008 / ix + 147 pp. / ISBN 978-1-55458-021-7

Lines Drawn upon the Water: First Nations and the Great Lakes Borders and Borderlands / Karl S. Hele, editor / 2008 / xxiv + 352 pp. / illus. / ISBN 978-1-55458-004-0

Troubling Tricksters: Revisioning Critical Conversations / Linda M. Morra and Deanna Reder, editors / 2009 / xii+ 336 pp. / illus. / ISBN 978-1-55458-181-8

Aboriginal Peoples in Canadian Cities: Transformations and Continuities / Heather A. Howard and Craig Proulx, editors / 2011 / viii + 256 pp. / illus. / ISBN 978-1-55458-260-0

Bridging Two Peoples: Chief Peter E. Jones, 1843–1909 / Allan Sherwin / 2012 / xxiv + 246 pp. / illus. / ISBN 978-1-55458-633-2

The Nature of Empires and the Empires of Nature: Indigenous Peoples and the Great Lakes Environment / Karl S. Hele, editor / 2013 / xxii + 350 pp. / illus. / ISBN 978-1-55458-328-7

The Eighteenth-Century Wyandot: A Clan-Based Study / John L. Steckley / 2014 / x + 306 pp. / ISBN 978-1-55458-956-2

Indigenous Poetics in Canada / Neal McLeod, editor / 2014 / xii + 404 pp. / ISBN 978-1-55458-982-1

Literary Land Claims: The "Indian Land Question" from Pontiac's War to Attawapiskat / Margery Fee / 2015 / x + 318 pp. / illus. / ISBN 978-1-77112-119-4

Arts of Engagement: Taking Aesthetic Action In and Beyond Canada's Truth and Reconciliation Commission / Dylan Robinson and Keavy Martin, editors / 2016 / viii + 376 pp. / illus. / ISBN 978-1-77112-169-9

Learn, Teach, Challenge: Approaching Indigenous Literature / Deanna Reder and Linda M. Morra, editors / 2016 / xii + 580 pp. / ISBN 978-1-77112-185-9

Violence Against Indigenous Women: Literature, Activism, Resistance / Alison Hargreaves / 2017 / xvi + 282 pp. / ISBN 978-1-77112-239-9

Read, Listen, Tell: Indigenous Stories from Turtle Island / Sophie McCall, Deanna Reder, David Gaertner, and Gabrielle L'Hirondlle Hill, editors / 2017 / xviii + 390 pp. / ISBN 978-1-77112-300-6

The Homing Place: Indigenous and Settler Literary Legacies of the Atlantic / Rachel Bryant / 2017 / xiv + 244 pp. / ISBN 978-1-77112-286-3

Why Indigenous Literatures Matter / Daniel Heath Justice / 2018 / xxii + 284 pp. / ISBN 978-1-77112-176-7

Activating the Heart: Storytelling, Knowledge Sharing, and Relationship / Julia Christensen, Christopher Cox, and Lisa Szabo-Jones, editors / 2018 / xvii + 210 pp. / ISBN 978-1-77112-219-1

Indianthusiasm: Indigenous Responses / Hartmut Lutz, Renae Watchman, and Florentine Strzelczyk, editors / 2020 / x + 252 pp. / ISBN 978-1-77112-399-0

Literatures, Communities, and Learning: Conversations with Indigenous Writers / Aubrey Jean Hanson / 2020 / viii + 182 pp. / ISBN 978-1-77112-449-2

I Am a Damn Savage/What Have You Done to My Country? / An Antane Kapesh; Sarah Henzi, translation and afterword / 2020 / vi + 314 pp. / ISBN 978-1-77112-408-9